The next morning I came out of the bathroom, toweling off my hair after a hot shower, and I heard him say from the kitchen counter, "How was your concert?"

My concert! I knew he didn't like that I went. It was weird because, in one sense, he gave me a lot of freedom to own a motorcycle or stay out as late as I wanted, but in another sense, he seemed to want to be in control, to somehow be the arbiter of how much freedom I was or wasn't allowed.

I pulled my head out from under the towel and said, "We didn't see it. It was sold out."

I wanted him to feel bad that he hadn't loaned me the money to buy the tickets in advance.

Instead, though, he changed the subject. Glaring at me, he asked, "How long are you planning to grow your hair?" as if he were seeing my hair for the first time.

What does he think my answer is going to be? I wondered. Down to my ankles?

"Uhm...I don't know," I said. "Not much longer."

"You look like a girl. If I wanted a girl, I would have had a daughter." Like he had a choice in the matter.

I buried my head back in the towel, more in an effort to hide my annoyance than to dry my hair.

"If you're going to live in my house, you need to get a haircut," he said. It was more of an order than a suggestion because that's how Dad rolls.

WHAT READERS ARE SAYING ABOUT GARY SCARPA'S WRITING:

"I could not put the book down. The dialogue is spot-on, and the details of the events made me feel like I was there."

"The characters are so believable that I couldn't wait to turn the page. Fantastic book!"

"The author has great skill for writing dialogue, and many of the scenes are gems..."

"If you are looking for a great book for a group discussion, this is the one for you."

"...simply a beautiful story, told well and well worth reading."

"Like a binge-worthy TV series, I found myself flipping to the next chapter as quickly as one would press play for the next episode – often staying up a lot later than expected."

"I can't wait to see if the author has a sequel planned. The book did not disappoint!"

"The characters jump right off the pages and you fall immediately into their world."

"...the stories and characters will evoke nostalgia, especially for those who grew up in small towns anywhere in America, while lending a humanness, and humanity..."

"It is a tale rich in character development and believable conversation. We get to know and care about these people."

"I found myself invested in the characters and rooting for their individual success as well as their relationship."

"Life is very short and what we have to do must be done in the now."
- Audre Lorde

~

"The best songs are the ones that resonate with people and make them feel understood."
- David Crosby

~

"What art offers is space – a certain breathing room for the spirit."
- John Updike

~

"Writing is the passageway, the entrance, the exit, the dwelling place of the other in me."
- Hélène Cixous

~

"I paint my joy and I sing my sorrow."
- Joni Mitchell

Still Life

A Novel

GARY SCARPA

NEXT
CHAPTER

PRESS

Book cover design by Mario Lampic

Printed in the United States of America
Names: Scarpa, Gary, author
Title: a novel / Still Life
Description: First edition / Next Chapter Press
Identifiers: ISBN: 978-1-7365146-4-1
Classification: Coming of Age Fiction

For more information about books by Gary Scarpa, visit www.garyscarpa.com

For Dad

CHAPTER 1

We were gearing up for rush hour when the wall phone began ringing.

"That'll be $4.25, sir," I said to my customer before yelling, "Somebody get that, please," hoping to quell the monotonous ring.

"Please!" I repeated. "Tomaso? Bink? Les? Anybody?"

My plea fell on deaf ears, so I tossed my customer's money in the register and headed for the phone. Apparently, I was the only one who wasn't too busy to answer it.

It seemed like the black wall phone was the one thing at Duchess Drive-In that wasn't white, silver, or clear glass. The front of the building was encased in large, slanted windows, the food counters and cabinets gleamed with the polished silver of stainless steel, and the expanse of the front counter space where the customers placed their orders was an immaculate white laminate.

I had been working at Duchess for two years since I began in September of 1967, five months before I turned sixteen, when Howie Millea, the manager, suggested to my brother Michael that he hire me early and pay me under the table until my birthday. Not even a full two years later, at the beginning of my senior year, Howie had promoted me to "window man" just like my brother before me. I'm not one hundred percent on this, but at seventeen, I may have been the youngest window man ever.

As a window man, you had more advanced responsibilities. You not only took all the orders and rang them up, but when you worked at night, you counted the money and put it in the safe, locked up the place, and whenever the damn phone rang during working hours, you apparently had the responsibility of answering it when no one else would!

The mind is a strange thing because, as I walked over to the phone, something screwy popped into my head out of nowhere – a poem by Edgar Allan Poe that we had recently been studying in English class:

> *Yet the ear it fully knows,*
> *By the twanging,*
> *And the clanging,*
> *How the danger ebbs and flows;*
> *Yet the ear distinctly tells,*
> *In the jangling,*
> *And the wrangling,*
> *How the danger sinks and swells,*
> *By the sinking or the swelling in the anger of the bells —*
> *Of the bells —*
> *Of the bells, bells, bells, bells,*
> *Bells, bells, bells —*
> *In the clamor and the clangor of the bells!*

Crazy, right? But that's what I was thinking as I prepared to relieve my ears of the irritating *clangor*. I don't broadcast it, but I like poems. Blame my mother for reciting poetry to me my whole life.

Picking up the phone, I said, "Duchess Drive-In," real matter-of-factly, because that's how we all answer the phone. I mean, it's a business.

I figured it was Gino, the meat man. Gino wouldn't have said hello or anything polite. He simply would have ground out, "How many patties, junior?" in his low, gritty voice, in which case, I would have dropped the phone, letting it dangle from its wire, opened up the walk-in and counted how many frosty, brown cardboard cartons of raw hamburgers we had left, then relayed the number to Gino so he'd know how many to deliver the next day. He wouldn't have said goodbye either – but just an abrupt, "You got it, junior," and hung up. Gino isn't particular; he calls everybody "junior."

It wasn't Gino, though. A shaky woman's voice on the other end asked, "Is Tomaso there?"

"Aunt Lucia?" I said. "It's Gabriel."

"Oh, Jesus, Gabriel," she responded. "I'm so nervous, I didn't recognize your voice. Get your cousin for me, will you?"

Tomaso and I are first cousins, so we've grown up together, but we've gotten even closer in recent years since I started working at Duchess. Tomaso started working there a year before me when Michael convinced Howie to hire him too. Sometimes I wonder if anyone would have a job if it wasn't for Michael.

"Hey, Tommy Trouble," I yelled. Michael had given Tomaso the comical nickname because Tomaso is such a prankster, and like most everything Michael does, the name stuck. "For you. Your mom. I'll finish that twenty-four while you take the call." Tomaso was in the midst of dressing two dozen buns and grilling the same number of burgers for the upcoming lunch hour. None of us at Duchess ever minds helping another guy out.

After I got everything set and threw the big tray up on the counter to be wrapped by a couple of the newer kids, I turned and saw that Tomaso had disappeared. Oddly, though, the phone was hanging by its wire, just like if the call had been from Gino the meat man. Puzzled, I lifted the phone and listened, hearing the dead buzzing of a disconnected call, so I hung up. I opened the walk-in, but Tomaso wasn't there. *Maybe he went to the bathroom,* I thought, so I checked that out, but the door was wide open and the light was off.

"Guys," I yelled to the crew. "Watch the window for a minute."

Shaking my head, I looked around, and I was more than a little bit surprised to see Tomaso's solid legs sticking out next to the big work sink near the back door. He was sitting on the floor, which was unusual for any of the guys to do even if they were trying to get out of work. It wasn't like the floor wasn't clean because each night a member of the crew washed the entire floor with an old-fashioned industrial mop, the kind with the coarse stringed head. Still, it was odd for someone to be sitting on the floor.

I crossed past the sink so I could find out what the hell Tomaso was up to, and I saw him wiping away tears. A guy crying isn't everyday stuff. You don't cry at Duchess if you can help it.

"Hey, man," I said. "You okay? What happened?"

Tomaso shook his head and bit his upper lip with his bottom teeth. "My mother. She called to say...to tell me...I got drafted." He took this big gulp like he had a mouthful of soda and needed to swallow it fast or he'd spit it out. "She got the letter in the mail this afternoon."

"Oh shit, you're kidding."

"I wish I was kidding," Tomaso said.

"Wow." I saw there was room, so I sat down on the floor next to him. "That sucks."

"Tell me about it. That's my fuckin' luck."

This wasn't like when Jeff, who's been my best pal since kindergarten, enlisted more than a year ago, which was in and of itself bizarro. It seems like the longer the Vietnam War lingers, the fewer guys want into the military.

Jeff had his reasons for enlisting, though. Not even eighteen at the time, he needed to get away from it all for reasons he kept mainly to himself, so it was a big shocker to me. The Marine recruiter had told Jeff that he couldn't go to Vietnam until he turned eighteen, and the recruiter practically promised that by then he'd be assigned to some other duty or the war might be over. The bad news for Jeff was he got his orders to go to Vietnam on the day of his eighteenth birthday. *What a liar that recruiter was,* I was thinking as I contemplated what I could say to relieve my cousin's distress.

"What was your draft number?" I asked.

He grimaced as if in pain and replied, "Thirty-one. I knew it was low, but you know, I was just hoping that..."

Overcome by emotion, he couldn't get the words out.

"Geez...that is low," I said. I hoped I sounded sensitive to his predicament because it was sure how I was feeling.

The draft was newish. I say "newish" because I guess it had also existed years before, during World War II, but after the U.S. declared victory, it was no longer needed. Not until Vietnam. Not until just recently.

I grew up watching a steady diet of war movies with my dad. A favorite is *Yankee Doodle Dandy*, where James Cagney as the famous composer George M. Cohan tries to enlist, but they won't let him because he's too old, and boy, does he ever get ticked off about it. Instead, he stays home and writes a great song about going to war, "Over There," which has such a memorable melody that I even find myself humming it all these years later. I imagined my dad was like George M. Cohan, but when I asked him what motivated him to enlist, he said that he joined up because he was young and lost and didn't know what to do with himself. That threw me for a loop because I always figured it was because he had been super patriotic and wanted to be a hero like John Wayne or Audie Murphy.

Patriotism, or lack thereof, is something I think about a lot these days.

Obviously, Tomaso wasn't feeling very patriotic at the moment.

"What are you going to do?" I asked.

"What can I do?" Poor Tomaso just shrugged, hung his head real sad-like, and stared at the tile floor.

"Well...maybe you can get out of it."

"Yeah. Wishful thinking. How the fuck do I do that? I don't have any physical issues, I'm obviously not religious, and I'm not in college, which sucks. That would have been my out. I should have gone to fuckin' college, but you know me, I never liked school."

He was right. College was the easiest way to get out of going. Even when I became eligible for a draft number at nineteen, it was two hundred seventy-three, which is a nice high one. Add to my high number that I had a college deferment, and I was safe.

Truthfully, I think Vietnam is the main reason my father had pushed college down Michael's throat and mine, even though he never said it. I mean, Dad began talking about college when Michael and I stopped sucking our thumbs, partly because he never had a chance to go because of the Great Depression and partly because of his Italian peasant parents who didn't know college from a hole in the wall. But he's shifted college talk into high gear in recent years, probably because of Vietnam. It's a little ironic because he hates the hippies who protest the war. Dad can be confusing sometimes.

Tomaso wasn't so lucky. His only other option was to bolt and take off for Canada, but that was so radical that I didn't even suggest it.

"Hey, Gabriel, we need you!" someone yelled from the front.

"Oh, man...listen, Tomaso, sorry about this, but we've gotta get back to work."

I pulled myself up from the floor, and Tomaso followed suit, grabbing the side of the work sink and hoisting himself to his feet.

As we headed back to our work stations, it occurred to me that neither of us had mentioned something that was too delicate to bring up, given Tomaso's dilemma. It hadn't been more than three months ago that we had attended the funeral of Buster Brookes, who had stepped on a landmine in Vietnam.

Buster was a regular fixture at Duchess with Big Alfred who is our bouncer, responsible for clearing loiterers off the lot. Howie had hired Alfred about a month after I started working since some nights it seems like every kid in the Valley – and that's Derby, Shelton, Seymour, and Ansonia – hangs out in the parking lot, and with lots of them being drunk, things can get hairy. I'm not sure if Buster was on the payroll, but he and Alfred were connected like Siamese twins that no one would want to mess with.

I'll never forget the night Alfred told me about it at work.

"Yeah, I was with Buster's momma when it happened. Two men in uniform showed up right here at the projects. When she opened the door and there they was in their fancy uniforms with shiny brass buttons, she knew right away what they was there for. Her legs went right out from underneath her, and you never heard nobody cry like she did that day. I had to lift her up and lay her on the couch."

"Oh God," I said. "That must have been awful. Were you and Buster related or just friends?"

"His momma is my second cousin or somethin' like that, so yeah, we was kin." Alfred shook his head like he was trying to get rid of a headache. "Buster was a good boy. Strong as a ox but wouldn't never hurt even a baby fly unless he had to. I gotta help his momma get through this."

That's Alfred. Always trying to help people. I can always depend on him to give me good advice or gas me up by complimenting me on my basketball skills. And then there are the times he'll flash that charismatic smile and announce to the whole crew, "Gabriel DeMarco is the best white boy I know!" I don't know if he's serious or razzing me when he says it, but it sure makes me smile.

The whole Duchess crew attended Buster's funeral. A good dozen of us sat, crammed together in the little balcony of the Baptist church not more than a quarter mile up the road from Duchess. You might say we stood out, being the only white guys in the church.

I had been to other funerals, of course, but this one was different. When the pallbearers rolled Buster's coffin, neatly covered with an American flag, down the aisle of the humble church, I swallowed hard. When Big Alfred surprised us by breaking into uncontrollable sobs as the congregation sang the opening gospel hymn, my own eyes filled with tears. When Buster's mother, at the end of the service, draped herself over the coffin in a spontaneous display of raw emotion and Alfred gently peeled her arms off the shiny wooden box, I thought I would stop breathing.

Then, at the gravesite, two crisply dressed soldiers, with square chins and skinny noses under the stiff brims of their caps, ceremoniously removed the flag from Buster's coffin and folded it with detailed precision into a perfect triangle. Except for the vivid red, white, and blue of the flag, I felt like I was watching a black and white movie. I closed my eyes as Mrs. Brookes accepted the flag and came undone once more. And when, from a shallow snow covered incline behind the congregation, seven soldiers cocked their rifles and fired in a succession of volleys, breaking the morning stillness with three startling pop-pop-pops of jolting sound, and then a bugler played "Taps," I knew the war was real.

It all punctuated the sad reality that Buster Brookes was gone for good. I mean, you couldn't help but love Buster with his thick glasses, his rock-hard muscles, and his broad, affable smile. How could he be dead?

Neither Tomaso nor I were about to talk about Buster, that's for sure. What we were obviously going to do was pretend like it never happened and go back to work cooking burgers and waiting on customers just like we were doing before the phone rang.

CHAPTER 2

This may sound a little quirky, but every now and then I grab a volume of our Britannicas from my bookshelf and shove off on one arbitrary journey or another to who knows where. It's something I've been doing since Dad bought the set.

I can still picture the salesman with his bulbous nose and greasy comb-over, which did nothing to camouflage a bald head you could see your reflection in, sitting across from Dad at our kitchen table on Maltby Street, me on one side and Michael on the other. The salesman explained that with such a wealth of knowledge at our fingertips, our lives would be transformed and our futures guaranteed. The sample volume was impressive to the eye with its rich brown leather cover and gold embossed letters on the spine. I have to admit, I felt smarter just holding the weighty sample in my small hands, and after all, who doesn't want to be smart?

And all these years later, I still like to browse the information packed pages. Something recently occurred to me – an epiphany, if you will – so I grabbed one of the yearbook volumes that Britannica sends every year, updating our collection with the latest in current events, and I looked up two important dates. The first was the assassination of JFK on November 22, 1963, and the second was the Beatles' debut on *The Ed Sullivan Show* on February 9, 1964. Back then, I watched both events on TV with rapt attention. Crazy, right? I was eleven when Oswald shot Kennedy, and I had just turned twelve a few days before Ed Sullivan proudly announced, "Ladies and gentlemen, the Beatles!"

By my count, there were a mere seventy-nine days between the two events, not even three months. Anyway, what occurred to me is that, from my perspective, once Oswald pulled the trigger and, a few weeks later, the Fab Four sang five of their hits on the most-watched television program ever, things changed for good. The world suddenly seemed to be thrown into a wave of confusion and took me with it just for kicks.

I should have tried to find the date the Vietnam War started as well because, in a way, it wasn't that long after I sat on the carpet at my Nonna Alberino's house that fateful Sunday night, watching the Beatles sing "I Want to Hold Your Hand" with hundreds of girls screaming their heads off, that headlines about Vietnam were plastered on the front page of every daily newspaper in America. And now I was eighteen, and my cousin Tomaso got drafted.

Without meaning to sound too self-centered, his being drafted was not only a big setback for Tomaso but another in a line of setbacks for me. First there was Jeff enlisting, and now Tomaso getting drafted. My two best friends, gone in a puff of smoke. I mean that figuratively, of course, because there was the real possibility, with the war, that a guy could go out in a puff of smoke. I mean, Buster hadn't been the first. A few years ago, my brother Michael found out that a neighborhood kid, Jake Thompson, had gotten killed in the war. To tell the truth, I don't even know how it happened, but I do know that Michael was rocked.

I remember that Michael was fifteen when he met Jake, who was maybe seventeen. Jake was one of those guys who was always trying to copy James Dean with his blond pompadour and a pack of cigarettes rolled into the sleeve of his t-shirt. Having his license, he used to take Michael and some of his friends for rides in his '62 Plymouth Fury. But when *The Evening Sentinel* reported that Jake got arrested for shoplifting at Bradlees, the big department store on Pershing Drive, Dad put the kibosh on Michael going for any more joy rides with Jake. Still, that didn't change how Michael felt when he heard that a guy he used to hang out with had been killed in the war.

Back to Tomaso, though. At the time of him being drafted, I was a high school senior and Tomaso a year out. As kids, we had spent a lot of time together at our grandparents' house in Derby, but when we hit our high school years, we didn't hang out at first, being from different towns. Duchess changed all that.

And let me add that when I introduced him to Jeff, the two hit it off, and we became like the Three Musketeers until Jeff got his orders to go to Vietnam.

Of course, being who he was, Tommy Trouble had become a little bit of a bad influence on me. Nothing too serious, though. Mainly, just goofing around at work and introducing me to alcohol. A couple of years before, when all of our neighborhood friends had started drinking, I had avoided it, and Jeff had stuck by me, but Tomaso caught me at a vulnerable point in my life. At the end of my junior year, I was dating this girl at school, and before I knew it, everything went down the tubes, which was typically how things went for me and girls. When I told Tomaso about it, he said, "C'mon, I'll show you how to forget your troubles."

That night, he picked me up in his candy-apple red Chevelle, pulled into Duchess, and said, "I'll be right out." Sitting in the car like a guy who just had a lobotomy, I waited, and he came back five minutes later with two large empty drink cups and a big ketchup can filled with crushed ice instead of ketchup.

"What's that for?" I asked.

"You'll see," he said.

Then he drove down to the package store next door to the Texaco station on Pershing Drive, jumped out, and returned a few minutes later with a brown paper bag.

"Whattaya got there?" I asked, in my zombie state.

"Check it out."

I opened the bag, and there was a fat bottle of gin and two bottles of what looked like club soda, only the labels read Tom Collins.

"How did you buy alcohol?" I asked. "You're not twenty-one."

"That guy doesn't fuckin' care how old anyone is," he replied.

"But I don't drink."

"Correction," he said. "You didn't *use* to drink, and now you do. Trust me, you'll feel better, and I won't let you get too carried away."

What did I care at this point? Mixed drinks. It all seemed like a lot of trouble to get drunk.

Before I knew it, we were driving along a narrow dirt road near our grandparents' house, heading for what we call "DeMarco Mountain."

The backyard at Grampa and Nonna's house on Smith Street in Derby is like none I've ever seen. I'm pretty sure it was designed to resemble the landscape they had left behind in their native Italy. It was a series of about five terraces, each one several feet higher than the previous one, divided by stone walls and three or four stone steps leading to the next level. When I was growing up, each terrace was planted with a myriad of colorful vegetables. Grampa and Nonna were simple people – immigrant, peasant farmers, and even in their old age, they farmed the land. I say they *were* simple people because they both recently died, not even a month apart. I guess after Grampa died, Nonna decided she couldn't go on without him, even though all they did was yell at each other in Italian.

I can remember many a Sunday, while walking up the driveway to the back door of their house, seeing one or the other of them, ankle deep in a sea of green, leafy vegetables on the first or second terrace. At the bottom level, there was a gigantic cherry tree. As children, my brother and our cousins and I would stand on the flat roof of the garage and pick the crisp red cherries right from the tree. One terrace had a chicken coop with live chickens, providing us all with fresh eggs, and during the Depression, my father said they slaughtered chickens for cooking. The next terrace had a tool shed. Among the tools, there was an old .22 caliber rifle and a rusty old hand gun that my father had somehow shot himself in the finger with as a kid. A terrace above had a mulberry tree and a few rows of cornstalks.

The last terrace led to an open expanse of land where there was a small pond and a dirt road, leading to a densely wooded area with gigantic rocks with cave-like spaces in them. From this wooded space, being at a high elevation, it seemed you could see all of Derby. This elevation would come to be known to us as DeMarco Mountain. Somehow, and I don't know how, Tomaso's parents had come to own the top level – the DeMarco Mountain level.

We had all played there as kids, and now that we're older, it's where we take girls parking. That was Michael's idea. He's a real innovator. DeMarco Mountain is very secluded, and there's a private dirt road that leads to it. And the nice thing about it is, if you didn't know where the dirt road was, you wouldn't know where it was. So it's a safe place to hide away, and if someone catches us up there,

Tomaso can say, "Uhm...my father owns this mountain." And Tommy Trouble is such a wise-ass, that's exactly what he would say.

Well, that night, Tomaso and I downed almost half of that bottle of gin. It didn't taste too bad because the soda had a subtle sweetness to it, not like the awful taste of beer, which I had tasted once at a Sunday family gathering. I think my dad and my Uncle Sonny had this idea, a little kid will hate the taste of beer, and maybe that will stick with him for life.

One thing was for sure. That night with Tomaso was the first time I had ever gotten drunk. Then, while listening to sad love songs on his eight-track tape player, Tomaso and I drove back and forth between Huntington, where my ex-girlfriend lived, and Orange, where some girl lived that Tommy Trouble was pining for. We must have gone back and forth five or six times without saying a word before he dropped me off at home. Just two drunk kids, wishing we still had girlfriends.

What a dumb thing to do, but that's the kind of mood we were in. I didn't drink too much after that, just now and then...not just for kicks, either, but mainly when I was feeling down.

As I finished the night out at work, I thought about Jeff in Vietnam and now Tomaso, a sudden victim of the draft, and I felt more lonely than usual.

There's a difference between feeling alone and feeling lonely. I had never minded feeling alone. But feeling lonely scratched away somewhere in the pit of my stomach, like a mouse gnawing through worn baseboard. It wasn't like I was unpopular at school, exactly. It's just there was always this part of me that felt like I didn't quite fit in, the proverbial square peg in a round hole. So my school friends were exactly that – guys I hung out with in school.

It seemed the people who I did fit in with, the ones I hung out with outside of school, kept being taken from me. I didn't quite know what to do about that because it gave me that restless, lonely feeling.

Tomaso had asked me not to tell Michael about him being drafted because he wanted to tell him himself. That wasn't going to be easy to do, but I'd do my best to keep my mouth shut.

CHAPTER 3

After taking a long drive with Tomaso, was Michael ever disturbed. Way more upset than he was when Jake Thompson got killed. Not a guy who easily hides his feelings, Michael's reaction to our cousin being drafted was written all over his face in fluorescent red.

He gave me this concerned look and, real somber-like, said, "We gotta do something for Tommy Trouble before he goes." He almost never talks about or addresses our cousin in any way except as Tommy Trouble, probably because he's so proud of the nickname he created. I myself tend to call him by his given name because I'm not all that strung up on nicknames, even though I appreciate Michael's creativity.

"What do you mean?" I asked.

"I don't know. A party, I think. Before he goes, we'll give him a big sendoff. This summer. That's what we'll do. But we have to start planning for it pronto."

"I'll help in any way I can," I offered.

"I'm gonna miss the guy. It sucks that he got drafted. I hate this fucking war."

Understanding that war meant possible death, I also realized we had faced a slew of family deaths in the last year or two. In addition to my grandparents, two of my aunts had also recently died. It was enough to make a person's head spin, as my mother is fond of saying.

Aunt Phyllis, my mother's eldest sister, went first a few days after Christmas when I was a sophomore. Cancer. The following Thanksgiving, not even a year later, Grampa DeMarco passed away, and then, bang, my nonna died about a week before Christmas. To make matters worse, my dad's youngest sister and my godmother, Aunt Francesca, died about two weeks after Nonna. Cancer again. She was only forty-three. Not a sweeter or gentler woman ever walked the planet. Mom always says there's something about holidays, especially Christmas, that seems to invite people to die. For a while there, I felt like I lived at the funeral home.

I'll never forget that Christmas. My dad had been too busy to get a tree, and after the funeral, Michael, Tomaso, and I bought a six-foot tree, tied it to the roof of Michael's beat up Corvair, brought it home, and decorated it. It was actually Tomaso's idea because when he's not pulling a practical joke on someone, he can be a sensitive guy. When Dad got back from the funeral, my mother helping him to the bedroom like an invalid, he stopped and looked at us as we stood by the tree. Were we ever stunned when he burst out crying in loud, ugly sobs. I had never seen him cry or look weak before. Michael, Tomaso, and I didn't know whether to feel good or bad about getting the tree, but Mom later told me that it touched Dad's heart.

So, yeah, even though I'm young, I know what loss feels like. When your best friend enlists in the Marines, that is obviously one type of loss. I hope he will return safely. Death is another, the kind you can't understand...the kind you'll *never* understand. Not only my grandparents and aunts, but there were kids I knew, like Buster. And even before him, there was Arty Miklos from the old neighborhood who died in a car crash three years ago. I even remember my first experience of someone young dying, a girl in school when we were in seventh grade who died of Cystic Fibrosis. I mean, if you could have heard Maura Brennan sing "How are Things in Glocca Morra?" in our St. Patrick's Day show a year before her death, you'd know she's now singing with a choir of angels. And there were other kids as well – kids I don't talk about anymore. The point is, a guy's heart can get buried in pain.

And now here was our cousin and good pal, drafted. Another loss. Tommy Trouble who had pulled so many pranks on us and made us laugh. Tommy Trouble who taught me how to drive a stick and how to ride a motorcycle. Tommy Trouble who came to get a Christmas tree for my dad with me and Michael when our grandmother died.

What would happen to him now? Would he end up in Vietnam like Jeff? Tomaso wouldn't have to wait to turn eighteen like Jeff because he was already nineteen. If the Army sent him there, would he come back alive? Would Jeff?

I don't know what to say. Death is just *so* wrong, and it still makes me depressed on a daily basis to think about so many people close to us dying.

To top it off, I had come off of a junior year that hadn't gone too great, and I was in the middle of a senior year that wasn't any bed of roses either. They say that high school is the best time of your life, but if that statement is true, I was in big trouble.

Let me get this off my chest. I hate to admit it, but I was feeling more and more depressed and less and less motivated about everything. Sports, for instance, weren't going well for me. While I had broken track and cross country records as a sophomore, I never broke my records again. And the most important sport to me, basketball, ended up being a complete bust, which only left me more unmotivated and cynical.

A word comes to mind that adults, especially teachers, had been throwing around a lot while I was in high school, *underachiever*. It's something else I remember looking up in our set of encyclopedias. Yes, the good old Britannicas.

Not that I didn't understand what the word meant, but somewhere early in my senior year, with nothing else to do except contemplate what a loser I was, I felt an overwhelming compulsion to look it up – *underachiever: one (such as a student or athlete) that fails to attain a predicted level of achievement or does not do as well as expected*. That described me to a T. Scanning the listing, I saw in the etymology of the word that it came into being in 1951, just in time for my birth a year later. In any case, I had come a long way since I sat at the kitchen table listening to that salesman make his pitch. A long way downhill, that is.

Don't get me wrong. I won a lot of races in both cross country and track. As a senior, I had finished first in nine of fourteen cross country meets, which isn't too shabby. But I had achieved these victories and others in track without my heart being in it. It's just that I have that competitive thing that some guys have. But when I faced an elite runner, I typically choked.

I recall one race where I went up against maybe the best runner in the league, Chip Reynolds from Lyman Hall High School. As a sophomore, Chip had won the big Housatonic League race, beating well over one hundred runners from every team in the league. As a junior, he came in second. The best I did either year was, like, twenty-first, which isn't awful, but it's also nothing to write home about. Reynolds was distance running royalty to say the least.

On a chilly November Tuesday in Wallingford, I went up against him for the last time. I'll never forget, right before the race, as I was taking a leak in the men's room, Reynolds walked in and said, "Who's DeMarco?" which shocked the hell out of me because, truthfully, I didn't think that he knew or cared who I was. What a poindexter he was, skinny as a rail with thick glasses held on with one of those elastic bands stretching tightly across the back of his head from ear to ear. I mean, this guy was a gigantic dweeb, except he could run like nobody's business.

When the gun sounded to begin the race a little while later, it was Reynolds and me stride for stride for two-thirds of the 2.8 mile course, but the first problem was that the Lyman Hall course was almost completely on a road instead of through woods and across fields. It was a course devoid of imagination or personality which started to bug me. The second thing that bugged me was Coach Zelly and their coach kept driving by yelling out the window. Their coach kept shouting, "That's it, Chip. He can't stay with you," and Coach Zelly kept yelling, "Stay with him, Gabe! You're as good as he is."

When you're a distance runner, your mind starts to play games with you. Negative thoughts pound at your brain, and you can't stop them.

So my mind starts to go haywire. *You can't beat this kid, ya loser! He's Chip Reynolds. He's the best kid in the league. His coach is right, and your coach is wrong!* And then I say to myself, *I'm going to let him go, and I'll just settle for second place. Coming in second to Chip Reynolds is nothing to be ashamed of.*

So, of course, I just shut down and let Chip Reynolds and his elastic band go. And before I know it, three more Lyman Hall kids come up close behind me, and then my brain says, *What's even the point of running? What's even the point of life?*

Those are the kinds of games your mind can play. But that's not even the worst of it.

Soon, two of my own teammates come up behind me and pass me by.

I finish seventh – my worst finish all year and the one time in my high school running career that any of my own teammates beat me.

So listen to this. On the bus, Coach Zelly sits next to me which I wasn't too thrilled about, and the guy asks in his most gentle voice, "Gabe, what happened back there?"

I just shrug because I don't want to talk about it. I just want to be alone in my misery.

So Coach Z gives me this puzzled look, and he says, "I mean, you were right by his side for more than two thirds of the race."

I just shrug again, thinking, *Now tell me something I don't know.*

If Coach Zelly and the Lyman Hall coach hadn't driven by us a couple million times, he wouldn't have known how long I was with Reynolds. Boy, did I feel like a dumbass the last time they drove by and I was in, like, 137th place.

Then he stares at me with these understanding eyes again, like he's Sigmund Freud or the most perceptive psychotherapist on the planet. "Don't you understand? You're just as good as Reynolds. Don't you realize that? You just let him go."

I tried to look at him like he was getting through to me, but what I was thinking was, *Yeah, right. Chip Reynolds. Ok, buddy!*

Let's face it, if Coach Z knew what he was talking about, we would have had a better team. I mean, unbelievably, my senior year was the first time Shelton ever (that's right, *ever*) won a cross country meet, and even then, we only won half of them. Finishing at 7-7 isn't going to win any gold medals.

It probably seems like I'm making a bigger deal out of sports than I should, but the kids I grew up with were obsessed with only two things – sports and girls. I'll get back to girls later, though.

In the neighborhood where I grew up and at the Boys Club where I spent thousands of hours, most kids could get by pretty well in one sport or another. It was a survival thing. If you wanted any respect, you had better be able to hit a baseball or hold your own on a basketball court. It was, like, you *needed* to be good at something, even ping pong or pool. Personally, by the time I was in eighth grade, I had developed a crazy passion for basketball that drove me. I was quick on the court, had a knack for dribbling and passing, and a pretty good shooting eye. And in every game, whether in a league or the playground, I went all-out.

It hadn't hurt my reputation in school when I accidentally found out I was a good distance runner as only a sophomore. On only my second day of cross country practice, I beat all of the upperclassmen, which brought me immediate notoriety. The next day in school, just about every football player patted me on the back for this first accomplishment. And when I broke our course record and, the following spring, broke the two mile record during track season, I was held in higher esteem by all other school athletes.

But during my last two years of school, something inside locked up and blocked any further real progress in the world of distance running. My heart wasn't completely in it. That complacency for track and cross country was one thing, but basketball was another. See, I ran distance not because I loved running but because I was good at it, but I played basketball because I loved it. There's an important distinction between the two. Doing what you're good at is all well and good, but a guy *needs* to do what he loves, and when he can't, it's another type of loss.

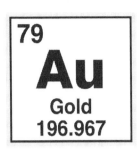

79
Au
Gold
196.967

I doubt if I'll ever forget Mr. Mown, my cool chemistry teacher during junior year. Mr. Mown was so cool, in fact, that he told us we could call him Mr. M. It sort of made you feel like he was your friend instead of your teacher. Mr. M looked like he was fresh out of college, and he sported a mustache and long sideburns like the Beatles have on one of my favorite albums, *Sgt. Pepper's Lonely Hearts Club Band.* His haircut was just a little more conservative than the Beatles and almost as long, but I think if he threw on a colorful military-style uniform, he would have fit right in the album picture, maybe right between Paul and Ringo. I don't know how he got away with the long sideburns because any time one of us kids grew out our sideburns, the assistant principal, Mr. Martin, walked up to us and said, "Hey, N-nutsie, d-d-don't come to school with th-those t-tomorrow," and, of course, we never did because who was going to mess with Mr. Martin? And who was going to make fun of his stuttering? That said, I guess the haircut rules were different for teachers. I personally never even tried for long sideburns because I had serious doubts they would grow in.

Anyway, I didn't think I was going to like chemistry because I was never into science, but Mr. M could talk about dust gathering on a bookshelf and make it sound like a matter of life and death, if you catch my drift. And if he could talk about dust that way, imagine what he could do with the periodic table.

I remember the day I walked into class and saw he had written the letters Au and the number 79 in bold chalk letters on the blackboard.

Once we were settled, he began, "Gold! An element you're all familiar with. Its symbol is Au; its atomic number, 79." He motioned to the board with his head. "You probably wouldn't have guessed that gold is far from the most valuable metal, yet it's been a symbol of wealth and prestige from time immemorial, presumably because of its warm, reflective color and because it doesn't tarnish or corrode."

He then explained that gold is also a symbol of eternal love which is why so many engagement and wedding rings are gold. I pretty much knew that because I didn't grow up in a cave, but Mr. M talked about it in such an engaging way, you couldn't help but pay attention.

There was something else about gold that he taught us that was new and that stuck with me, though. He sat on his desk, which is what he did whenever he got real serious with us, and he took off his college ring and tossed it up in the air and caught it. It was a Friday morning, the day of the Junior Ring Dance, and he said, "Take off your new class rings, hold them in the palm of your hands, and study them." So, we did like he said because we were wondering, *Where is he going with this?*

"What's fascinating about gold," he said, cocking his head and squinting at us with one eye, which is something else he did, "is that when you look at your ring, it appears to be permanent in form, but gold is highly malleable. You need to look beyond this application of gold. One ounce of gold from a ring like the ones you have in your palms can be deconstructed and then stretched into a thread fifteen miles long. A single milligram of the same gold can be hammered into a three-inch-square sheet so thin that light can easily pass through it. Can you imagine it?"

To be honest, it was hard for me to imagine my ring being transformed into a fifteen mile long thread.

"Furthermore," Mr. M continued, "the things gold symbolizes – wealth and prestige and, of course, love – are thought to be as permanent as the element of gold itself, but these qualities are, in fact, as often as not, ephemeral. While it's unlikely your *ring* will ever change its shape, your future wealth, prestige, and love very well may...or may, in fact, disappear completely. Give your rings a good look and think about that for a moment."

There we all were, staring at our rings "oohing" and "aahing" like we were watching fireworks on the fourth of July, when the girl sitting next to me, Jody Watkins, who has long, straight blonde hair, almost the color of gold, asked, "Wait, what does ephemeral mean, Mr. M?"

I could have told her what it meant, but I felt it was best to keep my mouth shut because I had a major crush on Jody.

Then Mr. M gave her this patient smile and said in a very low voice, "transitory," but Jody still had this puzzled look on her face, and I was thinking, *C'mon, Jody, get with the program so Mr. M can tell us the rest.*

Forever helpful, though, Mr. M clarified, "Short-lived...lasting for a very short time, maybe even a single day," in that same low, patient voice.

All of us nodded in agreement except for Jody, who said, "Wait! I don't get it."

"Anyone want to help Jody?" asked Mr. M.

Still looking at my ring like I'd been hypnotized by the thing, I raised my hand and took a stab. "Maybe it's, like, I'm looking at a class ring, and while it's a permanent object in one sense, in another sense the gold in the ring can be transformed into something very different from the class ring I think it is."

"Yeah, but what's that got to do with wealth or prestige or... love?" Jody asked.

I just rolled my eyes and looked at Mr. M for help because about the last thing I wanted to do was get on the wrong side of Jody Watkins.

"Gabe, you're on the right track. Let me suggest this – whenever you take your rings on or off, and as you celebrate today by turning your classmates' rings, and especially if you give your ring away to go steady, just give some thought to the permanent *appearance* of the things we see and experience in life. Are they really permanent? One of our biggest challenges in life is refusing to see that things change and sometimes, even, are gone forever."

For the rest of that school day and at the dance that night, I did what Mr. M suggested. As I turned each of my classmate's rings, I took Mr. M's advice and contemplated the ephemeral nature of life. At the same time, I also looked forward to a time when I would have a girlfriend to love and to give my ring to. I pictured a girl wearing it on a chain around her neck or making it smaller by wrapping colored yarn around the bottom of the ring and wearing it on her ring finger.

How perfect would life be if that happened? I mused.

CHAPTER 4

The beginning of basketball season in my junior year had a downside and an upside. The downside was that every senior on the football team chose to go out for basketball, and it wasn't like Coach Manzi was going to cut any of them, because like everyone else on the planet, Coach Manzi worships football players. It also meant that an insignificant distance runner like me was going to have to spend another year on the JV team. The upside was that I was the starting point guard as I had been as a sophomore.

In the first game against Trumbull, I found myself to be the victim in a chain of events that, in retrospect, I feel I had very little control over, like in *Romeo and Juliet*, except my story isn't romantic.

The way I see it is this – if I hadn't scored thirteen points in the first half, I wouldn't have been hoping to score twenty. And if I hadn't been hoping to score twenty, I probably would have told Coach Ruggerio that I injured my ankle at the beginning of the third quarter after landing awkwardly on it, battling for a rebound. And if I had told Coach Ruggerio about my ankle, I probably wouldn't have walked to River Restaurant in Derby after the game with Jeff who was home on leave from the Marines, thereby exacerbating the injury, making the damn ankle swell up like a balloon. And if I hadn't exacerbated the injury by walking to River Restaurant, Coach Manzi probably wouldn't have felt any need to call me a horse's ass. And if Coach Manzi hadn't had any need to call me a horse's ass, he probably wouldn't have told Coach Ruggerio to bench me even after the ankle healed.

Coach Manzi calling me a horse's ass took me by surprise because I had always been under the impression that he liked me. I remember freshman year when he saw me score eighteen points in a rec league game at the Boys Club.

After the game, he waved me over. "You go to the high school, son?" he asked.

"No, sir," I replied. "I go to St. Joe's."

He took a puff of his cigar. "Aw! Whattaya doin' there? You're a good player. We'd love to have you on the team at SHS."

I transferred after the first marking period in large part because of that exchange. And now what was I? A horse's ass!

Anyway, after spending the next five or six games on the bench, I was fed up. I had no idea why I wasn't playing.

Finally, in a game against Seymour, Coach Ruggerio put me in during the last twenty seconds of the game, and no sooner did I get in that I picked the pocket of the Seymour point guard, took the ball the length of the court, and laid it in at the final buzzer. At the blaring sound, I ripped my jersey off in front of the entire crowd and stomped off, banging through the locker room doors.

"When I saw the jersey come off," Michael would say later, "I knew you were all done." I could tell he felt bad about it.

A few days later, my Uncle Sonny said he heard I quit the team.

"Who told you?" I asked.

"I was at Over the Hill Tavern last Friday night, and Frank Ruggerio came in after the game and told me. He felt bad about it. Said he didn't understand why, but the head coach told him to keep you on the bench."

I was surprised to hear that Coach Ruggerio even knew I quit because it's not like I made a formal announcement. I just showered and went home. And to this day, I don't understand why Coach Manzi would have had me benched just because I made a bad judgment about my ankle problem. Can't a kid make a mistake?

I'm not trying to shirk my responsibility in the matter, but during that sprained ankle episode, when I would come home and complain that I suddenly wasn't getting any playing time, my dad would say stuff like, "You know what I'd do if I were you? I'd tell that coach where to stick it. Remember this. Never take any shit from anybody."

I guess it was true for him. A child of the Great Depression, Dad is a *never-take-any-shit-from-anybody* kind of guy, who slugged his way out of poverty and prejudice. He's fond of relating a story about how a boss of his had talked down to him when he was around our age, so he punched the guy out and sped away in his car, never to return.

I didn't envision beating up Coach Manzi, though, since he was a head taller and about eight hundred pounds heavier than me. Besides, Dad had also taught me to respect my elders. Talk about mixed messages.

If the basketball mess wasn't bad enough, the rest of junior year was a train wreck as far as girls were concerned.

After the basketball season ended, I miraculously had two romances, but neither worked out. First, I met a freshman named Kathy Duckworth at a dance at the Huntington Grange. I know that's a kooky name, Duckworth, but the truth is that Kathy doesn't look anything like a duck. In fact, she's a cute girl, so I asked her to dance, and before we knew it, we were making out in the corner of the hall next to a poster of Jim Morrison. I didn't even know her name yet. But Kathy couldn't shut up for ten seconds. A real chatterbox. She even kissed pretty good, and besides her cute face, Kathy had other physical attributes. But sometimes you just don't connect with a girl no matter what her bra size is. I just wanted to bust out of that corner and get away from both Kathy Duckworth and Jim Morrison, but what happened was I couldn't shake Kathy that night at the dance or for the next two months in school. So, we hung out and went out every now and then.

When I couldn't take the boredom any longer, I got rid of Kathy by not calling her anymore or meeting her between classes at school, which I realize was callous of me, and I started calling another freshman, Christine O'Hare. Or rather, she started calling me, which was a brand new experience for me because girls don't typically call guys. She must have heard about me and Kathy breaking up. Unlike Kathy, I fell hard for Christine. I have no explanation why I liked Christine so much because Kathy was way cuter. That's another weird thing. Everything with girls is chemistry. Or, if you listen to Mr. M, everything in *life* is chemistry.

Christine and I had a whirlwind romance where I saw her every Friday, Saturday, and Sunday for weeks. Two things happened to end it with Christine, though. The first was that my dad told me I couldn't give her my class ring.

One day after I got off the phone with her, out of nowhere he said, "Don't go thinking you're going to give this new girlfriend your class ring. Because I didn't shell out forty-five bucks so you could go give the goddamn thing away."

I don't know how he knew that had been my intention, because as far as I know, he's not psychic. He must have been listening when I talked to Christine about going steady on the phone, even though the door was closed and I was whispering.

My point is, not being able to give Christine my ring was a big setback as far as I was concerned. The next setback happened when Christine went to a picnic at Indian Well State Park with her friends on July 4th and cheated on me. Later that night, while talking on the phone, she dropped the bomb. I almost wish she had kept it a secret.

"You what?" I could feel myself breathing in short, rapid bursts.

"I...I don't know. We were all drinking, and I was a little drunk I guess, and before I knew it, I was making out with Eugene Kaminsky. You know who Eugene is, right?"

"Of course I know who Eugene is," I said.

I had seen the arrogant bastard around the Boys Club and in the halls at school.

So Christine continued, "Yeah, well, I mean...I didn't mean to. It just happened."

It just happened! Okay!

"Oh," I said back to her, because I had no idea how to respond.

"Yeah...so that's what happened. I feel bad about it. *Really* bad. Because you're such a nice guy and everything."

Then we both sat there on our own ends of the phone in complete silence for what seemed like, well, like about seventeen hours. I don't think there's anything more uncomfortable than silence. I was just breathing in and out as all kinds of craziness passed through my mind, like, *She's waiting for me to speak first* and *She's worrying I'm going to go ballistic on her* and *She must be hoping I'll forgive her.* Stuff like that.

Finally, I broke the silence. "Well...what I think is that...I just think...that...I'll forgive you, just this one time, I mean, but it mustn't ever happen again." I was thinking how unbelievably nice I was being about the whole sordid affair.

Another silence ensued, this one longer and more awkward than the first one, if that was possible.

Then, in an almost inaudible voice, Christine said, "I don't think so."

"You don't think so, what?" I asked.

"I don't think we should see each other anymore. It's just not going to work."

I won't lie. I felt pretty hurt. That night, I did what I always did when a girl hurt my feelings. I turned to music. Playing records on our home stereo had been an escape for me since being a young kid when I loved listening to albums by Doris Day and the film soundtrack to *The Sound of Music* – the only two albums my parents owned. When Michael began working and bringing new records home, I had a wider collection to choose from. Since seventh grade, I would listen to "Silence is Golden" by Frankie Valli and the Four Seasons and "The Tracks of my Tears" by Smokey Robinson and the Miracles whenever I felt heartbroken.

That night, as I spun those two old standby break-up songs over and over again, Frankie and Smokey helped me cope with heartbreak once more. In the process, I lay with my head fully under the base of the stereo cabinet, realizing I was rotating my class ring round and round my finger – the ring Dad had forbidden me to give Christine. And I thought to myself, *As usual, Mr. Mown was right. Love really is ephemeral.*

Not three weeks later, still smarting from being shot down by Christine, I watched Apollo 11 land on the moon, leaving Walter Cronkite, me, and the rest of the world speechless and in awe as Neil Armstrong and Buzz Aldrin walked across the lunar surface. I don't know. It made you feel how vast the universe is and how small you are.

Girl problems and moon landings aside, I went out for basketball again as a senior because I'm obviously a glutton for punishment. I knew I had to give it my *all* since I had quit a year ago. What's the old saying? Quitters never win, and winners never quit!

For me the old adage about quitters proved true because despite trying to have a positive attitude senior year, despite winning every wind sprint and just about every other conditioning drill, and despite going full throttle in every single aspect of practice, Coach Manzi found a way to get rid of me.

The day the uniforms were given out, I went to get mine, but Matt DeFerrari, the team manager, looked at his list like the thing was written in Greek and said, "Uhm...your name isn't on the list, Gabe."

The other guys were yucking it up in their excitement as they put on their uniforms, and I was trying to just, you know, hide somewhere. After they all left the locker room, I waited in my misery for Coach Manzi to come out of his office.

I was having trouble holding it together when he emerged. I don't know what I was expecting, but it wasn't this. Coach Manzi passes by, and he stops and gives me a look, like he's seeing something he doesn't recognize. "Something wrong, DeMarco?" he asks.

"Yeah," I say, "I don't understand what's happening."

"What do you mean?" he asks, still playing dumb.

"Well, the manager doesn't have a uniform for me. Am I on the team or not? I mean, you didn't cut me or anything."

So he leans over his fat belly and looks down at his own high top Chuck Taylors, like he's contemplating the meaning of life or something.

"It's just that you quit the team last year, remember?" he finally spits out, very grim and all.

"That was last year. This year, I'm here giving it one hundred and ten percent every day now. You must see that."

Then he takes another dramatic pause, once again drifting into the deepest recesses of his mind, and then he blurts out, "You know what? Go tell DeFerrari I said to give you a uniform," and just like that, he walks out onto the court.

The weirdest thing of all is when I got out onto the floor, Coach Manzi took me and the other five best players on the team to one basket and had us keep running offensive plays, alternating between me and Danny Oates at point guard, back and forth. Now I was thinking, *One minute he doesn't give me a uniform, and the next, I'm a potential starter. What the hell is going on? Is he testing me?*

As it turned out, it was a test, but one which I failed. At the game the next night, as we came out in our varsity uniforms for our layup drill, it was standing room only in the gym, and I felt dizzy. The raucous crowd, the other players, and even the hoop appeared tilted and blurry like when I was drunk with Tomaso. When the horn sounded to start the game, I wasn't on the starting roster. As the game progressed, I wasn't the sixth or seventh man – or even the eighth or ninth. In fact, Coach Manzi didn't put me in until the last minute of the game, and even then, he looked up and down the bench like he was pondering a life and death decision. As it turned out, for me, it was a death decision.

This time, I didn't make a dramatic steal or layup. It was all I could do to function because scalding tears were burning the corners of my eyes.

After a hot shower, I waited for him by his office. What histrionics would he pull this time? To this day, even though I'm in college now, I play this scene back in my mind like a movie.

Coach Manzi comes out and notices me standing there. "Got something on your mind, DeMarco?" he asks. At this point, I feel like I'm brain dead.

"Yeah, I guess I do," I say. "Would you mind telling me what's going on?"

"What do you mean?" he asks with a smirk.

Forging ahead in my nervousness, I say, "Yesterday, first you didn't give me a uniform, and then you had me practice with the starters. Then tonight, you barely played me. I don't understand."

"Oh yeah?" He looks down at me with those same grim eyes. "Well, if you don't like what's going on, DeMarco, maybe you should quit the team."

What do you even say to that? It wasn't what I was expecting him to say.

Unable to make eye contact, I said, "Yeah...I guess that's what I should do."

A little while later, as I was walking down the hill, Fran McDougal, one of the co-captains, pulled up, rolled down his window, and told me to get in his car. I wiped the tears from my eyes as I got in.

"What the fuck did you do, Gabe?"

I just shrugged.

"You didn't quit, I hope."

Another shrug from me because that's what I do when I can't speak.

"Aw, Jesus Christ, Gabe. You shouldn't have done that. We need you on the team."

But it was too late. I had quit. It's disappointing, I know. Believe me, the one thing worse than being disappointed in another person is being disappointed in yourself. Not that I mean to make the biggest deal out of high school basketball. Lots of people have bigger problems, I know. But just because others have bigger problems, aren't our own problems still important?

The next night, I spilled the whole rotten deal to Tomaso, who suggested we go up to DeMarco Mountain and tie one on. Being in the state of mind I was in, I didn't argue.

As we sat in his car on DeMarco Mountain with the dashboard lights glowing in our faces, he said to me, "You know my old man would never have taken any shit from that coach, and neither would yours have."

"Yeah, I know," I mumbled.

"Just sayin'."

"I know."

His dad and mine are, like, second cousins, which is why we have the same last name. See, Aunt Lucia is my dad's favorite sister. And my dad had grown up looking up to Tomaso's father. In fact, Uncle Buzz was the best man for my father when he and my mom got married. Not the other way around, though, because my dad was a kid, maybe twelve, when my aunt and uncle got married.

"I'm just sayin'," Tomaso continued, "that you should never forget you're a DeMarco and that guys in our family don't let people treat us like crap. Understand?"

I shrugged to show I understood because Tomaso and I were both basically drunk and because what else was I supposed to say? But the truth was, that kind of talk didn't make me feel better. I had worked too hard and wanted it too badly to have my dream of being a varsity basketball player go up in smoke. It felt like I could never catch a break.

That night, I felt so bad, in fact, that I got out of the car and threw up. It was the first time that I barfed from drinking too much. I'm not proud of it either.

The next morning, as I lay in bed, hungover, I contemplated my basketball experience and wondered if there was anything to be learned from it – perhaps a moral to the story. My father used to tell me stories about a fictional character during the Great Depression who worked hard to achieve his goals. I've forgotten what the guy's name was. Andy something or other. But the message was clear – success is the result of perseverance and hard work. Lying in bed with a pounding headache, I realized it simply wasn't true. Message received.

CHAPTER 5

When the third marking period began, I found myself in typing class, a course my mom had demanded I take.

"I'm not going to type all of your goddamn papers when you're in college like I did Michael's," Mom had said.

Mom doesn't generally say any bad words, but she can sure throw her "goddamns" around when she gets going.

But it was true. I can remember her at the kitchen table, pecking away in frustration as she tried to correct mistake after mistake with Wite-Out. Sometimes she'd get so rattled, she'd tear the paper out of the carriage of the typewriter like she was Bruno Sammartino ripping some other wrestler's head off.

So I responded, "Don't get all freaked out, Celia. I'll take typing if you want."

After Michael had dubbed our mother "the Big C" and himself "the Big M," naming them both after "the Big E," college basketball phenom Elvin Hayes, I felt like I needed a name for Mom too, so I used the shortened version of Cecelia, which is how her siblings address her. It's my own tongue-in-cheek game with her, and as far as I can tell, she likes it.

"I get too nervous typing," she explained. "You know I'm no good with my hands since those damned teachers made me use my right hand as a kid when I was born a lefty."

"Yeah, Celia. No sweat. I got ya covered," I assured her.

As it turned out, I was an all-star in typing class because I didn't know any of the kids, who were all girls, so instead of goofing off, I just minded my own business and typed. And unlike my mother, I'm pretty good with my hands. Add to that, the teacher was young and pretty, and she gave a handful of Hershey's Kisses and made a big fuss over whoever typed the most words in a speed test at the end of class. Why would I pass that up?

During the lunch wave on the back end of that class, I ate alone because I didn't know anyone in that wave. I didn't mind a bit because I could read while I ate.

One day, about a month after I quit basketball, I was sitting at a corner table, eating an overdone toasted cheese sandwich, slurping up a watery bowl of tomato soup, and reading *For Whom the Bell Tolls*, not for school, but just because I wanted to. I mean, the point is, I was minding my own business when I was interrupted.

"Anyone sitting here?" I heard a female voice ask.

With my back facing the corner of the big cafeteria, I looked up to find a skinny girl holding her lunch tray. She was wearing outdated cat-eye glasses, and she was decked out in forest green from head to toe. Scanning down, I saw her crew-neck sweater, matching plaid skirt and tights, and penny loafers, the only apparel that wasn't green. I wanted to say, *We don't wear school uniforms here.* Scanning back up, I saw a handsome face and poker straight brown hair, parted in the center and falling to the middle of her back. She was as neat as a pin, but otherwise someone forgot to tell her it was 1970.

"Uhm...no...no one is sitting there," I replied, as I wondered why she didn't sit by herself at any of the million empty tables around us.

"Well, do you mind if I sit there then, DeMarco?" I was surprised to hear her call me by my name.

"I...uhm...I...no, you can sit wherever you want, I guess. It's a free country." I shrugged, bit into my toasted cheese, and stuck my nose back in my book. I gave it a few minutes, pretending to read, and looked up. She was working on her own toasted cheese, chewing with her mouth closed in a tidy rapid rhythm and staring at me.

When we made eye contact, she said, "What are you reading, DeMarco?"

I was puzzled, to say the least. "Uhm...do we...uh...do we know each other?" I asked.

"Well, you obviously don't know me. But, of course, I know you,

DeMarco. I sit three seats behind you in typing. You sit in the first seat, second row, and I'm in the fourth seat, third row, so it's easy to see you typing away from my vantage point. And then, of course, you win almost every speed test. You're a real typing demon, aren't you?"

"I...guess, but –"

"Let me introduce myself. I'm Mary Elizabeth Kiernan."

Mary Elizabeth Kiernan reached her right hand across the table to shake mine. I noticed she was wearing a signet ring and also a simple, engraved bracelet on her wrist, like I'd seen a number of girls wearing.

After a firm handshake from her, I said, "That's one of those bracelets, isn't it? What's it say on it?"

She answered by reaching her wrist across the table and letting me read it for myself: George Howe – 1/10/68.

Looking into my eyes, she said, "Well, more specifically, it's a POW/MIA bracelet."

"Yeah, I know," I replied, almost defensively. "I've seen them before."

"POW, prisoner of war. MIA, missing in action."

"Yeah, I get it."

"I sent away for it."

"And this George Howe, is he someone you know?"

"Never met him, DeMarco. But I've promised to wear it every day until George's whereabouts is discovered."

"I see," I said and then shifted gears a little. "Uhm...so...you know me from where? From our typing class, sitting in the next row, three seats behind me? Is that right?"

"Come on, DeMarco. Everyone knows you."

"Everyone knows me? I don't think that everyone knows –"

"You've got to be kidding me, right, DeMarco?" she said, cutting me off again. "You can't be serious. I mean, you realize, I hope, that you can't be a big track star and have your name plastered on the school record plaque outside the gym without having everyone know you. Besides that, you're a basketball player. And besides that, every girl I know wants to go out with you."

I was now thoroughly confused. "Uhm...what year did you say you were?"

"I didn't say. I'm a sophomore."

With no small degree of irony, I said, "Right. Well, listen, first of all, if every girl you know wants to go out with me, I wish some of them would tell me. I wish even *one* of them would tell me. And, for your information, I am not on the basketball team, so if you don't mind, I'll just get back to my book."

I hadn't read a whole paragraph before she interrupted me again, "I think I offended you somehow, DeMarco, although I can't imagine how because I don't know why anyone would ever be offended by being told they're well known."

Her directness was, to be honest, irritating.

So I frowned and replied, "You didn't offend me, Mary Elizabeth Whatever Your Name Is."

"Kiernan."

"Yeah, right. Mary Elizabeth Kiernan. But, listen, basketball is sort of a touchy subject for me, and even though you sound sincere, I'd appreciate it if you wouldn't tell me that girls like me when they actually don't."

"Okay, DeMarco. I won't bring up basketball if you don't want me to, and I'll lie to you if you want and tell you that none of the girls I know like you."

"O-kayyy," I said. "Do you mind if I get back to reading my book now?"

"Not at all." A pause, and then, "Homework, is it?" Another pause, "For English class?" She interspersed these questions between little fastidious bites of her toasted cheese, careful not to talk with her mouth full.

This chick doesn't give up. "Not homework...just something I want to read."

"Because you like to read?"

"Right. In fact –"

"Weird. I don't know any boys who like to read."

In my impatience, I'm sure I grimaced. "Well, now you do."

"Hmmm, interesting. What's it about?"

"Well, if you must know, uhm, Mary..." I paused once again, trying to recall her name.

"Elizabeth...but you can call me Kiernan if you want."

"I'd rather not call you by your last name, because –"

"Okay, Mary Elizabeth is fine then. Or everyone calls me Liz if you like that better, DeMarco."

"And I'd rather that you not call *me* by my last name because –"

"You want me to call you Gabriel then?"

I couldn't remember the last time anyone had interrupted me this much.

"Well, how about this?" I said. "Why call each other anything? After all, we're not exactly friends."

"I can't think of any good reason we can't be friends now that we know each other," she said, matter-of-factly.

Instead of getting into a *thing*, I just said, "Gabe will be fine."

And there I was, through no conscious effort of my own, on a first name basis with a sophomore girl. I felt like I had almost been tricked into it. Then, surrendering to the situation, I related to her that *For Whom the Bell Tolls* is about the Spanish Civil War but that the protagonist is an American named Robert Jordan who joins the rebels in fighting against fascism.

The interesting thing is that while I was telling her about the book, she didn't interrupt me again or even say another word, but instead listened in a way that made me feel heard.

Before I knew it, I launched into an explanation that Robert Jordan was my idea of a true hero as I continued to summarize the plot.

"So Robert Jordan falls in love with a beautiful Spanish woman named Maria, see, who is supporting the cause. Wait, listen to this part that I just read a little while ago. He's, like, thinking to himself here."

I turned back four or five pages looking for the excerpt I had in mind where Robert Jordan contemplates the love he has for Maria:

What you have with Maria, whether it lasts just through today and a part of tomorrow, or whether it lasts for a long life is the most important thing that can happen to a human being. There will always be people who say it does not exist because they cannot have it. But I tell you it is true and that you have it and that you are lucky even if you die tomorrow.

No sooner had I gotten the end of the quote out of my mouth that the bell rang. I looked around and saw that the cafeteria had emptied.

"Wow, you're quite a romantic, aren't you, DeMarco? I mean, Gabriel...I mean, Gabe."

I think I blushed.

"Maybe you'll let me borrow it when you're through, but it looks like we have to get to our next class. I'll see you in typing tomorrow, though, okay? Just look three seats behind you, to your right."

Mary Elizabeth then half-smiled, got up, and returned her tray to the window near the kitchen. I, on the other hand, moved a little slower. As I saw her walk away, those green tights and loafers traversing the floor in small rapid steps, I shook my head. I'll probably go to my grave forever wondering what it was about Mary Elizabeth Kiernan that prompted me to read such a passage from *For Whom the Bell Tolls*.

As I walked out of the cafeteria, I heard Fran McDougal from the basketball team call out to me. "Get back, Jojo."

Fran and I had the next class, Advanced Math, together.

I turned around and replied, "Get back, Loretta!"

It was a private joke Fran and I had, repeating the lyrics from John Lennon's hit every time we saw each other.

"So what's going on?" he asked.

"Oh, nothing much." I almost laughed and added, "I just met some weird girl in the cafeteria. She just plopped herself down and had lunch with me."

"Pretty?" Fran asked.

"I don't know," I said. "More weird than pretty. Forget I even mentioned it, because I doubt I'll be talking to her again."

As we walked into Mr. Reagan's class, though, I had a funny feeling that I hadn't heard the last from Mary Elizabeth Kiernan.

CHAPTER 6

Toward the end of typing class the day after meeting her, Mary Elizabeth walked by my desk as she headed to the wastepaper basket, and she plopped a note on my typewriter keyboard, one of those folded triangles of words that girls love to write. On her way back to her own desk, she gave me a wide-eyed look and then winked and smiled. When the bell rang, Mary Elizabeth bolted out of the room and into the traffic of the hallway. Trailing far behind, I slowly unwrapped the tidy geometric note. In her impeccable handwriting, almost as if it had been typed, it said:

Hello Mr. Gabriel DeMarco,
I hope I've addressed you in an acceptable way! Meet me near the buses after school. I'm a walker like you. We don't live far from each other. Let's walk together. I think you need a good friend.
Truly,
M.E.

M.E.? I questioned, and then it dawned on me. *Her initials.*

I was dumbstruck by her note. I mean, it was presumptuous of her to assume I would meet her and walk home with her. How did she know I didn't already have plans or that I wasn't already walking home with someone else or that I had any interest in talking to her again? A ten minute conversation over a bowl of watery tomato soup and overdone toasted cheese does not constitute a relationship.

And how did she know that I was a walker or where I lived? But the truth was that, since quitting the basketball team, I did walk home alone, and an even greater truth was that I was, in fact, interested in talking to her after school, not that I was going to admit it to anyone that mattered. So after school, as I headed down the walk where hundreds of kids climbed into yellow buses, there stood Mary Elizabeth Kiernan on Shelton High School's frozen lawn. She seemed to be making a design with the toe of her shoe in a thin layer of snow from a recent snowfall which coated the lawn.

"Glad you could make it, Gabriel."

"How did you know I'd come?" It was cold, and I could see my breath in the air.

"Just a hunch," she said. Then she told me where she lived, on upper Kneen Street, about a quarter of a mile past Jeff's grandma's house, and she said, "You used to live on Maltby Street, but you moved somewhere."

I was starting to worry she was a crazy stalker, but she explained it further. "You lived on Maltby Street for a long time. I hung out at the playground at Fowler School when you and your friends used to play basketball and softball and football there. You just didn't notice me because I'm two years younger than you. Why did you move?"

As we headed down Perry Hill Road, I said, "I moved because... wait, what is it you want from me?"

"Not to have you be my boyfriend, if that's what you're hoping, Gabriel." Who the hell did she think she was? I didn't like her like *that*.

She took out a pack of gum and offered me a stick. I couldn't help noticing how comfortable she was in her own skin. As we both began unwrapping the shiny foil, she continued. "It's not about what I want from you but what you *need* from me."

"What do you mean, *need* from you? Listen, Mary Elizabeth, I don't need –"

"Don't go getting all huffy, Gabe," she interrupted as she chewed her gum. "I can tell you have problems that you need to talk about. I'm willing to be your psychiatrist. Like Lucy and Charlie Brown. You need someone you can open up to. A confidante who will keep what you say between us. So let's start with basketball. What happened?"

And, as we turned right on Bridgeport Avenue, I knew the route we were taking was a little out of my way, but I was happy to have the opportunity to spill it. I told her the whole ugly story of quitting the team and how disappointed and heartbroken I was over it. As good as she was at interrupting, she was even better at listening.

The next day, I told her about Jeff enlisting and Tomaso more recently getting drafted and about how Michael was growing up and almost ready to graduate college. I didn't tell her everything that's ever happened to me because there are some things that aren't just anybody's business, and besides, I hardly knew her.

"So, it sounds like you're feeling pretty alone right now, huh?" she offered.

"Well, yeah. Wouldn't you feel that way if you were me?"

Jutting her lower lip out and giving me a pensive nod, she said, "Yeah, Gabriel, I would. Well, listen. The best I can tell you is I can't fix what happened with Coach Manzi, and I know I can't be what your guy friends are, or were, to you, like Jeff or Tomaso or Michael, but I can promise you that you have a friend in me that you can always talk to."

I appreciated having a new friend to talk to. It even became a little bit of a joke between us. She would pass me one of her triangular messages in the hallway every now and then with a simple phrase inside. Just the words, *Psychiatric session after school? Be there or be square!*

And just about every day we walked, and I talked while she listened. I even got into a discussion of all the relatives and others that were dying around me or might be dying around me in the near future, but there were some things about death I didn't know how to talk about. Soon enough, our "sessions" drifted away from death and how alone I felt to my confusion over my relationship with girls. Because, the thing is, in general, there is nothing more confusing than trying to figure out how to navigate the treacherous waters of relationships with girls. I guess there are some things that stay bottled up inside you and that you can't even tell someone like Mary Elizabeth.

Mary Elizabeth called me out on it, over and over.

"Here we go round the mulberry bush," she'd say, "with the very cryptic Gabriel DeMarco."

But imagine what it might have been like to tell Mary Elizabeth that I was the only senior at Shelton High School who hadn't had sex yet – this girl who had *virgin* written all over her. How was I going to bring that one up? I *wasn't*, that's how. It was too embarrassing to talk about.

Not that I was completely without experience. In the last year, I had quite a few experiences kissing girls, ever since Lenore Ott had broken up with me freshman year because I hadn't kissed her. I vowed that'd never happen again. The problem was getting a relationship going because "good girls" didn't do more than kiss unless they were in love. That's the way I understood it. The girls I liked didn't seem to like me, and I didn't seem to like the girls who liked me. It figures.

My main hangout, Mosci's, was a guy's world, and it didn't take more than a few minutes, listening to other guys talk, to realize what a loser you were. You didn't even have to be part of the conversation. You could just be minding your own business, playing a pinball machine or flipping through a detective magazine or waiting for your turn at the phone booth, and the next thing you knew you'd hear some guy bragging about his latest sexual conquest. It made me wonder if maybe "good girls" weren't always so good.

Now that I was a senior, I had made a big decision for myself way back in September, months before Mary Elizabeth had intruded on my lunch wave in the cafeteria, that I was going to have sex with someone before graduation. It seemed fair enough since I had the whole year before me, but now that we were past the mid-year, I wasn't so sure.

I didn't share my secret with Mary Elizabeth because I don't think she would have liked hearing it. It's not like my goal in life was some noteworthy endeavor, like finding the cure for cancer or solving the problem of world hunger.

Then one day, when I was expounding on how confusing girls are, and while walking Mary Elizabeth home, she said, "If you're talking about Christine O'Hare, Gabriel, don't judge everyone by her."

I was stunned. "You know about Christine O'Hare?"

"Of course, Gabriel, we all know. Christine is our classmate."

"Well...uhm...I mean...what do you know? What does everyone know?"

"We all know she cheated on you."

That was thrilling to hear. I hadn't realized it had gone public.

Mary Elizabeth continued. "I can't speak for anyone else, but as far as I'm concerned Christine is insane. I mean, insane to pick Eugene over you...but that's just me. But, like I said, I wouldn't go judging all girls by Christine."

Anyway, there were a few other girls after Kathy Duckworth and Christine O'Hare, but no one worth talking about. Just "one-night stands" but not the variety where the couple has sex. Rather, they were encounters where I just fumbled one thing or another, not something I was about to discuss with Mary Elizabeth. My ineptitude with girls wasn't exactly something I was interested in broadcasting.

CHAPTER 7

In sharp contrast to Mary Elizabeth was a girl who hung out in the Duchess parking lot. Her name was Emily, but in my mind she was "barefoot Emily" because she never wore shoes. As someone who cleaned the lot during my first year working at Duchess, I can testify to the fact that no one should be walking around the asphalt parking lot barefoot. Emily's feet were always filthy, which personally grossed me out. The rest of her wasn't too clean either. Her clothes were soiled, and her hair looked like a stringy old bird's nest, frizzy and unkempt, just like Janis Joplin's. Otherwise, Emily wasn't half bad looking.

It was only a few weeks after Tomaso got drafted that a Duchess grill man, a guy named Sallie, took Emily parking one night. I know Sallie sounds like a girl's name, but it's a nickname based on his last name, Salfieri. And Sallie isn't a nickname given to him by my brother Michael, which is often the case, but one he grew up with as a kid.

Sallie and Michael had become good buddies, and Sallie is a good player on our Duchess basketball team. I say "our" because, since quitting the high school team, I had been playing on the Duchess team. Michael, as player-coach, let me join.

But back to Sallie. He's a real classic. I'll never forget how during a game we lost, I was sitting next to him on the bench during the fourth quarter, and as our guys missed shot after shot, Sallie sat shaking his head in dismay.

"Look, Gabe! Gabe, look! Will ya look?" he complained. "We're missing all these open shots. You can't miss open shots. You know that, right, Gabe? You can't win if you miss open shots. You understand what I mean, right, Gabe? Look at that – look! Another missed open shot. If you have an open shot, Gabe, you gotta make it. Open shots! You just gotta make 'em!"

Sallie could sure hammer away at a point. The thing is, after he carried on that day, it seemed like Sallie never missed an open shot again. I think there's a book, *The Power of Positive Thinking*. Just like that, Sallie became a dead shot.

That night, when he got back to Duchess with barefoot Emily, Sallie came inside, and we all crowded around him.

"So how did it go?" Tomaso asked.

"It went good," Sallie said. "Emily's a hot chick. It went really good. I had a good time. A really good time. Really good."

"Ya think she'd get together with me?" Tomaso asked.

I knew what was on Tomaso's mind. He had been moaning that he wanted to have sex before he went to basic training.

"Yeah, and how about me?" Robbie Latella added.

"Yeah...yeah. I think she'll get together with anyone who wants to get together with her because, you know, she likes to hook up. She really likes to hook up, and she's a good time. This chick loves hooking up with guys. I had a really good time. I mean, it was good."

Sallie explained sex like he explained basketball. So, now almost everyone seemed to want a night with Emily. Sallie grabbed a paper bag and made a schedule with a list of four guys on it. Then Sallie went out and showed the schedule to barefoot Emily, who apparently was fine with the whole plan. Within a day or two, there were seven guys on the list.

I, on the other hand, was feeling funny about the whole thing. In one sense, I get it. Emily thought of herself as practicing free love. In another sense, maybe this was pushing free love a little too far. So, despite my still unfulfilled goal, I didn't sign up because it seemed creepy to me, not to mention the vision of Emily's grimy feet. And I noticed that my friend Bink didn't sign up either because...well, because, if there was another guy who was a virgin in the Valley, it was Bink. I'm pretty sure Bink had never even kissed a girl, so I was way ahead of him.

Kevin Binkowski and I had started working at Duchess within a month of each other at the end of 1967. I wasn't even sixteen, but like I said, Howie, the owner, paid me under the table. It was my brother Michael who christened Kevin with the name "Bink" and, as is often the case with nicknames, it stuck. Besides Kevin's other obvious social inadequacies with members of the opposite sex, I'm sure being known as "Bink" didn't help.

I also remember when my brother saw the list hanging on the bulletin board near the phone and asked about it. When Sallie told him what was going on, Michael smirked and said, "Wow! You guys are even more fucked up in the head than I realized."

That was good enough for me. If Michael wasn't on board, then I wasn't either.

Then Michael came up with an interesting plan. We were driving home after work one night when he said, "I think I know how I can throw a wrench into this whole Emily thing."

"How's that?" I asked.

"Well, you and I know Bink doesn't have any experience with girls, right?"

"Uhm...yeah. Everyone knows that." Where was he going with this?

"Right! So if Bink goes out with Emily, I feel pretty confident he'll at least experience his first kiss. I don't think he has enough smarts to get further than that, right?"

"Well...no," I said, "but there're already seven guys on the list."

"Yeah? We'll see about that," he said with a confident nod.

A day later, without asking anyone's permission, Michael put Bink at the top of the list, scheduling Bink to take Emily for a ride the very next night. The first guy to complain was Tomaso.

"There's a list here! You can't just put Bink at the top," he argued.

"But I did, didn't I?" a supremely confident Michael replied.

"But there are rules," Tomaso whined.

"Don't sweat it. Rules were meant to be broken," my brother replied. "You'll just have to wait."

Tommy Trouble stormed away, threw the spatula across the grill and moaned, "What the fuck?"

But, see, Tomaso idolized Michael too much to push the matter.

When the next night came, sure enough, Emily arrived at Duchess to be with Bink and off they went in Bink's car. But when they arrived back at the place a few hours later, Emily came to the window, looking puzzled. As I was bagging some fries, I saw Michael take her down to the second window that was only used during rush hour. The two of them were talking in hushed tones, so I couldn't hear what they were saying. Bink must've still been out in his car.

The next thing I knew, Michael called all the guys who were working and hanging out over by the back sink and made yet another announcement. Or perhaps I should call it a decree.

"Listen up, guys, I have an announcement to make," Michael began in his most officious tone. "I hate to interfere in something that might not be any of my business, but it appears that Bink has fallen for Emily," he said. "She said they went to Osbornedale Park near the pond and had a really nice talk."

Tomaso knocked his fist into a wall and said, "A nice talk? What do you mean a nice –"

"Then, guess what," my brother continued. "Bink asked her to go to a concert at Yale Bowl. Grand Funk Railroad. Isn't that great?"

"What are you saying?" Tomaso said in disbelief. "The Yale Bowl concerts don't start until May."

Michael just shrugged. "That's right."

It was almost as if Michael had planned the entire caper.

"This doesn't mean the rest of us can't have our night with Emily, I hope," Tomaso moaned.

"Well," Michael replied, "at least not until after the concert, presuming things don't work out between Emily and Bink."

"You're shittin' me," Tomaso complained.

"I shit you not," Michael replied, ripping the list off the bulletin board and crumpling it up into a tight ball. "This 'good time with Emily' list is now defunct."

My brother has a way of bringing a conversation to an end with an air of authority I can only guess he inherited from our father. None of the guys who had signed up were happy about it, but my brother had taken over, and as far as he was concerned, barefoot Emily was now more or less Bink's girlfriend.

In the meantime, after work that night, I got signed up for something I hadn't expected. Hanging around outside by his Chevelle as we waited for Michael to finish counting the money, Tomaso continued to vent to me.

"Fuckin' Bink went and ruined everything, so now I need to come up with a new plan," he explained.

"New plan for what?" I asked, drop-kicking an empty cup on the ground across the lot.

"I leave for boot camp on June 1st. I need to get laid before I go, but now that Michael made Emily off limits, I need to come up with a new plan."

As I gobbled down a handful of fries, I mumbled, "Oh yeah? What's your new plan?" Tomaso was more experienced than me, for sure, but it wasn't like any of us could just make it happen with a snap of our fingers.

"Well...the way I look at it is this. Since I don't have a girlfriend or anything that resembles one at the moment, and since there's not a million Emilys running around, we're gonna have to pay for it."

"What do you mean by *we*?" I asked, still not catching on.

"What I mean is me and you are gonna have to pay for it. What I mean is me and you, and anyone else who wants to come, are going to New York and finding us some hookers."

"Hmmm...I don't know about that one," I said.

"What do you mean you don't know about that one? You're my cousin, and I fuckin' need you to do this with me. It'll be fun. I don't know what it costs, but how expensive can it be? It'll be an adventure. It sucks that I got drafted, and I want to do this...and you're doin' it with me. Capisce?"

The word *adventure* had a certain appeal. Besides, going to New York with Tomaso sounded like an easier way of achieving my goal with graduation getting closer. And it didn't seem as unethical as hooking up with Emily. At least I wouldn't be taking advantage of anyone. After all, it's how hookers make their living.

To make it even better, I'd be doing it for Tomaso.

"When did you have in mind?" I asked.

"As soon as possible, but I think we might need to wait a few weeks until the weather warms up. I don't want to freeze my ass off walking around New York. Are you in or out?"

"Ok," I conceded, "I'm in."

On the way home, I decided not to tell Michael about New York. I figured it might be best to let him find out when he found out.

Instead, I asked, "So what were you saying to barefoot Emily when you took her down to the second window?"

"I told her to try to look nice for Bink...that it's probably his first date ever and she should try to dress up a little...and put on a pair of shoes!"

"You did? Wow! Was she, like, offended or anything?"

"Nope. I mean, I tried to be diplomatic and all. I focused on Bink not having any experience with girls, which Emily liked. She kept saying things like, 'Aw, that's so sweet' and 'Bink is so innocent' and other stuff like that. It was almost as if I *wasn't* telling her to take a shower and comb her hair."

By the time Bink and Emily went to the concert at Yale Bowl, Sallie was on board for the New York trip. Of course he was. I didn't mind that, though, because Sallie was about the same age as Michael, maybe twenty-two, so I felt we would be going with someone who knew which end was up.

Tomaso picked the second Friday in May for the New York trip. Ironically, it was a week after Bink and Emily would go to the Grand Funk concert. I wasn't on the schedule to work that night, but Tomaso was, so I hung out alternating between shooting the bull with Tomaso inside and standing outside people watching. Before the concert, Bink stopped in to show off Emily.

She had obviously listened to Michael and taken a bottle of shampoo and a brush to her blonde hair, which now had a pretty purple ribbon in it that matched a choker with a peace symbol around her neck, and she was wearing a long-sleeved white blouse with frilly cuffs and a collar with wavy ruffles. The blouse was something right out of a Shakespearean play. To go with it, she was wearing a tight brownish leather mini-skirt, like cowhide, with tights the color of mustard, which only went down to the ankle. And, unbelievably, barefoot Emily was wearing shoes – open-toed sandals with big, clunky platforms. Best of all, her feet looked clean, which I felt relieved about.

I'm not going to lie; she looked pretty in a funky way. A major transformation, grungy hippie morphs into stylish hippie. Just as I had suspected, Emily was super cute, and I pretty much envied Bink.

It must have been about a half hour before closing when Bink arrived back from the concert with Emily. As they got out of Bink's car, I could see that Emily was once again barefoot, the index and middle fingers of her right hand hooked under the strap of her shoes. They came over to me near the side of the building and started filling me in on how awesome Grand Funk Railroad had been. Bink was less animated than Emily, though. He didn't seem quite right. His eyes were watery, like he was going to cry.

There was Emily, in mid-sentence, when Wayne Walker, a guy from my old neighborhood, pulled up with two of his buddies in his silver Mustang convertible. Without finishing her thought, Emily ran over to him, leaned over the driver's door, and gave Wayne a big hug like he was her long lost brother. Then, before Bink and I knew it, Wayne opened his door, pulled back his seat for Emily to climb in, and off they went. As Wayne tore out of the parking lot, I could see her feet up in the air. It was pretty depressing to watch Emily throw her shoes high into the air and see them come crashing down on the shoulder of Pershing Drive, as if to say, "I'm never wearing shoes again, and I'm never going out with Bink again either!"

The look of disappointment in Bink's eyes broke my heart. His big date had just gone up in smoke. Dejected, he sat down on the curb, and not knowing what to do, I joined him.

My relationship with Bink had changed a lot over the years. I remember our first weeks, cleaning the lot together and listening to him instruct me on the way to do it, parroting all of the advice he had received from the managers and window men. "You know what, Gabe? Howie will tell you and all of the window men including your brother will tell you...even if you see a single straw paper on the ground, pick it up...just pick it up."

Listening to him extol the virtues of picking up straw wrappers, I pondered, *This kid is hands down the biggest dweeb in the whole universe.* But when I became a window man this past year, my perspective began to change. For whatever reason, Howie and Will had chosen me when they could have chosen Bink who was a year older. Bink not only showed no jealousy, but he did everything in his power to make my job easier during rush hour in my first weeks on the window. If he wasn't in the midst of cooking a tray of burgers, he would come up to the front counter and help get drinks or wrap hamburgers or do anything that would help me. None of the other grill men had my back or would go the extra mile like Bink.

As I sat next to him on the curb, I asked, "So, what happened, Bink? It didn't go too good, huh?"

"I don't know," he said. "We both liked the concert. She was even dancing around, just, you know, into it. But after it ended, I suggested we race to the car, except I somehow got lost and it took me quite a while to find the car because, you know, there were hundreds and hundreds of cars outside the stadium. When I finally found the car, most of the lot had emptied, and her mood had changed."

"Yeah," I replied. "I don't think the race was the best idea you ever had, but..."

I couldn't go on. Poor Bink just tightened his lips and shrugged like he was trying to force back tears. I know how that is.

I tried to console him. "Well, don't let her get to you, Bink. She's not the right girl for you, is she?"

Bink just picked up a straw from the asphalt and dragged it on the ground as if he was drawing in sand on a beach.

"Listen, Bink, she's not worth it. She's a cute girl, but she's out there, if you know what I mean. And when I say out there, I mean *way* out there."

"I guess so," he said.

"Hey," I said, thinking of a good idea, "this is going to sound a little crazy, but Tomaso, Sallie, and I are going to New York to pick up some prostitutes later in the week. You wanna come with us?"

"Prostitutes?" he asked, squeezing his left eyelid shut, almost as if he had never heard the word.

"Yeah, next Friday. It'll be fun...you know...professional hookers, right in the middle of New York City. It'll be an adventure, and it'll take your mind off of Emily."

"Well," he said with a touch of hesitation, "if you're going, uhm, I guess I'll go. I mean, I don't think I'd know what to do with a prostitute, but...I –"

"That's the good thing about a prostitute, Bink. I don't think it matters if you know what to do because *she'll* know what to do. When it comes to sex, I think prostitutes are, like, basically experts."

When Tomaso found out how Bink's date turned out to be a bust, he suggested to Michael that he reinstate the list. Michael just rolled his eyes and said, "Not in this lifetime."

Tomaso wasn't as high on Bink coming on the New York trip as I was. Standing by our cars after work, I reassured him that I'd take full responsibility for Bink. "Besides," I added, "it'll be a good way for Bink to get it on with a girl."

"A good way?" Tomaso laughed. "How else would it ever happen? He just better not say or do anything fuckin' stupid."

"He won't. I'll make sure of it," I promised.

On the drive home, my mind wandered back to sitting in a booth at Mosci's, sipping on a cold milkshake and perusing the detective magazines. I pictured the girls we would be with in New York looking like the beautiful models in the glossy photos, dressed in nothing but black satin bras and sheer dark stockings with garter belts. I wondered whether mine would be a blonde or a brunette. Either way, it was going to be a blast.

CHAPTER 8

The plan was set. The four of us – Tomaso, Sallie, Bink, and I – would take a train to New York on the following Friday.

When I say the idea of going to New York appealed to me because it would be an adventure, I was in bad need of one. After the disappointments of my quitting basketball, my failure to break any more distance running records, and my utter ineptitude with girls, I not only needed an adventure, I deserved one.

Compounding my problems was the fact that I was going to have to go to Southern Connecticut State College, just like Michael had. Nothing against Michael, but I was sick and tired of always doing what he had done. I had wanted to go to an out-of-state college. I think I felt something like Jeff did when he joined the Marines to get away from home, only I'd be having a lot more fun in college than he was probably having in the military.

I had been getting letters from college track and cross country coaches who were interested in me since I was a junior. Coaches being interested in me made me feel like pretty big stuff. It was about the *only* thing that made me feel good.

By college application time in the late fall of my senior year, we had moved to the new house that Dad had designed and built, and I mean that quite literally. For the better part of two years, every night after dinner, he worked there until well after nightfall. I've never seen a more driven person. It was crazy. Dad saw building a house essentially as a do-it-yourself project. He not only put in the plumbing, but he did most of the electric and lots of other stuff. Often, he made me come with him to help, but I wasn't of much use to him. He's too much of a perfectionist to let some amateur like me do anything important.

From the very day we moved there, the house was the fulfillment of his dreams, his castle, and more than ever, he was king.

As senior year progressed, despite my lofty plans to go away to college, my father kept pushing for Southern.

"What do you want to be?" he'd ask. "What do you want to major in?"

I could tell he was using psychology on me. Ask some logical questions and break Gabriel down methodically.

"I don't know yet," I'd reply. I wasn't even eighteen for God's sake.

"Well, if you're going to be a teacher like Michael, you're going to Southern," he'd say, the great monarch delivering a royal decree to his lowly subject.

"Well, I'm not going to be a teacher." It seemed like a logical reply.

"Then what the hell are you going to be?" he'd ask, his voice rising in frustration.

"I told you. I don't know."

"Another good reason to go to Southern. We don't need to be paying a steep tuition to an out-of-state college for a kid that doesn't know what the hell he wants to be." His logic and mine were two different matters.

He did make one concession, though. Knowing how excited I was to be corresponding with college coaches, he gave me the green light to apply to one out-of-state college because, you know, he wasn't a complete dictator. I chose Bates College in Maine because their coach seemed the most interested.

I'll never forget discussing it with my guidance counselor, Mr. Gentili. What a classic!

The guy's office smelled like a Brylcreem factory. Though the commercial said, "A little dab'll do ya," Mr. Gentili's stiff hair looked like he dabbed the whole tube into it.

Looking at my transcript, he said, "Where are you applying to college, Gabe?"

"A few places – Bates College in Maine, UCONN, Fairfield University, and Southern Connecticut State College," I replied, mentioning Southern last, because I definitely wasn't going there. "But I already decided where I'm going."

"You've already decided without receiving admission letters? Where is that?"

"I'm going to Bates. The track coach has been writing to me, so I'm all set."

Raising his bushy eyebrows, he almost mumbled, "Hmmm. I don't know if you'll get into Bates. Your grades are pretty good, but your SAT scores are a tad low for Bates."

The first thing that popped into my mind was, *Yeah! Okay, buddy, you almost know what you're talking about,* but I just gave him the facts. "The track coach wrote to me last week, telling me to shoot him a letter back when I send my application, so like I said, I'm all set."

But when the rejection letter came in the mail from Bates, it was almost like I was reliving the day, four years before, when I had been rejected from Fairfield Prep, only this time my father wasn't disappointed.

I stared in disbelief at the embossed maroon school seal at the top left corner of the letter – a circular *Academia Batesina-1855* which not only signified in Latin where I *wouldn't* be furthering my education but also solidified where I would be going. I crumpled up the letter into a ball, dropped it on the kitchen table, and went to my bedroom. Mom and Dad had the good sense to leave me to my solitude.

The stereo that had once resided in the living room of our Maltby Street apartment had found a new home in my room. There was apparently no room for it anywhere else in my parents' interior design plan. I flopped down on the floor by the gleaming cherry wood stereo cabinet and blasted my *Sgt. Pepper's* album as loud as the volume would go, hating Brylcreem, controlling fathers, false promises, and hand-me-down colleges.

CHAPTER 9

A day after my rejection from Bates, Michael surprised me when he told me that Southern was closing down.

"What do you mean, closing down?" I asked. "The semester isn't over yet."

"I know. It's because they're predicting riots in New Haven. You should have seen the place today. The National Guard is moving onto the campus. A convoy of trucks, jeeps, and hundreds of soldiers in full combat gear. Rifles and everything. Bonkers!"

"But why the National Guard?"

"Who the fuck knows? To stop protests, I guess. It's always the same thing, isn't it? War or race. This time, I guess it's race. Something about a Black Panther murder trial. I don't know much about it. I just know they shut down the college and the military is moving in. It doesn't look good. I'll tell ya what. It's a fucked up world."

It was almost May 1st, and there were all kinds of articles about it in the *New Haven Register* with pictures of the military lined up on Chapel Street and across the New Haven Green, their rifles slung over their shoulders and ready for action. Other photos showed downtown businesses, their windows boarded up and splattered with graffiti. The paper said all of the excitement was related to an upcoming murder trial. Something about the leader of the Panthers, Bobby Seale, ordering a hit on a member he felt was an FBI informant.

Like Michael said, it wasn't anything new. There had been civil rights riots and Vietnam protests on campuses happening across the country. I was becoming numb to it.

It didn't seem like anything was boiling over in New Haven from what I could tell, but a few days later, four unarmed students were shot and killed by the National Guard at Kent State University in Ohio, and I felt like it was craziness layered on top of craziness. I could hear Sonny and Cher singing "The Beat Goes On," except in this case, the beat had to do with senseless killing. When kids your own age get gunned down, it starts to feel personal.

Trying to digest all these national issues went back to a string of political assassinations beginning with JFK when I was eleven, and then, a few weeks after I turned thirteen, Malcolm X. At the end of my sophomore year, Martin Luther King Jr. and Bobby Kennedy were shot within a few months of each other. The truth is, there's only so much a guy can handle.

Maybe this trip to New York would not only give me the shot in the arm I needed but would also be an escape from the insanity.

We asked Will not to schedule us on that Friday night. The four of us met at Duchess in the late afternoon before departing, grabbed an extra large bag of burgers and fries to take in the car, and headed for the Bridgeport train station in Tomaso's Chevelle. Sallie got in the front and Bink and I jumped in the back. Pulling out of the parking lot, Tomaso burned a long strip of rubber down Pershing Drive, his squealing tires announcing to all of the Valley that we were off for an exciting night.

No sooner were we out of the Duchess lot that I started to have misgivings. I mean, we weren't even out of Ansonia, and I was thinking, *I'm glad I didn't tell Mary Elizabeth about this, because she wouldn't approve of what I'm about to do at all, and she wouldn't hesitate to tell me so.* But then my next thought was, *Well, it's none of her damned business!* But then a second later I was wallowing in guilt, thinking, *She's been the kind of friend I'm supposed to share everything with. What a fake I am.* A conscience is a terrible thing.

Tomaso distracted me from thinking of Mary Elizabeth by turning up the sound on his tape player full blast, and we listened to his *Abbey Road* tape, one of my favorite Beatles' albums along with *The White Album*, which Jeff and I listened to while cruising all over the Valley when he was home on leave. We often marveled at one song, "Revolution 9," that was beyond weird, even stranger than "I Am the Walrus" if that's possible. While I can appreciate my parents' music, someone like Frank Sinatra never recorded a song that crossed new frontiers in music. It was always, more or less, "Come Fly with Me" to the same old place. The Beatles forged new pathways and opened new worlds.

Ironically, a few weeks before our New York trip, the news of the Beatles' breakup was plastered on every headline across the country. Personally, I was baffled. How could these four guys walk away from the best band that ever made a record? I just added it to a laundry list of things that depressed me.

Anyway, Tomaso playing the music full blast suggested to me that he didn't want to talk about what we were planning to do that night, he just wanted to do it, which was fine with me. I wasn't in the mood to listen to Sallie's repetitive analysis of any subject he brought up, never mind Bink's endless drivel.

I whipped out the latest book I had docked in my back pocket and started reading. It was *One Flew Over the Cuckoo's Nest*, which I was reading because I had read a magazine article about its author Ken Kesey who, along with a congregation of fellow hippies known as "the Merry Pranksters," experimented with psychedelics and traveled across America in a garishly painted school bus. I've been fascinated with road trips ever since reading my favorite book, *On the Road* by Jack Kerouac. Sal Paradise, the central character, hitchhikes across America. Being a local hitchhiker myself, I related to Sal in a big way, but he was an early beatnik, which predated hippies. Basically, I was curious to see if Kesey's book would speak to me in the same way.

I was realizing that there weren't many kids at Shelton High who were hippies. For me, between coping with my parents, playing sports, and trying to figure out what made girls tick, it was hard enough just to get through the day.

Most of us seemed caught in a surreal time warp, one foot rooted in a *Beach Blanket Bingo* movie and the other foot pulled forward by the music of the Beatles who seemed to be influencing everything from our hair styles to our clothing to our attitudes. Hippies seemed to take it to an extreme.

Kesey's book, it turned out, wasn't about hippies at all, but about patients in a psych ward. Who knew?

Once on the train, Sallie and Tomaso sat together, and the same for Bink and me. I got the message. Bink was my problem. The ride was a challenge for me, because how do you read when Bink never shuts up?

"Gabe, you think the Mets will make the playoffs again this season?" he asked, alluding to the fact that, last season, the Mets had won not only the National League Pennant but also the World Series.

"I don't know, Bink, maybe," I replied without looking up from my book.

"Yeah, last season, they shocked the world by upsetting the Orioles, so it's probably hit or miss this year, huh?"

"Yeah, sure," I muttered. "Hit or miss."

"If they do make the playoffs, you think they'll win it all again like last season?"

"Uhm," I shrugged, "I don't know. Maybe they'll win it all. Or maybe not."

"Who do you think is a better pitcher?" he persisted, "Seaver or Koosman?"

"I don't know...Seaver, I guess."

"Well, good point, because last season Seaver won twenty-five games and Koosman only won seventeen, but their earned run averages were almost identical, so doesn't that make them equal, in a way?"

"If you say so."

"Sorry if I'm bothering you," he said. "I see you're reading."

Very astute observation, Bink. After about a half second of peace and quiet, I realized it was futile to try to continue reading *Cuckoo's Nest.*

"Of course, I like Koosman because he's a southpaw. I think lefties are harder to hit than righties. Do you agree?"

"I don't know...I guess."

"Well, what's your personal experience with the two?"

"I don't know, Bink. I get by, but baseball's never been my game."

"Well, there's no denying Seaver's greatness, but when you think about it, Koosman came up with two wins in the World Series, and Seaver had only one, so that tips the scales in Koosman's favor, right?"

"Listen, Bink," I said, my patience draining like sand in an hour-glass. "I don't really care. I root for the Mets because they're from New York. Otherwise, I don't care about 'em. Michael and I are more Yankee fans than Met fans."

Mercifully, we arrived at Grand Central. The place was crawling with people like an infestation of insects. Tomaso asked a cop what the best way to get to Times Square was, and with a thick Brooklyn accent, the cop said, "The Shuttle. Follow the gray circles with a white S."

I felt like I was in a movie. Descending into the bowels of Grand Central as we traversed a concrete floor littered with hardened gum and flattened cigarette butts, I could almost hear the soundtrack – a lone jazz saxophone riffing, accompanied by pulsing brass accents. In the overstuffed and graffiti covered S train, I looked around and mused, *I'll bet we're the only ones looking for prostitutes.*

The last time I had been in New York was as a Cub Scout on a weekend trip. I had forgotten what it was like, but as we hit the street from the depths of the subway, I was quickly reminded. The chaos of bumper to bumper traffic, horns screaming, and flashing marquee lights in Times Square was an experience in sensory overload.

Hundreds of cars, trucks of all kinds, and yellow cabs criss-crossed through the intersection of Broadway and 42nd Street to the shrill tune of a police whistle. Horns beeped in short staccato bursts, and drivers shouted expletives at each other through their open windows in a dissonant symphony that was both off-pitch and badly out of rhythm.

After crossing, we noticed Bink was no longer with us. I stopped Tomaso and Sallie.

"Where the fuck is he?" Tomaso complained.

I spied him across the street at a pushcart with a multi-colored umbrella buying something from a vendor. When Bink caught up to us, he said, "I bought some honey-roasted cashews. Sorry, I was hungry."

"You were hungry, huh?" Tomaso said, turning to me. "It's gonna be a long fuckin' night." Despite the sarcasm, Bink offered us some nuts, and he was soon left holding the bag, now almost empty.

We continued past a row of movie theaters with their bright lights. I could feel the rum-tum beating of my heart and a rush of adrenaline wash over me as I inhaled the big city aromas and scanned the various movie houses.

I squinted into the kaleidoscope of glowing signs. The biggest one featured the latest major motion picture, *M*A*S*H*. A gargantuan poster hung above the marquee – a hand flashing the peace sign, the top of the index finger sporting an army helmet with an American flag insignia, and sexy women's legs growing out of the bottom of the hand in a sexier inverted peace sign. It was obviously some sort of war film.

Next door, a curvy Raquel Welch stared down at us wearing nothing but a skimpy red, white, and blue bathing suit with a white cowboy hat and matching boots. Above, patriotic lights flashed COMING SOON: MYRA BRECKINRIDGE.

I wondered, *Why the flag on both posters?* These uses of the flag seemed, I don't know, somehow sacrilegious, like the burning of flags at war protests. All I could think of was the soldier handing a folded American flag to Buster's mother at the cemetery.

Most other theaters on 42nd Street were playing X-rated films with titles like *Executive Secretary* and *Sensual Encounters*. I didn't recall seeing marquees like these when I was a Cub Scout, but maybe the leaders steered us away from 42nd Street, or maybe I was just oblivious.

When we got to the corner of 42nd Street and 9th Avenue, I noticed a lot of commotion. A crowd stood close together, listening to a guy who was speaking through a bullhorn. Curiosity got the best of me, and I scooted part way into the crowd.

"I tell you, brothers and sisters," he projected, "it's spelled out for us in Revelations 1:14-15." In the hand that wasn't holding the bullhorn, the man waved a black leather-clad Bible.

"His hair was like wool...his feet were like bronze," he shouted, a tinny sound emitting from the bullhorn. "Do you hear me, brothers and sisters? His feet were the color of *bronze*. The message is clear – Jesus was *not* a white man!"

A magnetic force seemed to pull me closer to the front of the crowd and closer to the speaker, who was surrounded by a half dozen other solemn men in suits and bow ties along with several women who were dressed in white, with veils like nuns. A variety of pictures hung on sheets of plywood behind them, presumably different renderings of what a black Jesus might have looked like.

With growing passion, the speaker continued, "The honorable Elijah Muhammad teaches us that Jesus did not have blond hair and blue eyes. The honorable Elijah Muhammad teaches us that the images of Jesus that are on the walls of churches worldwide are lies, that the white man –"

"Gabe," I heard an irritated Tomaso call. "C'mon, man!"

I weaved back out of the crowd. "Sorry, Tomaso," I said, "but that was interesting. That guy was just saying how Jesus wasn't a white man."

"Yeah, like I care," Tomaso replied. "We gotta get goin' and find what we're lookin' for, which is somethin' I don't think Jesus would approve of, no matter what fuckin' color he was." Tomaso has a way of putting things.

Despite being in my own world of *what-color-was-Jesus*, I followed the guys up 9th Avenue, even seedier than 42nd Street, as dozens of anonymous men passed in and out of businesses illuminated by signs with names like Paradise Alley and Peep-O-Rama.

When we reached the corner of 9th Avenue and 46th Street, I saw two policemen sitting atop majestic, chestnut horses. *So different from Shelton,* I realized.

Tomaso did a three-sixty. "You guys seen any prostitutes?"

"We're not going to see any here," I said. "Not with mounted police patrolling the streets."

Bink added, "I'm not sure if I'd know it if I saw one."

"Yeah, I guess you fuckin' wouldn't." Tomaso couldn't have been more annoyed.

"Hey, don't worry, Tommy Trouble," Sallie offered, "maybe it's too early. It could be too early. I mean, it's not even dark yet. So, ya know, Tommy, maybe it's too early."

Leave it to Sallie to shed a little light on a problem. But maybe he was right. Maybe street walkers didn't head out for the night until well after dark.

We took a right and walked for a few blocks, passing the 46th Street Theatre, the year *1776* plastered on the marquee. And there on the logo, once again, was the ubiquitous American flag (albeit the Betsy Ross version) in the beak of a comical looking, pie-eyed, baby eagle, hatching from an egg. I imagined the soldiers at Buster's funeral reverently taking "Old Glory" out of the eagle's mouth, folding it, and presenting it to Mrs. Brookes.

A few blocks later, when we turned left on 7th Avenue, I spotted the first thing I remembered from my Cub Scout trips up ahead. White, old fashioned lettering emblazoned the red awning over the entrance – Tad's Steaks.

Tomaso's face lit up for the first time that night. "Perfect," he said. "I'm starved. Look at this place. A steak dinner for $4.39. Not bad. Let's grab a bite and try to figure out what to do."

Tad's took me back in time. After we got our food, I sat at the table, remembering the last time I had eaten here. I was just some clueless little kid in a blue uniform and a goofy round cap. This time, what I was up to wasn't so innocent, and it made me feel sad.

CHAPTER 10

For me, if New York City was a meal, it would taste like a medium rare, flame-broiled T-bone, a piping hot potato dripping with butter, and a charred slice of garlic bread from Tad's.

Chowing down his steak, Tomaso whined, "There don't seem to be any hookers, which really sucks."

"Like I said before, Tommy," Sallie mumbled, shoveling a fork full of potatoes into his mouth, "it's too early. Maybe they come out late. You know what I mean? Maybe they wait until it's, like, late at night. I'm just sayin'."

Thanks for the clarification, Sallie.

"So what the fuck do we do in the meantime?" Tomaso asked.

"I saw the Ripley's Believe It or Not museum around the corner," Bink offered. "I like reading about the strange things they print up in the Sunday comics, like a goat with seven legs and stuff like that. We could go there."

"Goats with seven legs, huh?" Tomaso said, rolling his eyes at me. "Yeah, let's fuckin' rush right over there."

"I got an idea," Sallie said. "Let's go see a movie. You know? Let's kill some time. We'll go see a movie. To kill time."

"What movie?" Tomaso asked. "An X rated one?"

"That'd be fun," Sallie said, "but I got somethin' else in mind. A smaller movie theater on 42nd Street has a movie called something like *The Losers*. Looks like it's about Hells Angels."

I surprised myself when I chimed in with, "That sounds great!" All of us, except Bink, owned motorcycles, and it would kill a few hours, but I secretly hoped that after the movie there still wouldn't be any hookers.

The posters outside of the movie theater proclaimed, "They're a 'Dirty Bunch' on Wheels" and "The Army handed them guns and a license to kill."

In the film, the CIA takes a motorcycle gang of five criminals and sends them to Vietnam to rescue an imprisoned agent. The bikers, with machine guns mounted on their choppers and hand grenades dangling off their belts, ride through the jungles blowing away the enemy.

I wondered what Jeff, stuck in the real Vietnam, would think of a movie depicting Hells Angels as the true heroes of the war. The more the B-movie dragged on, the more I realized that a goat with seven legs was looking pretty good.

When the movie ended, we walked out into the night and turned left on Broadway. The towering buildings obscured the night sky, making it hard to see the millions of stars above us.

But the real stars were the hustlers who lined the sidewalks, hawking bronze statues of the Empire State Building and velvet portraits of Elvis and Marilyn Monroe and gold watches.

Despite the lateness of the hour, there were still no hookers. It appeared Sallie had been wrong. At the corner of 48th Street, Tomaso pointed to a sign across the street and said, "Let's go in there."

The flashing red bulbs spelled out, The Metropole Cafe, with smaller white lights advertising, "Topless Go-Go."

"What for?" I asked.

"Since it doesn't look like we're gettin' laid," he whined, "at least we'll get to see some nice tits."

He had a point. It occurred to me that this was going to be my first legal drink because the drinking age in New York was eighteen.

Before I knew it, we were sitting at a fancy bar, paying eight bucks a drink and looking at two girls up on a high counter behind the bar. Wearing white vinyl short-shorts and matching go-go boots but naked from the waist up, the girls undulated to the electric twanging of a wa-wa guitar on quaaludes. A mirror ball spinning in slow motion sprayed the pair with millions of dotted lights. It was

And when the swindler made eye contact with me at last, his wide smile and exposed black dappled teeth distorted like a reflection in a funhouse mirror, like a sheep I pulled out my wallet and handed the fake three tens.

Five minutes later, the man hadn't returned. Ten minutes later, we were sitting on the stairs in silence. Fifteen minutes later, Tomaso looked at his watch and moaned, "Fuck! That bastard ain't comin' back." When no one responded, Tomaso, ready to explode, said, "Gabe, let's go find that prick and kick his ass!"

"No way, man," I said. "I'll stay right where I am."

"Chicken?" he asked.

"I'm not chicken, it's just that –"

"Okay, chicken shit, don't fuckin' come then!"

"Oh, fuck you," I shot back. My cheeks were on fire and, at that moment, I wanted to kick my cousin's ass more than the con artist's. After all, it was Tomaso's fault that I was in this mess.

Luckily, Sallie had the presence of mind to intervene. "C'mon, Tommy, I'll go with you."

"Let's go, Sallie. You and me'll find him then."

Bink and I sat alone in soundless misery, Bink stupefied and me feeling bad I had lost my cool with Tomaso. Ten minutes later, the two returned.

"There's not a soul in the place except for a wino sleeping in the fifth floor hallway." Tomaso said. "That fuck must have gone up to the roof and crossed over to the next building with our dough."

When we walked out onto the street, I noticed something I had been oblivious to on the way into the building. Clusters of black people sat on steps and in lawn chairs, eating and drinking from coolers. Boom boxes blasted and children frolicked in a festive-like atmosphere. It was sort of like Memorial Day in Shelton, except it was after midnight and there wasn't going to be a parade.

The neighbors serenaded us with raspberries, whistles, and catcalls. "Whatsa matter, white boys, you lose somethin'?"..."Awww, the white boys look like they lost they best friend"..."You enjoy the whorehouse, honkies?"

Cabs zoomed by us like we didn't exist, and I felt crestfallen and foolish. Mercifully, we flagged down a cab and escaped back to Times Square.

Unbelievably, 42nd Street was now a veritable multi-colored

carnival of street walkers. In high-heeled platform shoes and go-go boots, girls of all colors, shapes, and sizes walked the wide sidewalks in groups of twos and threes. They glowed under the big city lights in their mini-skirts and low-cut blouses made of satins, sparkles, and beads. Wearing festive colored wigs of pinks and yellows and purples, their outfits appeared to be capped with swirling mounds of cotton candy. Tomaso looked excited and sick at the same time if that's possible.

"Okay, guys. The night's not over yet."

"It's over for me, Tommy," Sallie replied. "I only got nine bucks left."

"I'm broke," Bink chimed in.

"You got any dough left, Gabe?" Tomaso asked.

"Yeah, some...but –"

"Okay, then it's just me and you."

"No thanks," I said. "I've had enough excitement for one night."

"Oh no! You're not gonna fuckin' wiggle your way out of this one. You're my cousin, and I'm going into the Army. I need you to do this for me."

The other two guys stood staring at me. It was one of those moments in life when you're under a microscope, and you have to decide whether you're who you are or who others expect you to be.

Taking a deep breath, I wondered how many situations I was going to get into that didn't feel right. Then I said, "Okay, but I'll pick out the girls."

We headed across the street, just Tomaso and me, where I spotted some girls that looked good, as if I knew what I was doing. As we were approaching them, we heard Sallie yelling, "Guys...guys, come back! Over here! Over here!"

We jaywalked back over to him, and I could see that he was talking to two girls with the shortest skirts I've ever seen, fishnet stockings hugging their spindly legs, blonde beehive wigs, rouged cheeks highlighting their dark skin tone, and eyelashes extending like petrified spider legs from their tired eyelids.

"These girls'll do it for fifteen bucks," Sallie said. "It's a great deal."

"What're you talking abo–"

"We'll take it," Tomaso interrupted.

Take it? Take what?

That was it for me. "Alright, everybody, let's just hold our wild horses. Hold on, okay?"

This was no longer a fantasy I had cooked up. It was the real thing.

"If you'll excuse us, girls," I continued, "we need a minute."

We huddled together about ten yards away, and I said, "Okay... that's it, I'm out. I'm not doing this."

"Bullshit, you're doing it," Tomaso commanded.

"Look," I said with authority. "We've gotten taken once tonight, and I'm done! Finished!"

"I can't fuckin' believe you," my cousin said. "So what am I supposed to do?"

"Here's what!" I took out my wallet and slapped a ten spot hard into Sallie's hand. "You have nine bucks, right? Well this makes nineteen. That'll leave a few bucks left over for the cab or whatever you need."

"And what about you two idiots?" Tomaso asked.

"Don't worry. Bink and I will...we'll wait for you at Grand Central."

In a flash, Tomaso, Sallie, and the two skinny girls were off in a yellow cab.

As Bink and I watched them drive off into the night, I heard a voice from right behind us.

"Hey, boys, how come yer buddies went with them ugly girls?"

Before me stood a short, skinny guy with a thick head of disheveled hair, a faded Yankee t-shirt, loose-fitting sweatpants, and tattered sandals. His chin was covered with strands of sparse facial hair, his fingernails and toenails clogged with black grime.

"Well," I began, as if he deserved an explanation, "one of them just got drafted, see, so let's just say he –"

"But why does he want to have fun with them ugly girls?" he interrupted. "Don't he know no pretty girls?"

"He knows some pretty girls," I replied, giving Bink that *let's-get-going* look, "but...it's...it's, well, let's just say, it's a long story."

Bink and I were now on the move, but our friend kept pace with us.

"Hey, amigos. If you want some action, I know a pretty girl on the corner of 33rd and 9th. She'll give you some grass to smoke, free o' charge, and then she can, you know, make you happy too, entiendes? And, like I say, no charge, see, cuz she just wants some good times, same like you want some good times."

As we turned the corner at Broadway and 42nd Street, I saw the illuminated subway entrance across the street, but I wasn't keen on taking a subway this late at night.

"Yeah, thanks a lot, sir," I said. "We appreciate the offer, but –"

"Okay, no problem, man," he interrupted. I could hear the irritation in his tone. "No problemo. I'm just lookin' to hang out with some friends tonight."

I accelerated my pace and Bink followed suit, but I might as well have been back in high school racing Chip Reynolds.

"Hey, I got another idea," he said. "I know a back way behind them peep shows where there's a nice hole in the wall. You can take turns sneakin' a look. I don' even need to take no turns cuz I seen it lotsa times."

I realized I was going to have to be more assertive, so I stopped walking and confronted the man.

"Okay, sir, listen. We aren't going to any girl's apartment on 33rd and 9th, and no way we're going to some back door of a peep show. We already got hustled out of most of our money, and we don't plan to have it happen again."

"Okay, man," our friend said, hyperventilating through clenched, rotted teeth. "Sounds like you boys don' wanna be my friend. Fuck you then! All I was lookin' for was a little companionship. A junkie like me sleeps all day, and I'm up all night. The night is lonely and endless. Lemme tell you somethin' you don't know."

His voice was a harsh growl now. He lifted his forearms, displaying dark, craggy scars and sores. "You see these fuckin' arms, man?" he continued with unbridled passion. "When I need a fix bad enough, I kill people. All I was lookin' for was friendship!"

I could see we had now reached a less populated section of 42nd Street far from the crowded, well lit Times Square area. There was a tree lined park across the street, an abyss of black shadows and the perfect place for him to drag and abandon our bloodied bodies.

I suddenly felt unafraid, maybe because when you get this close to true danger, fear leaves you.

"Okay! Kill us if you want," I said, "but let me tell you something *you* don't know. I have about twenty cents left in my pocket, so if that's worth murdering us for, go for it."

"Awww, fuck you, man," he shouted, his voice carrying across all of New York. "Just – fuck you!" And he turned from us and stomped back toward Times Square.

We stopped and asked a passerby where Grand Central Station was. He told us we were three blocks away. Bink and I continued up the street without a word, moving at a rapid pace like two Olympic speed walkers. I could feel the adrenaline racing through my veins, and I'm not sure how loud I was breathing because Bink's breathing was deafening.

I almost felt sorry for the junkie, but instead, I morphed into survival mode. All thoughts of skimpily clad prostitutes, con artists, and junkies now left me. My solitary goal was to make sure Bink and I got home in one piece.

CHAPTER 11

Shell-shocked, Bink and I didn't speak. When we walked into the terminal at Grand Central, the place was a ghost town. I looked at my watch. It was after two. In my naivety, I had assumed we'd be home by now. Feelings of guilt filled my brain. *My mother must be worried about me.*

I gazed across the desolate vastness where, earlier, thousands of people had crossed every which way in a chaotic pattern of foot traffic.

As Bink and I passed a bank of phone booths, I suggested we sit on the floor nearby and wait for Tomaso and Sallie. I stared upwards at the gigantic leaded windows and the murals of constellations that decorated the ceiling high above our heads.

Bink broke the silence. "A penny for your thoughts, Gabriel?"

"Wow," I said, still looking heavenwards.

"Wow?"

"That's an expression I never heard anyone our age say. It sounds like something a guy would have said to a girl on a Ferris wheel in 1905. You're such a dork."

"I know," he said without the slightest pretense. Bink is among the few people I know who can be honest about himself without worrying about being uncool, a quality that has made me like him more than I ever imagined I could.

"You like astronomy?" he asked.

"I don't know a thing about it."

"Oh, I'm asking because you seem fascinated by the ceiling."

He was right. I was preoccupied with the celestial world above me, but I didn't know why. We continued in silence for maybe another ten or fifteen minutes.

This time, I spoke. "Did you know that guy earlier was a scam artist, Bink?"

"No, I didn't. Did you?"

"Yeah, pretty much."

"But then why didn't you –"

I shut him down. "I don't wanna talk about it."

When his eyes asked why I mentioned it, I turned away.

I couldn't remain quiet though. "What do you think about Jesus, Bink? You think he was black or white?"

"I don't know, Gabe. I never thought about it."

"Yeah, I get it. The thought never entered my pathetic little mind either – until today."

"Those guys in the suits got to you, huh?"

I sighed and felt my shoulders rise and fall.

"Does it make a difference?" Bink asked.

"No, I guess not. It's just that, you know, all the pictures in church and the movies and everything show Jesus as a white guy."

"That's true."

"I mean, did you ever see *King of Kings*? Jeffrey Hunter as Jesus? Talk about white! Even the crucifix above the altar at church – white Jesus."

Bink repeated himself. "I never thought about it."

I continued, choosing my words. "It just seems like so many things we're told are just a pack of rotten lies...and well, it's starting to bug me. Maybe there are a lot of...a lot of, well, *things* we never thought about that we should have."

Bink just nodded, staring at me with sky blue eyes. I looked away again because it made me feel uncomfortable to have another guy look at me like he cared so much.

"Ah, never mind," I said. "Who cares whether he was white or black or brown or purple or green – or *bronze*? What's the fucking difference?"

My irritation was obtrusive. We drifted back into a disquieting period of silence. I stopped staring at fake stars and closed my eyes as

72

my thoughts arbitrarily shifted to Ernest Hemingway. Fragments of the quote I had read to Mary Elizabeth flooded my mind.

What you have with Maria, whether it lasts just through today and a part of tomorrow...is the most important thing that can happen to a human being...I tell you it is true and that you have it and that you are lucky even if you die tomorrow.

I remembered the end of the story when, in an effort to allow Maria and other compatriots to escape, a wounded Robert Jordan gets mowed down by the guns of the fascists, an untimely death as his musing had foreshadowed. It hit me that I could end up dead at any time. It's something that I've always known, that everyone knows, but it's easier not to think about it, just like it's easier not to think about what color Jesus is.

The junkie could have killed us, just like he said. I was overwhelmed with the idea that I might die never having *lived* my life, never having known honest and true love – the kind that Robert Jordan felt for Maria, the kind that makes you feel lucky even if you die tomorrow.

"Gabe, are you okay?" Bink almost whispered, bringing me back to reality.

I didn't want to get too heavy, but it was hard not to.

"Let's just say that this night didn't go anything like the way I thought it would. It seems like nothing in my life ever goes the way I think it will."

"Yeah," he agreed. "Same for me."

"Oh yeah? How so?"

"Well, to begin with, there's girls. You know how bad I am with them, right?"

You had to bring up girls, didn't you, Bink? Because I wasn't depressed enough.

"Yeah, I guess," I mumbled.

"What do you mean, you *guess*? You were there last week when I got back from the Yale Bowl concert with Emily."

"Oh, don't let that bug you."

"It's the nearest I've ever been to kissing a girl, and I wasn't even close. Think about it. I'm going to be a college sophomore, and it's the only date I've ever had."

I didn't mean to be rude, but I found myself gazing up again, focused on a drawing set against thousands of little stars – a winged man, an ancient muscular angel, holding up a big club as a bull charges in his direction. *It's symbolic*, I guessed. *An archetype needing a club to fight through life.* I could relate!

Another long silence ensued. I slipped my hands under the back of my head all comfortable-like, and closed my eyes again. Lying on the floor in the eerily vacant Grand Central Station made me feel weird and more depressed. I stopped caring what time it was.

Bink, unable to remain quiet for long, asked, "Are you awake, Gabe?"

His tone was so soft and so understanding, I refrained from opening my eyes for fear of crying.

"Yeah," I said.

"If you want to talk about anything, I'm here," he said in that same empathetic tone.

I should have opened up. I should have told him. I should have spilled everything that was bothering me, because it's not every day another guy invites you to open up like that. Guys just don't. Jeff wouldn't have, and neither would have Tomaso.

I just shrugged and said what you say when you're a guy. "I'm fine."

I breathed in and out for a few minutes until I felt composed enough to open my eyes. The first thing I saw was Bink's look of utter confusion. I didn't need to say anything more because in the distance I recognized four legs walking straight toward us, and I knew they belonged to Tomaso and Sallie. I was relieved to be let off the hook because another half hour and I would have spilled my guts to Bink and probably sobbed like a three-year-old.

I glanced at my watch and saw that it was almost 3:30.

"How'd it go?" I asked.

"It went fuckin' great," Tomaso answered.

"Your tone of voice doesn't sound like it went great," I said.

"Well, don't fuckin' worry about it. It did!"

"Where'd they take you?" Bink asked.

"Well, let's just say it wasn't the fuckin' Ritz," Tomaso said, "but they were able to take care of business just fine."

"Where are they now?" I asked.

"They had to get back to work," Sallie replied. "You know,

because for them, it's still early. It's like at Duchess, when you're scheduled from eleven to six. Well, for them it's, like, still lunch hour. So they hadda get back to work because, for them, it's still early."

How many guys do they hook up with in one night? I wondered but decided not to ask, avoiding Tomaso's surliness and Sallie's redundancies.

"Let's go see what time the next train heads back to Connecticut," Tomaso said.

We walked out onto the concourse toward the big brass clock on top of the now vacant information kiosk, and the four of us stared upward at the gigantic bulletin board on the wall above the ticket booths. The next train on the New Haven Line would leave at 4:40 a.m.

"Shit," Tomaso mumbled. "We have to wait almost another hour and a half."

Trying to be helpful, Bink offered, "Perhaps we should have checked into that before we came."

Tomaso's eyes almost popped out onto the marble floor. "And *perhaps* you should shut the fuck up, Bink."

For a guy who just had sex, Tomaso was in a foul mood, so much so that I couldn't help feeling good that I had weaseled out of it.

Bink, of course, was deeply wounded by the barb. We dragged ourselves over to the grand staircase at the end of the concourse where we would wait for the train, the four of us keeping a protective distance from each other. Each of us curled up, finding our own private space, clinging to a brass railing here or a marble balustrade there, now wrapped in our personal, encapsulated cocoons after our big adventure.

If you've never been on a train leaving New York at 4:40 a.m. on a Saturday morning, you probably don't know how quiet it is. You probably don't know that there is no sound except the rattling of the moving passenger car. You probably don't know how it can make you feel. It's a loneliness that's empty and gray in color.

Tomaso's "shut the fuck up" to Bink continued to hang over us like a dark pall, and nobody had anything to say on the train. Not to mention, we were all bushed anyway, having been up all night. The three guys dozed off soon after the train started moving. Sleep eluded me, and I sat staring out the window at the blurry night images of darkened buildings and intermittent street lamps that flickered by as the black night gradually made way for the natural light of morning.

As the train made its way past New Rochelle, White Plains, Greenwich and beyond, it occurred to me that twice a day, night cross-fades to day and then day reciprocates and cross-fades back to night. It happens in such a seamless and imperceptible way that I almost never notice it. Riding on the train to Bridgeport, I wanted to start paying closer attention to things like sunrise and nightfall.

Bink, who had begun to snore, was slumped over the armrest, his wrist and hand dangling into the center aisle, and his mouth hanging open like a dead man. I should have been asleep too, but my mind shifted into overdrive, which is what it likes to do. First, I was thinking about how this was the first time that I had stayed out all night. *How am I going to explain this one at home?* I wondered.

I looked down and stared at my class ring, golden and malleable, and I turned it round and round on my hand, wondering how my life was changing and in what direction it was going.

CHAPTER 12

Having dozed off for a bit, I opened my drowsy eyes as Tomaso pulled into the Duchess parking lot. The sun, a hazy orange circle, hung low in the sky beyond the train tracks. The four of us grabbed breakfast at the New State Diner right next door to Duchess. The guys weren't in any big hurry to go home. I know I wasn't because I figured I was going to be screwed when I got there.

No one seemed any more interested in talking in the diner than they had on the train when they were dead to the world. Maybe everyone was silent because we were all famished. It felt like we had eaten at Tad's a thousand years ago. The four of us sat at the table, practically comatose – two guys who had had sex and two guys who hadn't, and no one seemed any better off than anyone else.

As we sat in the booth, I listened to the percussive clanging of the short order cook's spatula on the steel grill. There were a handful of customers in the place, a middle-aged couple in a nearby booth and two other guys sitting about five stools apart at the counter. One wore a red checkered flannel shirt and the other wore a tattered gray Giants sweatshirt. Typical Valley guys.

The only words any of us spoke came from Tomaso when he said, "I'm done. Let's get the fuck outta here."

I jumped in the Corvair and headed home. We had been living in the new house for over six months, but I still wasn't quite used to it.

Tired as I was, I almost drove to the old Maltby Street homestead before I realized we didn't live there anymore.

The big new house was quiet when I walked in. I could see Michael's door was cracked open, and he was out to the world. I assumed Mom and Dad were also sleeping. The new house, the product of Dad's design and hard work, is quite the palace. Friends and relatives still marvel at the place, saying it must have cost Dad fifty thousand dollars to build. The center atrium, with its twenty foot high paneled walls and its glass ceiling, is bigger than the entire Maltby Street apartment. Dad's and Mom's bedroom sits at the far corner of the atrium, secluded from the other rooms. I hate to say that I assume the reason for the seclusion is because of their sex life. It's gross to think about, I know.

Those two have always been a couple of night owls, and never early risers. I remember being a kid back on Maltby Street, and Dad tossed me an alarm clock one day and said, "You're old enough to get yourself up in the morning, so use this thing." And that's what I did. Mom would tell me to wake her so she could make me breakfast before I headed to school, but maybe Jesus could resurrect a corpse, but I sure as heck couldn't.

Sometimes Dad would have short-lived stretches where he'd get up and make me a couple of eggs. But after a few weeks, I was back on my own. I'll never forget the many mornings I served the early morning Mass before school. After a bowl of Cheerios, off I'd go down the outside stairs on Maltby Street and into the dark morning, street lamps lighting my way, my book bag slung over my shoulder, a hanger with my starched and ironed black cassock and white surplice clenched between my fingers.

It may sound like I'm complaining, but I'm not. Their laissez-faire (or should I say lazy?) attitude about my mornings fostered in me a love for silence and solitude. To this day, I often get up early and grab breakfast somewhere by myself. I learned it's important to know how to be alone with yourself.

When I woke up, I shook my head and gave the clock a double take. Morning was long gone. Sleep-walking to the refrigerator, I grabbed a carton of orange juice and began chugging it. Mom walked into the room and frowned at me. She makes faces at me all the time. I'd call it another of her games, but in this case I wasn't sure if it was because of being out all night or because I was drinking out of the bottle, and I wasn't about to ask.

Ours is a traditional household with, perhaps, some subtle differences. Dad is in charge of earning the money, paying the bills, and fixing anything that needs fixing. Mom, conversely, is in charge of cooking, cleaning, and laundering. She spends each day making sure that everything is spotless and that a balanced meal is on the table when Dad gets home from work.

But on Sundays, Dad transitions to cook, making us a delicious Italian dinner, the homemade meat sauce his very own specialty. And Mom looks more like a movie star than a housewife. I've seen my friends' mothers. My mother cleans the house decked out in trendy capri pants, jazzy gold lamé shoes, full out makeup, and her hair done just so, which is to say nothing of how glamorous she looks when my dad and she go out to dances and balls on Saturday nights.

Despite looking like she just stepped out of a Hollywood set, Celia is one hundred percent mom. When we were kids, Mom told us stories about growing up during the Depression, read and sang to us, and recited poetry, both by famous authors and verse she herself had penned. Mom, the storyteller, singer, and poet!

As we grew into our teen years, we had a lot of laughs razzing and teasing her. Michael began playing a game with her when he was about fourteen where he would pretend to disobey her, and I still chuckle when I remember Mom chasing a six-foot tall Michael around the table with a broom. The drama unfolded, but the three of us knew it was all a joke. Mom, our play partner!

And after school each day, we could count on her to listen to the travails of our day. She always says she could tell if Michael had had a good or bad day at school by the sound of his footsteps on the stairs to our second floor apartment. Mom, the listener!

The strange thing after my adventure in New York is that neither Mom nor Dad said a word about my being out all night. Here's my hunch. I'll bet that Dad intervened with Mom. I'll bet anything he said, "He's a boy, Cecelia. You need to back off and let him be a boy!" And I'll bet that ticked her off.

I did get in a little hot water, though, because when I wasn't working on a Saturday, I hung out with Mary Elizabeth. I would pick her up, and we'd grab a couple of coffees and glazed crullers at the

Dunkin' Donuts, then go hang out somewhere, like at the playground at Riverview Park. We'd sit at a picnic table and lick the sticky sugar from the donuts off our fingers and talk about anything and everything.

Anyway, after I put the orange juice away and grabbed a bowl of Rice Krispies, Mom said, "That Mary Elizabeth called twice this morning. You better call her back."

That's how Mom has always referred to my female friends – "that Mary Elizabeth" or "that Karen" or "that Jody," almost like she's jealous of them. I guess it's another of our games.

Mary Elizabeth skipped the hello when I called. "Where were you this morning, Gabriel DeMarco?" She calls me by my full name when she's displeased with me. Sometimes being friends with Mary Elizabeth feels like having a second mother.

With a yawn, I said, "Sorry...I was out real late last night...I must have overslept. Well, not overslept, because when you literally stay up all night, you get up late. Does that make sense?"

"Oh yeah...*so* much sense!" I could hear the acid in her tone. "May I ask what you were *doing* that caused you to stay up all night?"

"Uhm...you know how Tomaso is going into the Army next week?"

"Yes, Gabriel, of course I know how he's going into the Army. Have we not talked about it a hundred times?"

"Yes, well what I mean is...I was somewhere with him. I mean, we were somewhere with each other."

"*Somewhere*?" she said, unamused. "Are you trying to say you don't know where you were all night?"

"No, I'm not trying to say...well, what I am trying to say is, uhm, a few of the guys from Duchess and I took him out for...you know, for like, a little celebration."

"Oh? And where did you celebrate?"

"Well...nowhere special...but, uhm, just hung out here and there."

"Here and there, huh? Okay, I'm going to hang up now, Gabriel, because I am not loving this conversation and because I have a life. Maybe I'll see you in school Monday if you don't stay up all night and oversleep again."

I hated not being truthful. It wasn't that I lied or anything, but I was doing what my mother calls "evading the truth." I swear, Mom should have been a psychologist because she has a way to explain all kinds of behaviors. Hearing the disappointment in Mary Elizabeth's voice made me feel guilty, though, and I hoped she'd forget about it soon.

A week later, Michael and I threw a going away party for Tomaso on the patio at our new house. All the guys from Duchess, about twenty, were there, and Michael had invited an equal number of girls, some friends of his and mine and some girls who hung out in the parking lot. It wasn't like every guy there was going to pair up with a girl, but like Michael had joked, "It's going to be an even number of integers." After all, he is a mathematician.

Two weeks later in mid June, unbelievably, Tomaso was gone. My cousin was on his way to basic training at Fort Dix in New Jersey. Jeff had gone to boot camp at Parris Island in South Carolina, so I guess the Army and the Marines train in different places, but what do I know?

It boggled my mind how one minute you could be hanging out with a guy and the next minute he could be in the military doing something you can't even imagine. I didn't talk to God much, but when I did, I asked Him why He kept taking my friends away. Then I'd think, *Is there even any such thing as God?* Sometimes I wonder if I'm becoming an atheist. With my luck, I'll end up burning in hell for it.

Tomaso's leaving got me thinking. There are some things in life you just know. Things you learn as a little kid. Or maybe you're born knowing them and they germinate at a certain age. Maybe when I was seven or eight, I had this pervading sense that I was alone on this spinning ball of a planet. Sure, there were Mom and Dad and Michael, and there were the kids in the neighborhood and at school, and there were the grandparents and aunts and uncles and cousins – but one day, you go into a deep space and think, *There are all these people, and I'm still alone.*

It's weird, I know, but it's something profound. You realize that when push comes to shove, you can't depend on anyone but yourself. So, I had never minded being alone – but with each person who left my life for one reason or another, I was feeling lonely. And that's a whole other matter. So, yeah – like, there's *alone* and there's *lonely,* which aren't the same thing. It's a paradox because you can know you're alone, and at the same time, know you need friends to hang out with so you're not lonely.

I was looking forward to my senior banquet. It was about a week away, and ever since I was a freshman, a whole mythology surrounded the banquet, suggesting that you stayed out and partied all night and that the girls were hot to trot and all that crazy stuff. Every year, first thing in the morning after the senior banquet, a group of seniors would walk through the hallways in their tuxes, whooping and hollering, until the assistant principal, Mr. Martin, threw them out of the building. We underclassmen looked forward to drinking and making it with girls and getting thrown out of the building the next morning.

While I had failed miserably to score with a girl all year, senior banquet night offered a promise of redemption. The trick was to pick a girl. But who? It couldn't be a good friend because I wouldn't want to score with someone I liked a lot as a person. And she also couldn't be a girl I'd want to be my girlfriend because you don't have a one-night stand with a potential girlfriend. I would need someone I didn't know and someone who would know what she was getting herself in for because I'm not a guy who would ever take advantage of some unsuspecting girl. It was complicated.

At the time, Michael and I had chipped in two hundred bucks each and bought a 350 Honda. Michael was sleeping in because his semester had ended, so I got to ride the Honda to school.

As a senior, I had developed a problem with chronic tardiness, and I couldn't even get my act together and arrive on time for graduation practices. It's like my internal clock was always fifteen minutes off. I would pull my Honda up against the brick building and make a dramatic late entrance to practice.

As I walked into the gym, the guys in my class would call out, razzing the heck out of me, "Hey, Bronson," and "Here comes Bronson," and "About time, Bronson!" They were referring to a character on the TV show, *Then Came Bronson*, where the main character rides his Harley across the country looking for life experiences. Bronson takes off, living the life of a vagabond after being wrecked by the suicide of his best friend, and along the way he manages to affect the lives of those he meets in a positive way. I liked being compared to the character.

Mr. Martin would shut the guys down, though, stuttering, "O-okay-o-okay, okay...kn-kn-kn-knock it off, you d-donkeys!" Then he'd say something like, "DeMarco, have you ever be-be-been on ti-time for anything in yo-yo-your life?" Or he'd say, "How'd you wi-wi-wi-win all those, those, those cr-cr-cross country races? Weren't y-y-you late for the me-meets?" Despite his pronounced stutter and his more pronounced sarcasm, we all loved the guy, and we knew he loved us. I'll never forget that during those three graduation practices, as Mr. Martin reviewed the program for the evening, he practiced calling each graduate up to the stage. There wasn't a single kid in the class whose name he didn't know.

He had doled out a couple of dozen detentions to me during the school year for tardiness. I don't say it to brag, though. It was just another way I had changed for the worse over my high school career.

As for me, while my classmates walked up to the stage to receive make-believe diplomas and have their imaginary tassels turned, I scanned the girls' side, wondering who might be a good choice to help me make one final attempt to achieve my goal.

CHAPTER 13

It wasn't long before I noticed a girl at practice who fit my criteria: a foxy, hippie-dippy looking chick sitting across from me in the first row of the girls' side.

Decked out in a groovy, fringed leather vest over her paisley dress and those Greek style sandals with straps that wrapped around her lower legs, she looked like she just rolled in from Woodstock. I doubt she had gone to Woodstock, though, because my theory is none of us knew that Woodstock was going to be Woodstock or that the Summer of Love was going to be the Summer of Love until we heard about it on the nightly news. At least I didn't know about it until it was already up and running. Anyway, not many parents were about to give their seventeen-year-old kids permission to go off to a weekend rock concert where everyone was going to be drugging and walking around naked. There's no way my dad would have.

So, maybe she didn't go to Woodstock, but I suspected, with that flower child look, she worshiped at the Church of Free Love. Or something like that! Sure, I had seen her around, but we had never been in a single class together, and I realized I didn't even know her name. Perfect!

Even without having met, we already had a thing going, for sure. She and I were playing that game with our eyes where you check a girl out and she gives you that look that says, *I get that you're checking me out, and I don't mind it one little bit.*

When we got our yearbooks the morning of the banquet, the first thing I did was thumb through it, looking for her picture. There she was in the M section, Tina Moretti. I liked it. *Hippie Tina.*

I wasn't seeing Mary Elizabeth as often because she still had full days of school, and we seniors were sprung each day after graduation practice, around noon. We talked a little on the phone, though.

"What are your plans for the senior banquet?" Mary Elizabeth asked one night.

"Oh...you know, just go with my friends and have a good time."

I wasn't about to tell her that I was going to try to score with a girl I didn't even know. Not that I felt good about it either, but I just couldn't graduate from high school as the only guy-virgin in my class. If other guys would have just kept their own sexual experiences to themselves like they should have, I wouldn't have been in this pickle.

"What sort of good time, Gabriel?" she asked.

"Oh...I don't know. Just your everyday, garden variety sort of good time. Pete Jansen from the basketball team is taking six of us guys in his parents' station wagon. We all rented tails, with polka-dot bow ties and cummerbunds, because you know, we're trying to be funny. So, we'll go have a few drinks up behind the golf course, and then we'll head over to the banquet."

"O-ka-a-a-y," Mary Elizabeth said, with more than a hint of skepticism. "Well, don't do anything too stupid, Gabriel."

I wished she hadn't said that, because deep inside I knew my plan *was*, in fact, stupid. Mary Elizabeth could have that effect on me.

Another obstacle I had to overcome was communicating to my parents that I was going to be out all night again. Last time, I hadn't told them because I didn't even know. I'd play it safe this time.

A few days before the banquet, I tried to prepare my mother.

"Mom," I began, "Wednesday is the senior banquet, so I won't be home that night."

"Oh, like New York again," she shot back.

It was the first time she had brought it up. "Not like New York, Mom. That was just...just that we missed the last train, basically. There's no train this time. The banquet is different."

"Different how?" she asked. "Where will you be all night?"

"Well, I don't know yet. Just out."

"Just out?" she said, in a tone thick with emotion. "I don't like it at all, and I'm going to talk to your father about it."

"Now don't go getting a rash over it, Celia."

"Don't you Celia *me*, young man!"

It obviously wasn't the time to be cute. I hate when she gets emotional, and I hate disappointing her even more.

"Now, you don't need to be an alarmist about it, Mom. It's just, that's how it is on senior banquet night. We stay out all night. Not just me, but everybody. The whole class. Three hundred people. And then all of us guys meet at the school building in the morning and walk through the halls until Mr. Martin throws us all out. It's, like, a school tradition."

"Mr. Martin throws you out? What makes you think that's a tradition? And why would you want to get thrown out of school?" She waved her hand in the air like she was going to hit me. Not that she's ever laid a hand on me in my life.

"He knows it's going to happen, Mom. Geez, I think he'll be disappointed if we don't show up."

I don't know what she said to Dad, but oddly, there was no further discussion about it. I think maybe Dad came to my rescue again. I mean, the guy was in the Army Air Corps. He flew planes for God's sake. So even, like, when Michael and I got the motorcycle, Mom was against it, but I think Dad intervened there too.

My buddies and I did just like I told Mary Elizabeth. We went up in the woods behind the local golf course and had a few beers before heading for the banquet because that's what you do on banquet night.

When we arrived at the banquet hall, everyone was signing yearbooks before the meal was served. I weaved through the crowd, looking for Hippie Tina, and when I found her, I said, "Hi there, would you sign my yearbook?" trying to act like I had no ulterior motives but was just asking everyone to sign my book.

Hippie Tina smiled and handed me hers, and we got all serious and wrote each other a note.

I alternated between signing Tina's book and looking her up and down. She was wearing a mini-dress covered with large multi-colored daisies, with loud yellow tights. She reminded me of Goldie Hawn when she starred on *Laugh-In*, and I found it hard to concentrate on the note I was writing, but I managed to write something nice.

"Maybe I'll see you at the post-banquet," I said.

"Count on it," she said, with that Woodstock smile of hers.

That sure encouraged me. I felt even more encouraged when I got back to my table and checked out her neat, if not grammatically incorrect, handwritten note:

> *Your a cute kid I don't*
> *know too good, but wish I did.*
> *Love,*
> *Tina*

That's how kids sign yearbooks. They write dumb stuff like, "To a good kid..." or "To a kid who caused a lot of trouble in French class..." or "To a kid who needs to sober up..." and the girls all sign off with "Love," even if the two of you never said a word to each other. Oh, and seven out of ten kids write the word *your* when they mean *you're* or *too good* when they mean *too well*...but in Tina's case, I didn't need her to be an English scholar.

It made me feel great that Hippie Tina called me a cute kid and said she wished she knew me better.

Everything was going according to plan. The thing is, at the post-banquet, Tina and I didn't even talk to each other or dance with each other until the tail end, which sounds off the wall, but that's what happened. I hung out with my crowd, and Hippie Tina hung with hers, which were obviously two different crowds. Everyone was a little tipsy, and the girls in my crowd were generously giving all of us guys these big, wet kisses, which was making me sorry that I hadn't zeroed in on one of them. Like a girl named Hope Wells, who hung out at Duchess. I had a serious crush on Hope. But I knew my mission, and I was sticking to it.

At the end of the night, the lead guitarist from the band announced, "Okay, Class of '70, as you wrap up your high school career, we're gonna wrap up the night with something slow, so grab your favorite guy or girl and let's end this thing."

When the band began the song, "Something," by the Beatles, I made a bee-line to Hippie Tina, knowing exactly where she was.

"Hi," I said, "wanna dance?"

She just smiled and nodded, just like she had been expecting me to ask her. Girls are like that. Nine out of ten times, they know exactly what you're going to do.

We made our way onto the dance floor, and she wrapped both arms around me and put her head on my shoulder. *She's not even being subtle,* I realized.

About mid-way through the song, I pulled away from her so she would look at me, and I said, "Hey, Tina, wanna go somewhere?" Even though I didn't know where "somewhere" was, Hippie Tina knew what I meant.

"Sure," she said, with that same knowing, seductive smile.

"Except," I said, "I came with my friends, so I don't have a car."

She smiled. "That's fine. I have a car. I drove here, and I told my girlfriend she might need to go home with someone else."

See what I mean? The way I looked at it, Tina was a free love kind of chick just like I thought, and she knew exactly what she was doing. It wasn't like I was taking advantage of her. This was going to be a "no strings" arrangement, not some great love affair, which was just fine with me. My plan was working out just as I had hoped.

CHAPTER 14

My plan was working perfectly. When the song ended, I went and told my friends I had a ride, and Tina and I headed out to her car. Wouldn't you know it was a sports car? A Karmann Ghia, which wasn't going to give me much room to do what I was planning to do.

We started to make out for a while in the parking lot, and I was feeling pretty great about the way things were going.

"Where do you want to go?" she asked.

"I don't know," I said. "Just somewhere...like, you know –"

"Don't worry," she interrupted. "I know a private place in Stratford."

I tried not to show it, but inside I was feeling euphoric. *She knows a private place in Stratford! She's obviously done this before!*

On the way to Stratford, we didn't talk. She popped a Creedence Clearwater Revival tape into her eight-track player. It was the *Green River* album, and the title song was the first to play. Most kids would consider this sacrilegious, but I am no fan of Creedence Clearwater. I don't care for their country rock sound, and I can't stand John Fogerty's voice, but I wasn't going to tell Hippie Tina that. It's not like Hippie Tina and I needed to like the same music. We weren't going to get married or anything.

In about a half hour, the car bumped up and down along a woodsy dirt road in Stratford, with dark, low branches brushing against the windshield as we went.

When she pulled the car over, I asked, "Do you have any other tapes?" I didn't want to have sex for the first time in my life while listening to Creedence Clearwater Revival.

"Sure," she said. "There's a box behind my seat. Put in whatever you like."

I grabbed the box, and right on top I found a Crosby, Stills, and Nash album, my new favorite group since the breakup of the Beatles.

After I popped the tape in, Tina and I began making out. She was a great kisser, and because of the tight quarters of the Karmann Ghia with the stick shift on the floor and everything, she undid her sandals and kicked them off and then climbed over onto my seat, straddling my legs. To be honest, it was the first time a girl had ever straddled me, so I was thinking, *This looks very promising!*

A kiss or two later, Tina did something I *really* wasn't expecting. She hooked her thumbs into the waistband of her pantyhose, and somehow slithered out of them in that tight space, like a snake shedding its skin. Talk about a free love chick. I have no idea how she did it, but I was now convinced beyond a shadow of a doubt that I was going to, at long last, achieve my goal. Then we went back to passionately kissing again, and I kind of felt around here or there, not sure of what I was feeling for.

Since she was kneeling on the seat, her head above mine, I noticed for the first time that she was wearing a small gold crucifix which dangled a few inches below our chins as we kissed. Between each and every kiss there it was, a holy pendulum swinging back and forth. That's when my mind began to do its thing. *Jesus is watching me!*

About fifteen minutes into the tape, "Guinnevere" came on, and at first, I got lost in the tight harmonies, the haunting finger picking of the acoustic guitars, and the poetic lyrics. This feeling washed over me, *I am Sir Lancelot and this is my Guinnevere.*

But then my mind shifted gears. *Wait, Hippie Tina isn't my Guinnevere. I don't even know who she is!*

I realized this wasn't a good line of thinking at the moment, but I couldn't help myself. I was on an emotional roller coaster that was swooping downhill on the fast track. As Tina continued to kiss me, my mind clasped onto the lyrics of the song like a vice-grip, and I imagined another face, not Tina's but the face of a girl I had somehow known, having green eyes, and I pictured, not Tina, but this imaginary girl walking through a garden after it rained. And when David Crosby's voice rang out, asking the profound question in his crystal-clear tenor, "Why can't she see me?" I had a sort of epiphany. *I need to be with, not Hippie Tina, but someone who can "see" me.* At the same time, I still felt pressured to go through with it, but when Crosby, Stills, and Nash segued into a round of "doo-dum-de-doos," I worried I was going to cry.

Feeling depressed when you're about to have your first sexual experience is something I don't advise. I'm not certain if Hippie Tina noticed my crazy emotions, but she seemed distracted and stopped kissing me. Without warning, she slid back onto her seat and grabbed her pocketbook. It was like she had more than an inkling that I wasn't quite right in the head. Girls can tell. They have that "woman's intuition" thing where they know when something's amiss.

Hippie Tina then opened her pocketbook and took out a joint, already neatly rolled up. Sitting in her seat, her bare feet overlapping opposite thighs, she lit up and took a hit. Then she reached over, wordlessly offering it to me.

"No thanks," I said, awkwardly. "I...uhm...I don't smoke. You know, like, I drink, but I don't smoke."

Terribly unimpressed, Tina just grimaced and rolled her eyes.

I've blown it now, I realized as I watched Tina settle into her seat where she continued to smoke her joint. The next song that came on was "Our House." She looked over at me and said, "Did you know that Graham Nash wrote this song for Joni Mitchell?" The question surprised me because, a moment ago, it seemed like she didn't want to know me.

"No," I said, "I don't think I knew –"

"Yeah," she continued. "Well, you know they were a couple, right?"

"Right, of course –" I said, even though this was the first I'd ever heard of it. I had been more into the talent and musicianship of singers rather than their romances.

"And that they lived together at Laurel Canyon in California."

"Oh yeah –"

"You know...where a lot of the best rockers now live. You knew that, right?"

She was firing trivia at me in rapid succession now, not giving me a chance to answer.

"Oh, absolutely, I –"

"And Graham wrote this song for her. But then she broke up with him. That broke my heart."

"It did? I mean, she did? I mean –" I didn't know what I meant.

"Oh yeah...I was shocked because it was a match made in heaven. But I guess all good things come to an end, right?"

"Right...definitely." *Good things always come to an end for me*, I was thinking.

Then she examined me with curious eyes. "Do you like Joni Mitchell?"

"Well, yeah, I mean, sure...who doesn't like Jo–"

"Yeah, Joni's amazing, isn't she? There's nobody like her."

She finally paused, mercifully, to take a few more hits from her joint, holding the smoke in her lungs and then slowly letting it out.

We were just talking now. Or it might be more accurate to say she was talking and I was trying to respond.

"Yeah, you know how Crosby, Stills, and Nash sang the song 'Woodstock' at the festival?"

Thankfully, I did know that. "Yeah, sure I –"

"Did you know Joni wrote that?"

Another thing I should have known, but I shook my head like the dope that I am.

"Oh yeah, she wrote it. Hold on. Hand me that box of tapes." She rifled through the plastic tape cartridges and grabbed one that had a simple black line drawing of a lady on it with, like, a painted shawl draped over the arm of the female figure. At closer glance, the print on the shawl was a colorful collage of houses and cottages, which popped off the cover.

"So yeah, Joni painted this," Tina explained. "It's a self portrait. Put it in."

She handed me the tape. I studied the artwork before popping it in.

"So yeah, Joni went to art school, and she paints as well as she sings or plays musical instruments, if you can believe that."

Tina reached over and clicked the button on her tape player until I heard a moody jazz piano introduction begin Joni's rendition of "Woodstock," which was incredibly different from the Crosby,

Stills, and Nash hard driving electric version, which I was familiar with.

"So yeah," Tina said. (It seemed like she started everything she said with "So yeah.") "Joni was supposed to go with the guys to Woodstock, but she wasn't sure she could because she had to appear on the Dick Cavett Show, and when all those hundreds of thousands of people showed up, you couldn't very easily get in or out of the place, so she had to skip it."

"Oh," I said, going into one of my monosyllabic stupors when I didn't know how to respond, like when Jeff told me he was enlisting in the Marines.

"So yeah, I think she was super disappointed, but then look at what she goes and does. She watches the news reports from her hotel room in New York and writes this amazing song."

Where have I been? I thought to myself. Somehow I hadn't been paying attention to what was going on with Joni. I didn't even own a single one of her albums. I must have been too preoccupied with quitting the basketball team.

Strange as it may sound, I felt relieved that Hippie Tina and I obviously wouldn't be having sex. Instead, we were just talking to each other about music, just like two good friends. Just like me and Jeff, except for the fact that Tina was a foxy-looking chick and Jeff is just another guy. In a way, a guy could put too much pressure on himself trying to have sex.

Now we sat in the darkness, listening to Joni's angelic, emotion-filled voice, and it was at that moment that I fell in love. Not with Tina, though, but with Joni Mitchell whose voice penetrated my soul, cutting me to the core. In the darkness, I attempted to unobtrusively wipe tears from the corners of my eyes before Tina noticed. I try not to cry, especially in front of girls.

Tina leaned her head on the back of her seat and let out a long, contented sigh. "I feel so relaxed and peaceful now. Too bad you don't smoke weed. You're a cool guy; I think you'd totally love getting stoned."

"Yeah, maybe," I replied. "I don't know. I mean, maybe I'll try it someday."

"I'll tell you this, if you like music, it sounds even better when you're high. Everything is just...I don't know how to explain it...prettier and...and, like, heightened. Totally mind blowing!"

Then Tina asked me if I wanted her to take me home. I told her I was supposed to meet my friends at the high school before school starts, but that wouldn't be for more than an hour.

"Hm, we have time to kill then," she said. "There's a Dunkin' Donuts a little ways from here. Let's go hang out there and have a coffee and a donut."

"Sounds good," I said, feeling a twinge of disloyalty to Mary Elizabeth even though she was only a friend, but going to Dunkin' Donuts in Ansonia had become our thing. What was I going to say, though – bring me to the high school an hour early?

"But first," she continued, "could you hand me my stockings? I think they're on the floor by your feet."

I reached down and picked up the rolled-up ball of material, and with an apologetic look, handed the stockings, a symbol of my latest failed attempt, to Tina who stuffed them inside her pocketbook.

Ten minutes later, she and I were sitting at a little orange table in Dunkin' Donuts and talking about everything from music to our plans for the future. She wasn't going to college but said she was going to get a job as a secretary until she could save up enough money to take off.

"Then," she said, "I'm never coming back to this fuckin' hick town." She meant Shelton, of course, not Stratford.

Her use of the expletive jolted me. I wasn't used to hearing a girl say *fuck*, and I didn't care for it. The girls I was friendly with didn't.

"Where will you go?" I asked.

"Who fuckin' knows? (Jolt!) Any-fuckin'-where but here. (Jolt!) I'm thinking, the fuckin' West Coast." (Jolt!)

I told her how I had wanted to go to Bates College but that I got rejected and was going to the local state college in New Haven like my brother had. I was too embarrassed to tell her that my dad was making me go there. I did have the guts to say, though, that for once in my life I had planned *not* to do what my brother had done. I didn't plan to become a teacher like him, I told her.

"Yeah," she said. "I never heard of Bates, but getting rejected sucks. That must've hurt. And I can understand not wanting to copy your brother. I have two sisters – a lot older than me. Eight years and eleven years. I was an *accident*. And my parents always want me to be perfect like my sisters. It's such fuckin' bullshit! I can't take it anymore."

"We should probably head for the high school," I suggested.

Driving along Route 110 toward Shelton, Tina broke the silence. "You okay?"

"Me? Oh yeah...I'm great," I lied. "Just tired I think."

Then she popped a question that stunned me. "Do you want to talk to me about what's actually bothering you?"

"What're you talking about? Nothing's bothering me," I said, defensively.

She just took her hand off the stick shift and made the *okay* sign with her thumb and index finger. Then with a wry smile, she said, "Think about this, though. Whatever it is probably isn't worth freaking out over."

Wow! Just like Mary Elizabeth, Tina could read me like a book. What was it about me that made it so easy for girls to see through me?

When she dropped me off behind the high school, about fifteen guys were already there. Before I got out of the car, she reached into her bag and wrote her phone number on a gum wrapper. "If you ever need to talk to someone, call me," she said.

As she pulled away, I realized she had let me off the hook as far as sex was concerned. I should have thanked her, but I did the opposite. I could still hear the motor of her car fading away as the guys started patting me on the back and roughing me up a little by pushing me around from one to the other, all the while laughing and yelling, "You dog, DeMarco!" and "Bronson nails it!" and "It must be that motorcycle the chicks dig!" In their warped minds, I had scored with Hippie Tina.

Not having the courage (or whatever it takes) to tell the truth, I let them think what they wanted to think. Some guys can be such assholes, and in this case, I was an asshole too. Talk about pathetic. When we walked into the building, seizing our turn to be thrown out by Mr. Martin, I realized I still had Tina's phone number in my left hand. I stuffed it deep into my pocket, but I never called Hippie Tina. She deserved better than me.

CHAPTER 15

The morning after the banquet was a replay of the morning after our New York trip. Everyone was asleep when I arrived home. I slept the morning away, and no one asked any questions. I never told anyone about Tina either. Not my parents or Michael or Mary Elizabeth or the priest in the confessional. I'm just kidding about that last one because I haven't been to church in ages.

The beginning of the end happened when I was in eighth grade and I began to grow bored with church. I hate to blame Michael, but when he and I would go to church so that Dad didn't make a big stink, Michael would stand in the back against the vestibule door, not paying the slightest attention to the Mass, just off in his own little world. Before I knew it, I joined Michael in dreamland.

By the middle of freshman year, I was no longer going to church, which was a shame because for years, I had been a devout little Catholic. The strange thing about it was that while Dad had pressured us to go to church, it was a double standard, in my mind, since he and Mom had stopped going themselves by the time I was in the sixth grade.

Since Dad never met a thought he didn't want to express, one night he called me on it. "I'm disappointed," he said. "You used to be an altar boy and everything." As if being an altar boy made you a candidate for canonization.

"It just doesn't do anything for me," I explained.

Deeply troubled, he glared at me. "Are you trying to tell me you're not a Catholic anymore?"

I felt hesitant, but some inner voice spurred me on. "I don't know. Maybe."

"Well let me tell you something. My mother went to Mass every day of her life, and that's good enough for me."

I wanted to say it wasn't good enough for me, but I didn't. I wasn't about to argue with him any more than I would shove my finger into an electrical outlet. I just clammed up.

See, Dad has always been fond of saying, "I say what I mean, and I mean what I say." Truer words have never been spoken. When we were kids, whether it was going to bed on time, getting good grades in school, or doing our chores, we knew following the rules was the best path.

Another Dad-ism is, "I don't care if you like me, but you'll damn well respect me," and while I do think he wants us to like him and, of course, even love him, that respect piece has always been where his focus was.

I'll never forget the time, around fifth grade, when my friends and I sat on the steps of the Shelton Grange watching our brothers flirt with Maureen Malone on her porch across the street. Fascinated by their mating ritual, I lost track of time. When I turned the corner at Maltby Street, the street lamp shone down on me, and Dad's silhouette loomed large in front of our house.

When I got to him, he said, "Do you know what time it is?"

I shrugged.

"It's been dark for over an hour," he pointed out.

"Well, if Michael can stay out out after dark, so can I," I said, hoping he'd understand my point.

He leaned over, his face now inches from mine as he spoke very slowly and softly. "Maybe you've forgotten that Michael is four years older than you." Straightening himself, he said in a growing crescendo. "Now get the hell upstairs and go to bed and, in the future, don't ever again tell me what you can or can't do!"

And I never did because I'm not stupid.

Even the police didn't want to mess with him. Here's a good "for instance." When I was in the middle grades, Michael's rock band used to practice in an empty apartment at our house on Maltby

Street. The lady across the street called the police because she said they were loud and she had a headache.

Sure enough, a squad car showed up, and my dad was out the door like a shot.

"Is there a problem, officers?" he asked.

Standing there was a cop named Al DiCicco, a young muscular type who had been a star quarterback at the high school just a few years before, and another cop I didn't know, a middle-aged guy with a big belly. We kids all felt that DiCicco was a big deal, like he was Bart Starr or somebody.

"Is this your house?" DiCicco asked.

"That's right."

"Is that your kid holding a band practice?"

"It is," my dad said in a tone I myself feared.

"A neighbor complained about the music being too loud," DiCicco continued. "I'm gonna have to go back there and tell them to stop playing. It's late."

"I know what time it is," my dad said in a slow, menacing cadence. "They'll be done in a few minutes."

Even as Dad spoke, Michael and the boys were crooning "Hang On Sloopy" at the tops of their lungs.

"Well, like I said, I'm gonna go tell them they have to knock it off," DiCicco persisted.

"And like *I* said," my dad fired back, "they'll be done in a few minutes, as soon as this song is over."

I almost wanted to intervene, young as I was, and say, *He's not kidding, Officer! He says what he means and he means what he says. Really!*

DiCicco looked Dad in the eye as if sizing him up. "Sir, I'll say it one last time. I'm going back there and ending this thing now."

Well, my eyes nearly popped out of my head when, with a steely glare, Dad said, "You'll have to go through me first."

After a long, uncomfortable pause, DiCicco eyed the fat cop, and they turned, got back into their squad car, and drove away. For me, at that moment, my dad was Muhammad Ali, John Wayne, and Superman all rolled into one.

I don't mean to make Dad sound like some ogre who makes a habit of scaring cops out of the neighborhood. Dad has plenty of good qualities too, like if you need someone to take care of a wound, Dad's your man.

When I had terrible poison ivy, it was Dad who took care of the rashes and blisters. I remember how he'd sterilize a razor blade and, with great care, slice the big blisters on my hands, relieving the pressure, and then he'd wrap my hands in cool, wet handkerchiefs.

And when Michael suffered from nightmares, it was Dad who rescued him from his somnolent horror, wrapping Michael up in a calming embrace.

And, personally, I'll never forget the summer before I entered ninth grade. I had been on a three week bus trip to Philmont Boy Scout Ranch in New Mexico. After returning home, I had only one day before I had to go to camp in Goshen where I'd spend two more weeks. Upon arrival in Goshen, I remember coming down with a major case of homesickness, and Dad read me like a book.

"Let's take a walk," he said.

We walked in silence to the waterfront, and looking at the placid lake, he said, "Don't worry, Gabe. The two weeks'll pass quickly, and you'll be home before you know it. You'll be okay." In those few moments, Dad became a conduit, transferring a calming energy to me.

The way I see it is this. Working hard to support us, bandaging our wounds, feeding us, and calming us after bad dreams or long trips were the ways Dad showed his love. He may not always say it, but he shows it.

But for the everyday nuts and bolts of needing someone to talk to, Mom is our go-to girl.

One day, Mom, Michael, and I were having the best time talking at the kitchen table. Mom was reciting poems like "O Captain! My Captain!" and singing us old songs, like "Yes Sir, That's My Baby." Before we knew it, it had become a sing-a-long.

We were in mid-song when Dad came in, looking strangely hurt.

Yes, Ma'am, we've decided,
No, Ma'am, we won't hide it,
Yes, Ma'am, you're invited now –

We stopped dead as Dad said, "I hope you're having a good time because I don't like that the three of you always exclude me."

Then he did an about face and went back into the living room. We were all stunned. I decided that day to make an effort to strike up a conversation in the living room as often as possible. That was a pretty good decision because I could see that Dad enjoyed those conversations. I don't even think he realized that they were the result of a conscious decision on my part to throw the bull with him. It opened the door for him to impart wisdom and give me all kinds of advice.

Those conversations went on for months during my junior year, up until the day he told me I couldn't give my class ring to Christine O'Hare and shortly thereafter grounded me for getting a D in Algebra II, the result of what a huge slacker I had become. The fact that he didn't want me to go away to college didn't help either.

Sometimes you just get mad at someone you love and things change. I got over it, but it was quite a while before Dad and I got back to those nightly talks.

CHAPTER 16

Hippie Tina had inspired my newfound interest in Joni Mitchell. I had been familiar with some of her songs, but now I dove in, immersing myself in her music. A week after the senior banquet, I made my way over to Bradlees and bought all three of her albums: *Song to a Seagull*, *Clouds*, and *Ladies of the Canyon*. I bought the first two on eight-track, but for some reason I wanted *Ladies* on vinyl. Maybe because I liked Joni's cover art so much that I wanted to own the big square version of it. Whenever I had a little privacy, I sat on my bedroom floor, listening to Joni's melancholy sweetness, gazing at the cover art while trying to wrap my brain around the confluence of music, art, and life.

Of course, I told Mary Elizabeth all about my obsession with Joni at one of our outings at Riverview Park. It turns out she liked Joni's music as well. "Sure, Joni is amazing. I'm a big fan."

"I'm more than a fan," I tried to explain. "It goes way deeper than that."

"How deep?"

I shrugged. "I don't know. Lately, it's just so...so deep that I can't even explain it."

Putting on her psychiatrist persona, she said, "But you must have noticed her before this?"

"Yeah, sure I did," I said, looking out over the Housatonic River from a park bench we were sitting on. "But I hadn't really delved into her albums until a friend opened my eyes."

"A friend?" she asked.

"Yeah. A friend. Someone at the senior banquet."

"Oh!" Mary Elizabeth exclaimed. "A *friend* from the senior banquet – a night still shrouded in mystery."

"Alright, you don't need to be sarcastic about it."

"Would that friend have been a male friend or a female friend?"

I spotted a single white swan paddling far below in the tranquil water.

"Never mind. Her gender isn't important."

"Oh, *her* gender, Gabe...good one," Mary Elizabeth quipped as I realized my gaffe.

A week later, Mary Elizabeth came bearing gifts. Or should I say *gift*!

"I think you're going to like this," she said, as she slid a magazine out of a brown paper bag.

"For me?"

"Oh yes! From me to you."

I looked at it with more than a smidgen of surprise. "*Vogue*?"

"Yes *Vogue*, but not just any *Vogue*. Open to page forty-three."

I had never held a copy of *Vogue* before. It was thicker than any magazine I had ever read and, oddly, seemed to emit the scent of a pretty girl.

I did as directed and there on the glossy page, under the headline, "People Are Talking About..." was a photo of Joni.

"Holy...geez," I said. "Where the hell did you get this?"

"At a store. Where else, silly?" She looked very proud of herself.

"You read *Vogue*?"

"Well, I am a girl, Gabriel, in case you haven't noticed!"

"No...God...I mean, yes, of course I noticed you're a girl," I laughed.

"I don't buy *Vogue* as a rule. My parents wouldn't let me even if I wanted to. They don't know I have this. But I love Joni too...so I bought it a year ago."

"But you bought it for yourself, not for me."

"You're more obsessed than I am. I'm happy to give it to you."

"Wow! Wow! Wow! But wait. I can't take this home."

"Can't? Why not?"

"Oh yeah...what'll my parents think if I have a *Vogue* magazine at home? They'll think I'm...a little...well, you know..."

"Homosexual?" she said, flashing a sly smile.

"Well...yeah..."

Always in control, Mary Elizabeth said, "I'll take care of that." She took the magazine from me and ever so carefully ripped out the page featuring Joni and handed it to me.

"There...how's that?"

"That's perfect...just perfect!" I said in amazement. "Thank you. I love you!"

When I got home, I grabbed the J volume of the encyclopedias off the shelf and filed it between the front cover and the first page. For the time being, I wanted my Joni obsession to be my little secret.

September rolled in, and I was a freshman, commuting to Southern in Michael's Corvair which he had bequeathed to me a month before when he landed a teaching job in New Haven and bought a new car. My future, now sealed, was everything I had hoped it wouldn't be.

I took my studies more seriously, though, since Dad was paying tuition, and I got off to a fast start with an A on my first essay exam in my Western Civilization class.

When Dr. Rich handed back our first exams, he called my name, and I headed to his desk not quite knowing what to expect. As I approached the short, round professor, he looked up over his thick eyeglasses and handed me my blue book. On the cover, I saw the number 94 in bold marker.

"Congratulations, Mr. DeMarco. That was the highest grade in the class," he said.

I blinked my eyes in disbelief and said, "It was?"

Dr. Rich chuckled. "Oh come now, Mr. DeMarco. You and I both know you've never gotten anything below an A in your life." I was flattered, but it simply wasn't true. I almost smiled. *If this guy only knew what a slacker I was last year.* It was good to know I still had the right stuff, though, and Dr. Rich's comment redeemed my belief in myself.

I also found the professors to be people who talked about things that I hadn't heard about in high school. Dr. Rich, for instance, taught us how during the reformation, Martin Luther fought against corruption in the Church. It seems the leaders of the Catholic Church were selling something called indulgences. I guess it was, like, "Give me a hundred bucks, and you'll get out of Purgatory six months early." Something like that. Martin Luther tried to put an end to selling indulgences and other corrupt church practices, which didn't go over too big with the Papacy.

When I was a kid at St. Joseph's School, our history books portrayed Luther as a heretic because he sort of started a new branch of Christianity. As I came to learn more about him in college, I perceived him as a hero.

I wasn't as interested in my World Literature class, though, which didn't bode well since I'm now an English major. Reading the *Iliad*, *Beowulf*, the *Divine Comedy*, and other such antiquities didn't turn out to be my bag. I mean, *Beowulf* is so old they don't even know who wrote it, but I pushed through it. And it wasn't any fun lugging an anthology that looked like it had eaten a few too many french fries, but I was learning that when you're in college, you do what you have to do.

Then there was my Composition 101 teacher, Professor Forrest, who told us to call him Dan. I remember him telling us to question everything, even God. He said, "Think of all the hundreds of things you could do wrong. He could only think of ten?" Of course, Dan was trying to be funny, but his point was well taken.

Even my Music History teacher, Dr. Schmidt, used class time to talk about the Bobby Seale trial in New Haven. Somewhere between explaining the difference between *allegro* and *andante cantabile*, Dr. Schmidt would stop his lecture and look up at the ceiling, apparently distracted, and then he'd begin talking about the Seale trial.

Dr. Schmidt, in all respects, appears to be a white guy, except he wears his hair in a big Afro, just like a lot of black people do.

"You understand, I hope, guys and girls," Dr. Schmidt explained, "that because of this impending trial, this entire campus was shut down last May and made into a base for the National Guard."

Of course, I remembered Michael telling me about seeing the military moving onto the campus and explaining the students were not to report to classes.

Dr. Schmidt continued. "We're living in revolutionary times. You have been taught that America is a free country, but that so-called freedom is antithetical to the treatment of black people in this country, even today. History is being made right here in New Haven. The trial is public, you know, so you make it a point to get down to the courthouse and see it. You need to know what's going on in the world."

My Uncle Sonny is a sheriff in the courthouse, so I figured I'd talk to him about going to the trial.

With the first semester not even two weeks old, two synchronistic things happened within days of each other. First, I got a letter from Jeff. From Vietnam! After he had finished boot camp, he had been stationed at Camp Lejeune in North Carolina, and he used to hitch a ride home whenever he got a weekend pass. But this was the first time I had heard from him since he had flown off to Vietnam. Sitting at the foot of my bed, I tore open the seal of the dirty brown envelope to find not only a letter but a snapshot. With the blinding Vietnam sun in the background, Jeff stood bare chested, wearing camouflage pants, boots, and a wide-brimmed hat. Over his left shoulder were some tents, and over his right stood a wooden watch tower. It seemed surreal, almost like looking at a still picture from a movie. I unfolded the letter with care and blinked as I read.

Hey Partner,

I'm not big on writing letters, which you probably know already, but I had a little downtime, so I thought I'd shoot something out to you. How do you like this picture of me? I'm a handsome fucker, right? My uniform isn't exactly regulation but no one in Nam is too worried about being regulation if you catch my drift. How do you like my cover? It's called a bush hat because it's good to wear in the heat of the jungle and our heads blend in better with the leaves. You know, it makes our heads look less like a target for the Vietcong. We only wear helmets when we abso-fuckin'-lutely have to. I think the Australians started wearing these things years ago, or something like that. Sometimes they're called boonie hats too although I have no fuckin' idea why. Well that's it for now, brother, because I don't know what else to write. Hope you're having fun in college and maybe we'll see each other someday. Kiss a girl for me, will ya?
Your friend,
Jeff

I couldn't imagine what it was like to be where Jeff was or to do what he was doing, whatever that was because he obviously didn't say and I obviously didn't know. I folded up the letter and put it in my desk drawer for safe keeping, and I tacked Jeff's snapshot above my bed with some other important stuff I had on the wall.

Two or three days after receiving Jeff's letter, on a Saturday afternoon, Tomaso walked into Duchess in full uniform, shiny and starched and about twenty pounds lighter. I couldn't get over the transformation. And, boy, did the crew make a big fuss over him. Even Will Granger, who had done time in Vietnam and didn't seem to have any use for the military, was thrilled to see Tomaso. But no one was happier to see him than me.

At the moment, though, Tomaso was the center of attention, with all five guys shooting questions at him from every which way. I was even surprised that Karl Fischer seemed excited to see Tomaso. Karl, another of the older guys, had at one time in a drunken rage threatened to kick the asses of all three of us DeMarcos.

There was just something about a man in uniform that got people pumped up. I felt like I was a disembodied spirit, seeing and hearing the whole scene from above. Tomaso was charming, witty, and sharp.

"Yeah, I'm just home for the week"..."Oh, fuck you, I look good in my uniform and you know it!"..."Get lost! Boot camp was a walk in the park"..."They're sending me to Fort Sill in Oklahoma, so you assholes won't be seeing me for a long time"..."Yeah, that's right. I got my uniform on because when the chicks see me in this they won't be able to resist"..."Aww, fuck you, you're just jealous..."

And so the conversation went until we had a brief rush of customers and we had to man our stations. Even Tomaso threw on an apron and dressed hamburger buns because that's how we are at Duchess.

After I finished taking the last order, I heard Karl Fischer talking to Tomaso behind the grill in his unmistakable lisp. "Hey, Tommy Trouble, now that your cousin's in college, he thinks he's the hot shit."

"Is that right?" Tomaso asked.

"Oh yeah," Karl said. "He's too fuckin' good for everybody now."

Tomaso looked at me. "You're a big man on campus now, huh?"

"Don't listen to him," I said, nodding toward Karl. "He just thinks he's a funny man. I'm the same as I always was."

Then Tomaso asked me what I was doing tonight.

"Nothing. I'm hoping we can hang out," I said.

"Yeah, let's get drunk. I need to get drunk."

"Okay, that's fine."

"Perfect. We'll do what we always do. It'll be just like old times. Sometimes in boot camp, remembering those good times was the one thing that kept me going."

It occurred to me that the last time I had gotten drunk was with Tomaso before he left. Like he said, going drinking on DeMarco Mountain would be like old times. *Good times. Right!* Not to be a pessimist, but if they sent Tomaso to Vietnam, I wondered if there would be any good times to come.

After Tomaso went home and spent some time with his parents, we met at Duchess, got the necessary provisions, cups and the ice filled ketchup can, and then we swung by the package store for the gin and soda.

As I sipped my first drink, I said, "It's funny that you're home because I just got a letter and a snapshot from Jeff the other day."

"No shit! What did he have to say?"

"Not much of anything. The only thing he talked about was the hat he had on in the photo. He called it a bush hat and a boonie hat. Other than that, he didn't say a thing about what he was doing over there."

"Well, let me help you out. You don't want to fuckin' know."

"I don't?"

"No, you don't. Trust me."

"Ok, so then what about you?" I asked. "What's the deal with Oklahoma?"

"Well, Fort Sill is where soldiers are trained in heavy artillery, so I guess I'll find out what that means when I get there."

"Wow," I said because I couldn't think of anything else to say even though the words *heavy artillery* were like racing lights ricocheting against the contours of my brain.

We just sat in silence for a while, sucking down our drinks. I mean, *silence* except to say that there was the sound of the Temptations singing "Ball of Confusion" blaring through Tomaso's self-installed stereo speakers, two black protrusions on the shelf behind his back seat. He and I were both big fans of the Motown sound. As the Temptations' hit chronicled all the problems of the world from racial tensions to war to poverty in the coolest rhythmic groove, I started to feel bummed out.

Breaking the silence, he said, "Almost everybody who gets stationed at Fort Sill ends up in Vietnam."

Speaking of heavy artillery, hearing Tomaso could end up in Vietnam felt like a bomb going off inside my head.

I sighed. "Oh yeah?"

"That's what they fuckin' tell me."

I just sipped my drink.

He refilled his cup with ice and then poured in more gin and soda. "You know what I was reading before I left for boot camp?"

"What's that?"

"Letters my mother got from your old man when he was in the military."

"Where did you see those?"

"They're in a shoebox in our garage."

"No kidding."

He took a big gulp and said, "Yeah! But you know what he wrote about a lot? He told my mother to stop my father from joining up. 'He's too much of an individual,' your dad wrote. 'He'll refuse to take orders and then they'll just kill him.' Stuff like that."

I remembered the box of letters from my dad to my mom I had stumbled upon in the basement. Hundreds and hundreds of them. I had begun reading one, but it was too mushy for me.

I sat there as the eight-track clicked over to the next Temptations tune, thinking about how my dad was training to be a pilot when he was my age, high in the air while my feet were stuck on the ground.

"Maybe I'm not as big of an individual as my old man," Tomaso continued, "but I still take after him somewhat. I'm his kid, if you get me, and I hate taking orders."

"Was boot camp a walk in the park like you said?" I asked.

"Fuck no! It was the hardest thing I've ever done in my life."

His speech was slurred now. I think mine was too.

"But you did it," I said.

"Right! And damn proud of it. Still, I just hate taking fuckin' orders."

"Well, I guess you have to, right?"

"Yeah, I do," he said. "And if they send me to Nam, I'm gonna have to follow those orders too, but I ain't gonna like it."

"No," I said, "of course not."

"Maybe I'll see Jeff over there," he said with a sarcastic snort.

"Yeah."

We didn't say much of anything else. We just sat there in his car atop DeMarco Mountain, listening to the Temptations and getting drunk. It seemed like such a waste, in one sense, but I guess we had had an important conversation in another.

When my cousin let me off in front of my house well after midnight, I pushed myself out of his car and entered the house through the garage. My head was spinning. As I reached about the fourth basement step, I heard the high pitched squeal of his tires as Tomaso laid down a strip of rubber, and I smiled to myself. No matter what time it was, Tommy Trouble made sure the neighbors knew he was on our street.

CHAPTER 17

When you're not going to see someone you care about for a long time, you realize how short one week is. Besides, Tomaso had other people to see, including an old girlfriend who, like he said, couldn't resist a man in uniform. And I had to work three nights that week and read all my school assignments. The week was gone in a flash and Tomaso was on his way to Oklahoma.

In early October, I swung by my Uncle Sonny's house to ask about the Seale trial. I was a little nervous about going, but he told me to just look for him when I got to the courthouse, so I made a plan to go the next Tuesday.

When I arrived in New Haven, the city was swarming with Panthers in their black leather jackets and berets protesting the trial outside the courthouse. They were joined by lots of white Yale students. *Yale kids are so smart,* I thought. *They must understand what's going on better than I do.*

What I did understand were the basics, which I had researched on microfiche in the basement of the Buley Library at Southern – that some New Haven Black Panthers had shot a black guy named Alex Rackley in the head and chest and then had thrown him in the Coginchaug River in Middletown and that Bobby Seale was accused of giving the orders to knock the guy off because Rackley was an FBI informant. I guess I would have had to see the whole trial to know more, but it lasted for months.

Uncle Sonny and another sheriff brought Seale into the court-room in handcuffs. Big stuff! I was also impressed by the lawyers who were just as dramatic as Perry Mason. Months later, I read that all the excitement ended in a mistrial, which meant Bobby Seale wasn't convicted, which I'll bet Dr. Schmidt was happy about.

The Wednesday night after I had attended the trial, I was on the schedule at Duchess. In the lingering heat of Indian summer, we had the sliding double doors wide open in the customer vestibule like usual, and also like usual, the fluorescent lights drew flocks of moths. A middle-aged woman was waiting for a "special," a bacon double cheeseburger, when a kid with tangled, shoulder length hair and a glassy look in his eyes came to the window and ordered an orange drink. While I was taking his payment, the new drink man set the paper cup on the counter next to me. I slid it to the hippie kid and asked the next customer for his order.

Out of the corner of my eye, I saw the hippie kid lift the plastic cover off the cup, push it across the counter at me like it was a hockey puck, and look down in disgust.

"Hey, man! There's a moth in my drink. What the fuck?"

In one sense, I could see his point; in another, I had an issue with his bad language in front of our adult customer. Personally, I had been taught to respect my elders and watch my p's and q's in their presence. I opened the register, extracted a quarter and a nickel, slapped them on the counter, and said, "You know what, man, here's your money back. Take your business somewhere else!" The long-haired kid glared at me through dilated pupils and walked out.

I'm not sure if that was the best way to handle it, but he had pushed my button, and besides, I had seen Michael do the same thing with more dangerous guys than this winner. I remember in my first month at Duchess when two guys at the window were using some pretty raw language, and my brother refused to serve them. "Why don't you two get lost? We have real customers here," he said.

That night, I learned that Michael was sometimes fearless, not unlike our dad whom he had been named after, but I found myself doubting his judgment in this instance. One was a guy named Billy Robbins who we heard had served some time in prison, and the other was known as Beef Belsky.

Well, Beef didn't react well to Michael's self-righteousness.

"How about if I climb through this window and kick your ass, motherfucker?" he growled.

Michael stood his ground, though, not budging an inch. As for me, I went into covert operations of my own by surreptitiously taking a metal french fry basket and lowering it into the hot cooking oil. If Beef was going to come through the window at my brother, his face was going to come into direct contact with the hot fry basket. Surprisingly, Billy Robbins was the only one with any presence of mind, because neither Beef nor Michael had any. He clamped his strong hand around Beef's forearm and said, "Let it go, man. This fuckin' punk ain't worth it." Maybe Robbins had mellowed, or more likely, he was on parole and needed to be on his best behavior.

When Billy dragged Beef out of the vestibule kicking, shouting, and swearing, I breathed a sigh of relief. At the time, I hoped next time Michael wouldn't act like such a tough guy, and now wouldn't you know I was imitating the same behavior? In my defense, Mr. Long Hair seemed far less menacing than Billy or Beef.

In this case, after the kid left the vestibule, the matter seemed over. But a little after closing time, Big Alfred came in from the parking lot with a message.

"Gabriel, you know that boy you tossed out earlier?" he asked.

I nodded.

"He outside and tol' me to tell you to come out. He says he gonna kick your ass."

I felt that I was under the scrutiny of both Alfred and the other three guys on the crew. They were all giving me that *how-are-you-going-to-handle-this* look. I was, after all, in charge. At the same time, I didn't exactly feel like a responsible adult.

As a guy, there's a pressure you feel to answer the call when other guys are looking at you. You grow up needing to figure out how you're going to navigate the world of being bullied. Are you going to fight or are you going to allow yourself to be pushed around? I remember being about nine or ten when I was bested by another kid in a neighborhood scuffle. You know – the kind where whoever lands the first punch is the victor! At our kitchen table that night, Dad looked me straight in the eye through my teary face and calmly said, "It's not a problem if you get in a fight, just don't come home if you lose." I know. It sounds harsh, but I get it now. He wanted to raise a man, not a mouse. Still, it had mostly been my choice, growing up, to talk my way out of and around fights. If you're a good talker, you can avoid a fight without looking weak or stupid. I have a hunch I was more adept at talking myself out of trouble than my big brother was.

Confronted with a tricky situation, I headed for the back door. I heard Les Wilson, a step behind, warn, "Now don't do anything hasty here, Gabriel, baby. I feel you should just call the police."

"I'm good, Les," I said.

Les is an older guy, maybe forty. I've always liked him, but I felt I could handle the situation without calling the police.

Bink was also on that night and didn't say a word, but just followed me with curiosity as did Les and Richie Gagliardi, who everyone calls "Gag," a new kid on the crew that night. Everyone likes to see a good fight, even though my intention was to avoid one.

The long-haired kid was standing by his van, looking possessed and like he was as high as a kite. "Let's go, you prick," he said to me, lifting his fists into the air and staggering toward me. Looking at him, I wondered, *Aren't you hippies supposed to be all about peace and love?*

"Okay, man," I said. "Let's just get in your van and move along."

"Fuck you, asshole," he growled, and then the lunatic took a wild swing at me with his right fist. I could hear Gag yelling, "Don't take any shit from him, Gabe!"

"Just cut it!" I said, dodging his punch. "You need to get going, pal."

"I'm not your fuckin' pal!" he shouted and shoved me. I stumbled backwards right into Gag who pushed me back toward my attacker, saying, "Get him, Gabe! Get him!"

I appreciated Gag's support, but I *didn't* appreciate his support, if you know what I mean.

Now the hippie grabbed onto the collar of my white work shirt, and took a closer, wilder swing, which I deflected with my forearm. Before I knew it, we were in an awkward wrestling match, grappling with each other and trying to send each other down to the pavement. Everybody in the lot was yelling now, like the crowd calling for blood at the Roman Colosseum back in ancient times.

Our legs entangled, we fell to the ground and rolled across the asphalt, our arms swinging and our legs kicking and flailing. Luckily, I somehow ended up on top, and if I was a guy with a killer instinct, someone like Beef Belsky, I probably would have whaled on him. But, before I even could make a decision on my next move, I felt hands and arms pulling me off of him. As I was dragged to my feet, I saw that it was his two friends who had me in their secure grasp. Mr. Long Hair looked pleased, and with wild eyes, lifted himself off the ground and stumbled toward me.

Amid the chaos, I realized, *He's going to beat the hell out of me while his friends are holding me. Shit!* But I'd forgotten that there were other people in the lot. As my opponent entered my space, a big figure stepped between the two of us. I saw that it was none other than Big Alfred.

"The fight be over," Alfred said in a measured monotone.

"Listen, Alfred, this ain't none of yer business," the long-haired kid said, slurring his words.

"The fight be over, my man," Alfred repeated, in case he hadn't been heard the first time.

"Get out of the way, Alfred. I told you, this ain't yer business," the kid shouted.

Alfred repeated himself one last time, "The fight be over," and with clenched teeth, he grabbed the hippie dude by the shoulders and lifted him off the ground. Walking five or six steps, like he was carrying a sagging bag of garbage to the dumpster, Alfred smashed the jerk into the side of his van.

I don't know if I've ever seen anyone's eyes register greater fear and stunned surprise as the long-haired kid climbed into the driver's seat and his friends released me and hurried to the van as well.

As we walked back into the building, I felt grateful that Alfred was there to bale me out of a fix. It also occurred to me that even though Alfred was black and I was white, we shared a true friendship.

The next day, all the guys at work talked about the fight, razzing me for beating up a customer.

"Alfred told us all about how you kicked a hippie's ass last night, right Al?" Will Granger joked.

"Tha's right," Alfred said with a proud grin. "My man Gabriel's a badass!"

"But we can't have you beating the shit out of the customers,

Gabe," Will added, and when he flashed that Pepsodent smile of his, I could tell he was somehow proud of me.

"I didn't beat anyone up," I laughed.

"Well, the guys on the crew said you got the best of him," Will said.

"Don't you worry, Gabriel," Alfred added. "If those other boys didn't butt in, you wouldn't have needed me."

I just laughed. "He was so high he couldn't even see me."

Even though there was tremendous truth in what I said, I still felt a measure of pride in having perhaps bested another guy in a fight no matter how high he might've been. But despite what Alfred said about the other guys butting in, the fact is that they did, and I was grateful that Alfred was there to take care of business when I was in trouble.

CHAPTER 18

Meanwhile, nothing was happening on the local front that improved my level of happiness. I was still down in the dumps. Continuing to feel supremely alone in the world, my burning desire to connect with Joni Mitchell persisted, which made me think of a song from one of Michael's eight-tracks, "The Impossible Dream" by Robert Goulet. One thing about Michael. He likes the music of our generation, like songs by the Beatles, the Rascals, and others, but he doesn't seem to care if the musical artists are from our era, our parents' era, or whoever's era. If he thinks it's good music, he'll buy the tape, in the process exposing me to everything from Robert Goulet to Roy Clark to Mantovani since the day Tomaso installed the tape player in the Corvair.

Anyway, you don't have to be a rocket scientist to realize that me wanting to meet Joni Mitchell was an impossible dream. But that was before late November when a gust of cool temperatures blew in. With most everyone important in my life gone in one way or another, Bink and I had continued to bond. Maybe it was partly about how we had opened up to each other at Grand Central. Maybe it was a case of two people who needed each other. Maybe it was because I felt so damned alone.

We were both college commuters, me at Southern in New Haven and Bink at Housatonic Community College where his parents made him go in order to save money. A straight-A student, he was already accepted at UCONN for his junior year, which meant I'd basically be losing him too.

On a chilly November evening, Bink arrived at work and seemed to have something pressing to tell me. "Gabe," he said. "Guess what!"

"I don't have any idea."

"Joni Mitchell is going to be giving a concert at Carnegie Hall," he said, obviously pleased with himself.

"Carnegie Hall in New York?"

"Do you know of any other Carnegie Hall?" he responded.

"Wait! Isn't Carnegie Hall a place where, like, symphony orchestras play, like all the classical stuff I'm learning about in Music History?"

"Yeah, that's true," he replied. "But it's not all classical. Before she died, Judy Garland gave a concert there. And I think Johnny Cash did too. I saw an ad in the Sunday *Times* today."

"Wow! When is it? How do we get tickets? You wanna go with me?"

"Slow down, Gabe. I can only answer one question at a time. It's on the fourteenth of January. We'll both be on semester break. And, yes, I'll go with you. It should be better than our last trip to New York, right?"

"Hell yeah! Anything would be better than that."

My excitement turned out to be short-lived, though. Bink had cut the ad out of the *Times*, which indicated we needed to pay for the tickets by mailing a check with a self-addressed, stamped envelope. And the thing is, neither of us had a checking account. To make matters worse, neither of our fathers would buy the tickets for us. I don't know about Bink's father, but my conversation didn't go well with my dad who handles all the money in my family.

"I'm not writing a check for tickets to a rock concert, like that fiasco at Woodstock last year," he responded when I asked him.

"It's not Woodstock, and it's not exactly a rock concert, Dad, and I'll definitely pay you back," I pleaded.

"You're not going to be paying me back...because I'm not writing a check for you to go hang out with a bunch of pot smoking hippies. Besides, this noise you kids listen to isn't music as far as I'm concerned, so you have a lot of balls calling it music."

In frustration, my voice was shaking now. "C'mon, Dad. Be

reasonable. No one is going to be smoking pot at Carnegie Hall! And Joni Mitchell doesn't make noise. She's an acoustic musician with an angelic voice."

"I've heard some of the shit you kids listen to. The Beatles screaming, 'yeah, yeah, yeah.' You call that music?"

"Dad," I said. "The Beatles haven't screamed 'yeah, yeah, yeah' in years, and besides, if John Lennon or Paul McCartney were from your era, they would have been famous and would have made music you would have liked."

"Bullshit!"

My mother chimed in, "The music of our era can't be beaten. Glenn Miller. The Dorsey Brothers."

You're a big help, Celia!

"Well, you guys won't even give our music a chance," I complained, "and you've never even listened to Joni Mitchell. Her songs are deep and totally unique."

I knew I was pushing the envelope, but I had enough presence of mind to realize there was no point arguing any further about what constitutes good music or in trying to get him to write a check.

The next night, Bink and I talked it over at Valley Bowl. Bink isn't the world's greatest athlete, but bowling is something that we are similarly bad at.

After he lofted a ball into the air like it was a bocce ball and watched it slide into the gutter just before it hit the ten pin, he shook his head and came back to the scorer's table.

"Yeah, my parents won't buy the tickets for me either, so maybe we can't go," he said resignedly.

"Oh, no," I complained. "We're going. One way or another, we're going. We'll just take the train like we did last May and buy the tickets at the box office. It's a pretty big place, right? We should be able to get tickets."

"I'm not so sure about that."

"Don't give me that," I said. "I'm going to meet Joni, and you can take that to the bank!"

I was going to get tickets no matter what Bink thought. I had an inner feeling that there was nothing and no one that could stop me.

CHAPTER 19

I stayed home the night before the concert because I wanted to be well rested, which didn't do me much good since I had one of those restless nights of sleep when, at four in the morning, you don't have the slightest idea if you're awake or asleep. Still, it was all good because I spent the evening immersed in Joni's music, priming myself for the big day.

I sealed myself off in my room and played Joni's albums, one after the other on my stereo, flipping from one side of an LP to another, back and forth. I picked up my guitar which I had been teaching myself to play for the last year. After expressing an interest in the guitar, Dad had bought me a Kay guitar for Christmas during senior year. Personally, I had never heard of Kay guitars. I'd heard of Gibson and Gretch and a few others, and I mean, not to be ungrateful, but the tone was hollow, and the strings seemed too far from the fretboard which killed my fingers pressing them down to form chords. But you end up developing calluses, which I guess is the price you pay.

So, like I said, I sat in front of the shiny door of the stereo cabinet, trying to figure out Joni's beautiful chord progressions, but I couldn't do it. Not a single one. I guess her guitar chords are part of her genius, almost her own unique musical language, like a math proof that Albert Einstein had developed and no mere mortal like me could figure out.

The other part of her genius, of course, are her lyrics. I had enough of a feeling for language to know great poetry when I read it, or in this case, heard it. I understood that the lyrics of Beatles songs were often poetic, like "Lucy in the Sky with Diamonds," for instance, that Jeff told me he read was about an LSD trip. I don't know if that's true, and don't get me wrong, if the Beatles want to write about acid trips, that's cool, but Joni's songs are poetic in a different way – a more grounded, *I'm-not-high* kind of way. Her songs create imagery that you can relate to. Thirty seconds into a song like "River," you're right there with Joni ice skating away from your troubles...or else toward them. And that's my other point. There's something about her lyrics, even if you don't know exactly why she's feeling sad, that makes you feel sad right with her because, after all, we all have problems, right?

After giving up on the guitar, I sat down at my desk and I took a clean sheet of paper out of a notebook and just started writing her name over and over again, sort of like the nuns used to make us do, *I will not talk in class, I will not talk in class, I will not talk in class.* In this case, *Joni Mitchell, Joni Mitchell, Joni Mitchell.* Crazy, I know.

Then I had another idea. I grabbed that J Britannica volume and took out her picture. And then for what must have been more than two hours, I sat there staring at the *Vogue* picture. It's a photo I loved from the moment I saw it. Joni is sitting cross-legged and barefoot on the floor, decked out in a perfect white bohemian dress, her acoustic guitar resting comfortably on her right leg like it was born there. The best part is her face, beautiful but serious, framed by her radiant blonde hair, looking right at me, saying, "I know you, Gabriel DeMarco."

Sitting there listening to songs that had now become a soothing poultice to my troubled heart for months, I just sat staring back at Joni, outlining the contours of her face with my index fingers over and over again.

And here's the funny thing about it. I knew my train had gone off the tracks, but I didn't care because I felt good for a change. After all, the next day I would be meeting Joni, so what's the difference if I was acting a little kooky?

The day of the concert was bitingly cold with a wind chill factor that felt like 150 degrees below zero. Bink and I headed for the Bridgeport station in the late afternoon.

On the train, Bink was a barrel of laughs, saying all of the corny things that make Bink Bink.

"Gabriel, how do you get to Carnegie Hall?" he asked with this dumb look on his face.

He suckered me because I said, "I don't know yet, but we'll figure it out. We'll just ask someone for directions."

"Yeah, but *how* do you get to Carnegie Hall?" he repeated.

"We'll ask someone, I told ya."

"Yeah, but how do you *get* to Carnegie Hall?"

"I *don't* know," I said, hardly containing my anger.

"Practice," he said, very pleased with himself. "Practice...practice...practice!"

"Hilarious," I said sarcastically. "I'm happy you're proud of yourself."

We got to Carnegie Hall two hours before the concert. Luckily, there were no other customers at the box office window.

"We'd like two tickets for tonight," I said.

The box office lady didn't even look at me. Shoving some tickets into small envelopes, she said in a thick New York accent, "You're kiddin' me, right? This concert has been sold out for a month."

"But...but...we came all the way from Connecticut," I said, glancing helplessly at Bink.

She just shrugged. "Yeah, it's tough all over. Ya shoulda bought your tickets by Thanksgiving if you wanted to see Joni."

What do you mean, 'if I wanted to see Joni'? You'd think that a box office employee at Carnegie Hall would be nicer. I was so mad, I almost swore at her. Bink, sensing my irritation, grabbed my forearm and led me through the exit.

"Now what do we fucking do?" I asked, steamed. Frustrated and steamed. Disappointed, frustrated, and steamed. Of course, Bink didn't have a solution.

"I saw a McDonald's a few blocks back on 7th Avenue," he said. "Let's grab something there and talk about it."

It got us out of the numbing cold, but I felt a little like a traitor, sitting in McDonald's and eating the enemy's burger and fries.

"Maybe we could sneak in," I suggested.

"Sneak in?" he asked, stuffing his mouth with a handful of fries. "What do you mean, sneak in? How would we do that?"

"I don't know. Sneak in, the way Jeff and I used to do at the movies when we were, like, twelve. We just tried to blend in when everyone was heading through the double doors and we'd rush in, like we had already been inside. You just have to act natural. There's gonna be a huge crowd. No one'll notice."

"We're not going to be able to sneak into a concert at Carnegie Hall, Gabe."

I hate it when people talk too much common sense.

"Well, how am I going to meet her?" I asked.

"How did you think you were going to meet her?"

I also hate it when people answer a question with a question.

"Well, I don't know...wait at the stage door after the concert, I guess."

"We could still do that," he said.

"Yeah, we could."

"We'll just have to figure out what we're going to do while the concert is going on."

We walked around people-watching for an hour in the bitter cold, and then, before I died of frostbite, I suggested we head back to Carnegie Hall and see if we could catch Joni heading into the place.

"I would think she arrives at the venue *more* than fifteen minutes before the concert starts," Bink said skeptically.

"Well, you don't know everything, Bink!" I wasn't making any attempt to hide my frustration, and Bink reacted with this hurt puppy-dog face he's famous for.

When we got there, lots of people were streaming into the theater. We walked back and forth around the corner of 57th Street and 7th Avenue looking for the stage door. When we found it on 57th, I didn't see anyone who looked like Joni Mitchell heading in.

A guy in a trench coat and a knit cap heading past us held up an envelope and said, "I got a couple of extra tickets."

"Wow," I replied, "how much?"

"I'll let 'em go for fifty each," he said, not looking us in the eye.

"What? Fifty? But the tickets only cost fifteen bucks each," I complained.

"That's before they were in such great demand. Now, if you wanna see the concert, it'll cost you a little more."

"A little more?" I said, incredulously. "Okay, Bink, how much do you have on you?"

"I've got twenty-eight, but we've got to have money for the train fare back to Bridgeport too."

I had nineteen myself. Calculating the train fare, I looked at the guy and asked, "Would you take twenty-five for both of them?"

"Not in this lifetime," he said, and he went on his way toward the corner where there was more foot traffic.

After watching him move on down the sidewalk and attempt to sell his tickets to another patsy, I turned toward the brick exterior of Carnegie Hall, and seeing a large glass case which displayed a beautiful picture of Joni holding her guitar, an angelic smile on her face, I furiously pounded both of my fists against the glass. It felt like the entire building shook. Luckily, the glass didn't shatter.

Pulling me by the arm, Bink said, "Gabe, what the hell are you doing? Are you trying to get us arrested?"

"Yeah," I shouted, "I'm trying to get us fucking arrested, Bink! That's what I'm trying to do!"

With burning cheeks, I walked away, crossing the street at the corner of 56th and 7th. Halfway across the street, I heard Bink yell to me, "Gabriel, the sign said don't walk! You're going to get yourself killed!"

I was halfway down 7th Avenue before Bink caught up to me.

"Gabe," he whined. "You're acting nuts."

"Yeah, I'm acting nuts. So fucking shoot me!" When I get in a bad mood, it's hard to talk any sense into me, which Bink was finding out.

"Gabe, you need to calm down. Please calm down."

Luckily, in a sane corner of this pea brain of mine, I realized he was right. I also felt sorry for him because the last thing Bink needed was to be stuck in New York with a head case. I was obviously ready for the looney bin.

"Ok, I'll calm down," I conceded. "How sane was it, after all, to try to get into a sold out concert while simultaneously thinking I was going to meet the star?"

"Hey, listen Gabe. Maybe we should get on the train now, okay?"

"We're not getting on the train now, Bink. We're going to be at the stage door when the concert ends because I'm still going to try to meet Joni."

"Okay, Gabriel," Bink said, meekly. "What do you want to do until then?"

"Whatever you want to do, Bink. I don't give a shit at this point."

"Well, how about this, Gabe? How about we go to Ripley's Believe It or Not?"

That seemed fine. After all, the night we came into the city seeking prostitutes, Tomaso wouldn't let Bink go to Ripley's, so why not?

"Okay, Bink, let's go to Ripley's and see the seven-legged goat or whatever you're so excited about. Anything to get out of the cold." These days I swear more than I used to but mainly when I am mad or upset.

We asked a guy selling nuts on the corner where it was, and then we headed for 42nd Street. Before we knew it, we found the Ripley museum nestled right in the heart of the X-rated movie district.

Ripley's cost $2.25 to get in, which wasn't too bad. Much to Bink's delight, we saw the seven-legged goat and lots of other weird stuff. Like a full sized model of a Harley-Davidson chopper made out of the bones of roadkill. So strange. And then there was an eleven inch bird-eating tarantula. I mean, I couldn't picture the hairy monster eating a bird, but I wouldn't want to run into it on a camping trip.

The thing about Ripley's is, while in a sense it is interesting in a bizarre way, it isn't the world's biggest museum. In fact, it might be the smallest. The point is, we weren't going to kill two or three hours there, so before we knew it, we were back out in the bitter cold. Luckily, my coat had a hood because I'm not big on wearing hats.

"Now what do you want to do, Gabriel?" Bink asked. He's so annoying sometimes.

With a deep sigh, I said, "I don't know, but we gotta kill another hour and a half, and I'm freezing my balls off out here."

Across the street, Bink spotted our answer. "Hey look, we could go bowling!"

Across the street in mammoth red neon lights, the word Bowl-a-Rama flashed on and off, like a reverse oasis promising relief from the cold instead of the heat.

"You know what, Bink?" I said. "Once every ten years, you come up with a good idea." It may have seemed like a mean thing to say, but Bink appeared to be flattered, as if he had just been paid the highest compliment of his dull life.

Bowling was the perfect solution. It was inexpensive, it filled the time, and it got us out of the unforgiving January freeze. We ended up playing three games, and taking our time in the process – or at least I was taking my time – with me winning all three, which isn't that impressive since my highest score was a modest 134.

At 9:30, I suggested we head back to Carnegie Hall. It'd take us fifteen or twenty minutes to get there, and I didn't want to miss Joni coming out of the stage door. It turned out that the people didn't start pouring out of the theater for another hour. Joni must have given them their money's worth. While we were waiting for the concert to end, I was so cold I involuntarily danced an Irish jig to keep myself from freezing to death.

Before we knew it, there must have been over a hundred people gathered to see her. Since we had arrived first, we stood at the front of the crowd, closest to the door. *But how am I going to have a conversation with her with all these people here?* I wondered. *Maybe I can ask her if she would spend a few extra minutes with me after everyone leaves.*

The stage door swung open, and a guy about our age, dressed all in black including a black baseball cap, came out and he set up stanchions with chrome poles and red velvet rope (like the ones you see in banks) between the door and the curb. I wondered how he got the job working at Carnegie Hall and wished I were in his shoes.

The next thing I knew, a limousine pulled up to the curb, and it hit me. *It's for Joni.* I mean, who else would it be for? Then without a word, the guy disappeared back into the warmth of the building while all of us fans continued to freeze to death. After, like, another twenty minutes, the guy came out again, thank God. The crowd had thinned out a tad but not much.

"Ladies and gentlemen," he called out, projecting his voice. "In a moment, Miss Mitchell will be coming out of the building. Now, I'm sorry, but it's too cold to ask her to sign autographs. What's going to happen is she's going to come out of the stage door here and walk to her limousine." He pointed to the stage door and then the limousine, thank God, or I might not have understood what the words *stage door* and *limousine* meant.

"Then," he continued, explaining things to us like we were four-year-olds, "then, she'll wave to all of you, and you should feel free to wave back and to applaud for her. But *no one* should make any

on would wake me up since my bedroom was right off the kitchen. I'll bet they woke Michael up too, although neither of us let on we were awake.

Now getting drunk was a consistent thing. I remember talking to my mom about it.

"He feels a lot of pressure from his business," she explained. "People sometimes take months to pay him, and I think he spent a lot more building this house than he had anticipated."

"He's been obsessed with this house for a long time," I said.

My mother just shrugged, seeming more or less indifferent to the matter.

"You don't like this house?" I asked.

"I was fine on Maltby Street."

"Well, yeah, but this house is so –"

"Listen," she interrupted, "this house, and all the things he buys me, the diamonds and the furs, are nice to have, but the truth is, I didn't need any of it. I grew up poor. I don't need much to be happy. He puts too much pressure on himself."

I was pretty surprised at this confession because Mom sure rocks out the diamonds and furs.

"Your father's changed," she added. "I wish you could have known him when I first met him."

I wished I had known him then too.

The next morning I came out of the bathroom, toweling off my hair after a hot shower, and I heard him say from the kitchen counter, "How was your concert?"

My concert! I knew he didn't like that I went. It was weird because, in one sense, he gave me a lot of freedom to own a motorcycle or stay out as late as I wanted, but in another sense, he seemed to want to be in control, to somehow be the arbiter of how much freedom I was or wasn't allowed.

I pulled my head out from under the towel and said, "We didn't see it. It was sold out."

I wanted him to feel bad that he hadn't loaned me the money to buy the tickets in advance.

Instead, though, he changed the subject. Glaring at me, he asked,

"How long are you planning to grow your hair?" as if he were seeing my hair for the first time.

What does he think my answer is going to be? I wondered. *Down to my ankles?*

"Uhm...I don't know," I said. "Not much longer."

"You look like a girl. If I wanted a girl, I would have had a daughter." Like he had a choice in the matter.

I buried my head back in the towel, more in an effort to hide my annoyance than to dry my hair.

"If you're going to live in my house, you need to get a haircut," he said. It was more of an order than a suggestion because that's how Dad rolls.

Of course, it wasn't the first such ultimatum he had ever given me. Ever since I was big enough to question him, he had said, "If you don't like my rules, don't let the door hit you in the ass on the way out."

I realize now that it was an interesting way to communicate with, like, a ten-year-old. At least he hadn't changed his style much. He must have forgotten that I didn't want to live in his house, that I had wanted to go to Bates. It was Dad who wanted me to live in his house, and now he was ready to throw me out over the length of my hair. A day later, I expressed my concern to my mother, telling her the whole ugly story.

"I'm not cutting my hair, Celia, so you just better get him off my back." The tone of my voice made it sound like more of an order than a suggestion. I was realizing that, like Dad, apparently that's how I roll sometimes too.

"You know how he is," Mom offered. "I think he was just annoyed that you went to that concert."

"I'm almost nineteen years old. If I want to go to a concert, I'll go to a concert. Listen, I'm serious, Mom. I'm not cutting my hair. And if it means I have to live somewhere else, I'll figure it out. No joke!"

Not that I should have been surprised at Dad's reaction to the length of my hair. He's been against everything we're interested in since Michael was about fifteen. It started with small stuff, like when Michael used to drum on the kitchen table.

One weekend morning, Michael and I were talking, and Dad impatiently yelled, "Stop that!" At first we didn't know what he was talking about. Stop what? Stop talking? It's not like we were swearing or anything. When he saw the clueless looks on our faces, he raised his voice even louder. "Stop the goddamn drumming on the table. What the hell is wrong with you?"

But drumming is something that you do because you have this rhythm that's always beating inside of you. Maybe Dad's generation didn't have that inner rhythm. I don't know.

But besides dumb stuff like drumming on tables and the length of my hair, there are deeper ideological issues that sometimes make me feel like Dad's interfering with who I am and who I want to become. Something he said burned me up right when I started college.

"I just want to tell you something," he said one morning when I was frying some bacon and eggs for myself.

"What's that?" I said, not looking up because I knew from the characteristic imperial tone in his voice that I wasn't going to like it.

"Now that you're going to be a college student, don't ever let me hear you're protesting anything or else I'll never talk to you again."

Puzzled, I looked up from the frying pan. "If I protest *anything*, you'll never talk to me?"

"You heard me," he said, holding eye contact with me. He wasn't someone I was about to win a staring contest with.

Looking away, I asked, "What about this crazy war in Vietnam? Even that?"

I couldn't help thinking of the utter insanity of the Kent State massacre.

"Especially that," he shot back. "My best friend died in the Pacific when we were young guys. He gave his life for this country. That counts for something, and don't ever forget it."

How could I forget it? He'd told me about his childhood pal Scooter about a thousand times. But being stubborn, I made one more attempt to change his mind. "But, I mean, even if there's some other great injustice, I can't protest?"

"That's right! My kid isn't going to turn into some hippie asshole."

I just shrugged and went back to my sizzling frying pan. The food was cooked, but to avoid any further interaction with him, I let it basically burn in the skillet.

It wasn't like there weren't opportunities to join the world of protesting. No sooner had the spring semester begun when a guy I knew from Boy Scouts, Gordon Weed, stopped by my table in the student union. Gordon is a true hippie. Weed is an ironic last name since I'll bet he smokes a lot of pot, but you'll never meet a nicer kid. A year or two older than me, he knows just about everyone on campus, endlessly flittering from table to table with his shoulder-length hair and his tie-dye shirts, socializing with everyone in the student union.

"You're against the war, right, Gabe?" Gordon asked.

"Oh, yeah, definitely," I replied.

"We're trying to rally the student body here," he explained. "I'm starting an organization here on campus called Students Against War. SAW for short. We're having a big rally in the rotunda in Engleman Hall on Tuesday at 5:00. Why don't you join us?"

"Yeah, I'll try to make it if I can."

Gordon smiled, squinted, and said, "Thanks, Gabriel, that sounds great," but he had that *what-do-you-mean-**if**-you-can-make-it* look on his face.

What was I supposed to say, though? "I'd love to come, Gordon, but my dad won't let me"?

College, up until that point, hadn't been the life altering experience it was supposed to be. On the heels of my Carnegie Hall trip, I realized that, except for going to my classes, I hadn't done anything. Even though colleges had been recruiting me as a distance runner, my disappointment at not being accepted at the one out-of-state school my dad let me apply to caused me not to go out for cross country or track, which was a dumb idea because I might have actually made some friends. My college experience was limited to driving to New Haven five times a week, going to class, and then heading back to the Valley to work at Duchess.

I had initially questioned my decision to major in English, but a couple of courses in my spring semester turned me around on that one. One was 20th Century American Poetry. Celia had instilled a love of poetry in me, but the stuff we were reading was a far cry from what she had recited to Michael and me at our kitchen table. I felt like I was, more or less, in over my head in the course because it seemed like everyone else was an upperclassman – all of these long-haired, coffee-drinking intellectuals.

The professor for my poetry class was a middle-aged woman from Nigeria who wore floor-length dresses with colorful, geometric patterns accompanied by earrings, bracelets, and necklaces with jumbo matching beads, like succulent fruit ready to be picked. She's the only actual native of Africa I've ever known.

Dr. Okosieme is the real McCoy. She wears her hair cropped close to her head, very different from other women. I had never heard a Nigerian accent before, but she also sounds half British. Like, she pronounces the consonants at the ends of her words, especially T's, clearly and crisply. And she pronounces words like "after" and "ask" with British A's like she graduated from Oxford, and maybe she did.

You wouldn't expect someone from a foreign country to be teaching American poetry, but Dr. Okosieme said a "romance" began between her and American writers while she was doing her doctoral studies at Yale. I imagined it was sort of like an American falling in love with Roman architecture or French cuisine.

Not that I'm an expert, but there didn't seem to be a thing that she didn't know about American poetry. Besides her command of the subject matter, there was just something about her – a captivating presence.

I remember on the first day of class, the first words out of her mouth were, "Poetry is po-lit-i-cal." There was a rhythm in her delivery as she banged out each crisp syllable.

"How can it not be?" she continued in her hybrid accent. "To write a poem is a radical act of creativity. To write a poem is to say to the world, 'this is who I am in all of my authenticity and vulnerability, like it or not.' To write a poem is to demonstrate your God-given right to freedom of speech, and you must know, my good men and women, that not all of the citizens of the world have freedom of speech. In fact, all true art is a political act of freedom."

Dr. Okosieme had my attention. I learned quickly, though, that I was in trouble. As classmates interpreted poem after poem, I myself prayed that Dr. Okosieme wouldn't randomly call on me because I was more or less clueless. Not that I wasn't mesmerized by some of the famous poets, especially Beat writers like Allen Ginsberg and Lawrence Ferlinghetti and Gregory Corso. After all, I had already read *On the Road*, like, four times, and it's no secret that Kerouac is credited with launching the Beat movement. And sure, Kerouac is out there, and by out, I mean *way* out, but if you're patient and give him fifty or sixty pages, I promise he'll hook you and you won't be able to put him down.

Still, despite being a reader, I was hesitant to say anything in class, that is, until Dr. Okosieme asked me to meet with her in her office after class one day and called me out on it.

"Mr. DeMarco, I want you to come out of hiding," she said with a warm smile.

"Hiding?" I said, wanting to hide even more.

"Now, now, my friend. You know what I am talking about."

You had to love the perfect elegance of her accent and the warmth of her smile.

"Well, it's just that I...I'm younger than everyone else. I'm only a freshman, ya know. I should have taken this class next year or the year after."

"But you took it now," she offered, "and it is now that I want you to experience the poetry. It is now that these poems will impact you. We cannot wait for tomorrow."

"But...how can I talk about the poems if I don't understand them?"

"Don't try to understand, Mr. DeMarco, just *experience* and then share the experience."

I'm not sure if I understood what she meant, but I did try my best to begin participating in class, once in a while taking a stab at giving my interpretations.

On those occasions when I raised my hand, Dr. Okosieme would smile broadly and say, "Oh, wonderful! Let us hear from Mr. Gabriel DeMarco." I never felt like I had the insights that the coffee drinkers had to offer, but she affirmed me each and every time.

By the end of the semester, I realized that when you read some of this stuff, even if you don't one hundred percent know what's going on, you know you're reading something deep.

Poems like Ginsberg's "Howl":

I saw the best minds of my generation destroyed by madness, starving hysterical naked,
dragging themselves through the negro streets at dawn looking for an angry fix,

*angelheaded hipsters burning for the ancient heavenly connection to the
starry dynamo in the
machinery of night...*

Or Langston Hughes' short poem, "Harlem":

What happens to a dream deferred?
Does it dry up
like a raisin in the sun?
Or fester like a sore—
And then run?
Does it stink like rotten meat?
Or crust and sugar over—
like a syrupy sweet?

Maybe it just sags
like a heavy load.

Or does it explode?

Or T.S. Eliot's "The Love Song of J. Alfred Prufrock":

Let us go then, you and I,
When the evening is spread out against the sky
Like a patient etherized upon a table;
Let us go, through certain half-deserted streets,
The muttering retreats
Of restless nights in one-night cheap hotels
And sawdust restaurants with oyster-shells:
Streets that follow like a tedious argument
Of insidious intent
To lead you to an overwhelming question...
Oh, do not ask, "What is it?"
Let us go and make our visit...

Couple my adventures in 20th Century American Poetry with
the fact that I was also taking Creative Writing I, and the two courses
were shaking up my world. I started writing my own poetry because
besides having the kooky idea that I liked poetry, I now had the even

kookier idea that I could *write* poetry. That's when I got it in my head that maybe I could become an author. Maybe it was because I wanted to prove my father wrong since he had said, "If you're going to be a teacher like your brother, you can just go to Southern."

Or maybe it was because I wanted to have my own voice... because I had something creative and political and even radical to say.

My poetry probably isn't even any good. A hippie intellectual in that class critiquing a poem I wrote inspired by Buster's funeral called it, "Dynamite stuff, man, but without the blasting caps." Whatever that was supposed to mean. Obviously a left-handed compliment. I even wrote a short story about my trip to New York looking for prostitutes with Tomaso and the guys. When the professor asked that same hippie intellectual to critique it, he said, "Not the worst, but not the best, man. Just felt hackneyed. It's been done."

Maybe he was right, but I didn't care for the pretentious asshole.

Still, maybe there's a writer somewhere inside of me. Maybe I just need more life experience. Maybe if I can figure out who I am, I'll be able to put it down on paper. But a powerful gut feeling was born in me that semester – *I have something to say!*

Outside of taking my courses and dreaming that maybe I'd become a writer, I had no life at all. As the second semester reached its midway point and winter was nearing its end, I realized that Duchess was the one constant in my life and Bink my one and only friend. *Not much to write about there, Gabriel DeMarco.*

It's not that I felt I was better than Bink, but on my first night at Duchess more than three years before, as we cleaned the lot together, I could never have anticipated we'd be friends. So that's what my life had come to – being close friends with a major league dork.

CHAPTER 21

It wasn't the first time that I hung out with a dork. Back during the summer after eighth grade, something interesting happened. The biggest dork in our class, Walter Duborowicz, lived on the street where I delivered newspapers. While I was just minding my own business and delivering my newspapers, Walter started following me like a lost puppy. The first few days, I tried to pretend he wasn't there because I'd never known a bigger dork. Walter's thick glasses magnified his eyeballs, making him look like a preadolescent Quasimodo with spectacles. And no one in the history of Western civilization was more awkward. I mean, the kid couldn't walk to the chalkboard without getting one foot tangled in a loose shoelace and tripping, sending the whole class into spasms of laughter. Most of the boys addressed him as "Dumb-borowicz."

After about a week, though, I realized that Walter wasn't going to magically disappear, and I also noticed something else. In certain ways, Walter and I were more alike than different. Like the day he told me he had a crush on Colleen Carey, which blew me away because I did too. It can totally rattle you when you realize that you and a geek like Walter have a lot in common.

Well, before I knew it, we graduated from eighth grade, and that summer, Walter started calling me. "What are you doing after dinner?" he'd ask in his nasally voice. And I'd reply, "Oh...just hanging out with my friends." And Walter would say, "Can I come?"

What was I supposed to say to that? So, of course, I'd tell him he could come. Before I knew it, my friends were giving me a hard time because they didn't want "Dumb-borowicz" hanging out with us. That bummed me out big time.

One night Mom offered, "You know, Gabe. I know you're trying to be nice to poor Walter, but I think you have to ask yourself if it's worth losing your regular friends over."

If I was anything, though, I was stubborn. "Yeah, Celia," I erupted, "well, it *is* worth it because nobody's going to tell me who I can or can't hang out with."

I don't think Mom loved that answer because she didn't want me to lose my popularity with all the guys over one kid, which is what happened, but then and now, I can be an immovable boulder when I feel strongly about something.

Of course, Bink isn't one one-thousandth the dork that Walter was, and with Bink, it wasn't as difficult to stand by a kid who wasn't the coolest dude on the planet because the guys at work like him and accept him well enough because they aren't stupid eighth graders.

Still, Bink manages to muff things up now and then. Like this ice skating trip we went on about three weeks before the Carnegie Hall debacle. At the time, two new things were going on at Duchess. The Moscowiczes, who own the place, had recently built a dining room onto the business. The way I see it, the Moscowiczes had basically taken the McDonald's business model and improved upon it. Duchess is like McDonald's on steroids, part Burger Heaven, part Nathan's Hotdogs, and part Kentucky Fried Chicken. The Moscowiczes weren't about to be outdone by the advent of dining rooms on the scene.

The other thing that was new was, to go along with the dining room, Will had begun hiring girls. That must have come down from the top too. It was a little weird at first because Duchess had always been a man's world. Will started small, hiring two girls from Seymour. I remember turning away from the window to help a new girl wrap hamburgers because she was God-awful slow and realizing that she was so tall that my eye-level was at her shoulders. Her name is Candy, and is she ever, as my mother says, a tall drink of water! Her friend is a redhead with a billion freckles named Alice.

One thing I've noticed is, having girls around the place, we have to watch our language more. Another thing is, before you know it, you're hanging out with them. Like the night of the skating trip.

One night in late December, Bink and I found ourselves with Candy and Alice, just the four of us, ice skating on a little pond tucked away somewhere in Seymour. A perfect moon shone so bright that it was almost like the pond had lights like the one at Osbornedale Park. If I had a crush on Candy or Alice, I would even describe the night as romantic. The girls looked cute in their colorful knit hats, topped with fluffy pompoms and matching earmuffs. And their tight flannel leggings and dove white skates, as they glided across the glassy surface of the pond in the semi-darkness, illustrated the female form at its finest. It was almost like a double date which was nice I guess.

Nice, that is, until the middle of a conversation when I heard a crackling sound I didn't quite recognize. The four of us were standing not ten feet from the edge of the pond just talking when I heard that mysterious crackling sound again, and just like that, plop, Bink fell through the ice. Candy's eyes, at first wide as the moon above, blinked a couple of times, and before you knew it, a contagious giggle bubbled up in her and poured over Alice and me. The only one who wasn't laughing was Bink who stood waist deep in the icy pool, a half-baked look of chagrin on his face. What was bizarre was that the three of us, who were a mere few feet away from Bink, were still standing securely on the frozen surface. It seemed the universe had conspired against Bink alone.

I remembered reading stories of rescues in a Boy Scout magazine called *Boys' Life*, where after a kid went through the ice, the other Scouts ran for a rope and threw it to the kid and then as a team pulled him out of the frozen water. No such heroics were called for on this occasion.

Bink just hoisted himself onto the surface of the ice, which seemed solid everywhere else, his sopped pants making a puddle on the ice.

We packed it in and went to Candy's house where she gave him a towel to dry off and a pair of her jeans to put on. I couldn't resist teasing him after he was warm and dry again.

"Well, Bink," I said. "You finally got in a girl's pants!"

Bink's reaction surprised me. He punched me in the arm. It wasn't much of a punch, but we both cracked up.

I was happy when the first day of spring arrived, even though March 21st was a freezing cold day. It warmed up a little by the tail end of March, but when I arrived for work one night, the front page of the *New York Daily News* gave me an eerie chill.

The paper, like usual, was laid out on the back counter where we put on our aprons. In the boldest, blackest headline I had ever seen were the words – Manson Verdict: ALL GUILTY!

I hadn't been following the story because the murders were too creepy for words. But there was no escape, because every time I worked, staring at me from the lurid front page of the tabloid were the faces of Charles Manson and his disciples, three screwy chicks, whatever their names are. I don't know because they're all too unhinged for words, so who cares? I have to admit, I was happy to see they were convicted. But if I had any doubt about the utter madness of the world, a few weeks before, Manson shaved his head and carved a swastika on his forehead, announcing, "I am the Devil, and the Devil always has a bald head!" And now I was staring at a photo of his three harpies who apparently chose to hear the verdict with copycat bald heads and carved foreheads, leaving me with no doubt that the wheels had now completely become detached from the world at large.

We had our ways of escaping the world at large, though. By mid-April, with friendlier temperatures, some of the guys on the crew started a Wiffle ball league after work. We ended up with five three-man teams. We had team records, and we kept detailed statistics of batting averages and strikeouts. Everything.

Each night after closing, a game would convene under the lights in the parking lot. Guys were so into it they'd show up to play even if they hadn't worked that night.

Personally, I never missed a game. One night, Jack Murphy had a heck of a night on the "mound." Murphy is a former standout athlete from Derby, who at the time was a senior at Southern. The guy has a strange build. Like, his proportions are off. With a stout, iron torso, short legs and long arms, Murphy is built like an orang-utan you'd see at a zoo. He looks ever so slightly awkward when he plays sports, but he gets the job done in a big way because guys like Murphy just have the gift.

On this night, he was throwing fire. I was just glad my team wasn't playing against him. I've never seen anyone throw a better fastball with a piece of hard plastic. In the process, Bink struck out seven times. Murphy had a lot of strikeouts that night, but Bink never came close to even tipping the ball. It seemed like before Bink could get his bat around, the ball came smashing into the side of the red and white tile building. So what does the kid do? Feeling frustrated and embarrassed, he busts out crying.

"You're not actually fucking crying, I hope?" Murphy moaned.

That just made Bink feel stupider, and he ran behind the train tracks at the rear of the parking lot.

Murphy tossed the ball high up into the air and said, "Well, this is no fun if he's gonna cry over it. Christ, isn't he, like, a fucking sophomore in college?" Murphy isn't ever going to win any prizes for being Mr. Sensitivity.

With that remark, Murphy effectively brought both the game and the league to an abrupt end. As the other guys headed for their cars, venting about what a baby Bink was, the only thing I could think to do was go check on Bink. After all, hadn't he had my back when I first became a window man? Hadn't he told me about the Joni Mitchell concert at Carnegie Hall and put up with all of my emotional bullshit that night? Hadn't he been proving over and over again that he was a true friend?

At first I couldn't find him, but then I saw that he was curled up next to a rusted iron wheel on the far side of an abandoned boxcar. I took a seat in the gravel next to him. When someone is upset, I've learned the best thing I can do is keep my trap shut and give them some space.

But after the silence became too loud for me, I said, "Hey, you okay, man?"

Bink gave me one of those *no-I'm-not-okay* kinds of shakes.

"It doesn't matter, you know," I said.

"What doesn't matter?"

"Striking out, Bink. It's just a Wiffle ball game."

"I know. I just feel like...like such a big loser."

"Well, don't. It's no biggie. Who cares?"

"I care," he said. "Who likes being a loser?"

"Listen man. You're not a loser because Murphy struck you out.

I would never have been able to hit him either. And anyway, no one else was able to get any decent hits off him."

"It's not just that. It's everything. It's being lousy at sports. It's never having a girlfriend. It's home. It's just...everything sucks."

It was another of those Walter Duborowicz moments. "I know what you mean. I don't feel too different from you."

"You don't?"

"Nope. Life sucks for me too."

We could hear the engine of a muscle car roar as it circled through the lot behind us.

"What did you say?" Bink yelled.

"I said, life sucks for me too!" The car was back on Pershing Drive before I finished the sentence, and my volume echoed in the night.

Bink's face registered surprise. "Hmmm, you look like you always have it together. Well, except when we couldn't get into the Joni Mitchell concert."

I chuckled. "Looks can be deceiving. I don't."

"I can't wait until next year when I'll be up at Storrs."

"At least you have that, Bink. It looks like I'm stuck here in the Valley no matter what."

After sitting in silence for another good while, Bink looked up at me. "Hey Gabe, maybe when the semester ends, you and I could go somewhere. You know, just get away from it all."

"Go where?" I asked.

"I don't know. Somewhere. Anywhere."

"But where would we go?"

"How about Vegas? Remember when your brother and Will and some of the older guys went to Vegas?"

I did remember. Playing poker and gambling on sports had become a thing at Duchess. A window man, a guy around thirty-something-years-old, took bets on pro sports from us younger guys and called them in to his bookie, or so he said. And Will had had us at his house for poker games or for Monday Night Football where we'd watch the teams we bet on battle each other.

"I'd love to, but where would we get the cash to fly to Vegas?" I asked. "And what would we have left to gamble? Besides, I think you have to be twenty-one to gamble in Vegas."

"Wait," Bink said. "I've got an idea. How about a road trip? Yeah, a road trip. Let's just save up some money and take off for a few weeks. We'll just drive somewhere until we're out of money."

"Hmmm, you know, Bink, I'm not hating that idea."

I almost couldn't believe that I was agreeing to take off to nowhere with Bink. Hadn't I already been on two disastrous trips to New York with him? Inherent in the utter failure of those excursions, though, Bink and I had grown closer. Maybe, sometimes, good comes out of bad.

"The sixty-four thousand dollar question is," he said, "can Will do without both of us here at Duchess for, like, a full week or more?"

"He'll have to," I said. "We're not going to ask. We'll just tell him we're going away whether he likes it or not. If he can go to Vegas, why shouldn't we be able to go somewhere too?" There was that stubborn part of me again.

It was hard to believe that my wish to make like Sal Paradise and take off might come true. Of course, Sal Paradise seemed to be on the road indefinitely, and our trip would have a time limit, but at least I would see what it felt like to have a taste of freedom. With a little luck, I would discover America – not the America you see when you go on a Boy Scout trip or a trip to the World's Fair with your mom and dad, but the America you can only discover by following your own heart.

What I hadn't pictured was traveling the road to nowhere with Bink. I always figured it would be Jeff and me. Or if not Jeff, then Tomaso and me, or maybe some somebody who wasn't Bink and me. But fate decided my time was now and my traveling companion was Bink. And, why *not* Bink? Without even knowing it was what I wanted and needed, Bink had suggested it. Besides, Bink is a good egg, and I made a conscious decision going forward to stop thinking of him as a dork. I just hoped I could do it.

CHAPTER 22

As I anticipated our adventure, I learned a life lesson about fate and conflicting goals. Fate is a trickster that likes to play head games with idiots like me.

My latest conflicting goals were that I now wanted to save up money for our road trip, but I also got the looney idea that I was going to buy a sports car. One night, I noticed that a guy who regularly hung out at Duchess had a for sale sign in the window of his Triumph TR4. I have a thing for sports cars in general and the British-made Triumph in particular. When this tall, skinny kid came into the building, I asked him about it.

"What year is the Triumph?"

" '62, but it runs like a dream."

That made it about nine years old. It was red with a black convertible top. I had been admiring it now for a few years as I watched the skinny guy cruise in and out of the lot.

"How much?" I asked.

"I'm looking to get nine hundred bucks for it, which isn't a bad price. You want to give it a whirl?" he asked.

Did I want to give it a whirl? Did Queen Elizabeth want to ride in her Rolls Royce limo? Did Mario Andretti want to race in his Ferrari Spyder? Of course, I wanted to give it a whirl. I asked Bink to watch the window for me, and I ran out the back door. We aren't supposed to take off like that, but none of the bigger bosses were around.

Tomaso had taught me to drive a stick, and as I nestled into the driver's seat, I felt like Mario Andretti himself. The clutch was a little tighter than Tomaso's Chevelle, and the engine announced itself in an intentionally obnoxious manner when I pumped the gas. Girls wouldn't only see me in this baby, they'd hear me coming.

As I pulled out on Pershing Drive, I was in seventh heaven. I headed south on Route 8 and got off at Exit 14, then swung back toward Ansonia. The little car had "balls" and I had no doubt that my love life would seriously improve if I had a car like this instead of Michael's hand-me-down Corvair with the gas fumes and a heater that didn't work.

When we arrived back at Duchess, the skinny guy said, "Yeah, so think about it and let me know if you want it."

Let him know. Right! It wasn't as if I had any money at all, never mind nine hundred bucks. And it wasn't as if Dad was going to give me any or let me take out a loan to buy a sports car. After all, he wouldn't let me go away to college because he had said I wasn't going to be taking out any student loans. Geez, he wouldn't even give me a check for fifteen lousy bucks for the Joni Mitchell concert.

The sad truth is that it's Dad's fault that I like cars so much. Dad *loves* them and has been pointing out cool cars to me since I was a dumb little kid. It's funny how a parent can influence your thinking, your likes and dislikes. "Look at that Thunderbird," he'd say, or "Wow, what a nice Corvette," or "How about that little MG?" If it wasn't for my dad, I wouldn't know that an Avanti is the sharpest car out there, at least in my opinion.

That's why Dad is such a paradox. He brainwashed me to love cars, yet he lets me drive around in a bomb.

Look, I get it. Dad's goal is to teach Michael and me to be independent, and one of Dad's tacit rules is, "If you can't afford it, then you can't afford it." Conversely, he gives us Christmas gifts, and very nice ones, and he pays our college tuition, but otherwise it's pretty much, "Make your own way in the world financially, boys." It's been that way since I had my first paper route.

But I wanted that Triumph something fierce. I agonized for a few weeks about talking to Dad about it, but I couldn't do it. Things were tense enough between us. I could just picture his response. *The answer is no, I'm not buying you a Triumph TR4...and no, I'm not signing for a loan...and, in the meantime, get that goddamn haircut I told you to get.*

There was no point in even going down that road with him. And with my measly $2.10 per hour at Duchess, it would be hard enough to save up a couple of hundred bucks to go on the road trip with Bink. Owning a sports car would have to wait. A guy needs to set priorities.

The first person I told about the road trip was Michael. We talked about it one night while Mom and Dad were out visiting relatives.

"Where will you bird brains go?" he asked.

"We don't know...maybe just get in the car and drive south or west. Florida. Maybe Mexico."

"That doesn't sound too smart to me," he said.

"Yeah, well, I know it doesn't sound smart, but it feels like a cool idea. You just take off, but you don't know where you're going."

"You're not reading that beatnik book again, I hope."

"No, but I've read it enough to know a lot about road trips."

"Well, Gabe, I've got some bad fucking news for you. Life isn't always like what you read in books."

"I'm willing to take that chance," I replied.

"And what do you think you're going to drive?" he asked.

"The Corvair, I guess."

With an incredulous smile spreading out across his face, Michael said, "Oh, that's going to be good."

"I'll make it work," I replied.

"Well, it'll take some doing. You'll be lucky if that shitbox makes it to Greenwich."

I could see he wasn't taking me or our road trip seriously. Feeling determined, I made a decision. *I'll show him.*

"So, let me get this straight," he persisted. "You think it's a good idea to go on a trip to nowhere of all places, with Bink of all people, and in the Corvair of all cars."

"Well, Bink is basically my only friend," I began, "the Corvair is my only car, and nowhere is the only place I can afford to go. You have to work with what you've got!"

"I'd like to suggest," he said, "that you postpone this idea until you have some better options."

"No way. This is the time."

"Dig it. Well, you'll be alright someday." And then he just shook his head and chuckled.

What difference did Michael's opinion make, though? Just because he had a teaching job and a sweet new, shiny blue Dodge Charger and could afford to go on trips to Vegas didn't mean he knew everything.

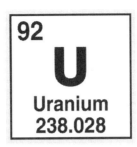

92

U

Uranium

238.028

It was in the middle of a late fall thunderstorm when I walked into class and saw that Mr. M had written a fat U along with number 92 on the board.

What's he got up his sleeve today? I wondered.

My curiosity piqued, I searched the room for whatever surprise he might spring on us. On his desk, I noticed a glass teacup sitting on a matching saucer. The glass, though, was transparent green rather than a ceramic white like most cups. It didn't seem like anything unusual. I had seen green glassware at my grandparents' house.

The bell rang, and Mr. M called out, "Uranium, atomic number 92," as he made his way to the windows. He moved from one window to the other, pulling the heavy opaque shades down, and then he crossed the room and switched off the overhead lights. Thunder clapped outside and shook the building as he did so.

Some of my classmates began to giggle nervously in the darkness. A moment later, Mr. M flicked on a black light bulb that he had attached to a bare wire and held it over the cup and saucer, both of which glowed in the darkness, fluorescing an eerie green color. It was a little spooky, even to me, considering the thunder accompanying his presentation.

After he allowed us kids to "ooh" and "ahh" for a few seconds, as was often the case, Mr. M simply said, "Radioactive!"

We sat in silence as I noticed the green color illuminating his face and reflecting off of his eyeglasses.

Without turning the lights on, he continued, "Uranium Oxide was used from the 1890s up to World War II to color glass and ceramic glazes until it was phased out for strategic as well as health reasons. But don't worry, the level of radioactivity varies by piece, ranging from less than one percent to up to twenty-five percent by weight, and there is no recognized danger to handling or using uranium glass."

I heard Jody Watkins speak out in the dark, "Why would there be any danger in having an empty teacup in the room?"

She sometimes asked dumb questions, but I have to admit, I was wondering the same thing.

"Well, we'll get to that in a sec," Mr. M answered, "but trust me that it's completely safe or I wouldn't have it here."

He then flicked off his black light and turned the overhead lights back on along with putting up the shades as he spoke.

"A uranium atom has 92 protons and 92 electrons, of which 6 are valence electrons. It is the largest naturally occurring element in the universe and is naturally radioactive as you have just witnessed on a small scale. Its nucleus is unstable, so the element is in a constant state of decay, seeking a more stable arrangement."

Now he was back to his desk, where he hoisted himself into a seated position, so we knew things were about to get serious.

"Uranium is among the more common elements in the earth's crust," he continued, "about five hundred times more common than gold. Small amounts of uranium are present everywhere – in rock, soil, water, even our bodies."

Jody Watkins said exactly what I was thinking, "Wow!"

Mr. M went on. "Uranium metal is a malleable and ductile element stronger than gold, silver, or platinum. Additionally, uranium does not rust, corrode, or tarnish."

Mr. M went over to the board and wrote a year and a name in chalk, which I jotted down in my notes.

"The 1789 discovery of uranium in the mineral pitchblende is credited to Martin Heinrich Klaproth, who named the new element after the recently discovered planet Uranus."

Then he wrote a second year and two more names down, and while tapping the white chalk on the board in a staccato rhythm, Mr. M continued, "Eugène-Melchior Péligot was the first person to isolate the metal, and its radioactive properties were discovered in 1896 by French engineer and physicist Henri Becquerel."

Feeling impatient, I thought, *Yeah, and your point is?*

Then, in letters three times the size of everything he had previously written, Mr. M wrote the date, August 6, 1945.

"Anyone want to take a stab at why this is an important date?" he asked.

I sure as heck didn't know, but then again, I'm not much of a date guy.

Out of the corner of my eye, I saw Timmy Ziamba raising his hand like he was a second grader – you know, one of those little squirts who stretches his arm way high, waving his hand like a flag and pleading, "Pick me! Pick me! P-l-e-a-s-e!" What a nerd Timmy is.

"Okay, Tim. Let's hear it," said Mr. M.

"Truman dropped the bomb on Hiroshima on that date."

You should've seen the look on Tim's face, basking in the glory of his correct answer.

"Exactly, Tim. What was discovered in that era is that uranium can do a lot more than make glass glow in the dark. Spearheaded by a theoretical physicist, J. Robert Oppenheimer, now known as 'the father of the atomic bomb,' it was discovered that uranium's ability to store and release explosive energy made the element very useful, especially in the production of nuclear weapons. Uranium is among the heaviest natural elements. In its nucleus, as I mentioned, there are 92 protons and a variable number of neutrons, ranging from 140 to 146. But we'll be talking more about that in upcoming days. Anyone know the name of the bomb dropped on Hiroshima?"

Everyone remained silent. Even Timmy didn't know that one. For me, I didn't realize that bombs had names, certainly not during the Cuban Missile Crisis when I was only ten years old. I remember sitting on my porch steps with Jeff, and we asked Bobby Chukta who was about fifteen if the Russians were going to bomb us.

Not getting any takers, Mr. M said, "Little Boy," and then he flashed a one-eyed squint before adding, "ironic!"

"Ironic," Jody said, "why ironic?"

"Ironic because, for one, 'Little Boy' weighed 9,700 pounds, and two, because it had the equivalent power of about 16,000 tons of TNT, and three, because it is estimated that it killed more than 80,000 people, mostly civilians, tens of thousands from radiation exposure."

He let us sit with those numbers for a moment.

"I think you can see why the name is ironic. You all seem pretty stunned, and we haven't even talked about Nagasaki and the second bomb, 'Fat Man' yet. But we'll save that for another day."

The thunder outside appeared to have stopped, and the bell would be ringing in another minute.

"I know none of you were born, but your parents were only a few years older than you are now. You should ask them how they remember that time. You might learn something interesting."

I remember I walked home alone after cross country practice that day, considering whether I would ask Mom and Dad about it. Dad had, after all, been in the Army Air Corps at the time. But for some reason, I never asked. Even now, almost three years later, I've never brought up the subject. I don't know why. Whenever I've heard mention of the dropping of "Little Boy" or "Fat Man," though, I think of the teacup and saucer glowing bright green in the dark.

CHAPTER 23

On a perfect spring night in mid-May, I was walking out to my car after work when who pulled into the lot in his Chevelle but Tomaso.

"What the...Tomaso!" I yelled, running over to him as he got out of his car. I grabbed onto his shoulders and I spun him around and around in an exuberant homecoming dance.

"Whoa! Whoa!" he yelled. "Easy does it, asshole!" But I could tell he was secretly pleased by my excitement to see him.

"But, I mean, what the hell, man? What are you doing home? Why didn't you tell us?"

"I wanted to surprise you guys," he said. "It looks like it worked."

Despite my exhaustion after a busy night, seeing Tomaso really recharged my batteries. "Wow! Are you done with the heavy artillery training?"

"Yeah, sort of. But listen to this. They ended up training me on nuclear howitzers."

"What the hell are nuclear how–"

"*Howitzers.* They're big artillery guns. You know the big cannon outside of the Derby Armory? That's a howitzer. But, of course, that one's a World War I model. Stone Age! These bastards are *nuclear* howitzers, so you can imagine the fuckin' havoc they can wreak. They can hit a target, like, twenty miles away."

At the second mention of the word *nuclear*, I recalled Mr.

Mown's discussion of uranium, and like a scrolling electric sign, the words *Hiroshima* and *Little Boy* and *80,000 dead* flashed with sudden brightness in the dark corners of my mind.

"Crazy!" I said, "And now what?"

"Next stop for me is Korea."

"Korea? Holy shit...Korea!"

He told me about how he had bought a bike out in Oklahoma and had been riding it home when, cruising through the Ozark Mountains in Missouri, he cracked a piston.

"Get out," I said. "What did you do?"

"Well, first of all, I had to push the fucker uphill and then coast downhill, up and down like that for about fifty miles until I finally found civilization in Kansas City. Then I found a Honda dealer, but he told me he wouldn't be able to fix it for at least three days, and shit, man, I only have a little time before I get shipped to Korea, and I was anxious to get home."

"So what did you do?"

"What did I do? I convinced him to buy the bike from me."

I couldn't believe it. "You what?"

"Yeah, I explained that I had bought the bike for six hundred and fifty bucks and if he gave me three, he could fix it and turn a profit."

"Wow," I said, "that's crazy! But listen, without the bike, how did you get home?"

"Took a plane out of Kansas City. Remember, I had an extra three hundred bucks in my pocket. My sister picked me up in New York, and then I drove here as soon as I got home. I didn't even say hi to my parents yet."

"Crazy," I said. "And now your next stop is Korea, huh?" At least it sounded better than Vietnam.

"Yup."

"How ya feelin' about that?"

"How would you be feeling?"

Like a cat, I climbed up and settled myself on the hood of his Chevelle. "Probably not good. Probably nervous."

"Yeah...well, the same for me."

I tried to offer some consolation. "But they must be sending you with your platoon or battalion or whatever ya call it. With guys you know."

"Yeah, right," he said. "No one I know is going."

"Wow, that sucks. But what will you be doing there? Because there's no war there, right? Nuclear whatchamacallits?"

"Howitzers. I'm not sure, actually. I'll find out when I get there, or so they told me."

"Doesn't sound like they tell you very much," I said.

"That's how the military works. They do whatever the fuck they want. They'll let me know what my duty is when I get there, and I'll have to fuckin' like it or lump it."

I realized how lonely being a soldier must be. I couldn't picture being in Tomaso's shoes and shipping out to Korea without a single friend. Or, even worse, being Jeff in the middle of the jungles of Vietnam. It made me feel grateful to be in college and have the life that I had here.

When I arrived home, Dad was sitting up in his chair, the room in darkness except for the TV screen and the glow of his cigarette.

"What were you doing so late?"

"Tomaso surprised me. He just showed up at Duchess," I said. "We've been sitting in the parking lot throwing the bull for more than an hour."

He sipped his drink. "So, what's next for Tomaso?"

"When his furlough is over, he's headed to Korea."

"Interesting," he said, looking as if he was about to drift off to sleep. Thinking about following orders, I remembered Tomaso, on his last visit, telling me about the letters Dad had written to Aunt Lucia years ago, something I hadn't mentioned to Dad.

"A while back," I began, "Tomaso told me about letters you wrote to Aunt Lucia. About warning her not to let Uncle Buzz join the Army."

He yawned. "Yeah, it wouldn't have gone too good for Buzz."

"Tomaso told me. He said you warned her that the Army would have killed Uncle Buzz if he didn't listen. But you meant that figuratively, right?"

"No, I meant it like I said it. Literally. Buzz marches to his own drummer, not anybody else's. They wouldn't have put up with him."

"But what about you? Did you listen to their orders?"

"Yeah, I did. I had to." He didn't seem happy to admit it, and then he changed the subject. "When do you have to declare your major?"

"I have until the middle of next year."

"That's not far off."

"I guess not."

"Got any ideas?"

I sighed. "Well, I'd like to be a writer."

He paused, deep in thought, and echoed, "A writer."

"Yeah. I feel – inside me – I have something to say."

"Is there a major for that? For writing?"

"No, not at Southern," I replied, "except English."

"And can you be a writer with an English degree?"

"Oh yeah, sure, a hundred percent! I mean, you can be a writer without a degree if you're good at it."

He took a long drag on his cigarette and blew the smoke into the air. "There's no guaranteed living at that, though, is there?"

"I guess not," I said, "but lots of things in life aren't guaranteed, wouldn't you agree?"

"I suppose."

"It's something I feel deep inside of me."

His eyes somehow looked sad, as if he knew what it was like to feel something deep within, and then in a soft voice, he said, "I think you'd make a damn good writer."

I almost couldn't believe my ears. I wasn't expecting such a vote of confidence. It reminded me of when he comforted me after my Scout trip to Philmont.

"Well, yeah, I do too," I offered. "I think Mom would have loved to be a writer. Maybe I can fulfill her dreams."

"Don't worry about her dreams," he said, "just worry about your own. But I have to warn you, dreams often turn into disappointments. Unfulfilled dreams can devastate a guy. I know. If it doesn't work out, you'll need to be strong."

I wasn't sure what he was talking about and wondered if it had something to do with his flight training when he was in the service, which he never finished, he said, because the war ended. But maybe there was a deeper, hidden story behind it.

"I think I'm strong," I offered, hoping he believed me.

He looked at me, or maybe I should say, looked *into* me and said,

"I think you're strong too. You just keep writing and let's see where it leads."

Then he picked up the remote and turned the volume up on the TV. He had a John Wayne movie on, ironically about pilots, *Flying Leathernecks.*

I said good night and headed to bed, realizing it was the best talk we had had in a long time.

CHAPTER 24

One thing I was learning about college was that I don't like lecture halls. Psychology 100 was my third lecture hall during freshman year, following Zoology and Probability and Statistics in the first semester, and even bigger and more boring than those if that was possible. Engleman 122 is a sprawling auditorium, and the place was packed to the gills. The professor, whose name I've blocked out of my brain (because why should I remember hers when she didn't know mine?) stood at a lectern on the stage and droned into a microphone all period in a high pitched monotone. Worse still, the class was at 8:00 in the morning. Try doing snoresville when you're barely awake.

My friends and I sat near the back door, and if she didn't give a quiz, more often than not we would slip out and go grab a coffee. One of my friends was a guy Michael had played Little League with who was back from Vietnam and in college on the G.I. bill, and the other was a former Derby football star. The three of us were a bad combo.

Skipping out of class wasn't a good idea, but I sometimes not only skipped out but downright cut classes. It was all part of the college culture and sometimes you even bragged about it. Like, "Yeah, I cut that class like it was my job and still got a B."

One time, neither of my friends were in class, so I skipped out on my own because I felt sleepy and irritable and couldn't cope with

Professor Monotone. I remember enjoying the early morning solitude of the student union, sipping hot coffee, and reading *Sir Gawain and the Green Knight* when I was interrupted.

"Hey, Gabe."

I looked up to see Gordon Weed sitting across from me, his smile exposing a gap between his front teeth and his stringy, unkempt hair reaching well below his shoulders.

"Hey, Gordon. What's up?"

"You look nice this morning," he offered.

I wasn't used to other guys telling me I looked nice. "Oh, yeah? Well, uhm, thanks, I guess. You do too." He didn't, but it seemed like the thing to say.

"Thank you," he said, closing his eyes and blushing. "Studying, are you?"

Isn't it obvious?

"Yeah. I'm cutting psychology."

"Aw, not psychology. I love psychology!"

"You wouldn't love this psychology. This is mind-numbing psychology. The prof is a drag, and I hate lecture halls."

"You'd probably be better off at a small college where there aren't any lecture halls. I'd hate to see you go, but maybe you should transfer."

Yeah, that'd be nice. It made me wonder if Bates was a small college. Even though I had wanted to go to Bates, I didn't know a thing about the place.

"Forgive me for giving you advice," Gordon continued, "but don't make cutting class a regular thing. It's a bad habit."

"Yeah...you're right. I won't," I promised, not meaning it.

"Oh, by the way, I don't think you've ever come to one of our SAW meetings, have you? We're working hard to get Congress to change the legal voting age to eighteen, and the more people who vote, the sooner we can end this bloody war."

"I see."

"We're meeting in the rotunda at 5:00 today. Can I count on you to join us?"

I was surprised when I heard myself promise him I would attend. Why not? I could hang around for another hour after my last class.

When I arrived at the rotunda, there were clusters of students spread across the vast space. There must have been at least a hundred sitting on the sweeping staircase. Signs had been taped onto the towering paneled walls, GET OUT OF VIETNAM NOW...BRING THE TROOPS HOME NOW...HELL NO, WE WON'T GO. Most looked like hippies, but that's the style. With the length of my hair, I suppose I do too, even though I don't feel like one. Everyone was chattering away in their various nests, some even strumming on guitars, and it felt noisy and disorganized.

Gordon appeared out of thin air with a red, white, and blue bullhorn.

"Thank you for coming to this important meeting, everyone," he began. "Students across the country have been tirelessly working to get the twenty-sixth amendment ratified. That'll lower the voting age to eighteen, and it'll mean that everyone in this meeting will be able to vote in the next election."

I couldn't help but love Gordon's sincerity.

"We don't know who Nixon'll be running against in '72, maybe George McGovern," he continued, "but the election is about a year and half away, and the only way we'll get out of Vietnam is if we defeat Nixon. If we can shake enough people our age out of their apathy, we can do it."

The crowd hooted and hollered, "Yeah, right on"..."Fuck Tricky Dick"..."Vote the asshole out"...

"That's the spirit," Gordon said. "Now, what we need you to do is to write to or call your representatives in Washington. Now, some of you don't even know who they are, but that's okay. We're here to educate, not criticize. We'll give you their names and contact information. All you have to do is let them know you want to see the twenty-sixth amendment ratified. If you're old enough to fight in a war, you're old enough to vote, right?"

That last sentence was greeted with an even bigger reaction, with kids pounding their feet and hands on the rotunda walls and floors. In the meantime, a platoon of students walked around the room, handing us mimeographed copies of our senators and congressmen, their addresses, and phone numbers.

"Speaking of fighting in a war, I want to turn the horn over to Dennis Blake, who served a tour of duty in Vietnam. Dennis?"

In sharp contrast to skinny Gordon, Dennis was as sturdy and thick as an NFL linebacker – a Dick Butkus with long hair, round spectacles, and a beard covering his ruddy face. He wore an army shirt with cut-off sleeves.

"Hey, everybody. You can call me 'Duke,' which is what everyone called me in Nam. Thanks for coming to the rally. I want to tell you what a shit show it is over there," he began, and I listened to his story as he described in graphic detail the atrocities he'd witnessed – about guys stepping on landmines and losing a limb or their lives (*Like Buster*, I thought); civilians being shot and killed by G.I.'s because "most of the time, we don't even know who the fuck the enemy is"; about the rape of Vietnamese women; about screaming, "Why God?" as he held a dying friend in his arms.

The crowd was silent, as if we were at a gravesite after a funeral. Some of the girls in the rotunda sobbed and wiped away tears as they listened. I was getting a little choked up myself.

On the drive home, I had Dad on my mind. He wouldn't like that I had gone to the meeting, but another way to look at it was that I didn't protest anything, I just observed. He didn't have to know I attended.

What he *did* know a few weeks later was that I barely squeaked through Psychology 100 with a C-. Dad wasn't thrilled about it, but he was now more diplomatic than in the past.

He said nothing about my A in Creative Writing II or my other three B grades, but asked, "What's this psychology course?"

"Oh...it's just a core requirement," I said.

"Hard?"

"Well...more boring than hard." I didn't share that I had habitually cut the class.

Dad let it go at that. Two years before, I would have been grounded. Maybe things were different now because he wanted to treat me like an adult. But a burning question was, would he treat me like an adult if I told him I wanted to protest the war?

Thinking about our road trip and planning for it propelled me through the month of June, giving my life some purpose, or as the French say, *raison d'être*. Four years of French in high school, and I walked away with a handful of phrases. *Où est la bibliothèque?* and *Je te rencontre au café* and the ever helpful *Je ne comprends pas*. Pathetic!

When I told my mom and dad about the road trip, it was my mom who was, as usual, more skeptical than my dad.

"Gabriel," she said. "Do you think this is a good idea...to just drive off without a destination?"

"That's why it's called a road trip, Celia. That's why it's exciting. Because you don't know what you're going to discover."

She gave Dad that distressed *say-something* look, but he just looked me square in the eye and said, "Just find a phone booth every day and make sure you call your mother and let her know you're alright. And don't do anything stupid."

Ne sois pas stupide! Fran McDougal and I used to tease each other with that one whenever our French IV teacher reprimanded one of us.

That seemed fine with me. That's the interesting thing with Dad. Even though he wouldn't let me live away from home, he knew enough to allow me a certain amount of freedom.

In a way, Mom seemed to be a bigger influence on me when I was a kid, but now that I was approaching adulthood and having these nightly conversations with Dad, his influence was growing.

For instance, despite my high school blunders with girls, I had had a paradigm shift since entering college. Some might call it maturity, but I had realized that maybe what my parents had taught me was true – that sex and love go together. I suppose I always knew it to be true, but under the influence of peer pressure, I had been sidetracked.

Now as a freshman in college, I dated a lot. Mary Elizabeth had even begun teasing me, addressing me as "Casanova." I'm not going to lie – I myself was surprised at my sudden success with girls.

Despite this newfound success, I realized something. A number of girls I dated would have gone all the way with me. It became evident that some girls only needed to hear the magic words, *I love you*, but I couldn't say something that wasn't true. In a few instances, such a declaration was not even necessary, which also didn't feel right.

In truth, I had been gaining a maturity that I didn't have in high school. My attitude about girls was changing. Now I found myself struggling, not so much with my virginity, but with *theirs*, should it still be intact. My parents had taught me to value a girl's virginity, and my existential problem was, who was I to want a virgin for myself if I was going to take the virginity of a girl I wasn't ready to make a full commitment to?

So what did I do? Let's just say that every time I came close to surpassing the speed limit, I exited the highway.

That might have changed in the spring semester when I fell hard for a girl from St. Raphael's School of Nursing. I met Joanne at the student union at Southern where she took core courses. I mean, the relationship had barely gotten off the ground, but I knew I wanted to fly with it.

She was very cute, and before I knew it, I was skipping my American Renaissance class to hang out with her. We'd sit in the grass outside of Engleman and share our deepest feelings. I randomly began visiting her at her residence hall at St. Raphael's, which, except for the parlor, was off limits to men, and I loved it when she would come downstairs and spend an hour with me.

I knew I was gone on Joanne. On our first date, she slid right next to me in my car, and it felt like we were already a couple. When I stopped to get gas on the way to the Showcase Cinemas and the gas station attendant remarked, "Your girlfriend's beautiful, man. I wish I had a girl like that," I'm not going to lie. I felt proud.

When one date turned into two and two turned into ten, I was feeling pretty good about the burgeoning relationship.

One night, after arriving home from a date with the nurse, Dad asked from his easy chair, "You like this girl?"

"Which girl?"

"The one you talk about all the time, according to your mother. The nurse."

"I don't know. I mean, yeah, I guess. She's great."

"Jus' be careful," he said in his intoxicated state.

"Careful?" I didn't know what he meant.

"Careful you don't do something you'll regret. Do I need to spell it out?"

"No, no...don't spell it out, please," I said, feeling irritated. It was an old story.

After a dramatic pause, he continued. "You want me to tell you what the problem is with your generation?"

"I mean," I said, not wanting to hear it, "I –"

"The problem with your generation," he interrupted, "is that nobody values virginity anymore. Where does that get anyone? I'll tell you where. Pregnant! Like two of your cousins. They got knocked up and had to get married. You know who I'm talking about."

"Yes, I know, but –"

"I'd hate to see that happen to you. It's a shitty way to begin a marriage. Life is enough of a struggle without starting off on the wrong foot. Understand?"

"Yes, I get it." I wasn't exactly able to argue the point.

He sipped his drink and took a drag on his cigarette before continuing. "Of course, should you get a girl pregnant, marrying her is the right thing to do, but what if she's not the right girl for you?"

"Well –"

"Or, instead of being stupid, you could get to know her without jumping in the sack with her. I'll tell you this. Your mother was a virgin on our wedding night, and we're both damned thankful we waited. The same for most of the women of our generation. Believe me when I say you'll be better off if you marry a nice girl like your mother or your Aunt Connie...or any of your mother's sisters or mine."

I've heard other dads almost brag about their sons' sexual escapades, but that isn't my dad. When it comes to morality, he knows where true north is without a compass and isn't afraid to let me and Michael know. He may be outspoken, but it's hard not to admire him.

It turned out he didn't need to worry about Joanne, though. A few weeks before my road trip with Bink, she came to the window at Duchess and asked if I would come outside for a minute because she needed to tell me something. I asked Bink to watch the window.

Through the window of her Dodge Dart, I could see that she looked sad.

"Everything okay?" I asked.

"Not exactly," she said, biting her straw.

"What's the matter?"

Then, in the quietest, mousiest voice, she said, "It's...it's just that I can't see you anymore."

"What do you mean, you can't see me anymore? I thought we *really* liked each other, maybe even that we lo–"

"Don't say it," she interrupted. "It's my ex-boyfriend...he...well, it's complicated, but he wants to get back together...and I just feel so freaked out and confused."

She looked out of her window, her beautiful, sad eyes pitying me, as if she wanted to save a stray cat but couldn't.

I was dying inside when, acting purely on instinct, I said, "Oh, yeah. Hey, listen, no problem. I didn't know there was an old boyfriend in the picture...so, yeah, don't worry about it. No sweat. I'll be fine."

Joanne seemed surprised by my response. I was a good actor, I guess. But despite trying to act all cool about it, I wasn't.

She started her car and pulled out of the space, giving me one last farewell glance. And I, for the hundredth time, feeling like an unrequited lover in a Shakespearean play, watched her take a right out of the parking lot and drive out of my life forever.

When I got back to the window, Bink asked, "Everything okay?"

"Yeah, everything's great...just fucking great." I went back to work, immersing myself in rubbing the stainless steel counters down with polish, but no matter how much elbow grease I put into it, I couldn't rub away the pain I was feeling.

Joanne breaking my heart synced perfectly with the release of Joni's latest album, which came out in June. I'm guessing she called it *Blue* because of the blue album cover and the sad feeling the color evokes in a person's heart. Her songs sure made me feel blue, not that I needed songs to do that. That's what girls were for.

It's not an album you listen to with a friend, like the way Jeff and I wore out *The White Album* as we cruised around the Valley in the Corvair. I feel *Blue* was meant to be listened to in solitude. After all, white and blue are two different colors.

In the weeks before our trip, I must have taken off alone more than a dozen times on the Derby Turnpike, driving along the river through Seymour and Oxford on my way out to the Stevenson Dam while Joni's truth-telling and raw emotion performed open heart surgery on me. I would pull into the hotdog stand at Lake Zoar and stare at the placid water, allowing Joni's soaring multi-octave vocals and flawless acoustic accompaniments to work their alchemy on me. Every song was a killer, but the title song, especially, cut me to ribbons, transporting me to new and unexpected emotional vistas every time I listened to it. She seemed to touch upon every nook and cranny of my feelings as if she knew me personally. I'm guessing that's what Joni was going for on this album...what she had always been about. It was on those drives that I felt certain that if I could ever figure out a way to meet Joni in person, it would help me in inexplicable ways.

CHAPTER 25

Bink and I decided to leave on the first Friday in August and go for about two weeks or until our money ran out. Getting away would give me a break from nurses with ex-boyfriends and from drunken conversations with my dad.

I got a tune up and an oil change and hoped for the best. I picked Bink up at his house and loaded his suitcase into the trunk which is actually in the front of the car, like a VW bug. We swung by Duchess before we hit the road, hoping for a nice sendoff from the crew.

"So what's the plan, Stan?" Will Granger asked me.

"I don't know," I said. "Just take off and see where the road leads us. It's sort of like I'm hoping to discover America, in a manner of speaking."

"In a manner of speaking?" Karl Fischer mimicked. "You realize, I hope, that Columbus only discovered America because he was lost. And I bet you two fuckin' winners'll be lost before you're out of Connecticut."

That gave the crew a good laugh, but to be truthful, I didn't care what Karl thought. When you work at Duchess, you learn to deflect the barbs.

"Don't worry, Karl," Bink offered, "I'm the co-pilot, and I bought an atlas."

I hadn't noticed, but Bink had an atlas tucked under his arm. I cringed as he proudly whipped it out to display its shiny cover featuring a graphic of a car on a highway with a drawing of a yellow road that said, *Rand McNally Road Atlas.* Across the bottom of the cover there was an orange band that said: *United States - Canada - Mexico.*

Karl let out an ear-piercing guffaw and joked. "If you morons end up in fuckin' Mexico, don't call us to come rescue you."

Don't worry, Karl. You'd be the last person I'd call.

It figured. Our sendoff had turned into the Karl Fischer Comedy Hour. Bink didn't know when to leave well enough alone.

I doubted we'd make it to Mexico, although that would be cool since it's a destination Sal Paradise traveled to in *On the Road.* He even found himself a Mexican girlfriend on that leg of the trip. I wondered if I would find a girlfriend on our road trip.

Thankfully, Les chimed in and said, "Don't you sweet boys listen to him. You just drive safe and have yourselves a lovely time."

"Yeah, exactly," Will added. "You guys just have fun and don't worry about anything."

I felt a little better as Bink and I took off and got on Route 8 South, headed for the Merritt.

I had decided on a few rules, which I laid out for Bink.

"First of all, Bink," I began, "we aren't going to be in any big hurry to get anywhere. I don't love driving, and besides, I want to take our time and see the sights. I've done a little traveling on Boy Scout trips, but I was too stupid to pay attention. This time around, I want to soak it all in and get a feel for what it's like to travel from one state to another."

Bink took a bite out of a chocolate-covered donut and nodded.

"Wipe the chocolate frosting out of your mustache," I said. "Okay, moving on, we need to be frugal and have our money last as long as possible, even if we have to sleep in cheap motels, campgrounds, or in the Corvair itself."

"Roger," Bink replied, like he was my co-pilot in a plane.

"And last, we need to promise not to get on each other's nerves."

"Sounds good," he said, new chocolate frosting once again on his mustache.

"But I want to hear you promise," I said.

"I promise."

"Good. Now wipe the chocolate off your stache again!"

In a box on the floor, behind the front seat, we were well stocked with eight-track tapes, because music was going to be important as we drove. Of course, I had plenty of Joni Mitchell to listen to, but we started our trip listening to a new album called *Tapestry* by Carole King. I'm not in love with Carole King like I am with Joni, but I'm sure in love with her singing voice and the songs she writes. Like Joni's music, Carole King's songs touch me right where I live.

We weren't even twenty minutes into our trip when one of my favorites, "So Far Away," played, and before I knew it, I was asking myself why no one stays in one place anymore, not even me. With my eyes glued to the broken white lines charting our course on the Merritt Parkway, I reflected on my yearning for independence and change, things that had eluded me since I was rejected from Bates College. *Damn them!*

Maybe this trip would give me the sweet taste of liberation that I craved like a drug. I drove along the open road imagining myself living on my own.

Out of the blue, Bink said, "I wish I had a serious girlfriend, don't you, Gabe?" rousing me from my daydream and reminding me of something else I didn't have.

I nodded.

"You ever had one?" he asked.

"Almost. Joanne. The nurse. But I'd rather not talk about her."

"I understand. But what if you were like me and never even had a date? Well, except Emily, but I suppose that doesn't count."

"It counts." I felt even sadder now.

"Maybe I'm gay," he offered. It was a revelation that more than surprised me.

"What the hell are you talking about?"

"Yeah," he continued. "Sometimes I seriously think I'm gay."

If he was trying to get a rise out of me, it was working.

"Why would you even say that?"

"Because, I don't know. If I wasn't gay, maybe girls would go for me."

"But you aren't gay," I said. "I mean, are you?"

"Well, I've never been with a guy or anything, but I don't know. Why don't girls go for me then?"

"They don't go for you, Bink, for all kinds of reasons...because you're a big dork and because so many girls are stuck up and stupid and because it's just not your fate yet to have a girl go for you right now. How are we supposed to understand girls, anyway, or why they go for and don't go for who they go for and don't go for?"

His eyes seemed to question the frustration in my tone. Hell, in my mind, even I questioned it. Why was I so rattled?

"Well, I just think I must be gay or things would be different."

"That's the nuttiest thing I've ever heard." Then, trying to digest whatever made this guy tick, I said, "Wait a minute! Are you, like, attracted to guys?"

"Well, no –"

"There! Then you're not gay...so don't go saying you are. You hear me? I don't want to hear that crazy talk anymore on this trip."

Bink just shrugged and frowned, apparently unsatisfied with my response. I continued to listen to Carole King, and at the same time, I started to wonder why the mere idea of being gay had pushed my button the way it did. It wasn't like he was going to try to kiss me or anything. At least I hoped he wasn't! But it made me wonder about having chosen to go off on this jaunt with him. I would never have been having this conversation with Jeff or Tomaso, that's for damn sure. If Bink had talked this way to Tomaso, he would have pulled over and made Bink walk home. Still, what made me so uncomfortable with the idea of homosexuality? Thinking it over, I concluded, *It must be because I don't know any homosexuals except for maybe Gordon Weed and Les at Duchess, who doesn't count because he's so much older than me.*

As we drove past the Darien exit, I saw a girl hitchhiking near the shoulder of the road right near a stone bridge on the Merritt Parkway. I then spotted another figure sprawled out in the grass nearby. As we got closer, I could see the girl had on a long floral skirt, a tie-dye tank top, more like a half-shirt that exposed her midriff, and a hat that looked just like the bush hat Jeff wore in the photo he had sent me. The one sitting in the grass was a guy with long hair and a beard. His head rested on a guitar case, and it looked like he was wearing a military shirt. I slowed down.

"You're not picking up these two hippies, are you?" Bink asked.

"Of course I'm picking them up," I said. "I know what it's like to hitchhike and have people fly past you like you don't even exist. I'm not going to do that to anyone."

"But...but what if they're dangerous?"

"Bink, please!"

In my rearview mirror, I saw the pair trotting toward the car. I could now see that the guy's army shirt had cut-off sleeves. *No one in Nam is too worried about being regulation*, I remembered.

Bink had to get out to let them in because the old Corvair is a two-door. They piled into the back seat, a tight fit for them with the guitar case and tattered rucksack. She was a wisp of a thing, and he was a bear with dark glasses that obscured his eyes.

He somehow looked familiar, and then it hit me. *Gordon's war rally.*

"Thanks for stopping, man," the guy said. His shirt was unbuttoned, and I could see his dog tags against his hairy chest.

"You got it. Where you off to?" I asked. For some reason, I decided not to mention I remembered him.

"We're heading into New York City," he said. "We're gonna crash at a friend's place tonight before we move on. Can you help us out?"

"I guess," I replied. "We're just taking a road trip, so we can drop you off in the city before continuing."

"Far out," he said. "That's cool. My name is Duke and this here's my girlfriend, Sparrow."

Right, Duke, I recalled.

Hearing their names, Bink eyed me with raised brows. "I'm Gabriel and this is my friend, Kevin, but everyone calls him Bink. What're your real names?"

Duke chuckled and said, "Well, I got my name in the military, but Sparrow and I came up with hers together. We chose it for her a few months ago. We don't consider these nicknames, though, but our real names now. We prefer names we've taken ourselves instead of names someone imposed on us when we were too young to make a choice, which we think is a drag, right Sparrow?"

I glanced in the mirror and saw Sparrow nod and flash a genuine smile. And what a smile she had with straight teeth, except for one slightly crooked one that turned away from the others at a perfect angle.

"So you guys are going on a road trip to where?" Duke asked.

"Oh, just nowhere," I said.

"That's the best fuckin' kind, man. Me and Sparrow are doing the same. The difference is we're thumbing it. You never know where the road'll take you."

"Yeah," I said, "I guess that's what's exciting about it."

I noticed Bink was flaking out on me. *You could at least shift your body a little and look at them,* I wanted to say to him.

"Where'd you get that bush hat you're wearing?" I asked Sparrow.

"Oh, this? It was Duke's when he was in Nam. It keeps the sun off my head when we're hitchhiking." She had the cutest voice, just like a cartoon character.

"Yeah? My best friend sent me a picture of him wearing an identical hat."

Except Sparrow's hat had a little patch with a peace symbol on it, I noticed, gazing again into my mirror. I realized I was peeking at her reflection in the mirror a little too often, and I hoped they didn't notice.

"Your friend's in Nam?" Duke asked.

"Yeah. A little over a year now. In a recent letter from him, he explained about the bush hat, but he didn't say anything about what it was like to be in Vietnam."

"Not surprised. Most guys don't want to talk about it. Who could fuckin' blame 'em?"

Somehow the last exchange ruined the momentum of the conversation.

Finally, Duke asked a question. "You guys in college?"

"Yeah," I said, "I commute to Southern, and Bink here is going to be at UCONN in the fall. How about you?"

"No shit. I just started at Southern last January. The G.I. Bill, which is the only good thing I got out of the fuckin' military. Of course, I'm twenty-two now, so I'm older than mostly everybody, but it's cool."

I wanted to say, *I know, Duke. I heard your story at the peace rally,* but I remained silent.

"How about you, Sparrow?" I asked.

"Me?" she said. "I quit high school because it was such a drag, and then I met Duke at a concert in Bridgeport, and we've been a couple ever since. Crazy, right? Maybe I'll get a G.E.D. some day, we'll see."

"Hey, Sparrow," Duke said. "What do ya think we invite Gabriel and Bink to hang with us tonight in the Village?"

"Groovy," Sparrow said.

"Hang out where?" I asked.

"A little club in Greenwich Village. The Psychedelic Menagerie. Very cool place. They're having an open mic night. You know, people read poetry or sing or expound on whatever they want to. Me and Sparrow plan to do a few tunes."

"That sounds cool," I said. "What do you think, Bink?"

Bink continued to look straight ahead, shaking his head "no" in the most imperceptible way. *What's your problem?* I wondered in frustration. To me, it sounded like a good enough prelude to our adventure.

"Count us in," I offered. "After all, it's not exactly like we have anywhere to be."

When we got off the Hudson River Parkway, we hit the Greenwich Village neighborhood close to noon. I saw that it had a different vibe than Times Square. There were no skyscrapers, and the buildings were homey brick structures with stone steps leading to the front door. The sidewalks were lined with trees, and it didn't have the cold concrete, neon energy that I had noticed around 42nd Street.

After about twenty minutes, I miraculously found a parking space. The four of us got out and headed down the walkway. At the corner, I saw street signs that said Bleecker Street and MacDougal Street. Duke headed left on MacDougal, and I asked where we were going.

"We'll go to the park and hang out," he said. "It's a beautiful day. We can get a hotdog from a vendor if you're hungry."

As we walked, Sparrow asked Bink what his major was, and the guy came to life like Jesus resurrected on Easter Sunday. A history major, he started ranting about the Spanish-American War like he was lecturing to a class at UCONN. Sparrow seemed transfixed. Go figure.

I also noticed a few things I had never seen before. One was that every now and then, a couple passed by holding hands. But they weren't always guy-girl couples, which felt, well, odd. Greenwich Village appeared to be a place where homosexuals could be affectionate without anyone picking on them. I thought about Bink saying he was gay, and I wondered if the gayness of the neighborhood would rub off on him.

On top of that, we passed by all kinds of small businesses, some of which had pretty unusual window displays. Some even had male mannequins all decked out in stockings, bras, and other women's underthings. It occurred to me that I had lived a sheltered life. Towns like Shelton and Derby were tame in comparison. And then I pictured Dorothy in *The Wizard of Oz*, a film I had seen just about every year since I was old enough to think. I could hear Dorothy's voice, after the house crashes to the ground and she surveys the land of Oz with wonder: "Toto, I've a feeling we're not in Kansas anymore."

"I don't know...maybe we'll just rest a little and then get something to eat. The Psychedelic Menagerie doesn't open the doors for a couple of hours, and it doesn't groove until later."

And so, much to my surprise, Duke and Sparrow snuggled up together on the lush grass carpet under a big old maple tree, and the two appeared to drift off to sleep.

Staring at the two of them, Duke's big arm wrapped around Sparrow, I was a little miffed.

"Now what?" I asked Bink.

He shrugged. "Shall we take a nap too?"

"What the hell are you talking about? I'm not taking a fucking nap in the middle of a park."

Feeling sorry for myself, I took off, walking the perimeter of the park with Bink trailing me. We passed a caged-in basketball court, and I stopped to watch, pressing my envious face against the chain link fence. The players were all black, their dark skin glistening in the summer heat as they flew up and down the court. The swish of the metal nets was music to my ears, and I wished I could play with them.

After about ten minutes, Bink gave my shirt a tug. "We should go," he said.

"Yeah, right...we should go," I echoed, wishing I had never quit the high school team.

At the park's edge, we came upon five or six cigarette smoking chess players, looking half-stoned, sitting at small rickety tables, their pieces arranged on worn black and tan boards in tight regimented lines like British soldiers ready for battle.

"What's up, bro?" a chess player with thick eyelids half covering bloodshot eyes asked. "You play?"

"A little," I said.

"Three bucks a game," he offered.

Bink's head went into his patented negative shake. I knew he was right. We had been hustled once before in New York, and we needed to keep our wits about us and conserve our money so our trip would last as long as possible. I declined, but we did watch some chess games, and just like I figured, the glassy-eyed players hustled person after person. They'd let their opponents win one or two before they took them to the cleaners.

We made our way back to Duke and Sparrow who were still dead to the world. Hungry and impatient, I woke them.

We found a delicatessen, and we all ordered club sandwiches, except Sparrow, who ordered something called a quiche because she claimed to be a vegetarian, which struck me as funny because I had plainly seen her eat a hotdog earlier in the afternoon.

"So what are you cats running away from?" Duke asked as he chomped on his sandwich.

"Running away from?" I said. "We're not running away from anything."

"Sure you are, man. Everyone's running away from something."

Puzzled, I turned the tables on him. "If everyone's running away from something, what are you two running away from?"

"Easy," he said. "Sparrow here is running away from her wealthy parents, and I'm running away from the larger Establishment with a capital E."

"What do you mean by the establishment?" Bink asked. I was glad he got involved because I felt a little intimidated to be left alone in the forest of Duke's confidence, maturity, and intelligence.

"The Es-tab-lish-ment, man," Duke said, punctuating every syllable. "Like Madison Avenue, like Wall Street, like the White House, like the Military Industrial Complex. The Man! He's fuckin' us all over, dude. Can you dig that?"

Bink shook his head, obviously not digging it, and I sat there looking just as clueless.

"Let's take Vietnam. Why are we fighting a war there?"

I found myself back at Gordon's rally listening to Duke speak.

"Because war makes money, man. Because the Military Industrial Complex wants to manufacture war machines...ya know, jets and helicopters and missiles and other death-creating shit so that *the Man* can keep rakin' in the dough hand over fist."

"But, uhm...who is the...the man?" Bink asked.

Duke grimaced and said, "The Man is *the Man*! Not just one man unless we want to talk about one corrupt and powerful fucker like Nixon, but when we talk about the Man we mean the power center. We mean the entire government or the entire rich white establishment. Where the hell did you guys say you came from? A monastery? A cave? Don't you see what's happenin'? Somebody like

me or your buddy goes and gets drafted and maybe gets his fuckin'
head blown off or loses an arm or a leg, and for what?"

"My buddy didn't get drafted," I said. "He enlisted."

Hearing that, Duke shook his head and rolled his eyes. "You're
shittin' me, man. That's a bummer. Let me suggest that neither of
you follow in your buddy's footsteps. In fact, if your number gets
called, if I were you, I'd beat it to Canada. It's a nice country."

All the while, Sparrow continued to eat her quiche, not saying a
word but just chewing and listening attentively.

"Listen, you guys aren't kids anymore. It's time you woke up."

Duke reminded me of Will Granger, who is similarly cynical
about his experiences in Vietnam, although not as intellectual or
political as Duke. *What ever happened to patriotism?* I wondered. I'd
never heard a guy from my father's generation talk about World War
II this way.

I wasn't surprised by Duke, though. I was well aware of the war
protests. How could I not be? For years, I had seen protestors burn
draft cards and American flags on the news. Not to mention a lot of
the songs I listened to were songs of protest and rebellion against the
establishment. Songs like "For What It's Worth" by Buffalo Spring-
field and "Draft Morning" by the Byrds, which depresses me every
time I think of Tomaso or Jeff.

So it's not like I was in the dark about the issues Duke was
expounding on. But when he called us to wake up, it left me with an
important question. *Am I, in fact, asleep?*

CHAPTER 27

In his frustration, Duke terminated the conversation and suggested we take a walk before going to the Psychedelic Menagerie. The Village was beautiful and peaceful at dusk. Maple boughs hung low, casting leafy cutout shadows on the brick buildings. Lush green leaves appeared to grow right out of the brick on the brownstones. Dozens of lazy bicycles shackled to telephone poles rested near the curb. The narrow streets were dotted with kitschy little businesses like Zito's Bakery, its store window stacked with crusty loaves of Italian bread, and cafes with French names like Croque Monsieur. Many of the businesses had park benches right outside their doors on which local residents, customers, and lovers sat, making plans and solving the world's problems over a croissant or an almond roll.

It hit me that Greenwich Village was more similar to downtown Shelton than to Times Square. There were no skyscrapers here, and the buildings, in some cases, were no more than three stories high, just like back home. The Village was just more expansive than Shelton – more of everything and more unusual names for each shop or business. I pictured taking Mosci's with its soda counter, jukebox, and pinball machines and plopping it right in the middle of the Village, perhaps giving it a hip name like The Pinball Palace. It would have fit in perfectly.

Unlike Shelton, the people passing by us on the street were of every color, age, and persuasion – a real mixed bag. Some were little old people, foreign looking types, who reminded me of my nonna and grampa, mixed in with a lot of younger artsy types. Among those were what I believed to be guys dressed as girls, their size and bone structure a dead giveaway, and still others whose gender was unidentifiable, so much so that it became a guessing game for me. People-watching can be so fascinating, and nowhere more fascinating, I learned, than in the Village.

I was so busy staring at the places and people, I was a little surprised when Duke announced, "Well, here we are."

There was the sign on a big awning before us. Behind a rendering of zoo-like bars, distorted neon-colored faces of animals of every kind poked through, hungrily looking down on us. The lettering, Psychedelic Menagerie, reminded me of artwork that I had seen on a lot of posters and album covers by groups like the Byrds or Cream, the kind that make you feel like you're high as you read the words, not that I had a clue what it was like to be high.

This ought to be interesting, I mused. Bink gave me an apprehensive look, but I just shot him a wordless shrug as if to say, *Why the hell not?*

The inside of the joint wasn't anything special. The brick walls were painted in black with random bricks here and there popping out in fluorescent pinks, yellows, and oranges. There must have been a couple dozen eclectic wooden tables and chairs, all painted black, practically piled on top of each other. A miniscule stage sat at the end of the room, illuminated with a warm pool of light shining on a solitary stool.

Duke led us to a little table, and the four of us took a seat. The place had alcoholic drinks, and since the legal age in New York is eighteen, I ordered a gin and Tom Collins. Thank you, Tommy Trouble!

Soon enough, things got rolling. The first act featured a muscular guy with an Afro making love to a tenor sax, which I found interesting since my brother and I had grown up playing sax. I remember learning songs like, "You Belong to Me" and "Stardust" and "Midnight in Moscow," but this guy was blowing something foreign to my ears. It sounded like a lot of high and low pitched notes to me, some long and a bit overzealous and others fluttering like birds fleeing a telephone line and still others punched out in short staccato beeps. We listened as his horn howled and cried and yelped. Most everyone seemed turned on by it, though. Sparrow was closing her eyes and moaning in ecstasy. Bink, of course, had that *deer-in-the-headlights* look on his face. He appeared to be as confused as I felt.

After about twenty minutes of way out sax dissonance, a hippie girl with a fire engine red headband and yellow granny glasses got up and began reading her original poetry. Even a semester of 20th Century American Poetry hadn't prepared me for this chick's off the wall verse.

Sitting on the stool in a liquid pool of light, she stared down at one of those black spotted composition notebooks and began her recitation with perhaps a bit too much emotion:

A dreary fence screams
In my sedimentary dreams
While fragile twigs
And highway rigs
Bite my postal strawberries
Come to me, guardian fairies
And dried goods
Alienated in the woods
Aborted sea shells
A shingle swells
Eerily linear
My aborted interior
Inviting cardboard teeth
Save me from the trash heap...

And it went on this way for another fifteen minutes or more. I thought to myself, *It's like she put a couple hundred words in a paper bag, shook it up, and then reached in and took one out at a time, and wrote it in her notebook.*

Sparrow and Duke reacted as they had to the sax player, emitting little affirmative sounds of approval. Once in a while someone in the place let go with a "Right on!" or an "Oh yes!" or a "Groovy!" like they had been living in darkness and had at long last seen the light. If Bink's eyes had radiated wide-eyed surprise at the sax player, they were now ready to pop out of their sockets on the little round table before us.

Duke and Sparrow were up next. We had already heard them sing in the park, so it felt like a welcome relief was on hand. And, more or less, I was right. That said, they didn't do any songs that were hits like out in the park. Instead, they sang originals that Duke had written. They were just like our conversation in the deli, politics set to music. Songs protesting the War and the Establishment and the Man...and just about anything that was worth protesting. I smiled to myself and pictured my father. *He'd just love this!*

In my humble opinion, Duke and Sparrow were the most talented act so far, and the customers loved them. I couldn't help noticing how cute Sparrow looked as she made a dainty curtsy, her cheeks blushing a rosy red as everyone whooped and cheered.

The next act was a Jamaican guy with dreadlocks and one of those knit hats, I forget what you call them, like Bob Marley wears – green and yellow and red stripes across a field of black. He dragged a huge conga drum onto the stage and went to town on it.

I then smelled a familiar aroma. I shifted toward the source, and there were Duke and Sparrow, passing a joint back and forth.

When our eyes met, Sparrow offered the joint to me, "Here, take a hit or two," she offered, although I don't know why she was whispering because Mr. Jamaica was beating the hell out of his drum in loud rat-a-tat-poom-bams.

I shook my head. "No thanks. I don't, uhm, smoke."

Sparrow gave me this very concerned look as if it was pretty much the saddest thing she had ever heard. I almost wanted to apologize. Then she offered a hit to Bink, who looked like he was about to cry. He just did that thing he does, shaking his head "no" in little controlled beats, like, no (four shakes), no (two shakes), no (three shakes).

After another two hours of poets, folk singers, musicians, drummers, and one ventriloquist with a Richard Nixon dummy, we walked out into the therapeutic darkness of the neighborhood, and I felt relieved to breathe in some fresh air. I looked behind me and saw Bink carrying Duke's guitar like he was his roadie, and Sparrow and I found ourselves walking side by side about fifteen yards ahead of them.

Sparrow, who was feeling no pain, asked me why I don't smoke. I'm not going to lie. Her question knocked me off balance and made me a little anxious.

"Well," I began carefully, "first of all, it's, uhm, illegal."

"Yeah? And?" she said, like she was waiting for a valid reason.

"What do you mean, *and?*" I asked. "Isn't that enough? What if we got arrested in there?"

Then she gave another sad look and said, "C'mon, Gabriel, I highly doubt the fuzz are gonna raid us."

"Okay," I said, and then I shrugged like I do when I don't know what to say next. At the same time, it wasn't lost on me how fantastically adorable Sparrow looked, and how her name suited her perfectly.

"Okay, what? Tell me the real reason." She was just so sincere, like her one true goal in life was to understand me – a level of sincerity that I wasn't sure what to do with.

"Let's see...the real reason. Uhm...well my parents wouldn't exactly condone it."

She nodded her head, squinting, like she was mulling it over and trying to process what I had said. "You do everything your parents say, then?"

"I don't know. I guess. I mean, I guess not. I mean...well not always."

She nodded again as we walked in silence.

"By the way, where are we going?" I asked.

"Oh, we're all gonna crash at Black Rosco's pad a few blocks from here."

"Who's Black Rosco?"

"The sax player," she replied.

Now it was me who was deep in thought. Now I was the one who was nodding and mulling things over. "Why do you call him Black Rosco?"

"Simple, because he's black and proud. After all, black is beautiful, you know."

As I chewed on a statement that had become an anthem for black Americans, I noticed Sparrow taking this gigantic breath through her little nose, a breath so big you wondered if she had enough room in her lungs for it. Then she let out a long sigh, the cutest long sigh ever, and went, "You know what?"

I'll play along, I figured. "What?"

Then, with the sweetest but most mischievous smile, she said, "I'm gonna get you high. Yes! I'm gonna turn you on!" She said it like she might have said, "We're going to have a party for your birthday," like it was a foregone conclusion.

"Oh you are, are you?" Sparrow just nodded yes, so I asked, "And how do you figure you'll do that?"

"Hmmm, I don't quite know yet," she said, holding onto each word, like they were all long notes on a page of sheet music. "But I'll figure it out. Sparrow always gets what Sparrow wants. Always! Anyone who knows me knows that. Ask Duke." Then she let out a playful giggle.

Looking at her under the street lamps of the Village, I asked myself, *Can I be falling for this girl?* And then one for the ages, *Can a guy fall in love more than once?* I had fallen for one girl after another – from just regular local girls to Joni Mitchell and now to this playful little sparrow who said she always gets what she wants. Boy, was I in trouble.

CHAPTER 28

The heady odor of dampness intermingled with the fragrant scent of cooking spices and the musky aroma of marijuana permeated Black Rosco's apartment. An upholstered chair and two overstuffed, worn couches with batting poking through holes in the faded fabric, no doubt pilfered from some junkyard, sat on the dull hardwood floors. The cracked walls were adorned with posters from rock concerts (the Who, the Stones, the Grateful Dead) as well as a few colorful tapestries, one with a big round sun smiling at me, another with a silhouette of a meditating genderless figure covered from the base of his spine to his head with small colorful orbs, and a third one with a great big circle made up of many smaller concentric circles.

As Duke passed by, I asked what the pattern was, and without breaking stride, he said, "A mandala, man!" I didn't know what that meant. I didn't know what any of it meant.

In the next room, a large poster with a picture of an American flag hung on the wall, except that, instead of stars adorning the field of blue, the word THINK was printed. I didn't understand that either, but I guess it worked because just staring at it made me think.

The whole scene at Rosco's reminded me of those worksheets we did as little kids in kindergarten, the kind where you have to draw a circle with your crayon around the thing that's not like the others. Like, there's a rake and a shovel and a hoe, and then there's a squirrel.

I looked around the apartment, and it hit me. *Bink and I are the squirrels.*

At least a couple dozen people showed up at Rosco's place and a party-like atmosphere ensued. It looked like an equal mix of guys and girls, all of them hippies. Well, all except Bink and me. The people were dressed in a fascinating array of bohemian colors and fabrics, Indian inspired batik and fringed macrame and peasant shirts. Once inside, most everyone kicked off their shoes, especially the girls.

People broke into little groups and began talking, drinking, and smoking. Some were smoking from pipes while others smoked joints, fat ones, wrapped in what looked like cigar leafs instead of rolling papers. I think they're called *blunts* or something like that.

I was afraid that Sparrow was going to seek me out and try to make good on her promise, but that wasn't the case. It seems she had vanished.

I now moved from one pocket of people to another, listening to conversations. Mick Jagger's voice singing "Brown Sugar" blared from a stereo, and it all felt a little overwhelming to me.

Sitting in the tattered upholstered chair, Duke was holding court for six or seven guys and girls who sat at his feet like he was their guru. His guitar sat in his lap, and he was expounding on how we needed to end the war in Vietnam, emphasizing that we'd all need to rally together to get it done.

"That's right, man," I heard Duke say. "Nixon being re-elected in '68 was concomitant to the prolonging of this immoral war. If Humphrey had won, this fucked-up bullshit would have been over by now."

As he made his case, he intermittently struck the metal guitar strings, which rang out in dissonant chords in sharp contrast to Mick Jagger's ear-splitting singing. Listening to Duke expound, I realized that guys like Duke and Will at Duchess, having witnessed the ugliness of war up close, were more against it than people like me who had avoided the draft in one way or another.

I moved across the room and noticed that Rosco, who had four other guys clustered around him, was talking about some famous sax players I had never heard of. As Rosco guzzled a beer, he argued, "No, man, I ain't disputing the greatness of Getz, I'm just sayin' there's never been a cat blow the horn like my man Coltrane and there ain't never gonna be no other like him. You dig? Dude was only forty when he died, and I still ain't fuckin' recovered."

I passed by other groups and into the kitchen, and who did I find deep in conversation but Bink and Sparrow. I had been wondering where they were. Bink talking about what else – history, of course. About the assassination of Abraham Lincoln. So, I kept a little distance, but listened in.

"Yeah," Bink said, "so, John Wilkes Booth, see, planned to kidnap Lincoln, take him to Richmond, which was the Confederate Capital, and use him as a bargaining chip for the South."

Bink may not be certain things, but what he is is a real smart guy, and he knows more trivia about American history than any human being should know or that any human being would want to hear about. But you couldn't tell it from watching Sparrow. As good as Bink was at talking, that's how good Sparrow was at listening. I stood there focused on her, those big, green eyes connected to Bink like emerald lasers, her head tilted in fascination, with that Mona Lisa half smile. She made you feel like what you had to say was important. And there she sat, cross-legged on the kitchen counter, holding her small feet with her hands, marveling at Bink's every word and saying things like, "cosmic" and "wild" and "far out, man!"

Every now and then, Sparrow took a hit from a little pipe that looked like it was made of marble. It appeared that Bink was no longer bothered by the pot smoking as he basked in the glory of female attention.

I was already bored and found myself staring at a collection of empty little glass bottles gathered on the windowsill above the sink, some clear and some brown but most of them green. *Uranium glass*, I thought to myself.

Focusing back on Bink and Sparrow, I heard him ask her, "And you know what else?"

"No, what else?" Sparrow asked, hanging on his every word like he was the Second Coming of You Know Who.

"Well, get this. General Grant was supposed to be at Ford's Theatre with the Lincolns that night, but he ended up backing out. I forget why…but think about it. If he had been there, he might have gotten shot too, and then it would have changed the course of history as we know it. Maybe it would've meant that the Union would have lost the war. Imagine that!"

"Yeah," said Sparrow. "Imagine that! Wild!"

Then she smiled at him and said, "You know so much about history. You are freakin' blowing my mind," and Bink's face washed all red, like he had a bad sunburn, and I just rolled my eyes. *He's blushing like a schoolgirl.*

Feeling jealous and alone, which is par for the course for me, I headed outside and sat down on one of the big stone steps of the building, contemplating life and love and death and war and parents and school and road trips and girls like Sparrow.

I lost track of time just sitting there alone under the stars when the weirdest thing of all happened, something even weirder than randomly picking up Duke and Sparrow or going to the Psychedelic Menagerie or hanging out at a pot party.

A guy came out and sat down on the brownstone steps next to me. Not that the Psychedelic Menagerie or the party at Rosco's had an age requirement, but this guy looked older than the others. I hadn't noticed him until now. He was wearing bell bottom jeans and sandals with a collarless white embroidered Nehru shirt. I had seen such styles on TV. In the dark of the night, his hair, tied back in a ponytail, looked like it was blond.

"What's happenin', man?" he asked, blowing a puff of smoke into the summer night.

"Not much," I said.

"Loud in there, huh?"

I chuckled. "You got that right."

"Too loud for me," he added. "And for you too, I'm guessing."

I just nodded.

"You look like you're feeling blue."

"Do I?" I asked, knowing he was right.

"I get it, man. Life can be a bummer."

"Is it that noticeable?" I asked, making no attempt at pretense.

"I noticed you inside," he continued, "bouncing around the room like a squirrel who's looking for a place to hide but can't find a tree anywhere."

"I was, uhm...just trying to, you know, like, remain anonymous because I don't know hardly a soul in there."

He sat there nodding and smoking, but he didn't reply.

"Yeah," I continued, "I'm just here because I picked up a couple of hitchhikers back in Connecticut. Their names are Duke and Sparrow."

"Duke and Sparrow," he repeated. "Yeah, I know them. I mean, I've known Duke for a few years. Smart dude. Fought in Nam."

"Yes, he told me."

"Connecticut, huh? I grew up in Connecticut. What part of Connecticut do you hail from?"

"Shelton."

"Wild, man. Seymour, here. The Valley, baby!"

I felt that surge of excitement so typical of bumping into someone on a trip by happenstance who hails from the same orbit as you.

"Wow," I said. "How long ago did you leave Seymour?"

"Oh, God, a l-o-o-o-n-g time ago." He stretched the word out with great irony in his tone.

"You didn't like the Valley?"

"Well, let's just say that the Valley didn't like me." He flicked ashes on the step below and then ground them into the stone stair with the toe of his sandal.

"How come?"

He parroted me once again. "How come?" and then repeated it again and again, "How come? How come? How come?" as if it was an unsolvable mystery.

I just figured that he was high like everyone else, so I left it alone and looked up at the moon hanging in the sky like a distant street lantern.

It surprised me when he broke the silence because I figured we had said what we had to say to each other.

"So what brings you to the Village? What are you looking for?" he asked.

This guy had the good looks of a movie star...of a Robert Redford or a Paul Newman.

His questions knocked me off balance. "I'm not looking for anything exactly...or, I don't know, maybe I am, but I don't realize it."

"I dig it, man. So, you're traveling alone?"

"Oh no, not at all. I'm traveling with a guy. He's inside talking to Duke's girlfriend, Sparrow. His name is Kevin. Well, I call him Bink, actually."

He chuckled. "Bink, huh? Interesting name."

"Yeah, I guess."

"So you and this Bink. You're a couple, huh?"

That was when an alarm went off in my head, and I realized what he was suggesting.

"Oh! You mean, am I...am I...am I..."

He could see that I couldn't get it out, so he smiled and said, "Yes, that's what I mean. Bink is your boyfriend, right?"

"Oh, no! No...no...no – not at all! Not me! Not even a little bit! Sorry. I didn't realize that's what you...I mean, when you said –"

"Relax, man...relax. It's okay. It's cool. It's just – a hunch I had about you."

What are you talking about? I wanted to say. *A hunch about me? Why would you have a hunch about me?*

He needed to have a hunch about Bink, not me. Bink's the one with a crazy notion in his head about being a homosexual.

"Sorry," I said. "I didn't mean to get so worked up. It's just that I'm as straight as an arrow, like the saying goes. I'm surprised it wasn't, well...obvious."

I felt stupid, knowing I was rambling.

With some amusement, he said, "Well, not *completely* obvious. It's not like all gay people have the same traits. But, look, it's cool, man. Let's drop it. I was just making conversation. I wasn't hitting on you. I just wondered if...well, forget it. Let's just shake hands and forget I even mentioned it. Let's just be friends. My name is Vincent Demski. Yours?"

It hit me that Vincent was, in fact, what I was so vehemently trying to convince him I was not.

"I'm Gabriel DeMarco," I offered tentatively. He reached out and gave my hand a good, firm shake. I was pretty sure shaking his hand wouldn't turn me gay.

"DeMarco from Shelton?" he said, tilting his head as if he was trying to recall an errant memory. "Hmmm...I used to know a girl from Shelton. She had a boyfriend named DeMarco. As far as I know, they got hitched after the war. Her name was Cecelia."

"I'll bet it's a coincidence," I offered, "but Cecelia is my mom's name."

"Her name was Cecelia Alberino, right?"

"Exactly!" That surge of excitement born of familiarity ignited again.

"Wow! What a coincidence."

"It sure is," I said.

"Who would have ever thought? We stayed in touch for a while after I moved here to the city, but after the war ended, we stopped seeing each other and writing. You know how those things are. People always say they're going to stay in touch, and then they don't."

"Oh yeah," I said, able to relate. I had lost touch with people.

"Yeah, sure. You look a lot like her." Then he chuckled. "She was very beautiful...and, well, so good to me."

I could see him picturing her in his mind, and his eyes reflected, even in the semi-darkness, a genuine affection.

"I loved your mother."

I wondered if he had once liked girls.

As if reading my mind, he continued, "But not like that. Your dad had nothing to worry about. Hey, listen. Would you do me a very big favor? Would you tell Cecelia that we met? Tell her that I'm doing well...that I'm making art here in the Village and selling some of it...and that I'm, well, getting by. Tell her that for me, will you?"

"Sure, I'd be happy to. I can't wait to tell her."

Our conversation was interrupted by the sound of Bink's voice behind us. "Oh, there you are. Whattaya doing?"

"Nothing much, just talking. Bink, this is Vincent. Vincent, meet my friend Bink."

The two shook hands as I added, "And listen to this one, Bink. Vincent is an old friend of my mom's. What are the chances?"

"Crazy," Bink agreed.

"Well, listen, you guys," Vincent said, as he dragged himself up from the steps. "Let me get out of your way. I'm so glad I followed you out here, Gabriel. I can't even tell you. Some things are just meant to be, aren't they?"

"For sure," I agreed.

"Okay, guys. I'm going to get back inside. Good luck finding whatever you're looking for."

As he entered the brownstone again, I wondered what my mother would say when I told her I had met an old friend of hers. It was hard to believe, considering how different he was from her. I'd have to ask her how they knew each other.

I also marveled at how Vincent appeared to know that I was looking for something. In two days, two people whom I had never set eyes on appeared to see through me. First Duke and now Vincent. Was I so transparent that utter strangers could see things in me that I couldn't see in myself?

CHAPTER 29

Bink sat down on the step vacated by Vincent.

"What happened to Sparrow?" I asked, not without a twinge of jealousy.

"Duke yelled for her."

"Oh."

A speeding police car, its siren screaming, rudely interrupted our conversation.

Finally, Bink said, "Yeah, I guess he wanted her to smoke a joint with him, so that's what she's doing."

"I saw her smoking a pipe while you were talking to her."

He considered my remark. "I guess she smokes a lot of pot, but it doesn't seem to change how nice she is."

"Didn't they invite you to join them?" I asked.

Bink just shrugged. He may have been holding back tears.

I realized that if we were back in Connecticut, we'd be hearing the sounds of crickets in the night instead of a constant stream of cars driving by, impatient horns beeping, and the police siren fading in the distance.

Forgetting Bink, I drifted off into some private cubicle of the mind. It's crazy how my mind often does whatever it wants, traveling to unknown places or playing tricks with me. The sound of the siren conjured up, for me, a poem by Wallace Stevens I had read in poetry class. At the time, it didn't resonate with me. But now, without warning, it did.

The night knows nothing of the chants of night.
It is what it is as I am what I am:
And in perceiving this I best perceive myself...

My mind drifted to some far off place, and Bink had to reel me in. "Gabe? Gabe? Gabe?"

"Huh...oh, sorry," I said. "My mind went some –"

"Hey, guess what, Gabe," Bink said, not missing a beat.

"What?"

"I think I have a crush on Sparrow. She's amazing." His face still reflected his pain.

I could relate. Despite meeting an old friend of my mother's, I was still feeling pretty down myself. And I wasn't going to admit it out loud, but I had feelings for Sparrow too.

I let out a deep sigh. "You're right. Sparrow's a gone girl. No doubt about it."

"What do you mean? Gone girl?" Bink had obviously never read Kerouac.

"Oh...it's just a beatnik expression. Forget I said it."

"Gone," he repeated. "Is that good?"

"Oh yes, Bink. It's good. It's *very* good."

Hearing him say he had a crush on someone I had realized, just a few hours ago, that I had a crush on too bummed me out big time. It didn't surprise me, though, since Bink and I had been vying for Sparrow's attention since meeting her. An image of Duke flashed through my mind. Competing with my friend for a girl that wasn't even available didn't make any sense.

"Yeah, well, good luck with that, Bink. If she breaks up with Duke, maybe some Saturday afternoon in September you kids can get hitched, then get yourselves a house in the suburbs, a station wagon, a cocker spaniel, and have a pack of kids."

The nuance and irony in my tone lost on him, Bink said, "I'd like that."

I controlled an urge to laugh out loud. *Wow, for a smart guy, he can sure be thick.*

Then I told Bink how I didn't feel we fit in at Rosco's and I suggested we take a little walk around the block. Bink didn't disagree, because besides Sparrow, who was he going to talk to there? As we strolled down the street, Bink launched into more amazing Civil War facts because he was so jazzed about his chat with Sparrow that he couldn't stop talking about it. He started spouting some nonsense about how the Lincoln assassination was part of a bigger plot. The murders of Grant, Vice President Andrew Johnson, and some other dude were all part of the plan. I forget the other guy's name, because truthfully, I was half listening. My mind was elsewhere – that dark hideaway that I alone have access to.

Besides, sometimes the best thing to do with a kid like Bink is let him blab on and on and just pretend you're listening. You just nod now and then or say something like "Oh yeah?" or "Oh, interesting." Either works. That technique is going to be in a book I'll write some-day, *How to Listen to Boring People*.

Speaking of acting like you're listening, that's exactly what I did when we got back to Rosco's place. For the next hour or so until things fizzled out, I sidled up to one group or another just like I had been doing earlier and tried to act like I belonged there, because what else was I supposed to do? Bink did pretty much the same thing, except at one point when he and Sparrow started talking again. I didn't have the stomach to listen in to their conversation. I had heard all I would ever want to know about the Civil War.

What bugged me most was that Sparrow never once tried to get me high. That may sound paradoxical given that I had no intention of ever getting high, but the least she could have done is *tried* like she promised. It's weird to wish someone would try to get you to do something you don't want to do, but that's how it was for me with Sparrow.

I don't remember what time it was when things finally calmed down. The truth is that I had gotten a little drunk after downing four or five beers. I don't even love drinking, but it's a way to feel less out of place.

I passed Duke in the kitchen when I grabbed my last bottle of beer from the fridge and, feeling no pain, I asked, "Hey, Duke. I was listening to you earlier talking about Nixon and the war and all that stuff."

"Yeah?" he said, a blunt in one hand and a bottle of Johnnie Walker Red in the other.

"Yeah...so I was, like, admiring your passion. I mean, you're against the war, you know, in a *big* way!" He still didn't know that I had heard him speak at the rally at Southern.

"Listen, man," he said, with a weary irony, "you probably won't get this, but nobody hates war more than an ex-soldier." I watched Duke stumble away and realized that he was wasted.

I don't even remember conking off, but when I opened my tired eyes the next morning, every part of me ached. That's because Bink and I slept on the floor atop a musty old Oriental rug. I scanned the room and saw that something like ten or twelve people had crashed at Rosco's. Duke and Sparrow slept on a couch nearby, and I noticed that neither of them had a stitch of clothing on except for underwear. There they lay in repose, a sleeping tangle of arms and legs, his thick and hairy, hers slender and soft. I wondered if, before falling asleep, they "did it" in full view of anyone who was still conscious. As I got my bearings, I began wishing it were my arms and legs wrapped up in Sparrow's, but I shook off that unlikelihood. I was dying for a drink of water because that dusty old rug had dried me out completely. The only one awake, I stumbled toward the bathroom, stepping over various bodies that littered the floor. There was even a girl curled up like a sleeping cat on the cracked tile floor in the kitchen.

As I guzzled water from the bathroom faucet, I prepared myself for the probability that I was never going to see Sparrow again. In fact, as people slowly rolled out of bed and off of couches and chairs or dragged themselves off the floor, I got Bink to hurry up and prepare to get back on the road. I hoped we could take off before Sparrow untangled herself from Duke, because I wasn't in the mood for any emotional goodbyes.

As Bink was brushing his teeth, though, Sparrow, wearing just her shirt and underpants, tip-toed over to me and said in a hushed voice, "Hey, Gabe, Duke and I were just wondering if you'd let us join you further on."

"Further on where?"

"I don't know. Where are you guys heading for?"

"Florida, maybe. I was thinking Fort Lauderdale...unless we run out of money first."

I was working hard to maintain eye contact and not stare down at her bare legs and feet.

"Florida sounds good. Or wherever." She pushed a ten dollar bill into my hand. "Duke says take this for gas. And if we get low on bread, we can find a city and sing on a street corner to get some more. Oh, and you know, if we decide to split before Florida, like if something catches our fancy, we'd like to do that, if that's okay."

What could I say? No? Duke was nobody's fool. He knew I wasn't going to refuse Sparrow. And I knew Bink would love the idea too.

We packed everyone's gear in the trunk of the Corvair and headed onto I-95 South. Lucky for us that Sparrow and Duke traveled light. *They probably just keep a couple pounds of marijuana and their toothbrushes in their backpack,* I thought to myself.

Now back on the road, I imagined myself marrying Sparrow, or it might be more accurate to say, I imagined myself telling my dad I was going to marry her.

"Right, Dad," I'd say. "Her real name is Sparrow."

Dad would reply in irritation. "What idiot would name their kid after a bird?"

"Well, I know it's a little unusual, but look at it this way. Frank Zappa named his kid 'Moon Unit,' so you never know."

"Who in the name of Christ is Frank Zappa?"

"Never mind," I'd reply. "Anyway, she goes by Sparrow now, and I love her."

"So you're saying I'm going to have a daughter-in-law named Sparrow DeMarco?"

"That's right."

"And what the hell are you going to name your kids?"

"Dad...Dad, you're getting way ahead of yourself. Let's take one step at a time."

"And where will this wedding take place? In a church, I hope."

"Well, that's the other thing. We don't believe in God, exactly, so we want to get married in the woods."

"What the hell are you talking about?"

"You know...in the woods, like at Boy Scout camp. Sparrow wants to feel in harmony with nature."

And the conversation would continue this way until he yelled at me and told me I had to go to bed.

As we crossed over the George Washington Bridge into New Jersey, I could see Sparrow nuzzled into Duke's muscular shoulder. She was out like a light. Duke must have tired her out. It occurred to me that, sweet as she was, maybe Sparrow wasn't the girl for me. At that moment, I questioned my deepest feelings. I thought of my mother who likes to say that someone is "in love with *love*." What she means is that a person isn't so much in love with another person but with the *idea* of being in love. Maybe it was true of me, I realized. Maybe I was mistaking infatuation for love. I'd have to mull that one over as I traveled on with Sparrow.

CHAPTER 30

Driving on I-95 has to be the most boring thing in the world. With cars zooming by on both sides and Mack trucks, their long trailers swaying in the thick summer heat like they're going to whip right into you, you could just about die. As we continued, my mind wandered. I wondered where everyone was racing to. Maybe to visit friends or relatives. Maybe a few were on vacation or on road trips like us, but I didn't suppose that was very many. Maybe some were on the way to work. Maybe some were already working. Especially those in trucks. Especially those in eighteen wheelers. You could lose your mind driving on a hot day, wondering about every stupid thing that enters your mind.

After two or three hours, I was getting tired of driving, and Duke offered to take the wheel.

"I love to drive," he said. "I can drive for twelve hours, no sweat, without even blinking."

My father's like that too. I feel most men are like that, and it makes me wonder what's wrong with me that I can't drive for hours on end without getting tired. Maybe Vincent's mistaken impression of me wasn't too far off.

The good thing is we pulled into a rest stop somewhere in southern New Jersey or Delaware, and the two of us switched places. Before Bink could make a move, I jumped in the back with Sparrow. Duke drove with just his right hand and stuck his hairy left arm out of the side window, letting it hang in the breeze like I've seen my father do.

It felt weird heading for nowhere because, without a destination or a goal, I was wondering where to stop and what the point of the trip was. Another game my mind was playing on me. A road trip had sounded like a cool idea, but now I was having my doubts.

The temperature must have been close to a hundred degrees, and the hot air was dense and oppressive. Since we didn't have air-conditioning, we had driven all that way without conversation, just the eight-track blaring. Talking would have been an exercise in futility. With the car cruising at seventy miles an hour and the hot air from the open windows blowing in our faces, it was next to impossible to hear each other.

It turned out I wasn't in the back with Sparrow for more than twenty minutes or so when she leaned over and rested her head in my lap, apparently still feeling sleepy. Or maybe she was tired of having the wind blow in her face like an overheated hair dryer. All I knew was that her head was in my lap, and I was having trouble thinking straight. Sparrow seemed comfortable enough, though. She snuggled up, her bare feet against the black upholstered armrest on one side of the car and her head nestled comfortably on my leg. I couldn't tell if she was awake or asleep.

And Duke must have seen, in the rearview mirror, that her head was no longer visible, but he seemed unfazed. Conversely, Bink couldn't have hidden his displeasure if he tried. He shifted his weight about seven times, and then turned away and looked out the passenger window.

But my pleasure was equal to his apparent irritation. In fact, I was just about the happiest I'd been since we left Duchess. Sparrow stayed right where she was for miles and miles as we passed by immense billboards, industrial plants, towering wooden water tanks, and infinite lengths of electrical lines, stretching across the landscape like oversized black licorice.

After what must have been almost two hours of silence, except for the music of the *Déjà Vu* album by Crosby, Stills, Nash, and Young blasting from the eight-track accompanied by the annoying duet of wind blowing and truck engines droning as they passed us, Duke pulled into a rest stop, announcing it was time to get something to eat.

Sparrow yawned and stretched, her hair on the side of her head wet from sweating on my shorts. She wiped the dampness with her little palm and said, "Whew...I fell asleep. I hope you didn't mind."

"No. It was okay with me," I said, which was the understatement of the year, but I played it down a little because I didn't want to seem too excited.

The rest stop had a McDonald's. You're likely to see a McDonald's pretty much anywhere. Michael had been to the Bahamas last summer, and he was surprised to see a McDonald's there. Even though Duchess is similar, I don't think there are any Duchess stores outside of Connecticut, never mind in Delaware or the Bahamas.

When we sat down in the booth, it seemed odd that Sparrow sat next to me instead of Duke. But I wasn't about to complain.

As we got started on our burgers and fries, Sparrow started a conversation about music, talking about how into Joni Mitchell she was, which sure surprised me.

"Wow, she's my favorite too," I said.

And Sparrow gave me one of those adorable pushes in the chest and said, "Get outta town."

"No, seriously. A year ago at my senior banquet, this girl I know told me a lot about her and I've been obsessed with her ever since. I've even got two of her tapes in my car. Did you notice?"

Bink tried to jump in with, "I like John Denver a lot. I've got four of his albums," which made me wince and elicited raised eyebrows from both Duke and Sparrow.

Sparrow overrode him, though. "Get lost. You have two of Joni's albums and didn't even tell us? You're gonna get it!"

"Oh, yeah. I have *Clouds* and *Blue*."

"Groovy," she said, "we'll have to listen to them when we get back on the highway."

Seeing how amped Sparrow was, I started telling her about how Bink and I had gone to Carnegie Hall to see Joni but how we didn't get in. I mean, I gave her the whole ugly story like I was describing the latest horror film to hit the silver screen, and when Bink threw in his two cents, chewing on his fries and saying, "Gabe was ready for the psych ward that night," and "He was one hundred percent certifiable," I found myself blushing.

Then the most interesting thing of all happened. Duke jumped in and said, "Well, I heard Joni's gonna be performing at the Blue

Ridge Mountain Folk Festival. I think it's happening right about now."

I couldn't believe what I had just heard.

"The Blue Ridge Mountain Folk Festival?" I said. "Where is that? What state?"

"Not sure. The Blue Ridge Mountains run through several states, but I think the festival is in North Carolina, maybe near Asheville. We can figure it out, but it's a little off the beaten path if you're heading for Florida."

"We don't care about Florida, do we, Bink? We'd rather see Joni Mitchell, right?"

"Not if you're going to flip out like you did in New York," Bink said, being totally unhelpful.

"Well, can we get tickets?" I asked.

"We could try," Duke answered. "What's the use of life if you don't try?"

It seemed like plan B had materialized with no special effort on my part. I couldn't have planned it better if I had tried, and I couldn't have been more excited.

Soon enough we were back in the car, but now Bink had jumped in the back seat, which threw me for a loop. As I tried to counter this chess move of his, Sparrow jumped right into her usual place in the back seat, relegating me to riding shotgun. I was miffed as I slammed my door shut. *I guess that's the end of Sparrow sleeping in my lap.*

As Duke navigated onto I-95, Bink struck up a conversation with Sparrow.

"It doesn't look like the Mets are going to win another pennant."

What the hell makes the guy think Sparrow cares about the Mets? I asked myself.

Sparrow was sitting behind me so I couldn't even see her. "Aw, that's too bad," she said, real concerned-like.

"Yeah, I'm bummed out because they might not even make the playoffs again."

"Again?" she asked.

"Yeah, well, they didn't make the playoffs last fall either." He couldn't have sounded sadder.

"Oh, I'm sorry," Sparrow offered, almost like it was her fault.

"Yeah, that's okay," Bink assured her. "But, I'm just disappointed, you know, because it's very unlike two seasons ago which was amazing."

"Amazing, huh?" she asked. "How so?" She had to ask!

Of course, Bink rambled on for, like, another hour, about how in '69 "the Amazin' Mets," huge underdogs, took the Orioles in the World Series in only five instead of seven games, singing the praises of pitchers Tom Seaver and Jerry Koosman and carrying on about great catches by center fielder Tommy Agee and other boring crap no one would want to hear about. No one, that is, except Sparrow who was unfathomably enraptured with the whole conversation.

When we stopped again because Bink had to use the bathroom, Sparrow went and sat on a patch of grass adjacent to the parking lot.

I flopped down next to her and said, "I'm surprised that you're such a baseball fan."

"I'm not," she said. "I don't know a thing about baseball."

"Well, you'd never know it. For the last hour, all you did was encourage Bink to keep talking about the dumb Mets."

She must have detected the irritation in my voice, because she said, "I was just trying to be nice. It doesn't cost anything to be nice to people."

She told me, I guess. Her remark made me think of Gordon Weed from Southern. Maybe there was, like, an oath flower children took, like the Boy Scout Oath:

A hippie is trustworthy, loyal, helpful, friendly, courteous, kind, obedient, cheerful, thrifty, brave, clean, and reverent...and interested in anything anyone has to say, no matter how boring or dumb it is.

It appeared to me that people like Sparrow and Gordon Weed, appropriately named, had smoked *so* much weed that they couldn't distinguish between an interesting person and a boring one. I buttoned up and withdrew.

When Bink got back from the bathroom, I told Duke I wanted to drive, which I hoped would take my mind off of my annoyance and also hoped would put Duke back in his rightful place next to Sparrow. But Duke manned the shotgun position, and it was more endless banter from Bink in the back seat. Now he was talking about working at Duchess and how he and I used to have to clean up garbage from the parking lot. And Sparrow continued to listen as if Bink was about to reveal the mystery of the afterlife.

As we headed toward Baltimore, Bink was somehow able to talk and keep an eye on the map at the same time. He told me to follow signs for I-495 and the Woodrow Wilson Bridge, which would take us into Maryland. It occurred to me that it would be expedient to try to find a place to sleep for the night. I suppose, with Duke and me taking turns, we could have driven on indefinitely, but I needed to get Bink out of the back seat and away from Sparrow.

CHAPTER 31

Passing through Richmond on the highway in the late afternoon, we saw a green sign that said Campgrounds. Duke said we could maybe rent a cabin or cottage, or even a couple of tents, which would be even cheaper. I had done my share of camping as a Boy Scout, so I didn't mind the idea. Maybe I'd be able to zip Bink up in a tent and slap a padlock on it.

When we got off the exit, we followed signs for Pine Meadows Campground. We rented two tents, a mere five bucks each. Then Duke suggested that he and Bink take the Corvair and go hunt down a store where they could buy some hotdogs and marshmallows to roast, if I didn't mind.

If I didn't mind? Being left alone with Sparrow? I didn't want to sound overly enthusiastic. "That's fine, I guess," I said. "That okay with you, Sparrow?" She smiled and nodded.

Once alone, she and I made our way down a woodsy path. She took her sandals off and walked barefoot along a carpet of golden pine needles, softened from age.

Walking a step in front of me, she said, "Don't these trees blow your mind?"

"Oh yeah...for sure," I replied, thinking about how I'd spent summer after summer in the wilderness and never thought of a single tree as blowing my mind. Now, I took a good look, marveling at the strong round trunks of some reaching skyward and the gnarled torsos of others growing crooked in zigzag patterns despite intermittent patches of rotted bark. *Trees seem to grow no matter what,* I concluded.

We continued under the leafy canopy until we saw a lake through the opening at the edge of the woods. I followed close behind her as she made her way toward the water. Except for the sweet sound of birds chirping, there were no other sounds. And there didn't seem to be any people.

After passing beyond the trees, Sparrow took a seat in the grass.

"Whew," she said. "It's so hot, isn't it?"

"Yeah, sure is," I agreed.

"Taking a little swim would sure be refreshing."

It wasn't the worst idea I'd ever heard, but I realized that neither of us had bathing suits.

"You wanna come in with me?" she asked. And then she stood up and let her long skirt fall to the ground. When she followed that move by lifting her tank top up and over her head, it startled me more than just a little, especially considering she wasn't wearing a bra. What a vision she was, standing about five feet away from me in just her underwear. But not for long because in a flash she dropped those too and headed into the water.

"C'mon," she called to me.

It hit me that this was the first time I had ever seen a completely naked girl in real life. I mean, I'd seen girlie magazines, but this was different because nudity in the light of day wasn't the same as nudity on a glossy page. It felt less seedy and forbidden.

Now chest deep in water, her small breasts were semi-obscured by the green lake water. "Are you going to be a drip or come take a dip with me?" she yelled. "C'mon, silly. It's refreshing!"

This is my moment of truth, I realized. *Am I going to stay on the shore all my life or am I going to jump in the water?* Part of my hesitation was due to the fact that I was feeling excited, which was embarrassing. So I took my shoes and shirt off, and I walked down into the water in my shorts until I was waist high.

"Not fair. You have to take off your shorts!"

Now feeling safer because I was in the water, I pulled off my shorts and underwear and flung them back onto the shore.

"That's better," Sparrow chirped.

When I reached her, she added, "Wow, you're majorly uptight, aren't you? You need to learn to live in the moment, Gabriel."

It seemed like good enough advice, but it occurred to me that no one had ever recommended that I try living in the moment before, not my parents or teachers or anyone else. Sparrow, on the other hand, seemed to live in the moment whether it was swimming in the lake, enjoying the trees, or listening to Bink ramble.

The two of us frolicked in the water, playing tag and swimming underwater with our eyes open, seeing who could stay underwater longer. At one point, she asked me to carry her, so I reached my arms out and held my right arm under her knees and my left under her shoulders. She was buoyant and weightless, so I just walked around, tip-toeing on the surface of the lake, thinking, *I have a naked girl in my arms.*

What surprised me, though, was that it wasn't sexual or anything like that. I had heard guys talk about girls and their breasts and nipples and pubic hair and the whole nine yards, but it was always about sexy stuff. But Sparrow had an innocence and a way of trusting me to just let go without it needing to be more than that, which helped me to feel less inhibited than I felt when she had first removed her clothes.

When we came out of the water, we sat on the grass beyond the shore letting ourselves air dry while we talked for a good, long while. The two of us relaxed in our own idyllic Garden of Eden, me playing Adam to Sparrow's Eve.

I ended up pretty much spilling everything, about my issues at home, about feeling like I had been forced to go to Southern, about girlfriends who didn't work out, about how Jeff and Tomaso were both in the military, and about how alone I felt. I even told her about relatives and friends who had died in the last few years and how death was freaking me out.

She listened to me Sparrow-style, but I hoped she found what I had to say more interesting than Bink's rambling. As usual, her eyes spoke to me, telling me she cared about how I felt and what I had to say.

I don't know how long we had been talking, but the sun was almost down now, and we had reached that moment when dusk was just about to segue into nightfall.

I shouldn't have been, but I was taken by surprise when Sparrow grabbed her bag and pulled out a joint.

"Remember how I said I was going to get you high?" she asked, holding it up, with a sincere smile on her face, like she was displaying it in a TV commercial.

"Yes," I replied, and it was weird, but I was now feeling a little vulnerable and a little emotional.

"I think this is the time, don't you?" A momentary silence was broken by the clarion wail of a loon sending a message from across the glassy lake next to the conical spires of evergreens. A moment later, another loon in the distance answered. In my mind, the two birds were calling to me. *Don't worry...it's alright.*

Sparrow didn't wait for my answer but instead took a lighter and held it up to the end of the joint. Then she closed her eyes and inhaled the smoke into her lungs like a sacrament, before releasing it. She looked at me with those big round eyes of hers and reached out her hand to me, offering the joint.

There was something so real about the placid water, the real moaning of the loons, and mostly, the real way she looked at me. Real, as in I lost all sense of time. Real, as in I wasn't hearing any voice in my head telling me what to do or not do. Real, as in I was naked and she was naked and we were also both, perhaps, feeling emotionally naked as well.

"It's not that I don't want to," I said, "it's just that...just that... I've never even smoked a cigarette...and..."

Sparrow just nodded like she understood completely, but she didn't withdraw her hand. She just looked into my eyes with a look that spoke for itself. *It's all going to be okay.*

I was planning to never smoke pot, but I gazed at her perfect naked body, her perfect breasts and her perfect stomach and her perfect pubic hair and her perfect legs and feet and her sparkling green eyes (*Guinnevere had green eyes...*) and, almost in a trance, I reached out and took the joint between my thumb and index finger and brought it to my lips.

"Just inhale and hold it in for a little bit," she whispered. "For five or ten seconds. Then release slowly. You'll feel better."

I did what she said, and then for the next twenty minutes or so, we sat together, talking and passing the joint back and forth, and the conversation turned to more intimate matters. Sparrow told me about her family life and how her parents got divorced when she was twelve.

"It sucked at the time, but like Duke says, it doesn't really matter. My mom and dad are just a couple of materialistic assholes, and I don't care if I never fucking see them again."

With her being so open, I told her how behind I felt, still being a virgin.

"Virginity isn't such a bad thing," she said. "I was only fourteen when I lost mine. A guy pressured me at a party. I mean, he actually forced himself on me, but I guess it was my fault because I didn't do anything to stop him."

"Wait," I said. "That doesn't sound like it was your fault to me." And I really meant it, but at the same time, I felt a loopiness – a contradictory, light-headed happiness that might have been the result of smoking pot. It felt different from being drunk.

Sparrow's eyes met mine. "That's nice of you to say. Anyway, after that, there were, well, lots of guys."

Then came the biggest surprise of all. Still maintaining eye contact with me, she looked vulnerable and sad. "Would you like to make love to me, Gabriel?" she asked, and it felt like the most honest thing anyone had ever said to me.

"Here? Now?"

"This is as good a place as any. And there's no better time than now."

"What about Duke?" My eyes must have been spiraling in their sockets.

"We have an understanding. Duke says if we want to 'be' with someone else, we always have that freedom. Trust me when I say I don't often feel like I want to, even though Duke does pretty frequently – but it's how I feel right now, Gabriel."

I let out a big sigh because, despite how good I was feeling and how magical the moment felt, I hesitated. "This may sound strange, but there's someone else I'm worried about besides Duke."

"Who?" she asked, puzzled.

"It's Bink." I heard my voice crack. "Bink is in love with you, and if we do this, I can't even imagine how hurt he'll be."

"What if he never knows?" she asked.

"He'll know. He'll be able to read it in my eyes."

Hearing that, Sparrow smiled and shook her head. "You blow my mind, Gabriel. I don't know very many guys like you. To think you care about a friend enough to pass up an opportunity to be with someone you're into. You are into me, right?"

I just nodded and closed my eyes because sometimes the truth can't be spoken in words.

She smiled. "A girl can tell these things. And I'm into you too. I was practically from the moment I met you."

Then Sparrow surprised me again. Moving onto her knees, she gave me one long, passionate kiss on the lips. "Don't let him read that kiss in your eyes," she whispered in the cutest way, breaking the tension and making us both giggle.

She hugged me, and the two of us laid down in the soft grass and held each other, wrapped in a safe, silent embrace for a long time. As I said, because I had heard guy-talk, and because I had seen photos in magazines, I had a picture in my mind of what lovemaking was going to be like with a beautiful, naked girl. But this was another kind of loving.

I'm not sure if she noticed, but tears welled up in my eyes and slowly rolled down my cheeks. It wasn't an ugly, sobbing cry or anything dramatic like that, but a soft, cleansing one. Sensing how emotional I felt, Sparrow held me in her wings just a little longer.

Finally, she took a deep breath in and then let it out. "You're a beautiful soul, Gabriel," she whispered. "And I want you to know that if you change your mind while we're traveling together, the offer still stands."

In life, there are different kinds of silences – early morning silences, sad silences, pouty silences, awkward and uncomfortable silences, even contemplative silences. This was a profound silence, the kind that words cannot fill. Our eyes stayed connected as we put our clothes back on. Sparrow took my hand in hers and we walked back to the campsite. It wasn't the first time I had held a girl's hand, of course, but I felt as if it was the most important time. I wasn't sure if I was high from the weed or from the experience we had shared.

My hand in hers, we walked in the near darkness. *The offer still stands* echoed in my mind. I doubted I'd take advantage of it, but I felt all warm and nourished inside. Sparrow made me feel like I mattered, like a pretty girl could like me, or maybe even love me.

CHAPTER 32

Approaching the campsite, I could see Bink and Duke, aglow in front of a flickering fire. In the darkness, I felt Sparrow release my hand. The tents were pitched and ready, although I guessed Duke was mainly responsible. They had also fried up some hotdogs which were scorched from the fire, the fat skin swollen and ready to burst. Duke remarked how hungry we must be, and he plopped a couple of dogs onto charred buns and handed them to us. What Duke didn't do was ask us a single question about what we had been up to. I guess Sparrow and Duke didn't ask each other questions. Bink's face, on the other hand, had accusations written all over it, but I tried to give him a look that said, *You have nothing to worry about.*

I couldn't worry about Bink now, though. I went to work on my hotdog, feeling very mellow as I bit into the juicy morsel. I wondered if I was high, and decided I felt so good that I wasn't going to worry about that either.

After we ate a few more hotdogs, we relaxed around the fire and roasted marshmallows. Of course, Bink wasted no time engaging Sparrow in another conversation, this time about Pearl Harbor. Personally, I was zoned out, just watching the orange flames pop and crackle.

With the fire burned down to hot glowing coals, Duke took his guitar and started strumming an unusual chord progression. With the faint firelight on his face, he sang out:

Hare Krishna, Hare Krishna, Krishna Krishna, Hare Krishna

Bink clammed up as Sparrow's sweet voice echoed the same lyric. Then Duke sang:

Hare Rama, Hare Rama, Rama Rama, Hare Rama

Once again, Sparrow bounced the tune and the words back to him. The melody didn't sound like anything I'd ever heard before. Rather, it felt like music from a strange and exotic place. The two of them, ever so calmly, continued to sing their call and response chant...from one to the other again and again. For me, it was like a spacy ping-pong ball floating from one side of a net to the other. Maybe it was the pot I had smoked, but their gentle, spirit-filled chanting lulled me into a trance. I was oblivious to how Bink was reacting, nor did I care.

After Duke and Sparrow faded into silence, Bink broke the serene mood. "Are you two Hare Krishnas?"

"We honor the divinity of Krishna," Duke replied.

"So, like, you're in a cult?" Bink asked, very defensively. "I've seen them on TV with their white robes and their shaved heads. But you guys don't have shaved heads."

"It's no cult," Duke said. I couldn't read whether he was amused or annoyed. "Krisha and Rama are Hindu deities, and Hinduism is one of the world's great religions, older than Christianity."

Bink persisted. "But by singing that, aren't you worshiping a false god?"

I wished he'd lay off.

"Wow," Duke replied, "you're even more brainwashed than I thought."

Now Bink squeezed his eyes closed tightly. "What do you mean brainwashed? How could we be brainwashed?"

Duke sighed and said, "Look, my man. Let me spell it out for you. Don't you fuckin' realize you're only Christian by birth – because you were born in America? I hope you have the intelligence to know that if you had been born in India, you'd be Hindu. You don't see it, but you've been brainwashed about everything since the day you were expelled from your mother's womb – by your family, your school, your church, your government...by all of it."

"How do you mean?" I asked, immediately sorry I spoke.

"Gabriel," he said, "did you ever think about how, in school, you said the Pledge of Allegiance every morning or you stood for the National Anthem at baseball games? Was that a choice you made yourself, or was it a choice that was made for you by your parents, teachers, and coaches? In fact, by your society? And what did you dudes do, go to Catholic schools? Did *you* decide to make Jesus your God, or did someone decide that for you?"

"I never thought of it that way," I said, still feeling a little woozy.

"Of course you didn't...because you don't think."

He couldn't hide his irritation. I felt bad because just a few minutes before he was immersed in a tranquil state while chanting.

"You know what, man? Remember how I advised you not to enlist like your buddy? Forget I ever said that. Both of you guys should fuckin' enlist. You'll make perfect little soldiers. They love guys like you in the military. Sheep who don't question anything... even the order to kill when you don't have the slightest idea who you're killing or why."

When Bink asked, "Did you make a perfect little soldier?" Duke looked like he was going to take Bink's head off, but he just got quiet for a minute.

Finally, he almost whispered, "You don't know what happened to me and you have no idea what I saw...so don't tell me what I fuckin' was or was not."

I probably should have kept my mouth shut, but instead I said, "Well, at least you came back alive. That's good, right?"

In the campfire glow, Duke's face went all dark and gloomy. "It might have been better for me if I hadn't," he muttered.

I was stunned and didn't know how to respond to that. We sat in silence for a long time now. I looked at Sparrow, who was poking the dying embers of the fire with a stick.

"Look," he said, seeming to gather himself a bit now, "your society doesn't want you to think. It doesn't want you to question anything. That's how brainwashing works. It's fucked up, I know, but that's how it works. What do you think? That brainwashing happens only in Russia? That's what the Man would have you think, but it happens wherever there are powerful people and weaker people, wherever there are rich people and poor people."

He spat into the fire, and the coals sizzled.

"And Krishna? Whether we call the divine intelligence from which the universe has evolved God or Jesus or Ram or Krishna makes no difference. They're just names. Just words! Words are inadequate in describing the ultimate reality, so why do you care? If the word *Krishna* works for someone in the middle of India or people in the Hare Krishna movement or for Sparrow and me, so what? Why should that bother you or the fuckin' leaders of your church? It doesn't change anything. We're all part of somethin' bigger than we are, aren't we? People have been killing each other for eons over what to call it. But it's so simple. There is a greater power in the universe, and it doesn't matter...it *shouldn't* matter what label we put on it."

Those last remarks left us speechless. There didn't seem to be anything more to say. Sparrow seemed to vanish and Bink retired to our tent when I approached Duke who was now sitting alone in front of the campfire.

"Hey, Duke," I began, "I just want to apologize."

"Apologize? What for?"

"Well, you know...for having allowed myself to be brainwashed like I did."

"Don't worry about it," he said, poking the last white embers of the fire with a stick. "You couldn't help it. You were just a kid. I shouldn't have flown off the handle. I just get frustrated."

"I understand."

"Yeah, it's fine. You grew up in a small town like most people, and small towns engender small-mindedness."

"Yeah, I guess you're right."

"But you're not a kid anymore, and it's never too late to change. Chew on that."

I crawled into our tent with a lot to think about that night. As I tried to rest, I couldn't sleep. It had been quite a day for me...from skinny dipping to smoking pot to, especially, *chewing* on everything Duke had said. Looking up at my canvas ceiling, I wondered if I was still high. I didn't think so. I heard Bink's gentle snoring and realized he had drifted off, the events of his day and Duke's remarks not causing him any insomnia.

About a half hour into my sleepless malaise, I heard the sounds of heavy breathing mingled with various muted giggles and moans, and I realized that Sparrow and Duke were in the throes of passion in their tent just a few feet away. I'd be lying if I said I didn't envy Duke for a good many reasons, not the least of which was his relationship with Sparrow. I didn't drift off to sleep myself until the only thing I could hear was the pulsing rhythm of crickets and the hushed sound of my own breathing.

Even though I was the last one asleep, I was also the first one awake. Bink was still comatose, and the canvas flap on Duke and Sparrow's pup tent was sealed tight. After shaking off the sleep from my head, I remembered I had seen a phone booth outside of the campground office. It was a glass booth, just like the one at Mosci's.

I thought I would call home like my dad said I should. My dad had also given me permission to reverse the charges, which was good since I'd be calling every day.

I leaned against the glass in the booth, and I have to admit, when Mom picked up, it was good to hear her voice.

"Hey, what's shakin', Celia?" I said, hoping to mask the gloom I was feeling.

"I'll give you, what's shakin', Celia," she said, and I could hear the delight in her voice.

"Sorry I didn't get a chance to call you yesterday, but guess what."

"What?"

"I met a friend of yours the night before last."

"Oh? And who might that have been?"

She asked the question like she seriously doubted I could have met anyone she knew on a road trip.

"Well, Bink and I were at a party in Greenwich Village and –"

"Greenwich Village!" she exploded.

"Don't get rattled, Celia. We were safe. It's a long story how we got there, but listen, I met a guy who knew you a long time ago. A super good looking guy. And very nice. He said his name was Vincent."

If it was possible, I could feel my mom's throat constrict through the phone line. "Vincent? Vincent Demski?"

"Maybe. To tell you the truth, I forgot his last name. He said he was from Seymour."

And then she just repeated the name again, as if in a daze, "Vincent Demski."

"Hey Mom, did you know the guy is gay?"

Once again, she paused. "Yes," she said. "Yes...I knew."

"I mean, I don't care. It's not like he hit on me or anything."

Mom didn't respond, so I said, "He wanted me to tell you he's doing well. That he's an artist now. Was he not doing great when you knew him, Mom? And how did you know him, anyway?"

"Oh," she began tentatively, "he and I worked together at the flight suit factory and became good friends. I'll tell you more about it someday."

I pictured sitting at the kitchen table while Mom was putting on her makeup on a Saturday night, and hearing her reveal the mystery of how she and a handsome gay man had become friends.

Mom didn't ask me any more questions. I could feel her emotion in the silence, though. I wasn't about to share much more actually, not about the Psychedelic Menagerie or the fact that I went skinny dipping and smoked pot with Sparrow. I just wanted her to know that I was in northern Virginia at a campground and I was doing fine.

When we hung up, I wasn't feeling anything like fine, so I called Mary Elizabeth too. It was Sunday, so she wouldn't be in school. Since I wouldn't be able to reverse the charges, I'd need change, so I ran to the Corvair and grabbed a handful of coins out of the ashtray.

I was glad when Mary Elizabeth answered the phone. "I hope I didn't wake you up," I said.

"Get lost, Gabriel. You know I get up at the crack of dawn. But where are you? And what are you doing? And are you having fun?"

"Wait...slow down...slow down. I'm at a campground outside of Richmond, and I guess I'm having fun, but...well, maybe not fun. I feel a little down."

"Why's that?"

Then I spilled everything and I mean everything – even about hearing the sounds of Duke's and Sparrow's lovemaking.

"Wow," Mary Elizabeth said, "I feel like I'm reading a story in *True Confessions.*"

Suddenly, the operator's nasally voice interrupted, "Please insert another fifty-five cents."

So I popped a quarter and three dimes in the round slots at the top of the pay phone and said, maybe a little too desperately because

I didn't want to lose the connection, "Mary Elizabeth, are you still there?"

"Of course, I'm still here, Gabriel. What did you think? That I was going to hang up on you?"

"I forgot what we were talking about."

"We were talking about what a wild child you are now, Gabriel."

"I'm not a wild child," I said. "It's just what happened. I didn't plan any of it."

"I'm just kidding, silly. You know you can tell me anything. But when you come home, don't think you're going skinny dipping or smoking pot with me!"

"I don't think that –"

"Good, cuz that ain't happenin', Mister Big Shot! I don't smoke pot, and there's no way I skinny dip."

I could almost feel myself blushing.

"So," she continued, not missing a beat, "what's the deal with you and this Sparrow girl? Are you in love?"

"No, she's great, but I don't think I'm in love with her."

"Good, because you have a habit of falling in love with every skirt that you see."

"That's not true."

"Okay...sure it's not. So, what's next on your itinerary then?"

"That's what I wanted to tell you about. We're going to a folk festival to see Joni Mitchell. In North Carolina."

"A folk festival," Mary Elizabeth said. "How did you find out about that?"

"Duke knew about it. I told them all about how I love Joni Mitchell, and he told me about this festival. I just hope we can get tickets."

Then the operator interrupted again. "Please insert another fifty-five cents." *Geez, this lady is going to fifty-five cent me to death.*

This time, I used three dimes and five nickels which took longer to insert. I felt impatient as I listened to each coin descend into the pay phone, making a little ding as it did.

"Mary Elizabeth?" I said.

"Don't panic, I'm here...but we better hang up before you go bankrupt."

"Yeah," I said, feeling disappointed because I wanted to keep talking to her for a long time, but I knew she was right about spending all my change. I'd need it.

When I walked back down the path to our campsite, I found Duke and Sparrow outside of their tent, sitting in a cross-legged position on the ground, their palms resting facing up on their knees, and their eyes closed. I sniffed, and thought for a moment that I was smelling pot, but then I saw a stick of incense burning in front of them. I realized that they were meditating, and not wanting to disturb them, I walked over to a nearby picnic table and took a seat.

Bink was nowhere to be seen, and I wondered if he was still asleep in our tent. Sitting there in silence, I became fascinated by the idea of meditation. It made me think of how the Beatles had gotten into meditation with some guru guy in India. Soon enough, certain other celebrities followed their lead and did the same thing. Other than that, I didn't know a thing about it.

A few moments later, I saw Bink heading back from the latrine, drying his hair with a towel. I brought my index finger to my lips, warning him to be quiet and not disturb our friends. The pair finished up their meditation by doing more of their call and response chanting. This time Duke sang out, "Om Namah Shivaya" and Sparrow echoed just as the night before. Their chanting went on for about five or ten more minutes, and then they opened their eyes to see Bink and me watching them like a couple of peeping Toms.

CHAPTER 33

Driving on the three-lane highway, I felt a strong urge to ask about meditation, so I plunged in. "So, why do you guys meditate?"

Sparrow answered, "It grounds and centers me. And it quiets the overactive mind."

"Same for you, Duke?" I asked.

"Pretty much," he said. "Besides, if I didn't meditate, there's a good chance I'd kill somebody."

I laughed, but I'm not sure he was kidding.

"And how'd you guys learn to meditate?"

"Duke took me to a retreat last spring in Upstate New York led by Ram Dass. He taught us." I could see Sparrow's sincere face in the mirror as she explained.

"Ram Dass? What kind of name is that?" Bink asked.

Now Duke jumped in. "His guru gave him that name. You guys might remember him as Richard Alpert. Does that ring a bell?"

Since it rang no bell for either of us, Duke continued, "Richard Alpert and Timothy Leary? The two college professors who got fired from Harvard in '63 for experimenting with psychedelics with their students."

"Oh," I said, "I think I do remember hearing about that."

"I fuckin' hope you remember," Duke continued. "It was groundbreaking work."

Duke mustn't have realized that I was only eleven in 1963. *And how old could he have been*, I wondered. *Fourteen?* In the cloudy recesses of my memory, though, I could hear my parents and aunts and uncles flipping out because college professors were getting students high. It was a part of a growing area of concern for my parents and other adults about drug use in America. Hearing more recently that G.I.s in Vietnam were doing drugs, my mom and dad are always asking what the world is coming to.

"So did this Ram Dass guy go to the same guru in India as the Beatles?" I asked.

"Nope. His guru's name is Neem Karoli Baba. He's known as Maharaji. I suppose I can see your confusion since the Beatles' guru was the Maharishi Mahesh Yogi. Only George stuck with it, though. In fact, today George is involved with the Hare Krishna movement, since you're so interested in it." Duke seemed happy as could be to educate us on the subject.

"Oh," I said. "So, like, that guy is Ram Dass' guru and then, like, Ram Dass is your guru? Is that how it works?"

"Not exactly. Ram Dass is a teacher, but Maharaji is our guru."

"Wait," Bink said. "So you two have been to India and met... what's his name?"

"Maharaji," Duke replied. "No, we've never been to India, but we don't have to meet him in the flesh. We meet with him on the astral plane."

Despite not having the slightest idea what he meant, I wasn't about to ask him to explain further. I shifted gears a little. "What was that thing you were chanting after you meditated?"

Now Sparrow joined the conversation, all excited. "Oh, I love that mantra. 'Om Namah Shivaya.' We sing to Shiva every morning. It's such a far out way to start our day because it centers my active mind after a long night of dreaming."

"What does the mantra mean?" Bink asked.

"It could have different meanings," Sparrow continued, "like, 'salutations to the auspicious one' or 'adoration to Lord Shiva' or 'universal consciousness is one'."

"I'm confused," Bink said. "Do you worship Krishna or do you worship Shiva?"

"We don't *worship* either," Duke replied. "Krishna and Shiva are one. There is one God who goes by many names, my man. You're just confused because you think God only has one name.

The fact is, your own religion has already proven that God has more than one name, God...Jesus Christ...the Holy Ghost. You've got three right there. Besides, in Hinduism we don't consider it worshiping the divine, but rather putting our trust into a universal energy. Let's just say the two of us are karmically predisposed to Hinduism."

Whatever that meant! I mean, I didn't know a thing about Hinduism. In fact, it occurred to me that until just a few years ago, I had never even heard of it.

I drove along in the heat questioning everything I had ever been taught. I had learned just about everything I knew about God at St. Joseph's where I had gone to grade school. I can just picture telling my sixth grade teacher, Sister Mary Andrew, that another great name for God was Krishna. She would have bounced my head into the blackboard. I mean, the nuns led us to believe that it was even a sin to go into a Protestant church where they called God by the same name we did. I remember that I went to a flea market in the basement of the Congregationalist church in my neighborhood with my friend when I was a kid, and I was almost sure I was going to fry in hell for being there. It didn't make any sense. But what Duke had just said did.

We continued on in silence for the next hour or more, just suffering from the heat and listening to music. As we approached signs that said Emporia, we also saw that the traffic ahead was at a standstill. It was too hot to sit on the highway, so Duke suggested we get off and drive on an ancillary road. When we got off the closest exit, Bink looked at the road atlas and directed me to get on Route 301 south, which he said ran parallel to I-95. We hit some traffic lights on 301, when we heard a loud clump and a dragging sound under the car.

"Oh shit, man," Duke said. "What the hell?" He pulled over to the shoulder of the road where we all got out. Duke crouched down on one side of the car and I did the same on the other.

"Bad fuckin' news," Duke said. "Your muffler and tailpipe."

I could see that the rusted and flaked tailpipe was almost three-quarters detached from the muffler, which was itself dragging on the ground.

"Shit...this sucks. It looks like that U-clamp there rotted away along with the rest of the exhaust system."

"What do we do?" I asked. I didn't know a thing about car mechanics.

Duke didn't answer and went right into action. He pulled off his belt and shimmied right under the car. I helplessly watched as he wrapped the belt around the muffler and tied it up to something underneath the car.

When he slid back out, I asked, "Now what?"

"Well, you can't keep fuckin' driving with it like it is. We're gonna need to find the nearest gas station and have a mechanic see what he can do about this. What a bummer."

We got back in the car, and without a functioning muffler, the wild engine roared like a racecar in the Indianapolis 500. We continued on 301, which was a wasteland of nothing. After about twenty minutes, we saw what looked like some feeble signs of civilization.

When we saw a rickety sign that said Welcome to Garysburg, Bink said, "Wow, we've crossed into North Carolina."

A Texaco sign atop a tall pole as rusty as my broken tailpipe sat at a corner up ahead. The two other businesses on the main drag were Moe's Spirits and the Village General Store. Talk about a ghost town.

The guy at the station looked like Gomer Pyle's cousin Goober from *The Andy Griffith Show* – just as goofy looking but not as friendly. He talked like him too, with a liquid Southern drawl. I was waiting for Andy, Opie, and Aunt Bee to come pulling into the station any minute.

I told Goober about the muffler, and he said, "Just pull 'er over there, yonder, and I'll give a look when I get time."

I noticed there wasn't another car in the place. His garage bays were vacant. A moment later, a local policeman pulled in, and Goober and the cop sat in two lawn chairs outside the garage and began shooting the bull. I could see the police officer wasn't the benevolent Andy Griffith type either. He wore sunglasses and his shirt had wet stains under each arm. I don't think Andy Griffith ever perspired.

We decided to go see if we could get something to eat at the general store and found out they made sandwiches. When we came out of the store, I saw that the Corvair was up on the lift. We sat outside on a patch of grass, and Duke clarified the situation.

"They don't like us," he brooded.

"Whattaya mean?" Bink asked. "They don't even know us. Why wouldn't they like us?"

"Don't you know they're still fighting the Civil War down here? They see your Connecticut plates and our long hair, and they've got it fuckin' in for us. They hate Yankees and they hate hippies."

Just great, I thought to myself. *Now what are we supposed to do?*

I went over to see what was going on.

"Looks like you need a new exhaust," Goober said, sipping on a bottle of cola and not making eye contact with me. "You best not be driving with this defective one."

"What time do you think you can do the job?" I asked, maybe a little too impatiently.

"Well, let's see." He seemed to be about to make a big decision. "I got me some important business here with the police, don't I, Officer Davis?"

And Officer Davis, who appeared to have a gob of chewing tobacco inside his lower lip, almost smiled. "Damn straight," he said.

"Then I got to drive myself over to Roanoke Rapids to get the parts, cuz we don't carry parts for no Corvairs here, do we, Officer Davis?"

"Damn straight," Officer Davis repeated, the only two words in his vocabulary I guessed.

"Well, is that far away?" I asked, sounding too whiny.

"Hmmm, lemme see now. I'd wager it's about twenty-five minutes each way. I'll have to wait til Virgil gets here, though. Can't leave the station unattended."

"When does Virgil get here?" My patience was wearing thin, but I realized I had better keep my cool.

"Lemme see now. I think he said he was goin' fishin' today, so he should be here as soon as he's done fishin'." That remark appeared to tickle Goober's funny bone because he broke out laughing.

Oh, perfect! I looked at my watch. It was late afternoon, and we had been on the road for a good seven hours. Then I had one more question. "How much is this going to cost?"

"Hmmm, now let me see. That's a good one. I'd say about somewheres like $175, wouldn't you say so, Officer Davis?"

Officer Davis, of course, had another "damn straight" for that one.

I realized that paying that amount of money would, effectively, end our trip, since it would wipe me and Bink out pretty good. I had no idea what to do about the situation. I felt, as my mother likes to say, "caught between the devil and the deep blue sea." I didn't feel that I could call home for help or advice. Dad would just say, "I told you so."

I thought it would be a good idea to report my findings to our group. Duke would know what to do.

CHAPTER 34

After I explained the situation to Duke, he just shrugged and went into Moe's Spirits, returning a few moments later with a six-pack.

He offered us each a cold beer, although Bink declined. Then we sat in the grass in silence sucking on our bottles while Goober and Officer Davis continued to chew the fat. God only knows about what.

The policeman at last drove away as Goober took the Corvair off the lift and parked it in the lot. The next thing I knew, he was locking the bay doors and the door to the office.

I looked at Duke who shook his head in disgust. I was up on my feet and crossing the road in a flash. "Excuse me, sir," I called before I was halfway across the street, "but what's the status of my car?"

"Looks like – wait til mornin' status. Closin' time."

"Closing time?"

"Yeah, my man. Virgil never showed up after all, so we'll see ya tomorra."

"But what am I...what are *we* supposed to do?"

"Like I said, can't fix it today," he said, without a shred of pity.

"But...but...but where will we sleep?"

He tossed the keys to me unexpectedly. "I guess y'all can sleep in the car. You'll be safe enough, I reckon. There ain't been no coyote sightings lately."

Very funny!

Goober then got in his pickup and drove away, and I wasn't sure whether I wanted to cry or punch something.

As I crossed back to the group, their troubled eyes conveyed that, without hearing my conversation, they understood what went down.

Was I ever surprised when Duke shrugged, yawned, and said, "Well, man, I think Sparrow and I better split."

"Split? Split as in *leave*?" A wave of anxiety washed over me, beads of sweat trickling down the side of my face.

"Yeah. Us being here isn't helping your cause any, obviously. I'm sure those bastards don't like what you look like, but at least you're not as freaky looking as we are."

"Don't leave," I said. "We don't want you to leave, do we, Bink?"

Bink, of course, had turned green at the idea of his precious Sparrow leaving. The kid couldn't even form any words.

"Yeah, I hear ya, but Sparrow and I appreciate how great you cats have been to us. Truly. But, like I said, we're of no use to you here. And besides, this shit's a drag."

"It's a drag for us too," I complained.

"I dig it, man. But it's your car...and your karma."

"But what about Joni Mitchell?" I said.

"Who knows? Maybe we'll see you there, if that's where the road takes us." Duke started gathering his gear.

"But I don't even know where it is!"

"Just ask for directions to the Blue Ridge Mountain Parkway, head toward Asheville, and ask around."

Sparrow prepared to say her goodbye to us, and I could see her eyes well up with tears. She hugged Bink first, and it was a nice hug, but the hug she gave me was the tightest, warmest hug I've ever gotten. She squeezed and held on like she wasn't going to let go, like it was the last time we were ever going to see each other, like one of us was going to the electric chair. I had never known a girl quite like her. She was all heart.

Bink and I stood at the corner of that barren intersection and watched Duke and Sparrow walk about fifty yards up the road. They used the same technique as when we had picked them up, Duke lying in the grass and Sparrow standing there in the bush hat with her thumb in the air. The extreme heat made them seem all wavy-looking, like I was seeing them through the heat of a charcoal barbecue. They almost didn't look real, and before we knew it, a pickup truck pulled over and the two got in. I saw the truck stop, and I saw them get in, but the blistering heat made it seem like a mirage...or a dream. The wheels of the truck created an enormous billow of dust and then disappeared. It was hard to believe that we might never see Sparrow or Duke again.

Left alone to our own devices, Bink and I sat, once again, in the grass in front of the package store.

"What now?" I asked.

Bink shrugged. He wasn't going to be any help. *Why is no one any help?* I asked myself in frustration.

"Well, look," I said. "We're going to need money to pay for the repair, right? Right! So I'm going to go call my brother, okay? Okay! Maybe he can help us. Sound good? Good!"

There's nothing like having a conversation with yourself. I got up and left Bink in his catatonic stupor.

A cockeyed phone booth with one pane of glass missing stood outside the general store.

Luckily, Michael answered the phone. When the operator asked if he would accept a collect call, I chimed in with, "Yes, he will, ma'am," in case he didn't know I had Dad's permission.

"Mom and Dad there?" I asked.

Michael told me they were visiting Aunt Lucia, which was a good thing. I needed money, but I knew asking Dad for it wouldn't go well. I knew the rules.

I explained the whole fiasco to Michael, who said, "How did you manage that one?"

"Well, it's not like I did something to ruin the muffler. It just happened."

"This guy is screwing you over, big time! A new muffler shouldn't be any more than seventy-five bucks, tops."

"Well, he doesn't like us. And he's not making any secret of it."

"Okay, if they have a Western Union office in that hick town you're in, I should be able to wire you the money. I think we have an office in downtown Ansonia. I never did it before, but it's not like it's fucking rocket science. But you're going to have to pay me back."

"No sweat, I will. I'll save it up and pay you back. Promise."

I had Michael hang on while I ran in the store and asked the ancient, gray-haired owner if they did Western Union, to which he replied, "You bet we do. We're all-in-one. Groceries, post office, Western Union, you name it. But you'll have to wait until mornin' because the Western Union office ain't open on Sundays."

"But aren't you still open?" I asked, "And aren't you the Western Union office?"

"Yessiree, but Western Union ain't open on Sundays."

"But –"

"No 'buts' – Western Union can't operate on a day when banks ain't open."

I ran back, grabbed the dangling phone, and told Michael the bad news.

"That's okay. What he said makes sense. Western Union won't be open here either. I'll do it in the morning."

Then, I told him the whole saga of Sparrow and Duke – about Greenwich Village and even about the skinny dipping. I didn't tell him about smoking pot because I knew he wouldn't approve.

"You're having quite a fucking adventure for yourselves," he said with a chuckle.

"Yeah, I guess so."

"Oh, by the way. Guess who we got a letter from yesterday. Tommy Trouble. He hates Korea. It was addressed to both of us, but I opened it. Hope you don't mind."

"No, that's fine. What else did he say?"

"I don't know. He said they've trained him on some new type of warfare and something about being transported to his work station over rocky unpaved roads in the back of an army truck every day. He said it's a forty minute bumpy fucking ride each way."

"Oh God! That sounds awful."

"Yeah – the worst. Well, I better get going," Michael said. "I've got a date tonight. Be careful sleeping in that car. Keep the doors locked."

I rushed back to the lawn outside the package store and delivered the news to Bink who continued to wallow in his self-absorbed despair. If anyone had a right to be depressed, it was me, but I tried to lighten the mood.

"That's cool that we might get to see Joni Mitchell, isn't it?"

Bink just shrugged his shoulders like it wasn't that cool.

"Maybe I can hopefully wander around and run into her, seeing it's outside and everything."

Bink gave me another shrug.

"You okay, buddy?"

Another shrug from Bink made me want to take him by the shoulders and give him a good shake like the nuns did to you when you zoned out in school.

"What's the matter?"

Finally he spoke. "It's just...Sparrow."

"Yeah, I know. I'm bummed that she left too." And I *was* bummed. What did he think, that he had the market cornered on liking pretty girls? Heck, I had seen her naked, and that counts for something.

"No girl has ever been as nice to me as Sparrow was."

"Yeah, the same for me. Not to downplay it, but I think she's that nice to everybody. I think that's how some hippies are. I know a guy at Southern like that."

"But...she's...not a guy," Bink said.

"Good point," I said, for obvious reasons.

"Yeah, and the thing is, I'm never going to meet anyone like Sparrow again."

I didn't even know what to say to that because I was feeling the exact same way.

"Can I ask a question, Gabe?"

"Sure," I said, as if he didn't ask a million questions a day.

"Do you think Sparrow will marry Duke?"

I had to think about that one for a minute, and the only thing I could think to say was, "I certainly hope not."

"What do you mean?"

I sighed. "Oh...I don't know what I mean. Or maybe I do. I just feel there's something not quite right in their relationship. At least it's not what I think a relationship should be. Duke's got demons. He's a little off, if you ask me. Maybe it's the shit he went through in Vietnam, I don't know. But I just hope Sparrow realizes he's no good for her because, well, he just isn't."

Talking to Bink about Sparrow made me feel more depressed than I already was, though, so I lay back in the grass and closed my eyes. I could feel the sunlight cover my face like a hot washcloth. I could almost see the bright sunlight through my closed eyes. I must have dozed off because Bink shook me, rousing me from the dead.

"Gabe, we should eat something."

We grabbed a couple of ham sandwiches and chips at the store, and sat on the hood of my car as we gobbled them down. Bink, luckily, had a deck of cards, so we played Setback for a long time, and then he read a sports magazine he had picked up at the general store, and I reached into my back pocket and grabbed a copy of the latest book I was reading, *The Grapes of Wrath*. I had read it for school when I was a junior, but there are some books you need to read more than once. For me, it was a good one to bring since the story is about a road trip, and even more depressing than ours was turning out to be, if that's possible.

I was glad that I had recommended that Bink and I both bring flashlights. I didn't read much that night, though. Secretly tucked away in the pages of Steinbeck's novel and folded tightly was my picture of Joni. I had brought it along to lift me out of any situations that might leave me feeling downtrodden and bereft. With Bink in the front seat and me in the back, I could be alone with Joni. In the warm glow of my flashlight, Joni and I looked into each other's eyes for a good long while, and I felt a sense of calm and reassurance that had abandoned me with the departure of Duke and Sparrow.

When I woke up in the morning, the first thing I saw was the dim bulb of the flashlight and then Joni's picture and my book only inches from my face. I folded the page up and put it away. I'd need to buy new batteries. The second thing I saw was Bink curled up in the front. His head on the driver's seat, his feet on the passenger seat, and his torso laying across the console. It was a rough night of sleep for both of us.

I rubbed the sleep from my eyes and looked out of my open window. I was also surprised to see Goober and Officer Davis back in their lawn chairs outside the garage.

I rolled out of the car and approached the two men.

Upon seeing me, Goober flashed his decayed teeth at me and said, "Good mornin', sunshine."

I yawned. "How's it looking?"

"Well, same situation as yesterday," Goober said. "Maybe Virgil'll show up at work this afternoon."

"This afternoon?" I was on the verge of exploding, when I felt a hand on my arm, pulling me away. It was Bink.

"Yup. He can't come to work til after school."

"Now listen you –"

"Excuse us," Bink said, while literally hauling me across the road toward Moe's Spirits.

"What the fuck are you doing?" I shouted.

"Shhh," Bink cautioned me. Then, pressing his mouth close to my ear added, "You're going to get us in more hot water if you're not careful."

"But Joni Mitchell," I moaned. "If we miss Joni Mitchell, I swear, I'll –"

"Shush," Bink almost shouted. "Just put a muzzle on it."

I had my wits about me enough to know that, at that moment, Bink had more presence of mind than I did. That's something important about a relationship with another person. I am reminded of a line from a favorite poem my mom used to recite to us, "If –" by Rudyard Kipling:

> If you can keep your head when all about you
> Are losing theirs and blaming it on you

And along with a big litany of "ifs" set to four more stanzas of rhyming iambic pentameter, Kipling concludes, *you'll be a man, my son.*

At this very moment, it was Bink, not me, who was keeping his head about him. It was Bink who was being a man, because I was ready to explode like a geyser.

"You just need to sit down in the grass and cool off," Bink said. "Let me take care of this."

Let you take care of it? Oh, perfect! Because you've been so adept at taking care of each challenge we've faced so far.

But before I knew it, Bink was three-quarters across the road and approaching the two men. I dropped down in the grass on my butt, and I could see Bink gesticulating and shrugging with his back to me. Goober and Officer Davis seemed to be listening attentively.

After he talked to them for about ten minutes, he made his way back across the road.

"What the hell were you saying to them?" I asked, feeling more than a touch of skepticism.

"I told him that we hoped he could fix the car soon because we were headed to Nashville."

"Nashville? Tennessee?"

"Why not? It's the next state over," Bink said, clearly proud of himself. "Get this," he continued in a volume that Dr. Schmidt had described in Music History 100 as *sotto voce*, "I told them that you're a huge fan of country music and that this trip to Nashville is a dream come true for you, but that we have to be back in Connecticut in three days."

I'm not quite sure what my face looked like as I listened and reacted to his conspiratorial tone, but I have a hunch my reaction was one of stunned incredulity. The next thing I knew, though, Goober set off in his truck, and we were back on the open road before noon. I was beginning to realize that having taken this trip with Bink might not have been the worst idea I ever had.

CHAPTER 35

I hate cars. They're just the worst. It's paradoxical, but I love cars too because of my dad. These days, he's driving a new Oldsmobile Toronado, which isn't my cup of tea, but it's not too bad if you like luxury cars with leather seats and air-conditioning and a built-in cassette player with AM/FM radio and power everything, not to mention a front end that stretches from here to Timbuktu.

But there is one car that isn't cool. A Corvair. How cool is it to have a junker where the maroon paint is faded, where the heater and defroster don't work, where gas fumes seep into the interior when you blow air in the car, and where the muffler rots off the bottom of the car when all you're trying to do is mind your own business and find the Blue Ridge Mountain Folk Festival?

Yeah, I just can't stand cars, except the ones I love, which I'm never going to be able to afford anyway.

My reality, though, is that I'm stuck with a hand-me-down car, which shouldn't surprise me since most things in my life have been hand-me-downs, whether we're talking about a bicycle, a clarinet, or a sled. Even the stuff I did, like joining Boy Scouts or going to Southern were just hand-me-downs from things Michael had done before me. It's lucky for me that Michael was always so much taller than me or I would have had to wear his old clothes too. Since he was over six feet tall by the time he was in seventh grade, that was something I didn't have to worry about. Not that being short was ever advantageous, especially as adults compared Michael and me. Like when my Little League coach, with a semi-disgusted look on his face, said to our dad, "How'd you grow one so tall," looking at home run-hitting Michael, towering over me in his pin-striped major league uniform, "and one so short," casting his eyes down at pathetic little me in my t-shirt, jeans, and oversized cap. Or when Mr. Bertini, the owner of a local grocery market near school said, "Hey, look! It's Mutt and Jeff," as Michael and I were buying a couple of Ring Dings. Even as a fourth grader, I wasn't amused. *Hilarious. I'm just dying laughing.*

I shouldn't complain, though, because Michael is a pretty terrific brother, and if he hadn't wired me a couple hundred bucks, our road trip would have died an early death.

Instead, we were back on the road. As my copilot, Bink pointed out that Asheville was west. *Way* west. Using the "inch to mile" guide, Bink estimated that from the tip of his index finger almost to his middle knuckle represented thirty miles. Using this method, he figured Asheville was over three hundred miles away. Going at about sixty miles an hour, it was going to take us, like, five or six more hours to get there.

Bink navigated us to US 158, heading west toward Interstate 85. US 158 was a narrower, winding road, but I assumed that I-85 would be a three-lane highway, more like I-95. The problem is we got lost on 158. Somewhere along the way, we must have missed a fork or zigged when we should have zagged.

When we realized we were no longer on 158, we pulled into a greasy spoon and asked for directions to I-85. Bink took copious notes, and then we grabbed a bite to eat. Chewing on a burger, I perused the map. Bink leaned in and pointed out something I'd already figured out on my own – how much bigger North Carolina is than Connecticut.

"See, the difference?" he said, flipping the atlas to its cover and pointing to North Carolina and then Connecticut. "So it's easier to get lost if you get what I mean."

It looked like you could fit about seven or eight Connecticuts into one North Carolina. It reminded me of our social studies book in fifth grade. There'd be a picture of Italy superimposed over California or a picture of Spain superimposed over Texas, and you'd be thinking to yourself, *Holy cow, that's weird. One state in the U.S. dwarfs a whole European country!*

What I was wondering at the moment, though, was if we'd ever get to Asheville. I was also wondering if we were going to see Sparrow and Duke there, and especially if I was actually going to meet Joni Mitchell. That's a lot of *ifs*.

It must have taken at least another hour to get back to 158, driving along rural roads, some of which weren't even paved.

It seemed like North Carolina was not only bigger than Connecticut but greener too. At least, in my state of mind, I was seeing a greater variety of shades of green even though I've never experienced myself as someone who notices subtle gradations of color. Maybe I was just bored with driving. The foliage seemed to hit just about every shade of green on the color spectrum, though. If that was true in Connecticut, I'd been oblivious. But maybe I was noticing lots of stuff I hadn't noticed before.

There was a lot of farm country as well. A lot more than in Connecticut. Not so much with crops, though, but more with livestock, especially cows. Mostly, though, we gazed at fields rolling on into infinity, interspersed with golden round hay bales and speckled patterns of brown and black spots – hundreds and hundreds of cows. I had seen some farms in Connecticut – but very few in Shelton.

On these farms, every now and then, I saw American flags painted on the sides of barns and the appearance of three crosses. It was like a merging of patriotism and religion. I realized the crosses represented the death of Jesus as He hung on His cross alongside the two thieves. I remembered how one thief spoke to Jesus, saying something like, "If you're God's son, have him save us," and the other just asked Jesus to be forgiven or to be remembered. Personally, I couldn't figure out what patriotism or the story of Jesus and thieves had to do with farming, though. I had a hunch these farmers wouldn't have been too keen with Duke and Sparrow chanting the name of Krishna.

We finally hit I-85. *Sweet Mother of Jesus, at long last.*

But it wasn't long before we ran into bumper-to-bumper traffic approaching Raleigh. It seemed like we couldn't catch a break.

When the traffic finally broke, I looked at my watch and saw that it was approaching 7:00. I was in no mood to keep driving to Asheville late into the night. I got off an exit and soon spotted a sign for the Sunset Motel, under which a smaller, yellow neon sign flashed the word Vacancy, only the electricity on the V was out, so it appeared to say "acancy."

I was tired and had seen enough bumpers, cow-spotted fields, American flags, and crosses for one day, so I pulled in. Bink and I went into the office, and a skinny lady with a cigarette dangling from her mouth looked up from a game of solitaire she was playing and told us a room would cost $11.00 a night, which sounded fine to us.

Everything in the room was dark brown, from the bedspreads to the worn carpet to the wavy wall paneling to the brown and tan curtains. Even the little television set was in a faux wooden cabinet. The room reeked of cigarette smoke, which I was used to since both of my parents smoke like chimneys. I guess Michael and I never smoked because Dad had put the fear of God into us. Dad is from the "Do as I say, not as I do" school of parenting.

At least the room had beds, which beat sleeping on the ground in a campsite or in the back seat of the Corvair. Bink and I were hungry, so I suggested we hop in the car and find a bite to eat. We didn't know what town we were in, but anything had to be better than Garysburg. On the drive, we saw an older man hitchhiking, so I pulled over.

"Here we go again," said Bink.

"Go again what?" I asked.

"Do you pick up every stranger you see?"

"Basically, yes."

As the old man hobbled to the car, I could see he was wearing long baggy pants and a t-shirt. He wore a ratty looking Atlanta Braves cap, and it looked like he hadn't shaved in days.

Opening the back door and getting in, he said, "Thank you, my good man, for accommodating ol' William with a ride."

I looked at him sitting in the back seat and saw that his caramel colored face was covered with blackheads. "You're welcome," I said. "Where would you like us to bring you?"

"Oh, you are most definitely a gentleman and a scholar. I live just a few miles from here if you happen to be heading straight for a spell. Or, if you might be drivin' down a short ways, you'll see a Piggly Wiggly where you can drop me off."

It was interesting to hear him speak because he had a resonant baritone voice and a genteel way of speaking to us. His speech reminded me of a dignified college professor, despite his impoverished appearance.

"Sure," I said. "We don't have anywhere to go. We're spending the night at the Sunset Motel, and we were just looking for somewhere to eat."

"Well, the only eatery here in Robbins is the Tar Heel Tavern, which is right on the way."

"The Tar Heel Tavern," I said. "That sounds like a bar."

"Of course, they do serve spirits, my good man, but they also have some mighty fine food offerin's."

Bink jumped in and asked, "Aren't the University of North Carolina's sports teams called the Tar Heels?"

"Yes, indeed," replied our guest with a chuckle. "The campus isn't an hour from here if you'd like to pay a visit to the esteemed center of learning. Just about everything in North Carolina is Tar Heels."

"What is a Tar Heel?" Bink asked. I was eager to hear the answer since I didn't know either.

"Let me see. That goes way back. The word comes from the North Carolina turpentine industry, which was worked by slaves and also poor whites. The workers had no shoes and the pitch or tar would stick to their heels. For a good long time, it was a derogatory term, calling North Carolinians Tar Heels, but during the War Between the States, North Carolinians repurposed the name, making it a matter of pride instead of a matter of shame."

I couldn't help but notice William's sincerity and kindness. I liked him.

"That sounds unusual," I offered, "to make the name a matter of pride, I mean."

"I suppose you're right," he replied, "but North Carolinians are an *unusual* breed, I can tell you. In other states, northern ones like where you boys come from, people wouldn't like being called a 'hillbilly' or a 'redneck,' but you call a North Carolinian one of those names, and he's liable to slap you on the back and buy you a beer."

Hearing himself explain it must have tickled William's funny bone because he burst out into the most genuine, bellowing laugh I've ever heard.

When he calmed down, William said, "Speaking of food, would you gentlemen mind if I joined you for a bite?"

"Well," Bink said, "I don't know about –"

"We wouldn't mind at all," I interrupted. "We'd love to have you join us."

"The thing is," our passenger continued, "I'll need you boys to order my food inside and bring it out to me. There's a nice picnic table outside next to a big ol' pine tree where the three of us can congregate and enjoy a nice meal."

"You mean they won't serve you inside?" I asked, feeling the heat rise up into my cheeks.

"No, well, not exactly. I wouldn't put it that way. Ten or fifteen years ago, there's no way they would have served me, but things have changed since then, in a manner of speaking. There's no more water fountains or bathrooms labeled 'white' or 'colored,' but just because Washington passes a law, it doesn't mean things change. People's minds need to change, you see. Let's just say at this particular tavern, white people don't particularly *cotton* to us negros stopping in for a bite. Pun intended." And once again, William burst into laughter. As he calmed himself, he added, "I been around a long time, almost eighty years now, and I've learned that it's better not to make waves. You boys might not know how things work here in the South."

He was right. I didn't know how things worked in the South, but I was learning.

"Well that stinks," I said. I felt like I wanted to give the owner of the Tar Heel Tavern a piece of my mind, but thinking back to our recent experience in Garysburg, I realized it would be better to tread lightly. From movies I've watched, I have a sense of the oppression black people have experienced historically, and I've noticed that there are segregated areas in Connecticut, in a way, like the black guys I work with living in a big apartment complex on Olsen Drive in Ansonia. All of them do – Big Alfred, Les, Lance, and even Buster who had given his life for his country. What I do know though is that if a black guy wants to go into a restaurant, any restaurant in Connecticut, he can freely do so.

Never one to miss an opportunity, Bink said, "Hey, William. Speaking of the War Between the States, you must know all about the Battle of Bentonville."

"I've heard of it, but I wouldn't say I know all about it," William replied.

"No? Well let me tell you, it was a pivotal battle, paving the way for Lee's inevitable surrender on April 9th, 1865."

With Bink in his glory and William occupied, I contemplated that, between our night in Greenwich Village and now our journey south, our road trip was turning out to be quite an eye opener for me.

Up ahead, I saw a sign for the Tar Heel Tavern. The exterior of the building was weather beaten and in obvious disrepair. The paint on the clapboard was peeling and flaky. A rain gutter hung loose from the worn roof, a rusty clamp broken and unattached. This would be a new chapter in our adventure, but I'm not sure I was looking forward to it.

CHAPTER 36

We sat at a picnic table that had seen better days, and William suggested we order the fried chicken with collard greens and grits.

"Tell the boss man the order is to go," he offered.

"I've heard of collard greens and grits, but I don't know what they are," Bink said.

"My sweet Lord!" William exclaimed. "Obviously, you boys have missed out on a culinary treat up North," and he, once again, broke into rolling laughter that seemed to originate deep in his belly.

"Now don't you worry about what they are," he explained, composing himself. "You just trust ol' William."

Inside, the place was dark and smoky. The jukebox was playing a country song. I'm not much of a country music fan, despite what Bink had told Goober and Officer Davis. My main exposure to country music was the television show, *Hee Haw*, which I could take for about a half second. Watching Minnie Pearl, a price tag dangling from her comical straw hat, repeatedly scream out "How-w-wdy!" wasn't my idea of entertainment.

There were eight or ten customers in the place, rugged looking types who looked like they'd had a long day working. I guessed they drove trucks or worked in farming or construction. We were able to order the food without a hitch.

Joining William at the picnic table, we all dug in. William was right. The chicken was the best I'd ever eaten, far more delicious than the Kentucky Chicken on Pershing Drive, and the collard greens and grits were different, but I didn't mind them at all.

"So, ol' William is willing to bet that you boys have a couple of nice girlfriends back in Connecticut," he said, as he chewed on a juicy drumstick.

"I wish," Bink said.

"Now don't you be modest. Two handsome guys like you!"

"Sorry to say," I replied, "but Bink and I are both losers."

"Now you stop right there, my man. No degrading yourselves. The Good Book tells us there is a season for everything."

"Well, I guess it just isn't our season, right Bink?"

Bink nodded, with a sheepish look on his face.

At that moment, a man with a cowboy hat and a face like leather came out of the tavern. "Evenin', William," he said.

"Evenin' to you, Mr. Robert."

Taking a deep breath, the man looked up at the sky. "Lovely evenin', ain't it?"

"Yes, indeed," William responded. "Lovely evenin', Mr. Robert. Yessiree!"

The man eyed us with a puzzled look.

"We don't see many Yankee boys in these parts," he said, his skeptical eyeballs fixed on the Connecticut plate on the back end of the Corvair. "They friends of yours, William?"

"Oh, these young fellas right here?" William laughed. "They's just a couple o' nice boys who picked me up hitchhikin' and give me a ride." I noticed that William's grammar now deteriorated as he spoke to the man.

"Well, I guess that's alright, then. You take care of yourself and have a good one now, ya hear?"

"Yes, Mr. Robert, I will. Indeed I will. And you do likewise, sir."

As the man drove away in his Dodge pickup truck, I was struck by the politeness of the exchange, yet something didn't seem quite right.

"Is he a friend of yours?" I asked.

"Oh, Mr. Robert?" William seemed embarrassed. "He's just a neighbor."

"And that's his name?" I continued. "Mr. Robert?"

"His name is Robert Grady."

I was puzzled. "You called him Mr. Robert. Why didn't you call him Mr. Grady?"

"Oh, it's always been our way, my whole life. It's just the way we colored folks talk to white folks. Or at least us older colored folks."

"Isn't that...I don't know, subservient?"

"I don't know about that. It's just bein' polite and keepin' the peace. That's all. But we were talking about this not being your season, am I right?"

"Yes, I guess we were," I replied.

"Well that's okay, then," William said. "Your day will come, as sure as ol' William is sittin' here. But you must have had girlfriends along the way, as you've grown up, I mean."

"A few," I said. "But nothing too serious. No real experience. Or at least none to brag about."

I watched as he peeled a slice of fried skin off of a drumstick and nibbled at it. "Nothing to brag about?"

"Well, you know what I mean," I continued. "Nothing has ever gotten too *serious* for me and a girl, and not for Bink either, if you catch my drift, right Bink?"

Bink came in on cue. "That's the understatement of the year if we're talking about me."

William laughed again. Bink and I laughed along with him, although we didn't know what was so funny. Seeing the stupid look on Bink's face, I realized that I must have had a similar look on mine.

"Oh, I sure do catch your drift, my man, no need to worry about that. I wasn't born yesterday," he said, pausing for almost every word as the curtain of his laughter slowly fell. "But that may not be the worst thing in the world. Would you like to know why?"

"I'd love to know why," I said.

"Well then, let me share a bit of wisdom with y'all. I know you boys are living in a permissive so-ci-e-ty, but..."

As he ripped off a strip of meat from the breast and began to chew, I thought about how much I liked his speech, the way he pronounced so-CI-e-TY.

"But?" I prompted him.

"But there is one thing you mustn't ever lose sight of."

"What's that?" I looked at Bink as if to say, *Where's William going with this?*

"Here's the truth of the matter. The female of the species is designed to make babies. Whether she knows it or not, and whether *you* know it or not. Bringing children into this world is her bi-O-logical destiny. That's how God made her and that's what she's all about. So, I don't care what she might *think* she's doin', every time a young woman gets *serious* with a fella, as you put it, she's on the path to fulfilling that destiny. You give me a good woman, and I give you a woman who is looking for love and the deep fulfillment of that love. And the fulfillment of that love is procreation, the way the Good Lord intended. That's not always so true with a man. You understand me?"

"You mean to say that when a girl has sex, she wants to have a baby?" I asked.

And Bink followed with, "...because my Aunt Catherine never had a baby. She's not even married."

"That's her," William replied. "I'm not talking about Aunt Catherine but about the vast majority of women. Listen close now."

I was all ears.

He continued. "Maybe you didn't hear me when I said, 'whether she knows it or not,' in which case I mean, a young girl might not know it and she's thinkin' she's just havin' a good ol' time, just like you're thinkin' you're havin' a good ol' time, but if the truth be told, she's on the path I'm talking about – the path of fulfilling that biological destiny...her God-given destiny. It's a merging of science and spirituality I'm gettin' at here."

Then he sighed and sunk his teeth into the chicken leg while Bink and I digested what he had said. "Yessiree," he said, dropping the bone into his carton, "I sure do think you boys are a couple of fine fellows, but if ol' William knows anything at all, he knows neither of you is ready to be no child's daddy. Just be careful. That's the big point!"

Then once more, like the tremor of an earthquake, laughter rose up in William, and he shook like the earth beneath him was undulating. There was nothing to do but laugh along with him.

When our stomachs were full, we headed for the Piggly Wiggly and dropped William off. He assured us he lived very close by.

"Many thanks, my good men, for your kindness and for your generous hospitality. And a final word about the female of the species. When you encounter a young woman, treat her well, because as the Good Book tells us, 'She is clothed with strength and dignity, and she laughs without fear of the future.' "

I wasn't sure what to say, so I just replied, "Yes, we'll do that. It was great having dinner with you."

"As it was for me, young brother. May God shower blessings on both of you as you continue on your journey. And may you never lose sight of His vision and purpose in your lives."

As we drove away, I glanced into my rearview mirror and saw William waving to us as I rounded the bend.

When we got back to the Sunset Motel, Bink flipped on the television, but the only channel that had any reception was NBC, if you want to call it reception. The movie *Patton* was airing on Monday Night at the Movies, but the snowy screen made it almost impossible to see George C. Scott as General George S. Patton carry on across Europe during and also in the aftermath of World War II. I remembered seeing it in the movies and being stunned when Patton wanted to keep the War going after VE Day so he could take over Russia. It made me think that maybe all military leaders are potential dictators, even American ones.

The poor reception made it more like listening to the radio, so I decided to dive back into *The Grapes of Wrath*. I was well into the book, and as I read into Chapter 16, it seemed oddly coincidental that the chapter I was reading was about Tom Joad's pregnant sister, Rose of Sharon. I found it moving when, deep in conversation about her future, Rose of Sharon said:

Well, we talked about it, me an' Connie…an' he says we'll see how times is, an' maybe I'll go to a hospiddle. An' we'll have a car, a little car. An' when he gets done studying at night, why – it'll be nice, an' he tore a page out of Western Love Stories, an' he's gonna send off for a course 'cause it don't cost nothin' to send off. Says right on that clipping. I seen it. An', why – they even get you a job when you take that course-radios, it is – nice clean work, and a future. An' we'll live in town an' go to pitchers whenever, an' – well. I'm gonna have an 'lectric iron! an', the baby'll have all new stuff – white an'– well, you seen in the catalogue all the stuff they got for a baby. Maybe right at first while Connie's studyin' at home it won't be so easy, but – well, when the baby comes, maybe he'll be all done studyin' an' we'll have a place, little bit of a place. We don't want nothin' fancy, but we want it nice for the baby…

I realized something that I hadn't noticed in my previous reading of the book. Most everything Rose of Sharon said or thought had to do with delivering and taking care of her baby – about her hopes for that baby's future and a better life for her child than perhaps she had had. I thought about my mom and dad and brother and contemplated how a family comes to be.

Is William right about women? I wondered. He was sure right about me. I wasn't ready to be any little kid's dad.

As I continued to read, I lost my concentration as I wondered what the future held for us, for Bink and me. For this trip and for life in general. It occurred to me, in my drowsiness, that maybe I was lucky that my attempts to lose my virginity had come to nothing. What if I had gotten a girl like Hippie Tina pregnant? What then?

As I drifted off to sleep, in the outer recesses of my consciousness, I felt my copy of *The Grapes of Wrath* gently slip out of my left hand and I heard it plunk onto the floor.

CHAPTER 37

I don't know what girls are attracted to in a guy's looks, and I'm not thinking about myself at the moment, but I'm willing to go down on record in saying that Kevin Binkowski is good looking enough. With a nickname like "Bink," you might think that he's a short, skinny, ninety-pound weakling, but it isn't so. I would describe him as being of average height and build, about 5'10" and 165 pounds, which makes him taller and heavier than I am. Bink has piercing blue eyes, not unlike Paul Newman's. I've seen photos of the statue of David, and Bink has a similar nose. Maybe that's called a Roman nose, I don't know. I don't like to talk about another guy's lips, but Bink's seem normal. With hair somewhere between brown and blond, wavy and longish with sideburns, he could be the fifth Beatle. Of course, if you heard him sing, you'd know why he isn't. Anyway, the point is, he's a decent looking guy.

Lack of intelligence isn't the problem. As I've said, he can dole out a billion and one history facts and baseball statistics. But my hunch is that girls like the strong, silent type. Maybe even the strong, stupid type. Bink's trouble might be that he just talks too much and asks a ridiculous number of unnecessary questions. That's why it didn't surprise me, as we headed back toward I-85, when he interrogated me like he was Perry Mason and I was the prime suspect in a murder case.

"Do you think we'll ever see Sparrow again?"

I noticed he didn't ask about Duke.

"I don't know, Bink."

"If they go to the folk festival, we should reconnect with her, right?"

"Maybe. I don't know."

"Do you think she's going to be there?"

"Uhm, maybe." I was a big help.

"What if we can't get tickets like that night at Carnegie Hall?"

"Right. Well, we better get tickets, Bink, or I'm going to end up in some Southern jail."

"Gabe, who do you like better, Sparrow or Joni Mitchell?"

What a question. "Well, obviously I don't know Joni Mitchell, and obviously she's a lot older than me, and obviously she's a huge celebrity, so how am I supposed to answer that one?"

"I don't know. I was just asking because I think, just like me, you have a thing about Sparrow."

"Well, yeah, who wouldn't? But I've got some bad news for you. I don't think either of us is going to end up at the altar with Sparrow. I think no matter how cute she is or how nice she is, her destiny and ours are, I'm guessing, two different ball games." I sounded like my mom who loves referring to life situations as "ball games," which is a little odd considering she knows nothing about sports.

"Yeah, I guess you're right."

"But I'll tell you what. If we meet back up with Sparrow, I'll let you have her – if you can wrestle her away from Duke. I have other problems."

"Like how you're going to meet Joni?"

"Exactly!"

"How *are* you going to meet Joni, Gabe?"

"How the hell should I know, Bink?" I must have sounded irritated because he clammed up. I popped in an eight-track tape, the Four Tops Greatest Hits, hoping the kid would give me a break for a while. But then, right in the middle of one of my favorite songs, "Bernadette," Bink got revved up again.

"Is something bothering you, Gabe?"

"No, why would something be bothering me?"

"I don't know, you seem annoyed and you're all quiet."

"Well, no offense, Bink, but you do ask a billion questions."

"Yeah. I'm sorry. You probably wish you were on this trip with someone else. Like, with Jeff or Tommy Trouble, right?"

I sighed. "I suppose."

"See?"

"Hey, listen Bink – I'm sorry that I've known Tomaso and Jeff practically my entire life and I've only known you for, like, three years, but I'm perfectly happy to be traveling with you. I mean, you're about as good a friend as I have left, with the possible exception of Mary Elizabeth, so you don't have to worry about it. Besides, it's not like you're my girlfriend or something."

"Do you wish Mary Elizabeth was your girlfriend?"

Wow, this kid never gives up. He didn't even know Mary Elizabeth. I had told him about her and he had seen her a few times, but she wasn't a regular at Duchess or anything.

"No, I don't have a crush on Mary Elizabeth," I said. "She's just someone I can talk to and who's always honest with me. It's different being friends with a girl than it is with a guy. And it's nice to have a friend who's a girl that I'm not interested in and who's not interested in me that way."

"Yeah, I can understand that," he said.

After we lapsed into another period of silence (well, silence except for the Four Tops), Bink had another question. He could only remain quiet for just so long.

"What are you thinking about now, Gabriel?"

I could have flown off the handle with him, but I didn't want him wallowing into that *I'm-not-good-enough-to-be-your-friend* crap again.

"I guess I'm just bummed that William felt he couldn't go into the Tar Heel Tavern and that he was acting so subservient to that white guy. And I didn't like it when that jerk called us 'Yankees' either. Did it bother you?"

"Well, yeah, of course it bothered me. But lucky we don't have that kind of prejudice in Connecticut, isn't it?"

"I don't know, Bink. Maybe we do – maybe it's just a different flavor."

"What do you mean?"

"I mean, there's no black people in my neighborhood. Any in yours?"

"Well...no –"

"There were maybe five or six black kids at Shelton High. Same with Derby, right?"

"Yeah."

"And you know how at Duchess Will always used to tease Buster and say stuff like, 'You coons need to come to the back door,' and Buster would laugh about it?"

"Yeah," Bink said. "I remember that. But Buster knew Will was just kidding, didn't he?"

"Maybe," I said. "But get a load of this. You know how Alfred asked me to play on a basketball team with friends of his in the senior leagues last winter?"

"Yeah."

"Well, everyone else on the team was black. I remember over-hearing a conversation in the locker room. Lance Jefferson was telling a story about some other guy from the projects, and he was saying, 'That nigger did this...and that nigger did that,' and yucking it up about whatever it was he was talking about. Big Alfred was like, 'Lance, don't you be calling brothers no niggers, that's disrespectful,' but Lance argued back and said something like, 'It ain't disrespectful for one brother to call another brother a nigger, Alfred. Don't give me that bullshit!' Alfred stuck to his guns, though, and said, 'Yeah, it is disrespectful. If we don't want no white people calling us names, then we can't call each other no names neither.' While Lance and Alfred were going at it, I remember Buster drying himself off and just digesting what they were saying."

"I don't know if I get your point," Bink said.

"My point is that it looked like Alfred got Buster thinking. Ever hear the saying, 'Much truth is said in jest?' How is it okay for Will to make racist jokes if Big Alfred doesn't think that black guys should be calling each other racist names?"

Bink scratched his unshaven chin and said, "I think I see."

"Yeah...race relations. Weird right?" I said, realizing that William had influenced me in the same way Alfred had seemed to influence Buster.

Bink nodded, and then I had a revelation that gave me an empty feeling in the pit of my stomach. *I guess Buster doesn't have to worry about race relations anymore.*

When we hit I-85, I felt good since we were once again headed for Asheville. Bink mustn't have slept very well in the musty motel room because he closed his eyes and passed out. Finally, a little peace and quiet.

It occurred to me that no matter how much I talked to Bink about race issues, or for that matter, any issues at all, we weren't going to solve anything. At the same time, a guy needs to have a friend – another guy to hash things out with and try to figure out this crazy world. Because if you don't have anybody like that, you could lose your marbles. I glanced at Bink, his mouth half open as he slept, and I smiled and kept driving.

CHAPTER 38

As I forged ahead toward Asheville, my mind continued to wander. It's crazy, but let's just say my mind has a mind of its own. It's a miracle that when I'm driving I ever get from one place to another in one piece considering I'm thinking about something else the whole time and not thinking about the actual driving.

What I was thinking about was something that happened when I was a little kid, maybe a fourth grader, and I was walking to school with Michael and his best friend, Paulie. When I say I was walking with them, I mean that Michael and Paulie were walking side by side, and I was about ten feet behind them because they considered me a second class citizen.

As we passed by Fowler School and took a left on Coram Avenue toward St. Joseph's, I noticed a group of four kids heading up the narrow sidewalk toward us. As they approached, I could hear the tip-tap metallic clicking of the cleats of their Cuban-heeled shoes against the sidewalk. They all looked alike with their pegged pants and pompadour hairstyles, slicked into big rounded bubbles of greasy hair on the front of their heads and tapered on the sides and in the back. Cigarettes dangled from each of their sardonic mouths. I couldn't picture Michael or Paulie smoking even though they were about the same age.

When they got close to Michael and Paulie, it was evident to me, even though I was just a little kid, that the sidewalk wasn't wide enough for both groups of boys to pass by each other.

The Fowler School boys just stopped and stood there looking tough. A few of them smirked and laughed like Michael and Paulie were pitifully funny to look at. Michael and Paulie tried to turn sideways to let the boys pass by, but the group didn't move. Then, Michael walked straight ahead, expecting, I think, for someone to create an opening for him. But no one did. Superior smiles flashed across the faces of the Fowler School kids.

Michael walked off the sidewalk and into the road, but the runt of the group moved with him and blocked his path. Cars zoomed by on Coram Avenue in both directions, so it was impossible for Michael to move further into the road. Michael towered over the shorter kid, but the kid glared into Michael's eyes with contempt as if to say, "Go ahead! Just try to go past me!" Michael wasn't about to get into a fight with the jerk. It was basic math. Four against two were bad odds. The sounds of more cruel sniggering echoed as Michael and Paulie seemed helpless. Watching the scene like it was a movie, I remember feeling worried and scared. The Fowler School kids finally continued up the hill to school, butting Michael and Paulie with their shoulders, knocking them way off balance, and passing me like I didn't even exist, laughing hysterically.

I never talked to Michael about the episode, but I think it toughened him up and made Michael someone who would fight his way through much of the rest of his teen years when he needed to. It made him the guy who wouldn't back down from the likes of Billy Robbins and Beef Belsky, two criminals.

What was mainly on my mind as I drove along I-85 in the heat, though, was how mean people can be to each other. That episode with the Fowler School kids was one of the first episodes of real cruelty that I had ever witnessed. As I listened to the sounds of Bink's heavy breathing as he slept, I contemplated, *If kids of the same race...kids who live in the same town...and who probably, more or less, have similar family backgrounds can be this mean to each other, why should we be surprised when people are cruel and bully people of other races?*

My thinking on that hasn't changed much. It's too bad, but it doesn't seem like there's any way to stop people from having an air of superiority and from hating each other, even when they have no good reason to do so.

Bink continued to sleep for a long time while I continued to daydream. After two more hours, I saw signs for Asheville, and just seeing the word made me smile. I hoped we hadn't missed the folk festival.

As I drove off the first downtown Asheville exit, a groggy Bink stirred. He shook his head and blinked his eyes.

"Where the...where are we?" he asked with a wide yawn.

"We're heading for downtown Asheville."

"Oh. That's good, right?"

"It's very good."

"Doesn't look like a festival is going on anywhere around here," Bink offered.

"Sure doesn't," I said. "Well, let's get out and ask someone."

I pulled into a spot, and we went into a small luncheonette. When I asked the freckle-faced waitress about the folk festival, she told me that there were two more days, as far as she knew. She said we needed to take the Blue Ridge Parkway, which we'd run into in about five or six miles, and we'd run right into the festival grounds.

"Do you know if Joni Mitchell has played there yet?" I asked.

"I think they're saving the big headliners for the last few nights," she answered, with a thick Southern accent.

"Who are the other headliners?" I asked.

"Some big names. I heard tell that Joan Baez and John Sebastian are also playin' there."

"Do you know how much it costs or how to get tickets? We're not from around here, so we don't know much about it."

"Oh? Where y'all from?"

"Connecticut," I said, hoping she wasn't prejudiced against Northerners like some others we'd met.

"You boys are a long way from home then, huh? Well, I don't rightly know about ticket sales, but it's outdoors and there's plenty of room, so I don't think they're turnin' anyone away."

Bink and I grabbed a quick bite at the counter, and then in a heartbeat, we headed back down the road in the direction of the Blue Ridge Parkway. As we drove into the mountains, I was struck by the beauty of the dense forests and the sweeping mountain peaks, like gigantic waves in the background. Covered in mist, majestic cloud formations hovered over the contours of the midnight blue peaks. Periodically, we'd see the foaming rapids of a small creek cut through the landscape or a small waterfall gushing into a blue-green pool below, or suddenly, the expanse of a placid lake reaching into what seemed like infinity.

Gazing at the natural beauty brought me back to my high school graduation. Our theme was "The Environment," and for our class song, we seniors sang Woody Guthrie's famous folk song, "This Land is Your Land." At the time, I felt the song choice was a little corny. I had hoped we'd have a song that was by the Beatles or some other more contemporary group. But now, as I drove the winding roads, I found myself playing the lyrics back in my mind and feeling a surge of optimism. After all, I would be meeting Joni and in a breathtaking setting.

About twenty minutes into our upward drive, we saw a sign – Blue Ridge Mountain Folk Festival Parking with a big yellow arrow drawn on it. The sign led us to a sea of parked cars. Hundreds of them. Young guys in orange vests pointed us down one lane and toward another, directing us to where we could park the Corvair. It was a long walk to a small log cabin style structure with a ticket booth. It wouldn't have surprised me if Davy Crockett or Daniel Boone appeared at any moment.

There were three ticket windows, so we approached the first one. The ticket seller told us that there were two nights left, as the waitress had explained, and that admission was $12.00. She said that the main performances began at 7:00, but there were other performers on smaller stages throughout the park.

When I asked her if Joni was playing, she said, "Not tonight. We got Joan Baez tonight, and it's going to be epic. Livingston Taylor, James' brother, is openin' for her. Joni is tomorrow night. John Sebastian is openin' for her. It's going to be like another Woodstock, but Southern-style."

"I'll bet," I said. "But it's Joni I came to see, so we'll each take a ticket for tomorrow night."

After tucking the tickets into our pockets, Bink asked me, "Don't you want to see Joan Baez?"

"I'd love to see Joan Baez," I said, "but I'm worried about running out of money. How much do you have left?"

Bink fished his wallet out of his back pocket and thumbed

through it. "Let's see," he said. "Uhm, I count $67.00." Then he jingled some coins in his pocket, adding, "And some change."

"Well, I have less than that, and we need to buy food, get a motel room, and then gas to get back to Connecticut. It looks like we'll need to go straight back in one day, but not until I meet Joni."

"And what are we going to do between now and tomorrow night?"

"Not anything that costs money. Maybe we can find out where Joni is staying and connect with her."

Bink shot me a look that questioned my sanity, but I didn't mind. My focus was one-pointed, and nothing was going to distract me from my quest.

It was approaching dusk as we headed back down the winding mountain road. Mountain peaks rippled against the purple sky in the distance. After passing a sign that said, Welcome to Asheville, I spotted another dumpy motel. The place was dark except for its neon sign, the words "Red Raccoon Motel" aglow, and a dim light in the office. I pulled up and said, "C'mon, let's see what the deal is."

I tried to open the door, but it was locked. "Hold on," I heard the raspy voice call from within. A man arrived on the other side of the door, and I saw him unhook a little chain like we had on Maltby Street when I was a kid.

"What can I do for you?" he asked.

"We're wondering if we can rent a room," I replied. "Are there any vacancies? The vacancy light on your sign isn't on, but I only see a few cars in the lot."

"There's always vacancies, kid," he said. He shut the door and released the chain. When we walked in, I was surprised to see he was heading back to the counter, tapping a red and white cane with a round tip.

Bink looked at me and mouthed the word, *blind*, as if I needed it explained to me. I just rolled my eyes. I'd never known anyone who was blind. When we reached the counter, I looked into his eyes, two round milky pools, his eyeballs not clearly visible. He was bald on top and had long, stringy white hair. His face was wrinkled and he looked like he hadn't shaved in a week.

"One night?" the man asked.

"Two nights, please," I said.

"Okay, that'll be $26.00 – $13.00 a night. Will it just be the two of you guys?"

I hesitated before saying, "Yes," and then Bink and I exchanged puzzled looks, wondering how he knew that there were two of us or, for that matter, that we were both guys. Then, I felt the need to offer, "Yeah, this is my pal, Bink – well, Kevin, and we traveled down here from Connecticut to go to the folk festival."

I knew it was too much explanation, and the man just nodded as if he knew exactly who we were and why we were there.

He made his way over to a side counter where he had an old single coil hot plate plugged into an outlet. A dented stainless steel percolator like Mom and Dad used to have at home was just starting to heat up. I could hear the popping of the coffee boiling and see the dark bubbles splashing against the small glass top.

"Can I pour you boys a cup o' java?" he asked.

Bink and I both said, "No thanks" as if we had rehearsed it.

"It hits the spot, but suit yerselves."

He reached up to a key rack on the wall with his left hand and felt his way from left to right before taking a key off a hook and saying. "Y'all'll be stayin' in room 104. It's just a few doors down."

I handed him a ten and a twenty, and when he reached into a cash drawer and gave me back four ones, Bink and I were once again mystified as if we were witnessing an act of inexplicable magic, as if we were in the presence of Houdini himself.

Walking out the door, Bink couldn't hold back, frantically whispering, "How did he know that we were –"

"Shhh!" I cautioned. "He'll hear us."

"He can't hear us from in there," he complained.

"Just shut up," I said. "He's blind. He isn't deaf!"

"But how did he know you gave him a ten and a twenty? You could have given him two ones! How did he know? How did he know it wasn't –"

"Will you shut the hell up?" I almost yelled, and then I shifted back to a whisper. "Maybe he just *trusted* that we wouldn't screw him over. Did you ever think of that? If the price was twenty-six and I gave him two bills, maybe he just assumed it was a ten and a twenty. Now put a lid on it until we're in the room for God's sake."

Once in the room, he continued to blather about the blind man for too long until I put an end to it. "Listen, I just think handicapped people, maybe, have ways of compensating for their problem. A blind guy can't see, but maybe his hearing or sense of smell is keener than ours. Or maybe a deaf guy can't hear, but he can see better than us. Who can explain it? Maybe we have greater limitations than they do."

That seemed to satisfy him, and he clammed up, thank God. The room was dingier than the last motel room we'd been in, and it reeked of cigarette smoke as well. Once we were settled, Bink and I took off in the Corvair to find somewhere to eat. Not a mile away, we immediately scoped out a Howard Johnson's, which looked just like the one in Derby, with its distinctive orange roof and blue spire.

As we sat in a booth chowing down our food, Bink asked, "What do you suppose the guys are doing at Duchess tonight?"

"Guys and *girls*," I corrected, biting into my greasy BLT.

"Yeah, right."

"They're doing what they always do," I said. "The same old humdrum stuff, cooking twenty-fours, dropping fry baskets in the hot oil, filling the ice bin, making sodas and milkshakes."

Then, after a pause, Bink asked, "Do you like having girls on the crew, or did you like it better when it was just guys?"

With my mouth full of chewed up fries, I said, "Guys."

"Really?"

"Yeah...with just guys, we could talk about everything more freely, especially about girls. Now we have to be careful, like when we're in school."

"I suppose you're right," Bink conceded. "But I'm hoping that maybe as more girls are hired, I'll meet someone."

"I understand," I said, and I *did* understand. We both wanted to meet someone. It was something that we had in common, something that bonded us. Hopefully, in the future, we'd zero in on two different girls instead of the same one, like with Sparrow.

When we got back to the motel, Bink disappeared into the bathroom, and I could hear him brushing his teeth. When he emerged, he mumbled a "good night" and in about a half second, he was out for the count. I wish I could say the same for me, but it wasn't so. After reading for fifteen minutes, I tried to sleep, but I could hear the rhythmic creaking of what was obviously a mattress and box spring and then the moaning of a female voice through the thin wall. I knew what I was hearing. The last time, it had been Duke and Sparrow in their tent at the campground; this time, it was an anonymous albeit noisy couple. *Just my luck,* I thought. It would be hours before I would fall asleep.

As I lay there, staring up at the ceiling and listening to the lovers' amorous rhythms intermingled with Bink's intermittent snoring, I pictured myself meeting Joni. Despite the noise that prevented me from sleeping, I stared up at the ceiling feeling optimistic.

CHAPTER 39

We spent the better part of the next morning cruising around Asheville, asking people – the waitress at the greasy spoon, a postman, a gas station attendant – if they knew where Joni was staying while the festival was going on. No one knew anything. I felt like I was King Arthur combing the English countryside, questioning every serf I ran into.

"Pardon me, my good man, but would you know where I could find the Holy Grail?"

"Oh, you moin the sacred cup Jesus quaffed 'is last drink from, matey? That one?"

"Precisely!"

"No, Oim afraid Oi don't, cap'n!"

Suffice it to say, finding where Joni was staying was a similar exercise in futility.

After we grabbed our second meal at Howard Johnson's, Bink and I found an outdoor basketball court and played one-on-one with a ball I had stowed away in the trunk. That, too, was an exercise in futility because Bink simply has no talent for the game. I tried to go easy on him, though, pretty much not playing any defense at all.

The afternoon hours were harder to fill with any meaningful activity. I called home and spoke to Mom.

"How are you doing?" she asked.

"Great...just great," I said.

"The car is running well?" It was almost like she was telepathic.

"Oh yeah. For sure. You know the Corvair. Always reliable."

The Garysburg incident remained a secret. I'll probably take it to the grave.

"Well, just be careful," she cautioned. "Don't get too big for your britches."

"Don't you worry about it, Celia," I teased. "I'm cool. I can look out for myself."

But could I? That was the question. Feeling a little shaky, I even called Mary Elizabeth, opening up to her about the debacle with the Corvair more than I had with my mother, but after ten minutes, I decided I couldn't afford to continue the call.

We killed more time by going back to the motel and reading, and then headed back up into the mountains when I couldn't stand waiting any longer. We arrived at the festival gates and parked the car.

As we walked into the park, young men at kiosks called out, "Festival t-shirts on sale here. Only two bucks!" as they hawked their wares. The shirts had colorful tie-dye designs with a circle in the center that housed a silhouette of a folk guitar and a pine tree. Neither Bink nor I could resist buying one despite our dwindling funds. A souvenir of our road trip.

It occurred to me, as we walked along a path bordered by mammoth evergreens, that this would only be the second big concert event I had ever attended; the first was Blood, Sweat and Tears at Kennedy Stadium in Bridgeport a year ago when Tomaso and I had doubled. I was with Samantha Getz, a girl I had met at Duchess, and Tomaso was with some chick he had gone to high school with. I remember how I loved the band but not the girl. And I also remember Tomaso needling his date on the drive to Bridgeport. "Why ya sittin' way over there? I don't bite!"

Bink and I entered a small clearing where an older man was playing the guitar, crooning "Puff, the Magic Dragon" for maybe twenty or thirty people. With shoulder length white hair, red plastic-rimmed sunglasses, and a tattered Derby hat, he looked garishly clown-like. We hung there for a while, listening to him sing in a raspy voice that sounded like it had smoked one too many cigarettes.

I was feeling impatient. It was that feeling you have when you want something so bad you can barely function. Bink must have sensed my agitation because he tapped me on the shoulder and asked me if I was okay.

"I'm okay," I said, "but I didn't drive all this way to hear some old hippie sing 'Puff, the Magic Dragon,' that's for sure. Let's go!"

"I don't know what your rush is," Bink complained. "Joni doesn't go on for almost three hours, and John Sebastian doesn't sing for almost two."

He had a point, of course. We just wandered the grounds, people-watching and, for my part, trying to figure out where Joni might be. Signs along the path were decorated with the festival logo and in bold multi-colored letters, THIS WAY. We found a refreshment stand where we grabbed a couple of burgers and fries. Eating something killed a little time, which always seems to drag when you want it to fly by.

We reached the main clearing, which must have been two or three times as big as a football field. Thousands of people were already seated on blankets in the lush grass or in lawn chairs. Circling back behind the big main stage, I noticed that there were a couple of trailers – long and white, like the ones that movie stars might have while making a film.

"Do you think she's in one of those trailers?" Bink asked.

"I'd bet my life on it," I replied. "At least later we'll know where to find her. C'mon, I want to get as close to Joni as possible."

"But there's no room anywhere close."

"We'll squeeze in somewhere."

We made our way around the perimeter of the crowd and spotted a small piece of real estate on the edge of the grass, right near the woods, about fifty yards from the stage. It would be a side view, but that worked for me.

Folk acts were already performing on the main stage. It wasn't that they weren't talented, and for a while I enjoyed listening to them, but some of them were corny, more Nashville than Woodstock. And they weren't Joni. After a short while, I made eye contact with Bink. He flashed a sly smile at me and withdrew his handy deck of cards from one of his pockets. We spent the next hour playing Setback before I got tired of playing, opting to lay back and shut my eyes. I rested in that exasperated state somewhere between sleep and wakefulness.

I'm not sure how much time passed, but Bink shook me awake

when a guy with a concert t-shirt and a straw hat, Gay 90s style, stepped up to the microphone and said, "Hello, folk music lovers! Are you all ready for our headliners?"

At the sound of his amplified voice, the crowd came to life, applauding and howling in assent. Without realizing it, I was up on my feet, making noise with the best of them.

"Well, here we go! Let's all give Mr. John Sebastian a warm welcome, everybody!"

The crowd erupted again. When he walked out on stage in tie-dye cut-off jeans and a short-sleeve shirt that was unbuttoned, revealing his hairy chest, a group of girls sitting right next to us lost their freaking minds and screamed, "Oh my God! Oh my God! Oh my God!"

I wanted to say, "Alright, let's just get a hold of ourselves."

Then when he began strumming his acoustic guitar and singing "Daydream," one of his oldies when he was with The Lovin' Spoonful, even I joined in the euphoria.

The end of his song was greeted by a standing ovation. Waving to the crowd, he said, "You guys are far out!" as whooping and hollering started again. "In fact," he continued, "this is such a poetic setting, and you are so beautiful, that I am reminded of a little concert I played at two summers ago up in Bethel, New York."

No sooner had the words escaped his mouth that the crowd carried on with even more passion and enthusiasm if it was possible. Bink and I were caught up in the emotion as much as anyone. If everyone else there was like me, they wished they had been to Woodstock in '69, and they hoped that the night might recapture some of the magic.

He surprised me when he then shared, "Now something that you might not know is that I was at Woodstock as a spectator. I wasn't on the schedule to perform. But after a rain storm delayed the crew from putting Santana's amplifiers on the stage, they asked me to do an acoustic set."

I certainly hadn't known that, and I suspected from the reaction of the crowd that many others also hadn't known.

"That's right," he went on, "so it was all very spur of the moment. Totally spontaneous and synchronistic. So, I started with this," and he began singing, in a most heartfelt way, "How Have You Been?" The crowd quieted in reverence, as if the vast field had been transformed into nature's cathedral. To make a noise would have been sacrilege.

When he let the last note of the song ring out, the pious crowd turned riotous, exploding into applause.

"How do you like my shorts?" he asked, and the crowd greeted his question with laughing and clapping and whistling. "I learned to do tie-dye from a lady when I was livin' in a tent in California. I tie-dyed my tent at the time." He smoothed out his shorts and added, "Now I tie-dye *everything!*"

His easy wit cracked up the entire crowd.

"Hey! Speaking of tents, I saw on the way in that some of *you* are stayin' overnight in tents. I like that. Like I said at the farm in '69, all ya need is a cloth house if ya got love."

That remark elicited a loving response from the crowd. I loved it too, and from what I could see, so did Bink.

As he continued his set, dusk settled in and the lighting instruments that hung from towering poles seemed more obtrusive.

After the fifth or sixth song, he said, "I see so many of you are enjoying this beautiful green place, and it's so incredible that you can smoke here and not be afraid, isn't it?"

I wondered why people could smoke so freely, but it was true. The group of girls next to us had been passing around a pipe the whole time. Having just smoked pot for the first time in my life, I wondered if I would repeat the experience. I somehow doubted it. *That time has come and gone,* I realized. *If I was going to become a pot smoker, it would have happened already.* But I pictured Sparrow and smiled.

John Sebastian sang seven or eight more songs, some old hits and some new compositions, before his set ended.

After a short break, the moment I had been awaiting arrived. Dusk had now given birth to nightfall, and I gazed up at the mountain sky dotted with millions of brilliant stars, and time ceased to exist.

The announcer manned the mic and said, "Our final performer for the festival needs no introduction. For me, I fell in love with her the first time I heard her utter a single note."

I wanted to yell out, "Yeah, me too!" but I contained myself.

The lighting dimmed to black, as the announcer's voice reverberated through the tall speaker cabinets: "Miss Joni Mitchell!"

When the thunderous applause began, a spotlight came up on a black stool. When she walked into the light, barefoot and clad in a long white embroidered dress, she picked up a small stringed instrument, and I felt my heart beating faster. She launched into "California" and sang with so much – I don't know what to call it – so much *heart* that I almost stopped breathing.

At the end of the song, after the applause subsided, with genuine humility, Joni said, "Thank you. I wrote part of that song in Paris and part in Los Angeles." The audience responded with warm applause, and she continued, "Yes, that's the story about that one." After fiddling with her stringed instrument, arbitrarily strumming or picking a few different harmonious notes, she explained, "If you're wondering, this is a mountain dulcimer, a true American folk instrument, from right here in the Appalachian Mountains. It was made for me by a wonderful girl named JoEllen from California who does beautiful work. She carved all the sound holes herself. There's so many of you, you might not all be able to see, but on the sounding board, she carved little stylized swallows, and on the tuning head, a hawk." She held up the instrument for all to see.

Something about Joni's authenticity made my eyes fill with tears. I don't know how to describe it except to say that you just knew that when she spoke, she was speaking her deepest truth.

"There are all kinds of myths about the origin of the dulcimer," she continued, still doodling, making little plings and plangs on the strings. "Different countries take credit, but no one knows the real story."

As I listened, she made me feel like we were alone, just Joni and me, maybe in a park or by a brook or maybe in a comfy room where she was strumming her custom-made dulcimer as she talked to me. That's how Joni talked to the crowd – just relaxed and friendly, drawing each of us in to a personal dialogue with her.

For the next hour, as she seamlessly moved from the dulcimer to the guitar to the piano, I couldn't comprehend her versatile talent. The crowd was less raucous than they had been for John Sebastian, but I realized it was Joni's serenity that had a calming effect on all of us.

As a fan, I had every one of her albums on either eight-track or LP, so I knew every song – so whether she sang "Song to a Seagull" or "Big Yellow Taxi" or "Both Sides, Now," I knew the lyrics to the songs and found myself mouthing the words as she sang. Hearing her recordings was one thing, but hearing her raw emotion live was another – strictly cosmic.

But the song that got me like no other was a lesser known tune called "For Free" from the *Ladies of the Canyon* album that Hippie Tina had introduced me to. As Joni sang about a man she saw playing his clarinet on a corner, I pictured myself as the man, actually, because I grew up playing the clarinet. And, in my mind, it was me she was observing. I was the man that everybody passed by because he wasn't famous. And in the song, Joni talks about herself, how she plays music for curtain calls and has a big limousine. I remembered that freezing cold night in New York when, with chattering teeth, I helplessly watched her escape the crowd outside the stage door at Carnegie Hall to her limousine. I was so upset that night. Continuing to listen to "For Free," it seemed to me that Joni, famous as she is, wished she could meet the clarinetist who played "real good for free," and I understood that she would have been upset if she knew how bad I felt that night. Tears were now streaming down my cheeks. I just felt an implicit understanding that, given the right circumstances, Joni would love to meet me as much as I would love to meet her.

I hoped Bink couldn't see that I was crying. I tried to wipe the tears away without being noticed like you do when you're watching a movie with a girl and don't want her to know that the sad parts are making you cry too.

I wasn't done crying for the night, though. For her last song, Joni sang one of her biggest hits, "The Circle Game," and I'll never forget what happened. After each verse, when she came to the chorus, everyone joined in singing with her. It just happened spontaneously, and all I can say is I never felt more connected to a group of people in my life. Thousands of strangers, all unified in song. And when she sang the last verse, mentioning that the central character of the story is now twenty, it hit me, *I'll be twenty on my next birthday*, and when I reflected on my own lost dreams and new dreams, my eyes started raining tears again. It was impossible to hide it from Bink this time. Thankfully, Bink never asked me why I was crying. It was good of him because if he had, I'm not sure I would have had an answer.

Joni bowed as her fans stood and showered her with love. After she exited the stage, the crowd wouldn't stop. "We love you, Joni!"

and "More, more!" and "Encore!" they yelled. I felt like we should all give up, but to our delight, she returned to the stage and picked up the microphone.

"Thank you, everybody," she began as the ovation quieted. "You're so beautiful. And I'd love to sing another one for you. I'd love to stay out here all night with you, until the sun rises, but I'm afraid I'm losing my voice, and I have another concert this weekend in Los Angeles, so I have to take care of myself. I hope you understand. But I love you all!"

Even though the crowd groaned, I sensed a collective understanding. And when Joni waved to all sides of the audience, everyone applauded and blew her kisses, and that was that.

The crowd gradually dispersed into the night to their cars or tents or wherever life was waiting for them.

Without a word to Bink, I headed straight for the stage. A step behind me, he said, "Uhm...where are we going, Gabe?"

"You know where we're going," I said, as if under a hypnotic spell.

"Oh, uhm...okay." I suspect he didn't have the energy to argue.

Strangely, there were no autograph seekers. Perhaps they knew something I didn't.

Behind the stage where we had discovered the trailers earlier, I saw a burly guy with long wavy hair and a bushy mustache standing by the door of one of the trailers. *That must be the one,* I realized. It had hardware with a heavy chain and a big metal ball on one end so that it could be hitched to a truck for transport.

I approached the man and said, "Pardon me, sir, but will Joni be coming out?"

"Nope." Obviously, he wasn't a big conversationalist.

"I was just wondering if maybe I could get her autograph."

He didn't make eye contact with me.

"Sorry, man, but if she came out here and started signing autographs, she'd be here all night. Joni needs to rest."

I could feel a tug on my back belt loop, and I knew it was Bink.

Miraculously, I maintained a lot more composure than I had months ago at Carnegie Hall. I calmly walked away with Bink still a step behind me, but then I turned back.

"Will she be heading to L.A. tomorrow?" I called to the sentry.

"No, she'll want to spend a day or two here in Asheville...to decompress."

"Decompress?" I said. "How does she do that?"

"She paints, man," he said.

I didn't want to push the envelope too much, so I accepted his answer and moved on.

She paints, I said to myself. *Of course, she paints!* I was left with one question. Where in Asheville would a celebrity go to paint?

CHAPTER 40

Walking across the field, Bink and I meandered through the litter left by the crowd on our way to the path that led to the parking lot. I could see a sprinkling of glowing campfires illuminating tents around the perimeter of the field and hear the distant voices of the campers. The only other sound was the tranquil, pulsing song of crickets contrasted by the occasional eerie call of an owl.

The Corvair was easy to spot with so few cars left in the lot. As I drove to the main road, Bink asked, "Uhm...Gabe? Now what?"

Feeling deeply reflective, the last thing I wanted to get into was a conversation.

"Back to the motel, Gabe?"

"Yeah," I agreed, "back to the Red Raccoon, and I'll hope for better luck in the morning. I think it's back home tomorrow."

Bink made an unintelligible sound. I think he was glad I didn't have some convoluted plan to try to connect with Joni that night.

"What a pathetic road trip," I complained. "It looks like it won't end up being even a full week long."

"Yeah...the guys'll make fun of us."

"Maybe," I said, "but maybe not. Maybe if...if..."

"If what?"

"If I meet Joni Mitchell, I doubt anyone'll make fun of us."

Bink didn't reply.

Back at the Red Raccoon, it was a replay of the night before with

Bink brushing his teeth and falling asleep and our neighbors in the next room back to their antics.

"Just my luck," I mumbled a little too loudly. Bink stirred at the sound of my voice but didn't wake up.

I decided that reading would help me relax, but I had forgotten to get new batteries for my flashlight, and I feared the ambient light from a lamp would disturb Bink. I had noticed a lawn chair outside the motel office. It was one of those old metal jobs like my grandfather used to sit in smoking his pipe outside his garage. *This must be where the blind man sits when he wants to get some sun,* I thought. Since it was the middle of the night, I felt it was safe to go sit in it. There'd be enough light from an overhead bulb to read.

I grabbed my copy of *The Grapes of Wrath* and slipped out of the room. I sat outside the office, but instead of reading, I took out my picture of Joni, unfolded it, and smoothed it out.

Sitting in the chair and staring at Joni, I lost track of time. The sound of the office door opening startled me.

The blind man said, "I'm just gonna have me a smoke if ya don't mind."

I had given up trying to figure out how he knew the things he knew, so I just acted all cool about it. "No, I don't mind." I quietly folded my *Vogue* page, hoping he didn't hear what I was doing.

Holding his pack out toward me, he said, "Smoke?"

I somehow felt embarrassed. "Oh, no thanks. I don't smoke."

"Smart," he replied and then lit up, took a drag, and blew a long puff. "Beautiful night, ain't it?"

"Yes, it is," I replied.

"Couldn't sleep?" He seemed like he was in the mood for a conversation.

"No, sir. Too much noise. My friend was snoring, and the people in –"

"Oh them?" he said. "Dang it. I forgot all about Cliff and Beverly. They're regulars, every Wednesday and Thursday night. Even got their own key. I should have given y'all a room farther away from those two lovebirds. My error. If y'all want, I'll switch up yer room for ya."

"No, that's okay. My buddy is fast asleep, and I'd rather not disturb him."

He stood there sucking on his cigarette, and I realized I was

weird feeling when you first wake up and you don't know what time it is or where you are or which end is up. But after I shook the sleep away, I realized it was just early morning in Asheville and that I had just enjoyed the first sound night of sleep since our trip began.

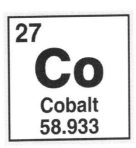

27
Co
Cobalt
58.933

When I walked into Mr. M's room, I was happy to see the letters Co and the number 27 on the board. You never knew when he was going to do one of his discussions, but those classes were always the most interesting, even more interesting than labs like the elephant toothpaste experiment, where we witnessed the reaction between peroxide, potassium iodide, and soap, resulting in a white column of foam shooting out of the beaker. I'm not going to lie, that rocked... but these discussions with Mr. M even trumped flashy lab experiments somehow.

On such mornings, my eyes searched his desk for whatever objects he had in store for us. On this particular morning, though, I didn't notice anything.

Once we were all seated and settled down, he smiled at us. He walked over to the bank of windows. Picking up a D cell battery that was sitting on the sill minding its own business, Mr. M began, "What does this have in common," and then moving to the back of his chair, he lifted up what looked like an old tablecloth with a blue geometric pattern and said, "with this," and then, bending over, he lifted an old window frame with a combination of clear and blue panes between narrow strips of lead, and once again said, "and this," and then, opening his desk drawer, he withdrew an old red and silver horseshoe magnet, and spoke again, "and *this*? What do these four items have in common? Anyone?"

I know I was clueless, and I could see that even Tim Ziamba sat in ignorant silence.

After surveying the room, Mr. M said, "Cobalt! Atomic symbol, Co."

Surprisingly, Jody Watkins blurted out, "One of the blue paints we use in art class is called cobalt."

"Exactly, Jody," Mr. M said, no doubt as surprised as I was that Jody had added anything meaningful.

Taking the tablecloth in his right hand, he continued, "For centuries, cobalt was used to make dyes and to color glass. Cobalt salts have been used, historically, to produce brilliant blue colors in paint, porcelain, glass, pottery and enamels." He picked up the window frame with his left. "The rich blue color that you see in these items, and yes, Jody, in the paint in art class, are the result of cobalt."

Jody turned to me, flashing a victorious smile. I couldn't blame her.

"Eventually, cobalt was used to make magnets," he said, picking up the horseshoe. "Alloyed with aluminum and nickel, cobalt creates a powerful magnetic force." He dropped his key ring on his desk, and we watched as six keys sprung skyward with a jingle and stuck to the magnet.

"In more recent history, demand for the transition metal has skyrocketed as it has become an essential part of lithium-ion batteries." Mr. M smiled and displayed the D cell battery between his thumb and index finger once again.

"As you can see, cobalt has many uses. Just a few more examples. Radioactive cobalt-60 is used to treat cancer and, in some countries, to irradiate food to preserve it. Cobalt has even been used in beer manufacturing to maintain a foamy head, but sorry, I'm not going to demonstrate that this morning!"

We all laughed. You had to love the guy.

He then became deadly serious as he offered, "Like gold and other elements, cobalt has come to exemplify deeper, more spiritual qualities. As a color, it is associated with transformation and inner growth. Additionally, cobalt blue has strong ties to communication, whether this means speaking your truth aloud or communicating with your inner self or your higher power. Also, cobalt blue represents tranquility and balance within oneself as well as within one's environment. Its calming energy helps bring peace into chaotic spaces while offering clarity when things feel overwhelming or out of control; this allows spiritual practitioners to stay centered even during periods of heightened stress and uncertainty."

You could now hear a pin drop in the room. I wasn't even sure if I was still breathing.

"So, as we continue our study of this element, I want you to think about the properties of cobalt in both the physical and the spiritual worlds."

Wouldn't you know that right at this dramatic moment, we had a fire drill, causing us all to exit the building. As I descended the stairwell, surrounded by dozens of students, I wondered how cobalt could be helpful to me through the times of stress and uncertainty I was currently experiencing.

When I walked out into the morning air, Jody was at my heels. "That stuff he said about cobalt was cool, wasn't it?" she said.

"Yeah...it was," I replied. "*Really* cool!"

There was a lot to digest about cobalt, but I think, for me, it really struck me when Mr. M spoke of communicating with my inner self and speaking my truth. I wasn't sure if these were things I always did. It was something I was going to have to think about.

CHAPTER 41

My eyes opened, and I blinked and looked at the glowing red numbers on the cracked face of an electric alarm clock. Digital alarm clocks are the latest thing, even though, to this day, I use the windup job my dad had given me when I was a little squirt. I rolled over and saw that Bink was still in a coma. It was early, but I had to get going. Slipping into my shorts and festival shirt, I scribbled a note on a small pad that was on the desk.

Bink,
I have to find Joni. Sorry to leave you here stranded, but I need to do this alone. I hope you understand. Checkout isn't until noon, so maybe you can watch TV til I get back. Wish me luck!
Gabe

I snuck out of the room, closing the door ever so quietly and drove out of the parking lot. I knew I looked like a mess and I'm sure I smelled none too good, but as the saying goes: desperate times call for desperate measures.

Following the signs for Downtown Asheville, I listened to a Joni tape as I drove. Ironically, "Woodstock" was the first song that came up, and I remembered Tina telling me how Joni had written the song even though she wasn't able to attend. A few months after Tina had enlightened me, while sitting in a booth at Mosci's, I read a quote by David Crosby in a pop magazine. "She captured the feeling and importance of the Woodstock festival better than anyone who'd been there," he had said.

Only Joni, I pondered as I approached Asheville's main drag where Bink and I had stopped at a luncheonette our first day in town. I noticed the name of the street was Broadway, which struck me as ironic because of the famous New York street. This Broadway was sleepy in the early morning, but I saw that the same establishment was open for breakfast, so I stopped in and sat on a round stool at the counter. It reminded me of Mosci's and a few other places in the Valley. *There must be greasy spoons like this in every little town in the country*, I mused as I scanned the menu.

I was happy to see the same freckle-faced waitress I had spoken to the day before. She shot me a friendly greeting. "Hey, it's my buddy from Connecticut."

"You remember me?" I said with some surprise.

"How could I forget? Did y'all make it to the festival?"

"Sure did," I said. "It was...amazing!"

"Aw! That's nice. What can I get ya – coffee?"

"Sounds great."

"How do you take it, cutie?"

Since she called me *cutie*, I responded in kind. "Light and sweet, somethin' like yourself." It was a line I had picked up from Will at Duchess.

And was I ever glad, even though I stole the line, because Freckle Face bubbled up with a giggle that lasted until after she had poured and served my coffee.

"What else, Mr. Smoothie?"

She looked at me like she was in love, but I didn't have time for love now.

"Maybe a bacon and egg sandwich?"

"Anything you want."

There was one other customer in the place, a black guy at the other end of the counter, eating his breakfast while reading the newspaper.

"So what ya got left on yer itinerary?" the waitress asked.

"Not much. We're running out of money and need to head back

home. But maybe you can help me before we take off. Is there somewhere around here where artists hang out?"

"Well, whattaya mean by artists?"

I wasn't sure myself.

"Uhm...I don't know...maybe somewhere painters make their art."

She squinted, and then she chuckled. "Hmmm! Let me see. I wouldn't call Asheville the hub of the art world."

"But there must be some artists who live here," I coaxed.

"Oh shucks, yeah, I s'pose so. I know there's some o' them oddball hippies and such, tryin' ta raise money to renovate the old factories and warehouses down by the French Broad River. I heard some of 'em go paint in abandoned buildings to show that those old wrecks still got life in 'em. But hold on, sweetie. Looks like yer sandwich is ready."

Now I was making progress. When she laid the small plate with my sandwich down, I asked, "So where is this French Broad River?"

"Lemme just show ya." She pulled the paper placemat from under my plate and drew me a map. "It's easy," she explained making fat lines on the paper, "just follow Broadway for three blocks and take a right and then go to yer, let's see, one...two...right, yer third light and follow it straight and you'll run right into it."

I did a pretty good job chomping down the sandwich while she was drawing, and then I thanked her.

"What is it yer lookin' for?" she asked.

She had been so nice, so I didn't want to blow off her question. "Let's just say that I'm looking for someone who can answer some questions I have."

"Oh, I get it. Yer some kind o' reporter."

"Sort of," I lied.

"Well, I sure wish you luck," she said, with such a big smile on her face I thought her freckles would pop off.

Using the placemat as my guide, I found the factories near the river in a matter of minutes. The buildings reminded me of the old structures on Canal Street in Shelton with broken windows and worn bricks. There must have been more than a dozen, and I wasn't sure where to begin. It was a ghost town of a street, somewhere I wouldn't have felt safe walking by late at night.

At the nearest corner, I saw a couple of parked cars and decided to do a little exploring. I felt a wave of anxiety pass through me. *What's the worst that can happen? I'll get thrown out,* I concluded.

I walked down a hallway with wooden floorboards, the wide planks dull and blackened from years of neglect. The ceilings were high with fat, exposed pipes. Suddenly, I heard some drumming, and I followed the percussive sound until I reached a staircase. Ascending the wooden stairs, the rat-a-tat sound got louder and louder. I arrived at an expansive space that must have once been a manufacturing assembly line of some kind. There were beat-up old machines and a rusty conveyor belt that connected one to the other like a train track joining a line of small towns.

A guy sporting a tattered top hat sat in the middle of the space banging away at a drum set. To get his attention, I would have had to yell, and I didn't want to startle him.

I stood there for about fifteen minutes, but I liked watching because he was lost in it. I'm surprised the top hat didn't fall off his head, given how aggressively he was beating the skins, alternating from one drum to another, exploding like machine gun fire and then slamming his sticks into one cymbal or another in complimentary rhythmic accents.

He looked up, beads of perspiration rolling down his forehead into his bushy eyebrows and streaming along the inner edges of his ears, and he stopped playing.

The silence was almost more deafening than his drumming.

His lips widened into a quizzical smile. "What's up, my man? Somethin' I can do for you?"

"That was great," I replied.

"Well, thank you, brother – I'm just gettin' in a little practice. Don't seem like nobody owns these ol' places, so nobody give a shit if I practice here. Add to that, there ain't no neighbors to disturb neither...so it's all cool."

"Yeah, I get it," I said. I hoped I sounded as cool as he did.

"So, like I said, what can I do for you?"

"I heard that artists hang around down here, and I was looking for someone."

"Oh yeah, young brother? And who might that be?"

I wasn't certain if I should tell him.

"Now, you got no need to be shy around me. Just lay it on me, and if I know the dude, I'll spill it."

"It's not a dude," I explained, and then, in my nervousness, I spilled the beans. "It's Joni Mitchell."

The drummer let out a long, "O-o-o-oh! I see! You a fan then, huh?"

"For sure," I answered.

"And I'm willin' to bet you're in love with her."

I just looked down, feeling embarrassed.

"Yeah...I dig it. You and jus' about every other cat in America. Well, you ain't gonna like hearin' this, my man – but Joni don't need no fans buggin' her."

"I understand," I said, "but I'm more than just a fan. I have some important things to talk to her about."

He pursed his lips. "I bet you do. And who tol' you Joni's here in this ol' good-for-nothin' factory?"

How was I going to explain who told me?

"A blind man...told me."

He smirked, gave his snare drum a rap, and shot me dead with an incredulous look. "What you talkin' about, brother? How's a blind man know where Joni is?"

"I don't know," I blurted out. "I'm confused, to be honest. But I know she's an artist and that she likes to paint, and I thought maybe she's here painting."

The drummer laughed out loud and struck his drums three or four more times with both sticks.

"My, oh my. You a funny mo-fucker," he said. "The fact is, I know Joni pretty good because me and her has played some clubs on the same ticket. Like I tol' ya...she don't, like, nobody, botherin', her. My advice is, abandon the search and forget about ever meetin' her."

"Yes," I said, "but I've come such a long way to talk to her. From Connecticut."

The drummer launched into a short drum roll and then laughed out loud again. "Oh, man, oh, man! You sound like Dorothy tryin' to see the Wizard."

I have to admit he was right, and I felt as vulnerable and helpless as Dorothy at the gates of Emerald City.

"No, I know," I said, "but...but you don't mind if I take a look around, do you?"

He flashed that mysterious wink at me again. "No, no, no, no, no! I don't mind nothin'. You do whatever you need to do, brother.

It's still a free country last time I checked. But you ain't gonna fin' her here, my man."

He winked at me, and there was an irony in his tone and a playfulness in his wink that suggested to me that he meant the opposite of what he said.

I thanked him profusely and headed back to the stairwell. The beating of my new friend's drums grew more and more faint as I ascended the wide staircase until, finally, I wasn't certain if the beating I was hearing was the musician drumming or the pounding of my heart.

At the entrance to the factory room, the open door was off its hinges on top and hung crooked, creating a little bit of an obstacle to the entrance. I wondered if I was barking up the wrong tree, but something within spurred me on. I straddled the lower end of the door and stepped into what appeared to be an observation platform that extended across one side of the room. *Maybe bosses stood here and watched the workers toil below*, I considered.

Lo and behold, there below me in front of a bank of windows at the other side of the cavernous space, a woman stood at an easel, painting with her back to me. I remembered my World Lit class and imagined how Sir Galahad felt when, because of his purity of heart, he discovered the Holy Grail.

It was hard to see, but it appeared to me that the woman was painting the windows, or at least a section of the windows just a few feet in front of her. I alternated looking from the canvas to the bank of windows, back and forth. Various panes were clouded, some were boarded up with plywood squares, while still others were broken, as if whoever had patched up the broken panes had finally given up. Broken glass lay strewn across the floor under the windows, and I couldn't see from my vantage point if she was trying to include them.

The woman was mixing colors on her palette then dabbing her paintbrush on the canvas before her. She wore sandals, pants, and an oversized t-shirt. At first it looked like she had a beret on her head. I don't know anything about art, but I think guys like Rembrandt always wore berets. Then I saw that it was an ordinary man's buttondown cap, wisps of golden hair dipping under the hat's edges. The rest, clearly, was tucked up inside.

Deciding the best thing to do was to keep my mouth shut and watch, I leaned against a rusty iron railing and soon lost track of time. Dizzy and uncertain, I was trying my best not to even breathe. I couldn't help but question if it could be her – if my dream was, in fact, materializing. *Can this be happening to me?* I wondered. But when she turned sideways and reached down to grab a different brush, I could see that the artist before me was unmistakably Joni Mitchell.

CHAPTER 42

I marveled at her uniqueness, even here, even alone, even unobserved. Unbelievably, I had found her, all by herself, creating a painting the night after a major concert. Something I had known subconsciously bubbled up in me like the coffee pot percolating on the blind man's hot plate. We were meant to meet.

After a short while, she addressed me. "You're an art lover I'm guessing."

I've heard of teachers who are said to have eyes in the backs of their heads, but I don't know if I ever encountered any. It appeared Joni had such a superpower because I swear I hadn't made even the slightest peep, and she hadn't looked at me once.

"I...uhm...y-y-e-e-s-s," I stammered. "Your painting looks, uhm, it looks great."

"Well, come down here and get a closer look," she said, still with her back to me. "I'd like to hear what you think of it."

I gulped and almost choked on my own saliva as I walked along the platform and descended a narrow brick stairway that led to the floor, stepping over unidentifiable debris, bits of metal and splintered wood, as I approached her. Joni didn't look at me, but seemed completely engrossed in her painting.

I suddenly wished I knew something about art because I knew I was going to sound like an ignoramus. What was I going to do if she asked me what famous artist influenced her work? *Let's see,* I thought to myself, *there's Rembrandt, and who? Who else?*

When I got closer, maybe only five or ten feet away, she stepped back, still not looking at me, and said, "So?"

What was I going to do? I had to say something, so I just confessed, "Gee, I don't know a thing about art. I took Music History, but now I wish I took Art History, so that I could give you some, you know, useful feedback."

"Don't know anything about art, huh?" she said, still engrossed in the image on the canvas. I couldn't tell if she was judging me.

"Not a thing," I responded. "I'm sorry for interrupting you. I shouldn't have come here."

"No," she said, "I'm glad you're here. I need feedback, and I don't need it from an art critic. Just tell me what you see and how it makes you feel. Art is meant for everyone, not just art majors."

Now she opened up, kind of like a door, and she finally turned to me, her eyes encouraging me to step closer to the canvas. Up close, she looked just like she did in magazine pictures – clean and natural and beautiful without a hint of makeup. Her fingers, though, were speckled with random paint colors.

For some reason, my nervousness dissipated, and it was as if I hadn't just made eye contact with one of the most famous recording artists on the planet. She was treating me just like a trusted friend who would give her an honest opinion.

"Well," I began, "as I said, I don't know anything about it, but I think maybe you aren't trying to do a realistic painting exactly. It looks more like a certain...I don't know how to put it, like a certain interpretation of factory windows."

Then I looked at her, hoping I hadn't in any way offended her. *Yeah, Joni, your windows suck, they're not even realistic looking. You can't even paint window panes!*

As that absurd reaction ricocheted off the walls of my brain, I tried to save myself. "I mean, what do I know, but I have a hunch you weren't trying to paint realistically, right?"

I breathed a sigh of relief when she smiled at me and said, "That's right. I can paint realistic windows, but that's not what I was aiming for. Anybody can paint realistic windows, right?"

I nodded, thinking, *Oh yeah, sure...anyone except me!*

She shrugged. "I'm hoping that the painting elicits feelings in people and makes them think. How does it make you feel?"

I inhaled deeply through my nose and brought my attention back to the canvas. "Let's see. Let, me, see! I think it makes me feel, uhm, sad..."

She smiled again, and her eyes reassured me. "Go on...tell me more."

"Yeah, it makes me feel that...uhm, this is probably wrong, but..."

She quelled my reluctance to continue, "There's no right or wrong with feelings. Go on, tell me more."

"You know, it's like you exaggerated everything...it's the jagged broken glass on the floor and the shattered panes of glass, and oh yeah, the ones that are covered over with plywood. It makes me think that the row of windows is the world and that...well, it makes me feel like the world is broken, that it's very badly broken, and maybe it's been neglected too long, like these windows, and maybe nobody's ever going to be able to fix it...and..."

I knew I couldn't say anymore without shattering myself, so I just helplessly looked at her.

Joni looked at me with those incredible blue eyes and said, "You're a pretty astute guy, uhm..."

"Gabriel," I said, knowing she was grasping for a name.

"Hi, Gabriel. My name is Joni," she said and reached out to shake my hand.

She gripped my hand firmly as I began rambling, "I know. You're Joni Mitchell, the famous singer. I was at the concert last night with my friend, Bink."

With a noticeable measure of amusement, she eyed my t-shirt which, obviously, was a dead giveaway.

"Yeah," I continued, mindlessly, "Bink and I work together at Duchess. That's in Connecticut. He and I tried to see you at Carnegie Hall last January, but it was sold out, and it upset me so much that...well, never mind that, but when we heard about the Blue Ridge Mountain Folk Festival, which Duke told us about...ya see, I picked up Duke and Sparrow who were hitchhiking way back in Connecticut, ya see...so yeah, when Duke mentioned the festival, we headed down here in my brother's Corvair, which is a real bomb... but..."

"Whoa! Whoa! Whoa! Please, Gabriel, let's not do this, okay?

Let's just keep doing what we were just doing. We're just two people, an artist who asked a nice guy for a reaction to her painting and a nice guy who gave her valuable feedback. Let's forget about who's famous and who's not because, honestly, who cares?"

And I realized she was right, but I didn't know what to say, so I just smiled.

"Do you drink coffee?" she asked. "I have a thermos here, and I could use a little break from painting."

"Yes, I like coffee," I said.

She sat down on the floor and poured some coffee into the cap of her thermos and handed it to me. It looked just like the thermos that my dad takes to work. Then she pulled a bagel with cream cheese out of a paper bag and ripped it in half.

"Here, have a bite to eat...and you drink out of this," she said. "I'll take it straight from the bottle," and then she let out the bubbliest giggle ever, so I laughed too.

I took a sip and I must have winced at the taste because she said, "Sorry I don't have cream and sugar. I like it black. I wasn't expecting company."

"No, it's fine. I like it black too, sometimes," which was a big fat lie, but I wasn't about to tell Joni Mitchell I didn't like her coffee. Instead, I changed the subject. "Yeah, so a girl I was with the night of my senior banquet told me you were a painter."

"She's right," Joni said. "My first love has always been art since I was a very little girl. I went to art college but dropped out."

"You dropped out of college?" I now took micro sips because I didn't enjoy black coffee. "My dad would kill me if I dropped out."

"At some point, you might want to consider," she said, "that you can't always do what your dad wants."

I remembered Sparrow saying almost the same thing to me.

"So why did you drop out of college, and what did you do?"

"The why is a long story and a little personal. What I did was I got more into music to support myself, and I started playing gigs at coffee houses or anywhere where people would listen to my songs."

"If art is your first love, how come you play music for a living?" I asked.

"It just happened. I can't explain how. My music just had an energy of its own. Some things are like that. Inexplicable. Besides, it's harder to make a good living from art."

"But you still paint," I said, "even the next day after a concert."

She smiled at me. "Yes, Gabriel, I will always be a painter first. Painting clears my head. I need both things in my life, painting and writing music. I love writing music, but writing is a more neurotic way to create, while painting is more meditative."

"So after a concert you paint?" I asked.

"When I can."

"It must be amazing to perform in front of thousands of people," I offered.

Joni's lips twisted into a sad smile. "I've never liked being a star or being the center of attention, but well, like I said, it happened. The truth is, the bigger the concert, the more of a problem it is for me. I've never fared well in front of crowds that are too big."

I was surprised because I always figured that big stars loved their celebrity, but as I chewed on the bagel contemplating Joni's words, I thought of how surprised I was at the deaths of stars like Marilyn Monroe when I was only about ten years old and then Judy Garland a few years ago and then, very recently, Janis Joplin. I didn't know the exact causes of their deaths, but in each case, the news talked about drugs and alcohol. I guess stardom isn't everything it's cracked up to be.

Joni seemed to have it together, though, and I found it hard to picture her drunk or strung out on drugs.

"So what's *your* deal, Gabriel?" she asked.

"My deal?"

"Sure, I create art and music to deal with my vulnerability. What do you use?"

It was a question that threw me. "I, uhm, I guess I don't use anything."

She smiled and held my gaze. "You mentioned your father. Do you and he get along alright?"

"Oh yeah! I mean, he can be, uhm, a dictator, and maybe I shouldn't say this, but I think he drinks too much."

"A lot of people drink too much," she responded. "*Most* people drink too much."

"I suppose so," I said.

"But you do whatever he says?"

"Well, not whatever he says, but it's hard to argue with him."

"And, you're how old now?"

"Nineteen."

"I see. Well, I'm not telling you to rebel against your dad, but sometimes a little rebellion isn't a bad thing. If you let people rule your life, you'll never find the real you."

I took a bite, shrugged, and then while chewing said, "I want to find the real me."

"What else is preventing it?"

"I'm a little embarrassed to say it, but for one thing, I'm still...still a virgin."

"So?"

That was about the last reaction I expected.

"So...how would you feel if you were me? I don't know another guy my age who's still a virgin, except for Bink."

Joni reacted with complete surprise, letting out a belly laugh. "Oh my! Oh my," she said through the laughter. "I don't mean to laugh at you, but that might have been the funniest, most adorable thing I ever heard a young guy say."

Feeling stupid, I related in words what I was feeling, "You can see how dorky that makes me. Right?"

"No, I can't," she said, her laughter now subsiding. "It doesn't make you dorky at all. And it doesn't matter."

"It doesn't?"

"Of course not. You're a sweet guy, and when you find the right girl, it'll happen."

"You make it sound so simple."

"That's because it *is* simple."

"But almost every guy I know –"

She interrupted and patted my hand. "Don't listen to all that guy talk. They're mostly full of it."

"But what about 'free love' and all of that? I'm not finding anything free about it."

"That's because love isn't free." She nibbled at her bagel. "Look, I don't buy into all of this hippie culture crap."

"But...you're...you're...I mean, you wrote..."

"I know I'm Joni Mitchell and I wrote 'Woodstock,' but that doesn't mean I buy into hippie ideology. Men have been trying to use women since the dawn of time," she said with an ironic laugh. "And the free love movement was made up by and benefits men."

"Wow," I said, not able to think of something more profound.

We sat in silence for a while chewing on our bagels and sipping the black coffee that was now beginning to cool, making it taste even worse. But I still kept drinking.

Sometimes when you sit in silence, you wonder how many minutes have gone by, but this was a very peaceful silence and time ceased to exist.

Joni apparently saw that I had stopped sipping my coffee. "I guess you've had enough, right?"

I smiled sheepishly and said, "I guess."

She reached over, took the cap out of my hand, walked over to a broken pane, and poured the leftover coffee out of the window.

"So what else?"

"What else?"

"Did you forget what we're talking about already?" she teased. "What else prevents you from dealing with your own vulnerability? What else is holding you back?"

"I guess...I don't know how to explain this. It's just that since I was, like, a sophomore in high school, a lot of people I know have died. Not just old people like my grandparents, but even people my age that I'd gotten to know at work or in the neighborhood or wherever. It just freaks me out, I guess."

Joni let out a deep sigh. "Yes, death – the great mystery. It's hard for everyone. I've faced my share of death, and I wish I could offer some deep wisdom on the subject, but I'm afraid I can't. What I can offer is this. 'A deep distress hath humanized my soul.' "

She must have read the puzzled look on my face. "Don't you like poetry?"

"I think so," I answered. "I'm an English major, you know, and I'm trying to understand poetry. Some of it is pretty, uhm, abstruse."

"Abstruse *shmabstruse*," she teased. "You don't need to try – just let it settle in and see how it makes you feel. Like my painting. All that matters is how it makes you feel. It's the same with my music. If you're all hung up about my fame, you can't meet yourself in my songs. But when you meet yourself in my songs, then they have real meaning."

"I see," I said, and somehow I felt like I *was* beginning to see.

"So, again, I offer you these words from the great poet William Wordsworth, 'A deep distress hath humanized my soul.' "

I don't know if anyone had ever looked at me like she did after saying those words, not even Sparrow. She didn't need to say it, but I knew she wanted me to just sit and let the words wash over me like baptismal water.

We sat in the same safe silence we had experienced a short while ago.

I wasn't about to speak, but Joni knew just how long to wait before offering, "I'm not a lot older than you, Gabriel, and I've been through some pretty sad times myself. I've come to feel that suffering is just another word for *growth*. I think that's what the poet is saying. This may surprise you, but I'm grateful for every bit of trouble I've experienced. What I've tried to do through it all is maintain a good heart. Looking into your eyes, I can see that you've managed to maintain a good heart through your distress too. That's all we can do."

It was a way of looking at life that I had never heard before.

"I don't know what to...what to say," I began slowly, "but I feel better than I've felt in a long time."

"Good," she said as she unexpectedly sprang to her feet. She took her painting of the windows off of the easel and carefully laid it on the ground, replacing it with a fresh new canvas. "I'm glad I brought a second canvas."

Then she took what looked like a fragment of a cardboard box, and she began squirting different colors of paint from jumbo tubes onto the cardboard surface. The fat paint looked like colorful squiggles of toothpaste.

"Let's see how you do," she said.

"How I do what?" I hoped she wasn't suggesting what she appeared to be suggesting.

"How you paint!"

"Oh, God. I don't know how to paint. I wouldn't even know how to begin."

"We can all paint. I'm sure you painted when you were a little kid. Just paint how you feel. Just slosh some colors on the canvas however you want. Don't think. Just get color on the canvas. Just let the colors say what you feel inside."

"But –"

"But nothing. Just do it," she commanded. "And don't think. Thinking only gets in the way. Your hand will know what to do."

I almost laughed as she put a thick brush in my hand. I dipped it into a glob of reddish-orange color and did just what she said. I sloshed it on the canvas.

"Oh, vermillion," she said with enthusiasm. "Good first choice."

"I thought it was, like orange or red-orange," I said.

"Red-orange, vermillion. It's all the same," she said. "What next?"

I spotted a yellow color and painted it on top of the vermillion, making what sort of looked like a sunrise on LSD.

"Wild! Cadmium. I like it," she practically cheered.

I smiled and blushed, while Joni looked around her like she had lost something. Suddenly, she picked up her thermos and skipped over to the windows, screwed off the cap, and set the thermos and cap down, side by side, on the brick ledge.

"Let's have you paint a still life," she said.

I was lost. "What's a still life?"

"A still life is when we paint a collection of inanimate objects. Go ahead. Let's see how you do with the thermos and cap."

I felt another surge of panic. "But...but I don't know how to paint an object. I have no idea how to paint a thermos."

"Like I've been telling you. Don't think about it. Just paint. Just create!"

"But it's...it's silver. I don't see silver on the cardboard."

"It doesn't have to be realistic. Remember? Life isn't always realistic. Pick a color that grabs you and make it that color."

Bewildered, I looked at the palate and dabbed my brush in blue.

"Cobalt! That's a good one!"

"Right...cobalt," I said, and I was suddenly transported back to Mr. M's chemistry class. He talked about Cobalt blue representing tranquility and balance. He spoke of its calming energy bringing peace and offering clarity when things feel overwhelming or out of control. He said it helps a person to stay centered during periods of stress and uncertainty.

What he had taught us suddenly rang true for me.

"Gabriel? Are you still with me?" I heard Joni ask.

"Oh...yes...yeah...I was just...sorry."

She giggled. "Wild! You went somewhere for a few seconds. Okay, just remember – don't think. Just paint what you *see*, what you feel."

So, I kept going. I spent the next half hour painting my version of the objects with Joni encouraging me every step of the way. When I was done, the canvas was covered with a big cobalt colored thermos and a green cap sitting next to it, set against a crazy sunrise. I somehow felt pretty good about it.

"How did it feel to make a painting?" she asked.

"Well, it's not real art, but –"

"Of course it's real art. Now answer me. How did it make you feel?"

"It felt...let's see...very, uhm, therapeutic. Yeah. And I forgot my problems while I was painting."

"Great," she said, and she hugged me. *Oh my God, Joni Mitchell is hugging me!* I wanted to shout.

As she released me, she asked, "What do you normally do to create?"

"Not art, obviously," I said with a laugh.

"You don't have to do art, but you need to create. We all need to create."

"I play some music. Clarinet and sax, and I'm learning to play a little guitar."

"Great, you like music, then...anything else?"

"Well, I'm thinking I'd like to be a writer. Maybe short stories or novels. I don't know."

"Good! We need creative pursuits in our lives, so be sure to take yourself seriously in your music or writing or whatever else you discover. Do things that you feel passionate about, that speak to your heart as well as your intellect. Never neglect the creative being within. We are all artists."

I looked at my watch and said, "Wow! I've been here for almost two hours. Bink must be worrying about me." Then, I looked at her and added, "Oh God! I'm sorry."

"Sorry?"

"For taking up all your time."

"No apologies are necessary. You're a sweet guy, and I had a great time. You need to take your painting with you, though."

I could feel my face go scarlet again as she handed me the canvas, and then she pulled her cap off her head, her blonde hair cascading around her shoulders, and put it on my head.

"What's this?" I asked.

"Something to remember me by," she said with a generous smile.

"Wow! My friends are never going to believe that Joni Mitchell gave me her hat," I said.

In what felt like a conspiratorial tone, she almost whispered, "Well, here's an idea. Don't tell 'em. Why not keep it between you and me?"

"Yeah," I said. "Why not?"

"Oh, and one more thing," she said, glancing at the ledge. She retrieved the thermos and screwed the cap on. "You'll need to take this too. Let it be a reminder that, when things are bad, you should never forget the words of William Wordsworth, and let your painting remind you that it is mainly the bad times that humanize us. And I hope you won't forget that, as human beings, we need to create – always!"

"I won't forget," I replied. "And I won't ever forget you!"

She then had one more surprise for me. Joni kissed me on the cheek, and as I made my way across the factory floor, I couldn't even think.

CHAPTER 43

I left Joni and headed down the factory stairs. It was hard to believe that I had just spent almost two hours with Joni Mitchell and harder still to believe that she had treated me just like I was a friend... just like Mary Elizabeth treats me. Life felt pretty good in that moment.

Opening the trunk of the Corvair, I carefully set the wet painting down, and I put the thermos next to it. The dazzling sun caused me to squint as I looked back at the dilapidated factory, knowing I'd always remember it. When I got back to the motel, Bink was sitting in the metal lawn chair outside the office with that same sick look on his face that reminded me of when we were both vying for Sparrow's attention.

Getting out of the car, I said, "Don't give me that look. I didn't mean to exclude you, but it was just something I had to do."

"So you met her?" he asked.

"Yeah, I'll tell you more about it in a minute, but I have to do something first. Did you check out yet?"

Bink shook his head.

"Perfect. Then give me the key."

I went into the office, and I found that the blind man was still there, thankfully.

"Hi," I said.

He was sitting quietly next to a small portable black and white television.

"You can just set the key down there on the counter."

How he knew it was me and not a new customer was one of a dozen mysteries about him that still puzzles me today.

"Yes, I'll do that," I offered, "but I also wanted to thank you."

"Thank me? Whatever for?"

"For pointing me toward the person I needed to see."

"Happy to be of service, young man," he said with a smile.

"But...but, how did you know who I was looking for...and where she'd be?"

"Truth is, I had no idea who you were looking for. Still don't. Hell, how would I know? I don't know you from Adam. But sometimes I get, how shall I put it, visions – pun intended." And then he emitted a raspy laugh, like his larynx was made of sandpaper.

"Wow! Well, I just want you to know that I appreciate it."

"Yer very welcome," he said. "But I gotta get back to *Sale of the Century*. I love watching the contestants' excitement when they win prizes, and I ain't ever got the slightest notion of who's gonna win, if you can believe that." And this time he howled as if he were the funniest guy on the planet.

When Bink lugged his duffle bag to the car, I said, "Just toss it in the back seat and I'll do the same with my stuff. I've got something personal in the trunk." Although he was obviously puzzled, I was glad he didn't ask. I drove off with nothing on my mind but getting home.

"Where'd you get the hat?" Bink asked.

"Oh, this dusty old thing?" I replied. "I found it on the floor of a factory where I met Joni." I hoped he couldn't tell I was lying.

"On the floor of a factory...but, wait, tell me what happened," he said.

And I did tell him what I felt safe to share. I avoided the nitty-gritty of what Joni and I really talked about, and I resisted the temptation to show him my painting. As I related encounters with our psychic motel clerk and the drummer with the top hat as well as witnessing Joni busy at work with paintbrush and easel, Bink listened with amazement, his jealousy diminishing with each part of the story. It made me realize what a good friend he is.

And then we made a decision to drive straight back to Connecticut. Looking at the atlas, Bink estimated it would take us about twelve hours, so barring any major traffic problems, we'd be back home around midnight. We agreed to take turns driving, switching every three hours, giving each of us time to rest. We had done what we had come to do, and besides, we only had forty-three dollars left between us.

As we hit the first major roadway, we talked about all the usual stuff – girls and sports and college and Duchess. Or I should say that Bink mostly talked and I mostly listened. After an hour, I had to tell him to stuff a sock in it, though, for two reasons. First, because it was important for the non-driver to rest, and also because I wanted to listen to music on the way home, which is exactly what we did the whole way.

As we left North Carolina, making our way through Virginia, Maryland, Delaware, New Jersey, and beyond, I felt like I was listening to the soundtrack of my life. In fact, there is something about the recording artists who wrote the songs I love, like Paul Simon; like Crosby, Stills, and Nash; like Bob Dylan; like James Taylor; like Carole King; and yes, like Joni Mitchell herself – the poets of my generation – that continue to make me feel that, while life may be sometimes challenging and while it may often be a mystery, it's important to keep on going, trying to figure out what our purpose on this spinning planet is.

While Bink slept, I kept replaying Simon and Garfunkel's "America." Since we were returning from a road trip, Paul Simon's music and lyrics resonated and felt poignant. It's not that we had discovered the America we were looking for, exactly, but we had a better sense of it than when we began. It occurred to me how sheltered guys like us, Bink and me, had been while growing up. *Small towns engender small-mindedness*, I remembered. But getting out into the world and meeting people like Duke and Sparrow and William and, of course, Joni gave me the feeling that there were lots of new people and new worlds to discover.

For a good long while, my mind wandered to people I already knew. Important people like Jeff and Tomaso. I wondered what time it was in Vietnam. I wondered if Jeff was in danger, and if he was afraid. I knew I would be. I wondered what Tomaso was doing in Korea. Was he shooting missiles from nuclear howitzers? I hoped not.

I also wondered what Jeff and Tomaso would think about my

meeting Joni Mitchell. I wondered if I would even tell them about it. Maybe, but Joni had suggested that it might be better to keep our morning together between ourselves.

When we drove over the George Washington Bridge late at night with Bink behind the wheel, I purposely popped Simon and Garfunkel back in and listened to "Homeward Bound." As one of my favorite duos crooned the moody tune, I wondered if my love was waiting "silently" for me. Joni had suggested that she was. Joni had talked about how music and poetry and art make you feel. A wave of emotion swept over me. Hearing the harmonious strains of Simon and Garfunkel and seeing the familiar New York skyline felt good. We were almost home.

As we motored our way from I-95 to each subsequent roadway – the Hutchinson Parkway, the Merritt Parkway, and finally Route 8, my anticipation grew and grew. When we got off on Pershing Drive, it was almost midnight and the lights at Duchess were still on. The guys were apparently just finishing cleaning up for the night.

CHAPTER 44

I wasn't surprised to see Michael's Dodge Charger in the lot when we pulled in. *Cobalt blue*, I thought to myself.

Even though he had been teaching high school for a year, Michael still couldn't extricate himself from the Duchess world. He loves the place too much.

When we walked in, Karl Fischer, a cigarette dangling from his mouth, was packing a dozen burgers into a bag to take home to his family. That's Karl's modus operandi – throw an extra twenty-four on the grill a half hour before closing, even if it's slow, so he can take a care package home to his wife and kids.

Bink, a step ahead of me, as if he were Moses returning from the mountain, announced our arrival. "Hey Karl, how ya doing?"

"Will ya look at this?" Karl said. "These two made it home. Have ya ever seen a sorrier fuckin' sight in your life?"

I suppose, after driving all day and night, we must have looked a mess.

The rest of the crew – Candy, Les, and of course, Big Alfred gathered around us.

"Hi guys!" Candy said. "How was it?"

"Yes, you darlings," Les added in his affected tone. "Tell us all about it."

Michael emerged from the office where he no doubt had just locked up the money in the big safe. "Well, lo and behold," he said.

"You two goofballs are the last thing I was expecting to see tonight."

Karl flicked his ashes in a trash can and said, "So that shitbox of a car made it, huh?"

"Sorry to disappoint you," I replied, winking at him to keep it light.

Michael remained silent, suggesting to me that our mechanical mishap was something he had kept to himself, which I appreciated.

"And how far'd you make it?" Karl asked.

Bink chimed in. "All the way to North Carolina."

"So, c'mon, guys. Tell us all about it," Candy said.

Quiet up until that point, Alfred jumped in. "How'd you boys like my home state? Beautiful, right?"

"Definitely," I agreed.

"And I'll bet you met some hot ladies," Alfred added. "There ain't nothin' like them Southern belles."

Karl sneered. "Are you shittin' me? These two losers?"

"Now, Karl! You just behave," the more kindly Les cautioned. "Let's just all sit down in the dining room with these two sweeties and hear all about it."

Bink and I sat on top of a table, and the five of them sat looking up at us. Karl tossed us each a couple of burgers, giving up a portion of his stash, which was probably the first nice thing he had ever done in his life. I appreciated it, considering I was famished, and for the next half hour we shared most of the details of our trip. They listened with rapt attention as we told them about our adventures and the people we met, from Greenwich Village to Asheville and everywhere in between. I even told them about Goober and Officer Davis, only I twisted the truth and made it sound just like a brief pit stop.

I didn't talk about my lakeside moment with Sparrow, though, and I definitely didn't mention meeting Joni. I was learning that we sometimes have experiences that not just anyone would understand. I felt conflicted about even telling Michael.

When Michael and I got home, it was so late Mom and Dad were asleep. I shuffled my suitcase and my wrapped up painting into my bedroom, hoping Michael wouldn't notice.

I curled up in bed, thinking I was going to conk off, when Michael walked into my room. "What's up?" I asked, my eyes half closed.

"Just wondering what's the big secret," he said.

"What're you talking about? I'm trying to sleep."

He motioned with his head at the painting, which was lying halfway under my bed. "The secret wrapped up in that blanket."

"Oh that," I said, realizing that, having shared the same bedroom on Maltby Street for most of our lives, he could see through me.

I remembered the many confidences in the small room on the second floor – the nights Michael would come home from a party or a date and toss his winter coat on my bed, purposely waking me up to tell me the tale about his evening. "Oh, sorry! Did I wake you?" he'd say, knowing full well that was his intent. But I loved those nights, hearing about how he had slow danced with a girl ("I put both arms around her, and she rested her head on my shoulder!") or his first kiss ("We were so busy we missed the whole movie!").

Those were conversations I still cherish. Michael was safe to share my secrets with. There's no bond like the one between two brothers.

So I rolled out of bed, unwrapped my still life, and told him the whole truth about Joni, about meeting her and about how she acted just like a regular person...that she was, in fact, just a person – an intelligent, warm, and friendly girl. Then I told him about the painting of the thermos and cap.

Michael simply shook his head in disbelief and said, "Well, Gabe, I don't think Renoir has anything to worry about." I didn't know a thing about Renoir, and I doubted Michael did.

"Lay off," I replied. "It's my first attempt. I'll get better."

"You're going to have to get a lot better. It doesn't look anything like a real thermos."

"That's how much you know, asshole. Famous paintings aren't always realistic."

I knew he was just razzing me, though, so there were no hard feelings.

"So, do you think you'll ever be in touch with her again?" he asked.

"That's a good question. Time will tell, I guess."

After Michael left my room, I further pondered his question. I seriously doubted that Joni and I would meet again. After all, Michael and Cecelia DeMarco didn't raise any dreamers. Almost without a doubt, it had been a one time experience. The stars were auspiciously aligned to allow the meeting, beginning with Duke telling us about the festival and leading to the prophetic blind clerk and the drummer at the factory. No such constellation of improbable circumstances was likely to happen again in my lifetime.

In the morning I put a couple of nails in the wall. I laid the canvas on my bed, taped my picture of Joni to the back of it, and hung my still life over the bed. I stepped back and admired my artwork, thinking back on what may have been the most important encounter of my life.

Mom would probably be the only other person to ever see my painting since no one else was in and out of my bedroom. I figured I'd tell her the story if she asked, but rather than asking, she teased me about it in her own special way.

"I like your painting, Mr. Artist," she said the next day, inferring that she somehow knew it was I who had painted it. A few weeks later she smiled at me at dinner and quipped, "I hope Mr. Picasso isn't planning to change his major to art," but Mom never asked about the conditions under which I picked up a paintbrush and created my first work of art.

CHAPTER 45

The next morning, the first order of business was to call Mary Elizabeth. We swung by Dunkin' Donuts and headed over to Osbornedale Park where we sat at a picnic table in the pavilion by the pond. She knew most of my story already, but even though Joni had suggested that I didn't need to tell people about our morning together, I couldn't resist telling Mary Elizabeth.

After hearing the whole saga, she said, "Well, I'll say one thing for you, Mr. Gabriel DeMarco. You are certainly persistent. I mean, when you want something, you go for it."

"Except that usually it doesn't work out in my favor," I said.

"This time it did."

"Yeah, I guess so."

"Well, what's next?" she asked, nibbling at her donut.

I sighed. "I don't know. Start the new semester. See what's in store for me. Try to be more awake and aware, like Duke said. Learn to be more independent."

"Sounds like a plan."

I looked into her eyes. "How about you?"

Mary Elizabeth chuckled. "I'm a senior now, so I have to figure out where I'm going to college."

"Got any ideas?"

"Somewhere good. I've worked hard. And I want to go away."

I could relate. I had wanted to go away too.

"Got anywhere in mind?" I asked.

"I think my dad will make me stay in the East, so I'm thinking maybe a Little Ivy, like Williams or Amherst or Middlebury."

While the names sounded familiar, I was embarrassed to admit I hadn't heard of Little Ivies.

At the risk of sounding stupid, I asked, "What are they?"

"Little Ivies?"

"Yeah."

"They're like smaller versions of Yale or Harvard. Similarly hard to get into."

"These are colleges you think will accept you?"

"I don't know. They're picky, but my class rank is good…I might even finish first or second, so we'll see."

I hadn't realized she was such a brain. You never actually know a person.

I smiled at her and said, "I suppose we'll be seeing less and less of each other, especially if you go away to college. I'll miss you."

"Oh, geez Gabriel, don't go getting all sentimental on me now. College is a year away."

But I knew that time travels quickly and that nothing is permanent, things I needed to start getting used to.

"So what do you have planned for the rest of the day?"

"Well, after I bring you home, I'm running down to Southern. There's something I want to check out in the library."

Even though it was several weeks before the second semester would begin, I drove over to Southern. I needed to delve further into the Wordsworth poem Joni had quoted.

What I discovered at the Buley Library at Southern was that the title of the poem Joni had quoted is "Elegiac Stanzas Suggested by a Picture of Peele Castle in a Storm, painted by Sir George Beaumont." What a mouthful!

I was in trouble right off the bat because, quite frankly, I had no idea what an elegiac stanza was nor did I have any clue who Sir George Beaumont was.

So the first thing I did was look up *elegiac* only to find it meant "of or relating to an *elegy*," another word that I wasn't wholly familiar with. Upon further investigation, I learned that an elegy was "a poem or song expressing sorrow especially for one who is dead." That worked for me. I looked at the poem, its fifteen quatrains spanning three pages, and I felt pretty intimidated as I read the first stanza:

I was thy neighbour once, thou rugged Pile!
Four summer weeks I dwelt in sight of thee:
I saw thee every day; and all the while
Thy Form was sleeping on a glassy sea.

Okay, let's figure out what pile means, I decided. I had hardly begun, and I was doing a lot of "looking up."

Pile: A large building or group of buildings.

Oh, that pile! Not, like, a pile of clothes. That accounted for the castle in the painting.

I forged on. "Thees" and "thous" and "thys" aside, it wasn't an easy poem to interpret. Joni had told me to evaluate a work of art by how it made me feel, but I needed a little help to decide. If nothing else, I was learning to research in college. Before I finished, I had three or four fat volumes that probably hadn't been opened in fifty years on my table, not only two with essays explaining the poem but also a hefty art history book which had a photo of George Beaumont's painting upon which the poem is based – a view of a dark castle on a cliff overlooking a stormy seascape.

In the fourth and fifth stanzas, Wordsworth suggests that if he had painted the castle instead of Beaumont, he would have placed the structure in a more peaceful setting.

Ah! then, if mine had been the Painter's hand,
To express what then I saw; and add the gleam,
The light that never was, on sea or land,
The consecration, and the Poet's dream;

I would have planted thee, thou hoary Pile
Amid a world how different from this!
Beside a sea that could not cease to smile;
On tranquil land, beneath a sky of bliss.

I got it. Wordsworth wished that life wasn't so stormy. Then, from a critical essay, I learned that the poem was, in part, inspired by Wordsworth's brother who had died at sea. I had known people who died, some close to me, but I couldn't imagine the death of my own brother.

And there, in the ninth stanza, were Joni's words:

A power is gone, which nothing can restore;
A deep distress hath humanized my Soul.

Ultimately, I understood that Wordsworth used the sea as a metaphor for life in elegizing the loss of his brother, and he suggests, especially in the final quatrain, that in the face of sorrow, we must have fortitude and hope.

But welcome fortitude, and patient cheer,
And frequent sights of what is to be borne!
Such sights, or worse, as are before me here.—
Not without hope we suffer and we mourn.

I understood. I had experienced a few storms in my own life, and I knew there was no telling how many I'd have to weather going forward. I felt grateful that Joni had shared the quote with me and happy that I had delved further into it. A lesson well learned. I closed the antique volumes, returned them to their shelves, and headed home.

CHAPTER 46

In the fall of 1971, the total number of American troops in Vietnam dropped to a record low of 196,700, the lowest since January of 1966. In the fall of 1971, my best friend Jeff's biological father, a man he hardly knew, died of a heart attack, and as a result, Jeff received notice that he would be released from his tour of duty in Vietnam and reassigned to a Mediterranean tour.

In the fall of 1971, the United States tested a thermonuclear warhead at Amchitka Island in Alaska, code-named Project Cannikin. At around five megatons, it was the largest ever U.S. underground detonation. In the fall of 1971, my cousin Tomaso had been stationed in Seoul, Korea for four months, where instead of manning nuclear howitzers, he had been trained on Hawk missiles, medium range ground-to-air weapons meant to protect the demilitarized zone, a neutral expanse of about one hundred and fifty miles that runs across the Korean peninsula.

In the fall of 1971, the Pittsburgh Pirates beat the Baltimore Orioles in seven games to win the World Series. Puerto Rican born outfielder, Roberto Clemente, was named the series MVP. Much to Bink's dismay, the Mets finished in a tie for third in their division, not making the playoffs for the second straight year. In the fall of 1971, Bink moved into a dorm at Storrs to begin his junior year at UCONN.

In the fall of 1971, John Lennon released a new song called

"Imagine," encouraging listeners to imagine a world of peace, without the things that separate us, like borders and religion. It quickly rose to number one on the Billboard charts. In the fall of 1971, after a heart-to-heart talk, I moved out of my father's house.

I'm beginning to think that the people we know and the things that happen to us are just meant to be, and that's all there is to it. As far as I'm concerned, that's why my mom and dad are my mom and dad, that's why Michael is my brother, that's why I have the friends I have, and that's why I have encountered the girls I've encountered, not the least of whom was Joni Mitchell.

That's how it was with Randy Duggan. It was only the second week of the semester when I was enjoying an early morning breakfast in the student union before my first class. I got a jump start on the day, contentedly enjoying my solitude and my breakfast – a couple of fried eggs, some rye toast, a juicy slice of orange, and a steaming cup of coffee – when Randy walked over to my table and said, "Mind if I join you?"

Now, the cafeteria in the CU must seat a couple hundred students. And I don't think there were even a dozen early birds there, so Randy had a million empty tables he could have sat at, but he picked mine.

"Yeah, sure. Fine with me," I said.

It wasn't the first time I had ever seen Randy. He had been a regular at Duchess for years. Of course, I've encountered hundreds or even thousands of kids while working the window, and most of them I don't know by name.

Wouldn't you know that Randy would bring it up right off the bat. "You work at Duchess in Ansonia, right?" he said, giving me an affable grin. "I'm Randy Duggan."

"Yup. I've been working at Duchess since I was fifteen," I said. "Good to meet you. I'm Gabe DeMarco," and I reached out and shook his big freckled hand. He squeezed my hand so firmly, I wondered if he had fractured any bones in my fingers.

Randy had straight red-yellow hair that fell just below his big earlobes, and a ruddy complexion that screamed out, "I'm Irish and proud!"

And right from the start, we were pals. There's no explaining it;

that's just how it is sometimes. And it's synchronistic that we met that morning at Southern because Randy and I had crossed paths at Duchess for years, and come to find out, we lived only about ten minutes from each other.

The next thing I knew, he and I were hanging out at a bar, Chick Henry's, in Ansonia not a mile from Duchess, right across the bridge on the corner before you get to Main Street. There was talk that the drinking age was going to be lowered to eighteen in Connecticut, but it hadn't happened yet. Whoever Chick Henry is didn't care, though, because we could sit down at the bar and drink without being carded. Randy was almost twenty-one anyway.

I've never been a big beer drinker, but Randy is. We'd sit there, and he'd knock down the first beer, and order us both a second one, and then he'd do the same thing with a third, fourth, and fifth. I couldn't keep up with him. For Randy, though, being buddies meant going beer for beer.

The first time we went to Chick Henry's, after a few beers, Randy shared, "Yeah, so I live alone up by Griffin Hospital. I deliver oil for Kasden Fuel real early in the morning to pay for shit – rent, utilities, tuition. That's why I didn't start college til just this year." And then he took a big slug of beer.

A few nights later, I had a question for Randy. "So, you live on your own. Do you mind if I ask where your parents are?"

That's when Randy opened up. "I don't mind. My dad died last May. A heart attack."

"Ouch," I said, not expecting that response. "Hey, I'm sorry, man. And what about your mom?"

Randy's face turned redder than it already was. "I don't talk to her. My dad and I stopped talking to her about five years ago when my dad found out she was sleeping with his best friend. Some kind of fuckin' best friend, right? And some kind of mom."

His words knocked me for a loop. That's the thing about Randy, though. He knows how to be real.

"Hey, man," I said. "That's too bad...what I mean is...you've been through a lot."

Randy just nodded, looking into his beer mug like he wished it was a crystal ball.

"But even though we've only known each other for a short time," I continued, "it's like I've known you forever. You're a cool guy, and...I don't know...to do what you're doing, putting yourself through school, making your own way. I'm impressed in a big way."

Randy almost blushed, and I realized that my words solidified our bond.

October picked up where September left off, with Randy and me hanging out a lot together. He owned a muscle car, a '67 Pontiac LeMans, and he liked to pick me up. In first gear, the LeMans sounded like a lion's grumpy roar, and by the time he shifted into fourth, the engine purred like a contented kitten. Otherwise, the car was a little worse for wear, but Randy was proud of it, and rightly so, because he bought it himself.

Randy himself is thick and muscular, not anyone to mess with, but clearly a guy with a heart of gold.

One night at Chick Henry's, he surprised me again. A few beers in, he looked at me and said, "Hey, Gabe, I got a good idea. How about you and me get an apartment?"

"Get an apartment?"

"Yeah, why not? Over near Southern. Maybe Dixwell Avenue in Hamden. We'll have a blast."

"But what about your apartment?"

"My lease is up at the end of the month. Then I'm free as a bird."

Sure, he was free as a bird, but was I? Frustrating memories surfaced of wanting to go away to college but my dad being against the idea. I also remembered Sparrow and Joni suggesting that, at some point, I needed to fly on my own instead of letting Dad control everything.

I loved the idea and decided to bring it up with Dad. I found him picking tomatoes in the big garden he had planted behind the new house. Like his parents, he was blessed with a green thumb, for sure. It was a perfect opportunity to talk alone, just the two of us.

After I told him Randy's idea, he looked up from his plants and said, "I'm not going to pay for you to live in some dive in New Haven when you have a perfectly beautiful home to live in here."

"But it's not about that, Dad," I explained. "Remember how I told you I want to be a writer? You liked the idea, right?"

"I suppose so."

"Well, the thing is, I think living on my own and making my own breaks will help me become a better writer. And I'm not asking you to pay for it. Randy has been making it on his own for months now, and I think, together, the two of us can make it work. I can work more hours at Duchess. I mentioned it to Howie, and he said they can give me hours both in Ansonia and at the Duchess in downtown New Haven."

Dad continued placing the juicy red globes in a weathered basket. He paused, finally, and said, "I'm not crazy about the idea. And your mother will miss you."

"Let me ask you this, Dad," I said. "What were you doing at my age? You were in the service. You said you were stationed all over – Nebraska, Utah, Ohio, Texas, other states – and what states you weren't stationed in, you said you passed through." I was pushing hard now. "Think of the adventures you had at the same age as me and how the experiences probably helped you to grow stronger and smarter. Doesn't that make sense?"

He shrugged and nodded.

"And as far as Mom goes, I'll talk to her, and I'll let her know that I'll stop by all the time to visit. But I don't want to go without your blessing. I look up to you, and well, I need to feel you're behind me."

A long silence ensued as Dad began brushing the garden dirt off his hands and nodding his head. He appeared to be concentrating deeply. I surveyed the entire expanse of the garden, his creation, and I admired his ability to grow things and fix things and make things better.

"Well," he finally said, "I want you to know that you're on your own. If you want to live like a grownup, you'll need to act like one."

I couldn't hide my exuberance. "That's awesome, Dad. I promise I'll make you proud of me."

Then he said, "And I want you to know something else. If this plan with your buddy doesn't work out...you always have a home here. That means for the rest of your life. Just remember that. And before you tell your mother, let me talk to her first."

Dad did a good job running interference with Mom because when I talked to her, she was behind the plan. Recalling the way she had fostered a love for literature and poetry in me, I felt it would be cool if I could achieve what, maybe, her circumstances during the Depression didn't allow. Even though Dad had told me not to worry about Mom's dreams, I will never forget the way her eyes lit up when I told her I wanted to become a writer.

CHAPTER 47

With everything sewn up on my end, Randy worked fast. In less than a month, he and I moved into a rundown, third-floor flat on George Street. Randy couldn't find anything on campus since the semester was well underway, and it was so cool to be so near downtown New Haven. The place was fully furnished, all second hand junk, but all that mattered was I was on my own.

Howie Millea introduced me to the manager of the New Haven Duchess, and I began working thirty hours a week, splitting my time between New Haven and Ansonia. It was a grind, but if Randy could make it on his own, so could I.

I worked in Ansonia every Saturday night, often with Bink who came home from Storrs to grab a few shifts on weekends when he could. He was surprised to hear I had moved out of my house.

"It's weird living away from home, isn't it?" he said one night after work.

"It's only been a few weeks for me, so the novelty hasn't worn off yet," I said.

"Yeah, that makes sense. And this guy Randy..."

"Duggan," I said.

"Yeah...Randy Duggan. Like, he's a good guy?"

I almost laughed. "The best. He can knock 'em back, though. How about you? You make any new friends in Storrs?"

"I don't know," he said, sheepishly. "Not many. I'm not that good at making new friends. It's the reason I come home on weekends."

Feeling an urge to reassure him, I said, "Well, you're always my friend. And I'll never forget our big road trip. It changed my life."

"I'll never forget it either," he offered with those sparkling blue eyes.

"Yeah...good times, man. And here's what I think. That trip bonded you and me for life, Bink. I'm not kidding. In fact, this may sound weird, but...well...when I get married, I want you to be in my wedding party."

Bink's face flushed a soft hue of pink. "Wait. You want *me* to be in your –"

"That's right, man. It sounds dumb since I'm not going out with anyone, but I picture you, Tomaso, and Jeff as my ushers. Of course, Michael will be my best man. You in?"

"For sure," he said, blushing a darker crimson now.

Bink was clearly flattered, but that wasn't my objective. I wasn't trying to make him feel good. I was just speaking the truth. Although it was premature, I was already making my wedding plans. Now, all I needed was a serious girlfriend.

At school, I had decided that I wasn't going to choose a college minor. Going without a minor opened me up to more electives and gave me the opportunity to study things I wanted to learn instead of *had* to learn. My summer road trip had made me realize that there was a host of interesting things I knew very little about, not the least of which was art. So, besides courses in my major, I took Art History because it was a prerequisite to take Introduction to Painting. With two courses in my major, Authors of the American Renaissance and Chaucer, as well as a core course in chemistry, I also squeezed in Contemporary Music with Dr. Schmidt because he not only sparked an interest in classical music in me but he had inspired me to attend the Bobby Seale trial, an eye-opening experience.

Dr. Schmidt covered important twentieth-century composers, most of whom I had never heard of – names like Igor Stravinsky and Béla Bartók.

It was only a week or two after Randy and I had moved to George Street that Dr. Schmidt said, "I'd like to let you all know about a great free concert this Saturday night. The Yale Symphony Orchestra – and, quite honestly, they're very good – will be presenting two works we've studied by Aaron Copland, *Rodeo* and *Appalachian Spring*, this Saturday night at Woolsey Hall on College Street. There is simply nothing that compares to live music, and this is a great opportunity to listen to and enjoy Copland's work. Of course, these are both quintessentially American works. If you've never experienced an honest-to-goodness concert hall, this is a wonderful opportunity. Just to hear great music at an historic venue like Woolsey Hall is reason enough to go."

I felt an inexplicable magnetic pull to attend the concert. Dr. Schmidt had suggested several other concerts, but I had been too busy or too lazy or too something. But I had to go to this one.

When I asked Randy if he wanted to go with me, he said, "Not in this lifetime, Gabe. If it was a Three Dog Night concert, it would be a different fuckin' story. Gimme a little 'Joy to the World' and I'm your man."

"Okay, wise-ass. I'll go alone then."

That Saturday night, I walked to Woolsey Hall, which was only a few blocks from our apartment. I felt a little intimidated as I approached the white, circular domed building. Passing by the mammoth exterior columns, I entered a rotunda only to find that the circular space was bordered by more immaculate white columns. This rotunda was different from the more modern one at Engleman Hall at Southern. I don't know how to describe its architecture exactly, but it seemed ancient and sacred and important, and it made me feel like I was in Rome or Athens instead of New Haven.

I ended up sitting by my lonesome in the balcony right next to what else? A column. If you like columns, you'll go bananas for Woolsey Hall. As on the exterior and in the rotunda, the interior is lined with columns, round and shiny and white, capped off in ornate gold. I had a cloudy recollection of studying types of columns in World History in high school – Doric, Corinthian, Ionic – or something like that. I didn't know one from the other. These columns reminded me of the columns at St. Joseph's Church where I grew up, only more like their big brothers.

Since it wasn't quite dusk yet, sunlight streamed through what must have been a dozen colossal, rounded windows on both sides of the wrap-around balcony. The majestic pipes of an organ spanned the wall above the stage, although no organ would be played in this concert.

The orchestra members themselves were busy on the stage, unpacking and tuning their instruments. Dressed in black tuxedos and long dresses, they looked spiffy and sharp.

Finally, a violinist tapped his stand, an oboe player let loose with a held note, and the orchestra tuned together just like you see on television and in films. When the conductor entered, the audience applauded for him and the entire orchestra stood, apparently a sign of respect. No doubt a professor, he shook his mane of white hair and raised his baton, signaling the rousing fanfare of *Rodeo*. Dr. Schmidt had explained to us how both of these pieces had been created for ballets, something I had never seen. It was hard to imagine cowboys dancing in a ballet, but I sure enjoyed the music.

It hit me that this was only the second time I had heard a live symphony orchestra. The first was when I was a Cub Scout on a trip to Radio City Music Hall. Strangely, I was sitting in the first row in the huge theater, way off to the side. But when the orchestra rose up out of the floor on a gigantic elevator, I was thunderstruck. Adrenaline pulsed through my veins, and the grandeur I was seeing and hearing excited me in a way I couldn't process at the time.

Now, years later and with more knowledge and maturity, it was different. I appreciated the individual sections of the orchestra – the strings, the woodwinds, the brass, and the percussion, each of which drew my attention throughout the piece. I imagined what it must be like to play in such an orchestra, or better yet, to conduct one – because the conductor himself was clearly the heart of the ensemble. I caught on right off the bat. The fifty something musicians pulsed effortlessly in harmonic unison, becoming the arteries and veins of the conductor's circulatory system.

When the conductor brought the piece to its rousing conclusion, the audience erupted into thunderous applause. He acknowledged the orchestra, directing them to stand in response to the ovation. I was seeing that there was a protocol and an order about the concert that I can only describe as "classy."

After a pause of about thirty seconds, once everyone was settled and ready, the conductor cued the first tranquil notes of *Appalachian Spring*. A solitary clarinet introduced the musical theme. I imagined myself playing those opening strains on my clar-

inet. Other musicians gradually complimented and echoed the clarinet – a bassoon here, a French horn there, a haunting oboe – and I
relaxed and felt the music. A few minutes into the piece, things
started to get more interesting and exciting, with strings and brass
and percussion passionately joining in.

Listening, I remembered Joni and her dulcimer, an instrument
she said was commonplace in the Appalachian Mountains.

I went with my feelings like Joni had suggested. Having recently
spent time in the Blue Ridge Mountains which were part of the
greater Appalachian range, I closed my eyes and pictured the
glorious peaks, covered with millions of evergreens, and the canopy
of purple clouds. The dramatic strains of music took me back to
my trip with Bink and the night at the festival that had caused a
shift in my life that I'm still trying to process. Music can do that
to you.

As the piece continued, almost without realizing it, I zeroed in
on a particular musician, a cellist. To this day, I'll never be able to
explain it. One of six cellists, the others all being male, she sat two
chairs over in the second row, a dozen violins in the row in front of
her and four towering upright basses in the row behind. I sat there,
suddenly unable to take my eyes off of her. The beautiful wooden
instrument appeared made for her, her knees and feet turned out,
creating the perfect space for it. I was hypnotized as she maneuvered
her bow in a graceful motion from right to left and the slender
fingers of her left hand fingered the fretboard, gently shaking back
and forth on long notes. She seemed lost in the music. Even when
the cello section was resting, she sat concentrating on her music, the
very definition of anticipation, focused and ready for her next
entrance, the next stroke of her bow.

I felt I had seen her somewhere before but couldn't recall where.
Her dark hair, her alert eyes, her elegant motion as a musician
became my obsession for the remainder of the evening. It didn't
make any sense because there were plenty of women in the orchestra
in each and every section. Why her?

When the piece reached a moment Dr. Schmidt had talked at
length about – how Copland "borrowed" an old familiar Shaker
song, "Simple Gifts," and when that same solitary clarinet that had
introduced the bigger piece earlier now introduced the Shaker tune,
my eyes stayed focused on my cellist. When other instruments – a

flute, a bassoon, an oboe – joined the clarinetist, I continued to stare down at her and only her.

Even in recalling how Dr. Schmidt had explained that Copland had incorporated the song into his work, based on the Civil War, to express themes of peace and remembrance, even as I began singing the lyrics inside my head: *'Tis the gift to be simple, 'tis the gift to be free*, I observed how free my cellist seemed to be, immersed in the instrument and the music and the moment. And I wanted to experience that freedom too.

Only moments later, when the entire orchestra joined in the "Simple Gifts" theme in a steady rhythm accented with a pounding bass drum, a crescendo of mellifluous sound filled every nook and cranny of the auditorium, and as tears filled my eyes, nothing existed except Copland's brilliance, the promise of a peaceful world, and my cellist.

Finally, a lonely flute softly took up a brilliant and emotional variation of the "Simple Gifts" theme as other sections supported her, as the entire orchestra grew quieter and quieter in symphonic prayer until we were at last left in reverent silence. I wasn't sure if I was still breathing as, for the first time, I averted my attention to the conductor who had allowed his chin to fall to his chest and his arms to drop to his sides. The audience joined the orchestra in what I believe was a collective moment of reflection before rising to their feet in a jubilant ovation.

It had been a short concert, not quite an hour, and I was sorry it was over. I made my way into the rotunda, lingering there hoping to see my cellist. I stood there, observing other musicians, carrying instrument cases large and small, greeting family members and friends. But finally, when I was the last person standing in the immaculate circular lobby, I realized the object of my affection must have exited another way. I gave a nearby column a gentle rap with my knuckles and left the building, feeling empty and disappointed.

On the way home as I strolled along College Street heading for George Street, I passed along Yale's campus with its gated courtyards and imposing gothic buildings. A million questions crossed my mind. I wondered who my cellist was and where on campus she lived and what state she was from. I especially wondered if I'd see her again any time soon. *Maybe the next time the Yale Symphony Orchestra gives a concert,* I hoped.

But, unbelievably, it was only two days later when, working the morning shift at the New Haven Duchess on lower Chapel Street, I called out, "Next please," and there she was, my cellist, standing at the counter in corduroys and a white, gauzy peasant blouse, her trusty cello case at her side. I mean, I almost had a heart attack – her in that peasant blouse with eyes like ripe olives looking right at me. It was almost too good to be true, but it dawned on me. *It was here that I'd seen her.* Having only worked in New Haven for a couple of weeks, I hadn't made the connection.

Trying to pour on some charm, I smiled and spoke again, "Yes, miss, what can I get you this morning?"

"I'd like a toasted hard roll, lightly buttered, and a medium coffee, please." She had an aura about her that was vibrant and authentic and alive, and it was all I could do to function.

I tried to think fast. "Will you be having that here?"

"Yes, please," she replied with a warm smile.

"Great! Why don't you take a seat, and I'll bring that right out to you."

We didn't typically serve customers at their tables, but it was slow, and this wasn't just any customer. I ran back to the grill and prepared the hard roll myself, making sure it was toasted and buttered to perfection. I poured the coffee and off on my delivery I went.

She was studying a math textbook when I arrived at her table.

Hoping to think of something terribly witty to say, I asked, "Have you figured out what y equals?"

"I'm trying," she laughed. "I'm afraid math isn't my strong suit."

"Here you go," I said. "How's that for service?" *Was I trying too hard?* I wondered.

"Best service ever," she commented.

I smiled and started to walk away, but realizing it was now or never, I turned back and went for broke. "I think I've seen you here before."

"You probably have. I've been coming here a lot since the semester started, so I've seen you."

"Yes," I replied, "but I think I saw you somewhere else and couldn't figure out why you looked so familiar. But it just hit me. Weren't you one of the musicians in the Copland concert this past Saturday?"

If her face was bright before, now it lit up like a neon sign. "Why, yes, I was. Were you there?"

"Yes, my professor from Southern recommended it. You're a cellist, right?"

She glanced at her case and teased, "How did you figure that out?"

"No, I know...I mean, the case...it's obvious, but what I mean is, I saw you playing at the concert, so you know, even if you didn't have your instrument staring me in the face like this...what I'm trying to say is –"

Helping me as I stumbled, she interrupted, "You're very observant to notice me in a big orchestra." *Notice her? There was an understatement for you.* "Do you like classical music?"

"Well, it's new to me," I said, scrambling to recover, "but yes... yes, I do. Very much. I play a little this and that myself – clarinet, sax, guitar."

"Awesome," she said. "It sounds like we have music in common. My name is Gia."

What an adorable name. I think I raised my eyebrows because she explained, "Well, Gianna, actually. Gianna Cipriani, but my family and close friends call me Gia."

"Sounds Italian," I said. "Something else we have in common. I'm Gabriel DeMarco."

"Nice to meet you, Gabriel DeMarco." She reached her elegant hand which had played the cello so beautifully across the table. After a smile, she added, "By the way, I'm only half. Italian, I mean. But that still counts, right?"

"For sure. Definitely! And the name is one hundred percent Italian. Gianna is beautiful, but I hope I'm a good enough friend to call you Gia."

"Of course you are," she answered. "Let's be *best* friends."

Let's be best friends! That response gave me one of those tingly feelings in the pit of my stomach like you only feel when something incredible happens to you. In my euphoria, I almost walked away at that point, but a greater force kept me rooted to the spot. "Would you mind giving me your...what I mean is, would you mind if I called you? Maybe we could do something together sometime."

Her cheeks shone with a warm glow. "That'd be nice. You can

call me at my dorm." She ripped a little strip off her bag, took out a pen, and jotted her number down.

"Thanks," I said, looking down at her neat handwriting. "Anything you'd enjoy doing?"

"Maybe we can go out for pizza. Naples makes a great pizza. Ever been there?"

"No, I'm new to living in New Haven," I explained.

"Well, it's right around the corner from Woolsey Hall. It's a real Yale hotspot. I think you'll love it. They encourage you to carve on the table and booths. And the graffiti on the tables and walls is strictly intellectual stuff, everything from Shakespeare to Marx to Nietzsche."

And after a beat, we both laughed.

"That sounds perfect! You'll be hearing from me soon."

"Promise?" she asked.

"Promise," I replied and then floated back behind the counter.

Being the impatient soul that I am, I called her that very day in the late afternoon. She told me she had a lot of studying to do, but she said she never passes up an offer to go to Naples. When I told her I lived on George Street, she suggested we walk, which was A-OK with me. I met her at the gate of her dorm, Vanderbilt Hall on Chapel Street, and we walked down to Naples. She was right about the pizza...and the graffiti. In fact, as we sipped birch beer, I added my own carving to our table. Heck, I had done plenty of carving and whittling as a Boy Scout. I etched out just the simple letters, G-i-a and punctuated it with a question mark. When I looked at her, Gia simply blushed.

It was the walk back to her dorm, though, that was most memorable. As we strolled the campus in darkness, Gia informed me of something I didn't know – that Yale had only been co-educational for two years, and that Vanderbilt Hall was strictly inhabited by freshmen women.

When she let us in the gate, she said, "I'll have to say goodbye out here. No men allowed." She winked at me.

Sad to leave each other, we parted with a gentle kiss, and then a longer, soulful kiss. Let me say, experiencing a first kiss in the courtyard of the U-shaped castle known as Vanderbilt Hall at Yale on an autumn night is an experience one never forgets.

For me, just to be sure I'd never forget it, I began writing a story when I got back to my place. I had been looking for inspiration to begin something, and now I had discovered my muse. I wasn't sure if it was going to be a short story or a novel. I'd decide later. I sat at my Smith Corona and began to type:

I'm learning that life is often a cosmic game of Connect the Dots, that to view the entire picture, you must begin by drawing lines. I'm discovering that drawing one line leads to the next line and then to the next. In actuality, the first dot probably goes all the way back to when we're born and the doctor slaps our bottom, causing us to let out our first big yelp. I don't want to go back that far, though. For me, my story begins with a road trip and a painting and a color, cobalt. It begins the summer I met Joni Mitchell, the famous singer. Had I not met Joni, I don't believe I would have ever met the cellist. But, like I said, one dot leads to another. Let me begin...

ACKNOWLEDGMENTS

The writing of my books is a true collaboration between me and my daughter, Mia. It would be an understatement to merely call her my editor. She is my partner in writing and publishing my work, not only editing, but formatting the interior of the book, brainstorming and advising on every aspect of the process from day one through publication. Together, we are our own publishing company, Next Chapter Press, committed to writing and publishing books written by me – and, perhaps, one day by Mia! As a team, we are getting better and better at writing, editing, and publishing our books – and we are super proud of *Still Life*. Mia and I have a wonderful, productive working relationship, and in the summer leading up to the publication of *Still Life*, when we weren't working on the book, we exercised together on a daily basis. Without Mia, I simply couldn't do what I do! For more about Mia, visit MiaGScarpa.com.

I want to also thank my wife, Francesca, who offered valuable insights throughout the writing process, as well as my daughter Gina and grandson Michael for their ongoing support, input, encouragement, and love.

Mia and I are grateful for our awesome team of beta readers, some of whom have been with us for all three of our books. Thank you to: Sharon Cayer, Sandy Morrill, Linda Welch, Mike O'Mara, and Nick Picknally. Each reader offered insights leading to meaningful revisions that improved our story.

I'd like to offer a very special thanks to our good friend, Liz Kennard, whom we have officially adopted as a member of Team Scarpa. Liz continues to generously offer her services as moderator for our major book signing events at local libraries. She is a real pro and adds a professional touch to these events. I even named an important character in *Still Life* for Liz, Mary Elizabeth Kiernan!

Also a big shoutout to my close friend Dave Presutto and his wife Patty for their input, as well as to my good friend Steve Gould for his help.

I couldn't be happier to have Mario Lampic from Serbia on board as our cover designer. Mario is simply the best. I wouldn't consider working with anyone else.

I also want to extend warm wishes to the many people who inspired various characters and situations in *Still Life*. My memories of the late '60s and early '70s are fond ones. The people, the music, and the experiences will stay with me forever. My later high school years were indeed a series of comical misadventures, my experiences working at Duchess in Ansonia were a blast, and my years as a college student at Southern Connecticut State College were culturally enriching ones that changed my life. That said, *Still Life* is very much a work of fiction.

Finally, we want to thank all of our friends and supporters who have been willing to give my books a chance. We appreciate all of those good people who not only read our books but who spread the word to others as well. Personally, I am eternally grateful that you are helping me enjoy this "next chapter" of my life.

Gary Scarpa is a lifelong resident of Shelton, Connecticut. He enjoyed a lengthy and fulfilling career in secondary education as an English teacher and a guidance counselor, and along with his wife, Francesca, founded a non-profit theater in Connecticut in 2005. After his retirement from both education and theater, he reinvented himself and began writing fiction. *Still Life* is Gary's third novel.

*To contact **Gary Scarpa** for speaking engagements on podcasts, at book clubs, and more, please email inquiries to ScarpaAuthor@gmail.com.*

For information on upcoming books by Gary, visit his website, garyscarpa.com and follow him on social media:

Facebook: @ScarpaAuthor
Instagram: @garyscarpa

∾

If you enjoyed *Still Life*, please consider leaving a review on Amazon, Barnes & Noble, and Goodreads.

Also by Gary Scarpa

In this captivating novel, the reader is transported to the turbulent wartime era and also given glimpses of the Great Depression as experienced by two young people growing up and coming of age during these historic back-to-back eras. ***What are the Chances?*** – dramatic, comical, and heartbreaking – is a story of what it meant to grow up as the children of immigrants during the 1930s and 1940s. It is a story of the complexity of dreams and the overcoming of obstacles. It is a story of love, of perseverance, and of destiny.

Made in the USA
Middletown, DE
10 November 2024

63803459R20196